The Kinship

BOOKS BY ERNEST HEBERT

Mad Boys

Live Free or Die

The Passion of Estelle Jordan

Whisper My Name

A Little More Than Kin

The Dogs of March

The
Kinship

A Little More Than Kin

•

The Passion of Estelle Jordan

Two Novels from the Darby Series

with a new essay by

Ernest Hebert

University Press of New England / Hanover and London

University Press of New England, Hanover, NH 03755
© 1993 by Ernest Hebert
Printed in the United States of America   5   4   3   2   1
CIP data appear at the end of the book

A Little More Than Kin first published in 1982 by The Viking Press.
The Passion of Estelle Jordan first published in 1987 by The Viking Press.

Contents

Author's Note

The Kinship includes *A Little More Than Kin* and *The Passion of Estelle Jordan*, the second and fourth novels of the five-book series revolving around the imaginary town of Darby, New Hampshire. Upon writing the last sentence of *A Little More Than Kin*, I knew the story of Estelle Jordan had to be told before the Jordan saga was complete. I brooded upon this matter all the time I was writing the third Darby novel, *Whisper My Name*. I'm glad that the two Jordan books are now where they belong, together, and that I have some space at the end of *The Kinship* to tell the story behind the story.

A LITTLE MORE THAN KIN

God chose those whom the world considers absurd to shame the wise; he singled out the weak of this world to shame the strong. He chose the world's lowborn and despised, those who count for nothing, to reduce to nothing those who were something; so that mankind can do no boasting before God.

The First Letter of Paul to the Corinthians, 1, 27-29

Ollie and Willow

Old Man Dorne gathered the phlegm in his throat and spat it into a handkerchief, and that was how the storekeeper knew he was getting ready to launch into a speech.

"The Jordans are no kin of mine, no kin of yours, no kin of God almighty himself," he said. "They ain't even a family exactly, not like you and I think of as a family, anyway. Just a collection of like-minded individuals, like communists or participants in modern art. Course the blood bond is there, right from the line of Cain, if you don't mind me speaking a little in a religious vein here. Not that I have anything personal against the Jordans, except maybe against Willow, who upset my missus over the matter of some petunias. I don't bear him any malice, however, not as Harold Flagg would. How that man could hold a grudge, God rest his soul. God rest all our souls. I wouldn't admit this in front of a bunch of strangers, but I'm getting a little atheistic in my old age. A man gets more impressed by the evidence and less by the arguments, older he gets. You could get mad at Willow Jordan, but you couldn't hate him. It's hard to hate an idiot. It's something that takes practice, and I never had the time.

"As I say, Willow Jordan is an idiot, but his father Ollie is another matter. There is something brooding and figurative about the man. A mind like his is dangerous to society, dangerous to itself, but there's an admirability about it too. That's why I think Flagg hated him so. Flagg was a big law-and-order man, and he was a smart man, but he didn't have much admirability. So, you see, he had double grounds to hate Ollie Jordan: philosophy and jealousy. It's not generally known, but Flagg's the one that got Ollie and his kin run off from that piece of land they were living on. I'm for private property and all that but they were on that land so long they had a claim to it.

"The land is owned by some feller from down-country. He rents out space for the Basketville sign that you can see from the Interstate across the river in Vermont—God bless that state and its crippled deer herd. He also rented to the Jordans. Nobody else would want to live up there, on that lonely road that the town don't—won't—plow. The Jordans arrived there maybe twelve, fifteen years ago, and through it all Flagg built up this animosity against Ollie Jordan. Flagg gave him credit, you know. Wanted the man to owe him something, so that when he took back from him, he could take back everything and call it interest. He bided his time. A man with a grudge don't like swift retribution. Then about in March, Flagg got the planning board to write the feller from down-country and tell him he couldn't rent his land no more, and Flagg called him up, all sweet, you know, and said hush, hush. The next week Flagg died of a heart attack but the wheels were set in motion. Last month the Jordans were evicted. Now I don't say that Flagg knew he was going to die, but I say each man has certain, er, call 'em cognitions, when his time is near, even if he don't see them for what they are, and he tries to put his house in order, or bring down somebody else's house, if he's the kind.

"Course nobody really likes the Jordans. But I don't go with those who say they don't belong in Darby. I say every town has its Jordans and moreover needs its Jordans so the people can take their mind off their troubles. Give a man somebody lower than himself to compare himself to, and I'll show you a man with a strong belief in his own being. Even Willow, I'll admit, was put here for some purpose. Your average Congregational minister will tell you that, of course, but I mean to say I know the purpose: somebody to wear the fun hat. Every man needs somebody to laugh at that he ain't related to, and there's no one on this earth more distant a relative to you and me than Willow Jordan. On the whole, I'll argue the town's poorer without the Jordans. I'm not saying I was happy to see Ollie and his idiot son this morning. I'm speaking theoretical here. Anyway, as Professor Blue would say, 'It's purely academic,' because I don't imagine they'll stay. When Ollie Jordan sees what's been done to his land, he'll run like any other lonely heart fleeing the scene of his hurt . . ."

A call on the storekeeper's CB from Mrs. McCurtin interrupted Old Man Dorne. The cops were headed for the Jordan place, she said. Heard it on the scanner. No confirmation. A code 9. Unfamiliar to her. Therefore, must be something considerable. She signed off temporarily to listen some more to the scanner. The old-timers in the store fell silent, waiting for more news.

Mrs. McCurtin was the town reporter, that is, the town gossip, but she lacked tenure, just as the storekeeper did. Old Man Dorne had explained the situation. The former longtime town gossip, Arlene Flagg, the old-maid sister of Harold Flagg, had committed an unpardonable act: She had mocked the town with her own secret. After her brother died suddenly, she sold the store through the Stout Realty people and then left town without telling anyone where she went. Someone said she had run off with Lancelot Early, the milk salesman from Walpole, but no one in Darby was sure. The fact was no one knew where Arlene was or why she'd done what she'd done because there was no one in Darby with the sources that Arlene herself had. Mrs. McCurtin had spirit, curiosity, persistence, and a darned good scanner, but she was inexperienced. She got overexcited. Her speculation was not put forth logically. Nonetheless, the town was giving her a grace period while she got some on-the-job training. The position of town gossip was an important and difficult one. It took time to break in.

Old Man Dorne was about eighty, slow-talking, with a heavy up-country dialect. His yarns revealed him as one who had read much but had had little formal education. He was the kind of man who could use the words "ain't" and "incur" in the same sentence and make it work. Others in the store included a teenager with a horse laugh, an out-of-work wallpaper hanger who made vile speeches against plywood paneling and women's liberation, and Dr. Hadly Blue, a college teacher, who was the only person in Darby, New Hampshire, with a Ph.D. Never mind that, of the customers, only Old Man Dorne was old. As far as the storekeeper was concerned, if someone came into his store and lingered a moment to chew the fat, he was an old-timer.

The storekeeper had few regrets about leaving Pennsylvania, but he was subject to a peculiar malaise. Back in Hazleton, he had nurtured his soul with a dream of running a country store in New England. Now he had the store. The dream, which had brought him some moments of ecstasy, was now an ache. He was homesick for a place in his mind that he had left. Back there in Hazleton he had created the old-timers, a composite mental picture of people he'd read about in *Yankee* magazine and heard about from his cousin Richard, who had settled in Claremont, New Hampshire, and who, ironically, had returned to Hazleton, divorced and alcoholic, about the time the storekeeper had moved himself and his family to the store in Darby. That had been the first hint that the dream could not be brought forth in anything like its entirety. The full realization came down on him shortly after he took over the store. Most of the people in town were like people anywhere else. As he had sought to regard them as quaint, so they were seeking to regard him. Everybody is part of everybody else's dream, he thought, and it's when we get to know each other that we get let down. Still, he was settled here, and he would not return to Pennsylvania.

Gloria, who had held up his move for ten years, now was saying it had been her idea. As wife of the storekeeper, a junior college graduate, and an obviously concerned parent, she had automatic status in Darby, and she was feeling surges of power. In fact, she was thinking about running for the school board. The kids were getting on after a period of moping. Nancy was crowned spelling champion of Darby. Victor was learning how to trap muskrats from Old Man Dorne. People came to his store and hung around to chew the fat, as they never had done when Flagg was running the place. The storekeeper figured he had awakened in them some long-forgotten pride in self and place by the interest he took in their town, by the reverence he showed for their ways.

He had never heard of the Jordans until Old Man Dorne said that he had seen Ollie and his idiot son Willow this morning driving up the road to where their shacks had been. The storekeeper sensed that in the Jordans was something both pure and tainted, and out of the heart of this region. Even now he felt kinship with this man he did not know who was returning to a place he had once called home.

The Sign

Ollie Jordan stepped from the family truck onto the soil where once his home had been, turned to his son Willow, and said, "Wiped clean." A bulldozer had scooped out a cavern in the hardpan and buried his shacks. All that was left were the caterpillar tracks of the dozer. Already some wild grasses had taken hold in the soil. Willow tugged at the chain that bound him to his father. Willow was looking at the back of the great sign—BASKETVILLE EXIT 8—in whose shadow the Jordan shacks had sprouted. He wanted to climb the sign, swing among the steel struts, holler, exercise what his father called his mysterious sense of humor. Someday, thought Ollie, I'm not going to be strong enough to hold him, and he'll drag me where he wants as now I drag him.

Ollie began at the north corner of the sign and walked thirty-two paces southeast. Here had been the sleeping shack, which he had built for Helen and himself and which he called the "boodwar." He had overheard the word "boudoir," and deciphered that it meant a place for lovers. He had analyzed the word and found it a good one. The meaning of the "-war" part was clear enough, for what were lovers but ceaseless battlers? As for "bood"—he figured that was one of the less ugly terms referring to copulation. He walked twenty more paces. Here his cousin Tooker had settled with his family in a converted schoolbus. To the right was the shack he had built for Adele and her baby, and behind that the room that his children, Turtle and the twins, had fixed up so that they could call it their own. Now, as the wind quieted and the early summer sun fell upon the earth—his earth—Ollie Jordan caught a remnant of his home that the bulldozer could not remove: the smell of his clan.

Ollie's place sat on half an acre on top of a hill. It was bounded by steep ledges and hemlock trees whose roots gripped the granite with all the determination of dying millionaires clutching their money. Here, where the porch had been, a man could sit in a rocking chair, drink a beer, smoke a pipe, hold forth. Here he had said to his friend Howard Elman: "A man fishes to catch his natural-born self. You'll see a banker casting a fly to a rainbow trout, a mailman throwing plug at a smallmouth bass, and a man like me offering a worm to a horn pout . . . You can keep your trout. I don't want no fish that walks on water when it feels the hook." If the sign blocked his view of the Connecticut River valley below and the Vermont hills beyond, at least he could listen to the music of the Interstate highway, which ran beside the river, and to the bitching and moaning of the wind like a woman too long without comfort.

Although the sadness of the loss of the place had settled in him before, and although he knew that later he would feel even more deeply the knowledge of its complete annihilation, Ollie Jordan did not bother to puzzle over why he had been evicted and why his works had been buried because Ollie, like nearly all the Jordans in Cheshire County, did not bother himself with causation. Perhaps this was all for the better. If Ollie had known that one man, Harold Flagg, had plotted to get him evicted simply because he didn't like him and then, as if to prevent any possibility of revenge, had died, and that another man, Alfred Rizzo of Cranston, Rhode Island, had demolished his works because it was the cheapest way to prepare the property for the real estate market—if Ollie had known these matters, he might have gone mad on the spot. As it was, he said to his idiot son, "Willow, there ain't no place left here for a man to sit civilized."

Willow tugged at his chain. He wanted to climb the sign.

Ollie's mind went blank for a moment and then, responding to an urge outside his consciousness, he hit the boy in the face with the flat of his hand. Willow dropped to his knees and began pawing at the earth. It used to be that Ollie would hit Willow when he did something wrong, but the boy learned nothing from discipline, and so now Ollie only hit him to relieve his own tension. Someday, he thought, my temper will lead to murder, either his or mine.

Ollie sat on the ground and put his arm around Willow. The earth was warm. It was going to be a hot day. He was grateful. He knew there were places where it was summer nearly year round, but he could never live there. He had not the will to move, nor—somehow—the right to such a luxury.

"What to do next?" he asked, bringing his mind to bear on the immediate problem, which was the only kind of problem that he considered. To Ollie the only truth of a clock was the ticking, and that was how he took life, tick by tick. Ollie Jordan had returned to his former home in the vague hope that he might sneak back onto his land with Willow. He never imagined that there would be nothing here but the sign.

After he and his family had been evicted, they had been offered succor by Ollie's half-brother, Ike. A professional man, in the Jordan sense, Ike was a successful burglar. Ike's wife, Elvira, introduced Ollie's common-law wife, Helen, to a social worker, and thus was born a great tension. Ollie was a traditionalist, in the Jordan sense. He feared welfare because he was afraid it would change him and change his family's ways. Not that he was proud of himself or the family, but he did believe in the rough integrity of distinction among creatures; and the Jordans, whatever else they were, were as distinct from the run of society as mongrels were from poodles.

Matters reached a crisis when Ollie learned that the "Welfare Department," which was Ollie's phrase for any social service agency, had found a place for them to live in Keene. Helen urged him to move with her. Ollie was about ready to go along with the idea, partly because, as he would say about certain women, Helen could always "cast a spell over this frog," and partly because he was willing to sacrifice a philosophical point to get away from Ike's succor. But then Helen said that the Welfare Department wanted to examine Willow. They said, she said, that Willow might not be as dumb as he looked, might even be "educable," a word that Ollie translated as a marriage of the words "edible" and "vegetable." No one was going to examine Willow as long as his father was alive. He couldn't explain it so it made sense, but he held a deep conviction that in his son's apparent stupidity and odd behavior there was a seed of genius that someday would sprout, provided it was kept away from meddlers such as the Welfare Department. Willow's place was with him, and that was that. As was his wont, Ike entered the argument. "It ain't good for a man's spirit to have an idiot chained to him," Ike said.

"Everybody's got an idiot chained to him," said Ollie. "Only difference is mine is here to see."

Ike smiled. He had the narrow-minded confidence of a successful man. Furthermore, while he was generous with his advice, he was cheap with his beer, which to Ollie demonstrated a poverty of style. That night Helen walked out on him with nearly all the family belongings and the children, save Willow of course. Ike drove the pack of them to Keene in his auctioneer's moving van. Ollie knew Ike's motives in helping Helen, and indeed in providing his family with succor in the first place. Ike meant to gain ascendancy over him. Ollie Jordan might allow his woman of many years to leave with everything they had made together, but he could not allow Ike, his inferior half-brother, to enjoy ascendancy over him. Therefore, the next morning Ollie absconded with Ike's considerable beer supply. He fled with Willow in the family pickup, an ancient four-wheel drive International that Ollie had outfitted with a salvaged church pew, where the kids would ride in warm weather. Besides the beer and his son, Ollie took only his tools, a few personal items, and the knowledge that he had prevented Ike from gaining ascendancy.

Now, broke and angry, and knowing that as soon as the anger wore off he would be sick with loss of his family, Ollie drove at random on the back roads of Cheshire County, like a bandit with no hideout to go to.

Ollie Jordan had never traveled more than one hundred miles from Keene, the hub of Cheshire County. The farther he got from the county, the more uneasy he became, like some sailor of old fearing he might fall off the edge of the earth. Once he had been to Hampton Beach, getting his first and last look at the ocean. He had been appalled by its immensity, which seemed designed specifically by the Creator to diminish humans. On a practical level, he couldn't understand why men and women would want to strip to their undies and lie on gritty sand under a harsh sun, unless it was that the ocean air had disturbed their minds. Certainly it had disturbed his, and he had rushed home.

This morning, every time he had approached the borders of the county, he had found a reason to turn around. He had had no destination, no plan, only Willow and the beer. By accident, it seemed, they had arrived at the narrow dirt road that wound up the mountain from Route 63 to the Basketville sign. For a second, he had thrilled to the thought of returning to the shacks he had built. Now the truth was upon him. All that was here of home was an old scent that the rain eventually would wash away.

Willow tugged at his chain, making a sound like a puppy.

"Oh, all right," Ollie said, and he slipped the key in the padlock that kept the chain around the boy's waist and released him. No doubt trouble would follow. It always did when Willow was loose, but at this point trouble seemed better than nothing.

Willow headed for the sign. At six feet, he was taller than his father by a couple of inches, but he seemed shorter because he walked hunched over like an ape. Ollie stood ramrod straight, except that he held his head bent sideways on occasion. Ollie Jordan smiled little, but when he did he revealed a mouth of black, jagged teeth. Willow smiled often, and his smile was white and empty. Both Ollie and his son had dark hair, slicked by their own body oils, coated with dust. Ollie kept his hair short, so that his hat would always fit correctly. He hated to shave, mainly because no one had explained to him when he was a young man the benefits of hot water, and he hated a beard out of a vague philosophical bias. He groomed himself with a pair of scissors, so that his face had a permanent stubble. He fancied he looked distinguished.

Willow, as his father had said, was "late getting a beard and he's late getting brains," and he sported sparse whiskers which his father would trim. Ollie's skin was pale because he wore a felt hat everywhere and stayed out of the sun as much as possible. The hat was Helen's idea, but Ollie had taken to it and considered the hat part of his uniform. Willow's skin was darkened by the sun because he kept his head up, looking at the sky. Most of the Jordans had pale blue eyes, but both Ollie and his son had drab, brown eyes, which up close revealed wormy markings like pinto beans drying in a musty pantry. There was only one other person in the Jordan clan with eyes like that, and that was the woman they called the Witch.

Willow paused before the sign to sniff the treats wafting on the air currents of morning. Satisfied that at the moment the world was good, he grabbed one of the steel supports on the rear of the sign and, with monkeylike grace and monkeylike foolishness, swung from strut to strut until he was nearly at the top. There he rested, draping himself in the crook made by two pieces of steel. Ollie watched Willow's performance, proud as any father would be before the athletic exploits of his son.

Ollie now prepared to make himself comfortable. He fetched a quart of Ike's Narraganset beer from the truck,

searched about for a patch of ground just the right temperature, sat cross-legged, and lit his pipe to await developments.
He figured that Willow, who like himself had not eaten breakfast, would realize he was hungry in about an hour and then
would come down from the sign. How they would eat with no
food and no money Ollie didn't know. He'd solve that problem
when the hunger came. He had nothing but contempt for men
who held full-time jobs, ate regular meals, and showed any
other evidence that they sought to order their lives in space
and time. "There ain't no other time but now," he would say.
Thus, his despair at seeing his works destroyed lost hold for
the moment, as the comfort of the day, the comfort of the
beer, the comfort of his thoughts settled in.

He watched white clouds gamboling in the sky, and they
reminded him of his dogs. God, he missed them—their wet
tongues and bad breath, their ridiculous insistence on protecting him from nonexistent threats. Dogs were loyal to undeserving men, as men were loyal to their own undeserving
ideas about how to live. He supposed that after he had abandoned them, the dogs had stayed around until the bulldozer
came. Some would raid garbage pails and thus would get shot.
Others would attach themselves to humans, and thus stood a
fifty-fifty chance of survival and a fifty-fifty chance of being
gassed by the county. Ollie imagined that such a death would
be without pain and also without the sweetness that follows
pain. Perhaps one dog, say the shepherd, would learn to hunt
alone again and return to the wild life to live in unacknowl-
edged glory until his teeth went bad and he slowly starved to
death or until he succumbed to his own parasites, eaten inside
out as a man is by his beliefs. The dogs stood no chance with
men, he thought. And men stood no chance at all. Men, like
the dogs that they made over as their own dark inferiors, were
neither wild enough to go it alone, nor civilized enough to get
along together.

To survive, the world needed some improved versions of its
creatures. He had worked on this idea long ago, when he had
sensed the strangeness in himself and had sought to give it

dignity and importance by contriving a theory around it. Soon, however, he realized he was not better than most men, nor fitter, but merely different. But in his son Willow, Ollie saw possibilities. Indeed, he had concluded that Willow's idiocy was a departure point. He had gotten the idea by observing caterpillars immobilize themselves in silky webs, to emerge later as butterflies. He had seen hints in Willow of the butterfly, in the boy's inscrutable and dangerous adventures, what Ollie called "his sense of humor." Lately, as more and more people—even Helen—had called upon him to shuck off the burden of his son, Ollie Jordan recognized the love he had for him as an instinctive, brainless duty, the human equivalent of a salmon swimming upriver to fertilize some eggs and die. But also he saw in Willow his own shadowy love of self.

For almost an hour, Ollie's thoughts passed in review like the clouds above, to thicken into meaning and then dissolve into nothing. He had finished his beer, his pipe had gone out, and he was starting to doze when he was startled by a thump at his feet: Willow's shoes and pants. Moments later the shirt, then the undies came fluttering down. The clothes, all in a bunch at his feet, reminded Ollie of a parachutist whose chute had not opened. He looked up to see Willow hoist himself to the four-inch-wide header at the top of the sign, stand, and—baldacky bareass—face the Interstate highway below.

"When you come down here, I'm going to beat you blue," Ollie said, but even as he spoke, even as he proceeded to give Willow holy hell, even as he shook his fist and jumped up and down at his own frustration, even so, Ollie Jordan thrilled at the sight of his mad son. "You stupid bastard," he shouted, but added under his breath, "My what a sense of humor that boy has got."

After a few more minutes of perfunctory ranting, Ollie fetched another beer, reloaded his pipe, and considered the situation.

The worst, and unfortunately most likely, thing that could happen next would be that someone on the highway would report seeing a naked man on the Basketville sign and in no time flat the Welfare Department would arrive and take Willow away in a white van with a red light and a siren that said *wup-wup-wup*. The second worst thing that could happen—and now Ollie was hearing himself voice his thought—"is that the little bastard will fall off and break his head on the ledges."

What to do? If he could go around the front of the sign, perhaps with a long pole—say a young maple sapling—he might be able to knock Willow off so he would land on the softer earth at the rear of the sign. "It won't work," he said to himself. "The little bastard is too quick." He calculated it would take a motorist twenty minutes to get off at the exit in Putney and find a phone. It would take the Mutual Aid dispatcher another ten minutes to get somebody to the scene of the crime. Let's see, he thought, twenty and ten is thirty minutes—half an hour, that ain't bad. Unless of course a state trooper saw Willow and radioed ahead. But Ollie, operationally optimistic if philosophically pessimistic, wouldn't consider that possibility. Half an hour, not bad, not bad at all. He had, oh, fifteen minutes to enjoy this show before he had to do some serious thinking. He took a swig of beer and watched Willow.

Willow, arms outstretched, tiptoed along the top of the sign, like some creature half-ape, half-dancer. He'd walk to one end of the sign, pivot, and walk the seventy-five feet to the other end. Through it all, he seemed to be keeping time to a music heard only by himself.

Suddenly Ollie Jordan heard a car churning up the dirt on the road that led to the sign. Moments later, Godfrey Perkins, the part-time constable of Darby, N. H., stepped out of his cruiser, paused to adjust his stomach, and with studied nonchalance said, "I see Willow's got himself in a pickle again."

"It's his pickle," said Ollie.

"Not quite. It's a public pickle. He's disturbing the peace of the good people down there on the highway."

"Do 'em some good to have their peace disturbed."

"If you won't get him down here, the law will," said Godfrey.

"Be my guest," said Ollie.

"He won't come down for you?"

"Nope. Got any ideas?"

"Not at the moment," said Godfrey.

The two men settled in, hands meditatively on their chins, like a couple of stand-up comics mocking intellectuals. Willow continued to perform. Occasionally, he would do a handstand on the top of the sign while giggling loudly at the upside-down world, and then, almost faster than the eye could follow, he would spring back to the world of right side up, and continue his walking. Or he would imitate Constable Perkins hoisting up his stomach by the gun belt. "If you could get a pair of pants on him, you could put him on the Ed Sullivan Show," said Perkins, who would have been surprised to hear that Ed Sullivan was deceased.

Godfrey Perkins was a passably tolerable man, for a cop, thought Ollie, who envied the constable for his stomach. It was a magnificent thing, a soft, basketball-sized, man's answer to pregnancy, especially remarkable in that it resided in the frame of an otherwise thin man.

As for himself, Ollie had never been able to cultivate an impressive gut. "You have to have good teeth to make good fat," he would say, and spit. His own blackened teeth punished him like a grief with a constant dull ache, unless he was drinking. They hurt him outright if he ate sweets, and they failed to serve him at all in chewing anything tougher than ground meat. Eating was such trouble he often skipped meals. But now, in the flush of noticing Godfrey's stomach, he was reconsidering his past ways. If he really wanted a nice-sized stomach, he said to himself, he would have to grind his food, and force himself to shovel three meals down the hatch. Was the product worth the labor? He glanced at Perkins, whose belly swayed to and fro, as if inside a lazy baby lolled. The sight inspired Ollie. He vowed silently to amend his life. The vow lifted his spirit for about thirty seconds, and then it vanished forever as he again heard the sound of a vehicle on his road.

A government car leading a cloud of dust came to a halt just behind Godfrey's cruiser. Ollie feared the worst—the Welfare

Department had come to get his boy. A woman driver and a male passenger stepped out of the car. Ollie watched them walk the hundred feet from where the cars were parked to the sign. To Ollie they looked like vacationers: tanned, pretty, dressed in colors instead of garments, it seemed, more ideas of people than actual people, the woman walking like a man, the man walking like a boy.

"Good morning," said the woman. "We're Kay Bradford, social worker, and George Petulio, intern, from the I-I? Independence for Independents in Keene?" Her voice traveled up-slope, so that it appeared she was asking a question instead of introducing herself. She glanced at Ollie, taking in his circumstance, he figured, like a loan company manager watching a stranger approaching his desk, but it was Perkins that she had addressed.

"Ma'am, you're talking to Constable Perkins and this is Mr. Jordan," said Godfrey, "and I must warn you that we've got a naked subject on top that sign."

The woman smiled. "Have you tried talking him down?" she asked.

"Not really; I just got here," said Godfrey.

Ollie could see that the woman was going to run the show. So it goes, he thought. Men talked big and fought big, and ran governments like fancy sportsmen's clubs, but when women chose to step in, they had their way. Women told you where to put the back door, what pan to spit in, and what pot to piss in, took, really, complete command of the important things. He believed that women were tough as oak knots on the inside, and that displays of tears and hysteria were more techniques of control than emotions. As for Polio, which was how Ollie heard the name "Petulio," there was something peculiar about him, and it took Ollie a moment or two to realize what it was. He was big, not bear-big or bull-big like some men, but merely unnaturally outsized, as though in the universe in which he lived, things came bigger.

"Mr. Jordan," said the woman. "We want to help your son, and we want to help you help yourself . . ." She knew him somehow, Ollie sensed, and he was alarmed. They had papers on him, he guessed. These government people knew everything and they knew nothing. They were more dangerous than Christian ministers. "We're going to try to talk him down, and you can stand by and help," said the woman.

She walked over to the sign, placing herself just below Willow, cupped her hands, and said to Willow in a strong voice, "Your mother and your brothers and sisters miss you. They want you to come home."

The word "mother" jarred Ollie into a fear that seemed for just a moment to transport him into a time past, and he saw Willow the infant playing in a pool of blood, if that's what it was, and then he was back into time present in the brightness of the day, the fear gone, and he was wondering how the woman had gotten on to him and Willow. Although, of course, she hadn't entirely. Willow had a mother, but she would not miss him. The woman must mean Helen, he figured; she must have talked to Helen, who had given her some of the facts of their life, but not all, of course, for Helen did not know all. He felt mildly disappointed. He had the idea (foolish, he realized) that the Welfare Department, if it did not know all, at least *could* know all. An idea came to him now that if the extraordinary events surrounding Willow's conception, birth, and upbringing were written down as official government record, the curse that had been put on his memory by the Witch would be lifted. ("I want to know," he had said to the Witch. "You don't want to know," she said. "I was there and you made me forget," he said. "You made yourself forget. All for the best.") How she could taunt him. Somehow, through her black magic, she had drawn curtains across his mind. ("You cut off parts of me. Makes a man lonely for his own self," he had said. "All for the best," she said.) Could the government help him? he asked himself, and he looked at the woman speaking to his son, and at the giant young man with the note pad, and he knew that they could not help. His past resided only in the mind of the Witch and in the region of his own bad dreams.

"Have you had anything to eat today?" the woman asked

Willow. "If you come down we'll buy you a biiiiig hamburger."

Willow continued his business on the sign, ignoring the woman.

"Willow . . . Willow . . . Willow," she called, but Willow seemed not to hear.

She continued for a few more minutes, but she had to step back when Willow turned toward her to urinate. Not that there was anything personal in his action. He just needed to take a leak.

Constable Perkins was disturbed. He had a daughter just a couple of years younger than the social worker, and it bothered him that there was not a trace of shame on her face at the sight of a naked man. The crazy idea was forming in his mind that himself witnessing the social worker watching Willow would somehow influence his own daughter toward depraved ways.

"Damn your soul, Jordan, get that subject down here," said Perkins to Ollie.

The woman turned a stern look on the constable. Clearly, she didn't like his approach, but then again hers wasn't succeeding. She seemed to consider the situation, and then she asked Ollie, "Why did he climb up there in the first place?"

"His reasons," said Ollie.

"Crazy reasons," said Perkins, as Petulio continued to scribble.

"He looks frightened to me," said the woman.

"He ain't, but he ought to be," said Ollie.

Kay Bradford thought she understood now. "Mr. Jordan, is that boy up there because you abused him?"

"I'm going to abuse him when he comes down," said Ollie. His voice was rough as granite. He was shocked by what he considered to be the woman's familiarity. It was clear to him before that they wanted to take his son away from him. Now it was clear that they also were looking for an excuse to put him in jail. They want everything, he thought. It wasn't the armies you had to fear. It was the truant officers and welfare people.

The woman caught hold of her emotions and said with a smile, "Mr. Jordan, you haven't been able to get the boy down. Why not give us a chance—alone? You just melt away. Maybe when he sees you're gone, he'll come down on his own."

"He always did like that sign. Course he never went up it bareass before." Ollie stood his ground. The smile on the woman's face demonstrated to him a lack of cleverness that heretofore he'd thought she possessed. She was dangerous, he said to himself, but ignorant as a stump. No way she could gain ascendancy over him.

It was Godfrey who worried Ollie now. The constable had lost his sense of humor; he was beginning to become professionally annoyed by the situation. Minutes later, Perkins summoned the woman and the note taker to the vehicles for a conference. Ollie could see that they were having a spat, and he could also see that Willow was not about to come down from the sign. When the woman returned, Ollie could tell by the urgency in her voice that something important had transpired at the vehicles.

"Willow, we don't have much time," she shouted. "Willow, it's hot today. You must be getting thirsty. If you come down, we'll buy you a . . . [she turned to Ollie] what does he drink?"

"Moxie." Ollie lied.

"Willow, we will bring you a Moxie," said the woman; then she turned to Petulio and said, "Go to the store and buy Willow a Moxie."

Petulio seemed uncertain whether she really meant what she said—as well he should be, thought Ollie—and his uncertainty seemed to shift from mind to body, so that he swayed like a tree sawed through but undecided which way to fall.

Ollie sidled up to Constable Perkins and launched an exploratory mission for information. "She ain't doing too good," he said.

"It don't matter," said Perkins. His hands were cupped under his stomach; his manner was distinctly self-satisfied.

Ollie moved off. He had no doubt now that Perkins had

called for help. He eased down to the vehicles, and there he heard the dispatcher speaking on the two-way radio in Perkins's cruiser. They were sending a fire truck with a hook and ladder from Keene, presumably to go get Willow. Ollie figured he had only minutes to act.

Back at the sign, Kay Bradford stood with her arms folded beside the sign. She had given up.

"A sad case," she said to Perkins. "Child abuse, parenting without goals or objectives." She spoke as if to implicate Perkins in the sadness of the case.

"He ain't no child, ma'am, he's as grown as you and me," Perkins said, defending, it seemed, himself.

"Mentally, still a child. Look at him," she said.

Perkins's small anger, small smugness had left him unexpectedly, and now he found himself blushing for the social worker, blushing because she could not blush herself. He simultaneously felt warmth for her, and revulsion. He didn't like this scene one bit. Too shifty. Give me a good accident, he thought, somewhere where I can be of service to the public. Oh, well, soon it would be over. "Retarded, I guess," he said.

"Possibly not. Possibly his development was arrested by a traumatic childhood experience."

Why, Perkins asked himself, did he get the feeling he was being implicated in Willow's problems? "Whatever—still an idiot," he said.

The social worker breathed a sigh that obviously was an accusation, and Perkins for the life of him couldn't understand what she thought he had done wrong.

At this point, Petulio, the assistant, put his note pad in his pocket and spoke for the first time. "Is that gas I smell?" he asked.

Constable Perkins was alarmed. It struck him that he had made a mistake in not keeping an eye on Ollie Jordan. Then he heard, or perhaps felt, a *wump!*—a thing of substance that seemed to engage him with a cloud of black smoke full of orange light and lift him off his feet and carry him into the sky. So this is death—not bad, he thought. Seconds later he came to his senses. The social worker and her assistant each had a hold of one of his ankles and they were dragging him along the ground. He could feel heat in the air. The indignity of being saved by a woman and a college student hastened a return of his manly bearing, and soon he was on his feet. The faces of his saviors—and his own, he guessed—were blackened. He thought about his brother, Andy, and how he would imitate Al Jolson singing, "Oh, Mammy, oh, Mammy . . ."

"He's taking him." That was the voice of the social worker and Perkins turned to see Willow scrambling down the un-burning end of the sign, saw his father corral him in some kind of rope getup with one hand, beat him with a stick with the other, until off they went like a couple of guys in old movies being chased by cops. Perkins, too, found himself running—dead last. Ahead of him were the social worker and the assistant. He saw the Jordans get in their vehicle and peel out. Seconds later the social worker reached her car, but Perkins knew somehow that this chase would not amount to anything. Sure enough, Ollie Jordan had taken the time to slash the tires of his cruiser and the government car.

Perkins turned to look at the burning sign. It was a pretty fire. The people on the highway would thrill to it. He deduced that Ollie Jordan had siphoned gas into a can, crept along the ledge, and doused the front of the sign with the gas while he and the social worker were busy yacking at the rear. Perkins now could hear the fire truck that he had summoned pulling off the hardtop onto the dirt road. There was a good chance it would be too big to negotiate the steep turns. Oh, well, that was of little importance. What was important was that the world, as he saw it, was becoming faintly orange around the edges. He began to taste the hot dog he'd had this morning from Joe Begin's lunch wagon. Nausea—sign of shock, he thought. He touched his face. It was numb, and left a dark, greasy smudge on his fingers. Under the black on his face would be red like a bad sunburn. Blow up a white man to make a Negro, he thought; wash a Negro to make an Indian. The social worker and the assistant had gotten out of the car, and they were moving toward him, floating it seemed on a carpet of orange light.

"Oh, my God, what's happened to our faces," said the social worker.

"Oh, Mammy, oh, Mammy," said Perkins.

The Charm

The first thing that Ollie did when he pulled his truck onto the main road was open the last quart of beer and with it salute the fire truck as it sped by. He drove about five miles and turned off a dirt road that led to a sandbank on the Boyle property, where he stashed his truck in some pucker brush. He tried to concentrate on what he should do next, but instead he remembered that as a boy he had conducted evening eavesdropping missions at another sandbank at the end of another road. High school boys in hee-haw voices came in packs to drink beer there, smash bottles, and talk about automobiles. Lovers parked in cars and struggled agonizingly for an hour to do what the young Ollie could do in two minutes. From his observations, he gained in knowledge. He concluded that people tried to imprison one another and in so doing imprisoned themselves. He was warned, and it wouldn't happen to him, he had told himself. He realized now that he had been wrong. Knowledge of error tended to make one error-prone instead of error-shy. Show a man the destruction a gun can bring, and the first thing he wants to do is fire it.

Undecided as to the proper course of action, Ollie walked his naked son through the woods a short way to Boyle's barn. He found an old army blanket in a stall and he wrapped Willow in it and took him up a ladder to the hayloft. Willow had drifted off into a walking-doze that sometimes came over him following his adventures. He'd be easy to handle until the next morning, when he'd awaken frisky and hungry. Ollie drank the remainder of his beer in the hayloft, but he dared not light his pipe. Farmers had good noses for smoke, especially in their barns. When the beer was gone, Ollie shackled Willow to himself and took a nap. Ollie preferred daytime sleeping because the demons stayed away. When Ollie woke, farmer Boyle was milking his cows below. "What's a matter with you?" he asked them. "Moon gotcha?" Ollie hungered for food, drink, and tobacco; his bladder cried for relief; and he was afraid that Willow might reveal their position at any moment. Guess I must be desperate, Ollie thought to himself, and was reassured by the idea since he didn't feel all that bad.

When night fell, Ollie tied Willow to a post in the barn and foraged outside. He swiped a pair of coveralls and a shirt from Mrs. Boyle's clothesline, dressed Willow, returned with him to the sandbank, and drove off in the truck. Time was running out. He had no money, no food, no drink, no place to dwell, no good ideas, and he was running low on tobacco. There was only one thing to do, what he always did when he was desperate: visit the Witch. He faced the prospect with loathing and excitement. It was as if he deliberately got himself into situations where he must turn to her. Oh, well, she'd have liquor, and she'd offer them succor. Had to.

The Witch lived in the tiny town of Dubber, N.H., named after Alexander Dubber, the founder of what is now the Boston law firm of Dubber, Dubber, Dubber, Grosbeck, and Dubber. The central feature in Dubber was Dubber Lake, which commanded a magnificent view of Mount Monadnock, which was only about 3186 feet high but gave the illusion of being higher because it was surrounded by smaller hills and because its peak was bare of trees. Dubber was dominated by a class of people who had lived the American dream in reverse. During the 1920s, the progenitors of this class had come to Dubber, drawn by the lake and the mountain, to build a couple of dozen mansions that lay hidden in the spruce and birch forests like mortal sins deep in the souls of clergymen. When the 1930s came, the money slowly evaporated; by the 1940s, all the servants had gone to war and returned affluent and arrogant; by the 1980s, the sons and daughters of the builders found themselves with huge real estate holdings that they could not afford to own or maintain. The town was also pocked with small populations of shacks and trailers, and in one of the trailers, on the edge of a bog, lived the Jordan Witch.

Ollie and Willow arrived under the blue light of a full moon. Stumps poked up through the stagnant water of the bog and immediately were transformed in Ollie's mind into the petrified remains of slouching, stunted men carrying sacks of their young to be drowned, the men rooted in the mud as punishment by the granite god of the mountain that loomed in the background. He could smell the cesspool as they approached the trailer. The edge of a swamp was a crazy place for a home, he thought. It would be windy and cold in the winter, stifling and hot in the summer; it would be infested by mosquitoes and birds that ruined a man's sleep first thing in the morning. And yet, the place had a beauty that took hold of him. The stars were so numerous overhead that he could feel a lifting of the weight of his own isolation. The Witch had gotten the place a couple of years ago from an old man whom she had screwed to death, or so Ollie imagined. The property included a trailer up on blocks that seemed to be sinking slowly into the soft earth, a shed that perhaps had been there before the trailer, a tiny lawn and garden. There were no other of man's works to be seen; the area was dominated by the immensities of swamp, forest, mountain, sky. A light was on in the trailer, but Ollie could see no sign of life. The Witch would be in the shadows, like a spider or a dirty book, or perhaps she was in the bedroom entertaining. He wouldn't put it past her. The idea suddenly outraged him. "And at her age," he heard himself say to Willow, who halted, looked up, and raised his arms. Startled, Ollie put his hand across his eyes, sensing a bat honing in on them. It took him a second to realize that Willow was trying to touch the stars. "Far away, you idiot," Ollie said cruelly, wounded, for the boy's simple gesture had made him realize his own smallness, and Ollie understood that wherever the boy went they would want to kill him out of jealousy for the purity of his expression and out of fear for the power of his strangeness.

He stood there with Willow on the doorstep, which consisted of a board resting on two flat stones. Ollie paused at the screen door. He could see into the kitchen, could see the cat staring at him from a basket on the dining table, could smell the smoke from the Witch's wacky tobaccky. He hated the idea of knocking on the door, of walking in. He wanted to be drawn in, to be absolved of the responsibility of acting. Finally, he heard the Witch's voice from inside: "Don't just stand there, come on in." He did as he was told.

The Witch was in the living room half-sitting, half-lying on the couch, as if in homage to the graceful "s" of ascending smoke from her pipe. "Stoned again," Ollie said.

"You got your habit for after dark. I got mine. Yours, by the way, is in the cupboard," she said.

A chill ran through him. She had been waiting for him. She had been waiting all along. She had told him once that sometimes though he might be miles away she could sense his moods and follow his movements in her mind. It was a lie, a typical tactic to keep him bound to her, and yet the idea haunted him like an unreasonable fear of poison in canned foods. She had probably heard of Willow's exploits on the radio, and then she had figured that he and Willow would come here. Not that she would admit such a thing. She'd spook up the explanation. A witch had to keep the world off balance, keep simple matters in confusion, find design where there was only blowing leaves, and keep the fear she raised in proportion to her real power, else they would burn her as in olden times.

She had thinned out some since the last time he had seen

her, aged as if from additional knowledge rather than just wear, but her hair was still boot black and her eyes writhed like snakes dropped in fire. She rose and came toward them, and Ollie caught the aroma of her and recognized the kinship between them. She shuffled past him and gave Willow a brief embrace. Ollie stiffened—with protective concern? With jealousy? He didn't know.

"I see you got electricity put in—you must be getting old," Ollie said, to fill a space.

"These days, I need good light," she said, leading them into the kitchen. Her voice had the raspiness of old women who smoke too much.

"Used to be you liked the dark," Ollie said.

"I still like the dark. Used to be you were 'fraid of the dark," she said, somehow leaving a vague threat that she could if she chose douse the lights at any moment.

"I get along," he said.

She stood there, saying nothing, imposing a moment of anxiety between them. Having made her point, she broke the spell by turning on the television.

"I got TV now. Makes the time go by for an old woman," she said.

She was very good to them, then. She washed Willow's face and brought him some milk. Later she led him to the couch and with a whisper, it seemed, put him to sleep. Ollie helped himself to the bottle of whiskey in the cupboard. He didn't dare buy hard liquor himself. He liked it too much. It would kill him some day, he knew, as it had killed or led to the murder of most men everywhere. The drink eased him down to a warm spot—at the gates of hell, he thought.

"Your whiskey?" he asked.

"I don't touch that piss anymore," she said, blowing some wacky tobaccky smoke at him. "Some old man left it here."

"And you can't remember which one, can you?" Ollie said.

"What difference does it make? You got the bottle."

"It don't make no difference to me," he said, knowing that he had left himself open.

"Course it makes a difference. It always did with you," she said.

She boiled him a potato and some carrots, mashed them with a fork, and added two tins of strained beef baby food, which he guessed she had shoplifted. She didn't have a tooth in her head, and the men loved her for it, she would brag sometimes, just to infuriate him.

She's fit as a fern in the shade, he thought, and his mind flashed back to his land and the burning sign and his old shepherd dog out there in the wild. Creatures died quick deaths from fangs, or slow deaths full of visions from starvation from lack of teeth—this was God's way, if there was a God. It was only humans that lived on without a tooth, to die of diseases unintended by God, if there was a God.

The food settled into him like a cheering, harmless lie. He was, he thought, darned near completely relaxed. They retired to the living room before the television—Willow asleep on the couch, Ollie in the easy chair with the bottle of whiskey and a glass, the Witch in a shadow, partly in the living room, partly in the cramped hall that led to the bedrooms. She was sitting in a kitchen chair she had brought in, and she lit her pipe as Ollie lit his. Soon the room was filled with the smoke of marijuana and Carter Hall tobacco. Ollie drank steadily, peacefully. From time to time he glanced at the Witch. She watched television as though trying to hypnotize it. As for himself, he did not seem to take in the programs. He would see a man rise up out of the ocean, as if born that moment, and then he would be watching some fellows in a bar drinking beer, and then some gunshots would draw his attention, and there seemed through all these fragments an unending automobile chase. Getting drunk, he thought. Wonderful. Isn't that wonderful? Occasionally, he would speak, out of character, even to himself . . . "Let us hope for a kindly summer, me lady." The Witch would say nothing, or tell him to shut up.

Soon he lost track of time. Reality was a blend of things that presented themselves, as if for introduction only, and then vanished. The television was off, and it was on, and it had been moved, or he had been moved. The Witch gave him some of her weed to smoke, and the colors from her dress burst toward him like exploding flowers. It seemed to him that certain secrets in familiar sounds were revealed to him—a volcanic rumble in Willow's snoring; something in his own jumbled speech that sounded like a chicken being strangled. He was talking to the Witch, or perhaps she was talking to him. Hard to tell the difference, he thought, vastly amused, and he laughed aloud and continued laughing until he had forgotten why. Ideas trooped in and out of his mind, like armies. For a moment it seemed to him that he was reaching into his past, into that lost mine of memory, reaching for the source of the unknown grief that had shadowed his being all these years. He was just at the door of recollection when the Witch touched his arm and jarred him into speaking. "Different facts don't change the same old shit," he said, and the door of memory slammed shut.

During part of the time they were in the kitchen, and here the Witch had sat him down for one of her little talks.

"That boy of yours is eating you up," she said. "Give him to the state. They can do more for him than you can."

"He'll die with the state," Ollie had said.

"Together, you both die. You think somehow he's your better half, but it ain't so, Ollie. He's your worser half."

He wanted to tell her of the enormous possibilities in Willow, possibilities of the kinship itself, but really he had no argument. Just a queer faith. And the conversation had dribbled away because they were both drunk and stoned.

He was back in the living room, and on the television there was a monkey dressed like a child, and Ollie was smelling the Witch's hair, a waterfall of aroma pouring over him, and the monkey seemed to reach out with desperate hands to its keeper, to ask why, oh, why, oh, why, and the Witch's arms were about his shoulders, and he wanted to say to her, "black flowers," but instead he said only, "whatever—" and she was speaking to him: "Admit it, you come to me for succor." And he was weeping, deep wracking sobs of childhood, and his face was in the cascade of her hair and he was on a boat, and he knew he was out of his senses. When they returned, the Witch was holding his head over the sink, and he was puking. She had planned this, he thought, and he had succumbed. He had succumbed totally to her and would continue to succumb, as it was meant. At the final reckoning, if there was one, the judge would say: "All parties are guilty."

"Stop crying," she said.

"I ain't crying," Ollie said in the voice of a child.

"Stop crying," said the Witch.

"Don't you have no feelings?"

"I don't feel nuthin'. It don't pay to feel. You don't feel nuthin', either. Drunk feeling don't count. Now shut up."

The Witch ran cold water over Ollie's head and cleaned him up. He was a little soberer then.

"What am I going to do, Witch?" he asked.

"You can't get by with that boy in the culture," she said, exaggerating her New Hampshire accent so that the word "culture"—"cull-cha"—had the impact of a curse word.

"I admit he's a nuisance," Ollie said.

The Witch burst into a mean laughter. "You're your own nuisance, Ollie Jordan. He's just something in your mind. Give him up. Be good for the both of you."

"As you say, something in my mind. Where he goes I go," Ollie said.

She laughed again, cackling like the old whore that she was. "You remind me of a case I heard about, an old man got elephant balls from a disease, and he carried 'em in a wheelbarrow everywhere he went."

"As you say, Witch," Ollie said, and something in his voice insulted her, and she turned on him and slapped his face. A moment later she was kindly again, and he wondered whether he had imagined that he had been slapped.

"If it has to be the three of you—you, him, and the chain—take him out in the pucker brush for a spell. He always liked it out there, and the culture don't care what goes on there. If you can't live off the culture, live out of the culture," the Witch said.

To the pucker brush: The idea took hold in him.

Having made her point, the Witch brought him to his feet and steered him into the bathroom. When he was finished, she led him to the tiny spare bedroom and shut the door. Outside, the crickets were calling in kinship. He heard himself giggle. He undressed. He felt pretty much whole—"Thank you, booze," he said. And then as if to remind him that no man is ever really one with himself, a stranger inside him said "*Plant thy seed and grow thy flower.* He lay down on the bed. Nice bed. He listened to himself make *em* sounds. He handled himself, discovering that at the moment he was not able. For the first time, he felt completely safe, and he fell into a dream that was the color green.

Later in the night he awoke, realizing at once that she had come and gone. She had bided her time, returning to the bed after the dulling powers of the whiskey had been transformed into a bile in his loins while his brain was still lulled by sleep. His thoughts took a turn: *Them ain't crickets, and these ain't bed springs a-squeaking, but oar locks a-creaking. The Witch she comes out of the sky rowing on an old flat-bottom boat.* And he was asleep again. Later still, the smell of the cesspool coming through the open window in his room shoved him like a mean brother, and he knew the Witch had visited Willow, too. He woke in the morning to the color green slowly fading into the yellow of sunshine, which diluted his memory of the night to a suspicion.

The Witch made a huge breakfast of scrambled eggs, sausage, applesauce, and coffee (Kool-Aid for Willow). The food freshened father and son. Willow began behaving like a puppy—a 180-pound puppy. At one point, he tried to embrace the Witch, who boxed his ears until he let go. Ollie was in such a good mood, he could only react with laughter.

"What are you going to do?" the Witch asked, turning the situation inside out with the tone of her voice, so that Ollie was suddenly on guard.

"Going into the woods, like you said, to live away from the culture," Ollie said.

"How do you figure your prospects?" she asked.

"I never had no prospects. I never had no luck. You know that," Ollie said.

"What if I said I had some luck for you?" the Witch asked.

She was up to something. She had softened him with a good breakfast and now she was going to eat him in her toothless mouth, like a mushy boiled egg. "I'd say, if it's luck you got for me it's bad luck."

"It don't matter, Ollie," she said. "Your luck has been so bad that any more luck either will be the same or worse."

He didn't like her using his first name. "If my luck could get worse, you'd be the one to do it," he said.

"I want to give you some luck," she said.

Ollie didn't know what to say. The Witch almost was showing affection. It curdled him inside. He found himself nodding. The Witch rose and then went to her bedroom. When she returned, she was holding a small wooden carving of flowers, roses maybe, the arrangement coming into focus now as a butterfly. The wood had dried and cracked, and the stain that had made the flowers red had gone bad and was now the color of dried blood. Still, he liked the carving, liked the way it felt in his hands.

"It's a charm. It will bring you luck," the Witch said.

"I don't need this. I need money," said Ollie.

"I've got money."

"I know you've got money, and I know how you get it."

"Take the charm."

"Looks like a butterfly, a goddamn butterfly. How did you come by it?"

"I'll say that you've seen it before, in the old days," she said, and it was as if he were trying to recall a dream bathed in orange light.

"I can't remember," he said.

"All for the best."

The Witch gave him some money, making it clear that if he took the money he was to take the charm. It was really very pretty, and it was light and could fit in a coat pocket. He didn't believe in her hocus-pocus, her astrology charts, her funny cards, and he didn't believe in this charm. There might even be some danger in it. Anything from the old days he had to suspect. But he couldn't deny that it felt good in the hand, that it seemed to belong with him.

Mrs. Clapp

The storekeeper was surprised when a black man came into his store, wiped his brow with a red handkerchief, remarked casually about the heat of the day, bought a six-pack of Coke in cans, and walked out. The storekeeper was so surprised that he followed the man outside, for what purpose he could not have told you. The man got into a svelte Oldsmobile and joined a wife and a couple of kids. The man smiled at the storekeeper, the kids smiled, the storekeeper smiled and found himself returning the good-bye waves of the kids as the car started moving down the road. The car had New Jersey plates. Tourists, he thought, and went back into his store.

It was the first time since he had arrived in New Hampshire that he had seen any black people and he found that black people now affected him in a different way from the way they used to. He was oddly at once sympathetic toward them and yet repelled, as though they were carriers of some disease. It was a while before he realized that his new attitude had been drawn unconsciously from the native world of Darby.

That afternoon, in the hour before the old-timers would start arriving to chew the fat, the storekeeper took stock of himself and his relationship to black people. It came to him that a big reason he had come to this town was that there were no black people here. Not that he would have admitted that at the time. Not that he was a bigot—then or now. There was no man, no thing, no idea that he truly hated in this world—except maybe the New York Yankees. Still, there was the feeling in him that he was a bigot. It took him about twenty minutes of stumbling about in his thoughts to find an explanation, and when he did find it, he acted it out in a passionate, glamorous, imaginary plea before the black man that had come into his store, the man, his dark skin like a judge's robes, standing there in the theater of the storekeeper's mind.

Every heart is a lonely heart, the storekeeper argued in his mind, unaware that he had cribbed the phrase from Old Man Dorne. Every heart seeks fellowship with his own kind to soften that loneliness. It's not that I'm against the black. It's that the black gets in the way of the fellowship of the white, just as the white gets in the way of the fellowship of the black.

Let me give you an example. I'm not from around here; I'm from Pee-Ay, and I was brought up, courtesy of my dad and my Uncle Chet, a Pirates fan. It was an honorable thing to be a Pirate fan, and any time I was rooting for the Pirates I was not lonely. Heck, I didn't complain when they got Clemente and guys like that. I applauded, because you see then the fellowship of the team was white. Well, there came a day when there were more starters on the team that were black than white, and that was the day that the fellowship of the team turned black. It was a lonely day for me. The hard part to understand is that there can't be a gray; the fellowship is either black or white. That's why the fellowship of, say, a neighborhood changes in a flash and catches people off guard. Overnight, they go from comfy to lonely. Then comes the hatred and the evil actions. I feel as bad about this situation as you do. There's but one way to stop the hatred and that's to reintroduce the security of the fellowships—yours and mine—and then all the hatred will pass and we can treat each other like polite strangers. The thing that tipped the scales when I was weighing reasons to come here—unconsciously, I mean—I mean, I just at this moment discovered this myself—is that the fellowship of the team they root for here, the Boston Red Sox, is white. Oh, I know they got Rice, and I root for Rice, but the fellowship of the team is white. See, it's like the Pirates got Garner, but basically the fellowship of the team is black. Come World Series time, I'll root for the Red Sox, you root for the Pirates, and we'll both be happy . . .

At that moment, the storekeeper was interrupted in his thoughts. Old Man Dorne came in the store, followed moments later by a man with a bandage on his nose.

"I see a family of coloreds down the road, stretching a bit by the lake," said Old Man Dorne. "Scare me to death every time I see those people. They've all got the shanks of chorus girls, tough hides, tough skulls, and brains untainted by all those past generations of inbred Europeans that afflicts us hearts here in Darby. Someday they'll rule the world. Mark my words."

"The world maybe, but not this backyard. They couldn't stand the cold here," said the man with the bandaged nose. He spoke with a slow, melodious drawl, accompanied by a small, secretive smile, as though minutes earlier he had bedded the wife of some prominent official. That smile elicited such a jab of concern in the storekeeper he was taken with an urge to lock his cash box.

Old Man Dorne sent the man a nasty look, but the man either did not notice or cared too little to respond. The storekeeper realized now that they had not come in together, but they knew each other.

"I expected to see Mr. Flagg here," said Bandage Smile.

"Flagg's gone—heart attack took him in the spring of the year," said Old Man Dorne.

"We all got to go," said the man, still smiling, making small talk, leading up to something.

Old Man Dorne said nothing, averting his eyes from the man.

The man, perhaps aware that he was wielding considerable influence merely by his presence, stood still silently smiling for a long moment before finally addressing the storekeeper.

"How about forking over some Carter Hall pipe tobacco," he said, and when the storekeeper took his money, he added: "You sell much of this tobacco, do you?"

"You own stock in the company?" asked the storekeeper.

"Nope. Just want to know where my kin are," the man said, and left the store. The parting comment puzzled the storekeeper and made him uneasy.

"That's Ike Jordan," said Old Man Dorne. "Kind of gives you the heebie-jeebies, don't he? He's an auctioneer by trade, but who knows what else he's mixed up in."

"Funny customer—my day for 'em. The black people first, then that one with the nose," said the storekeeper.

"School's out a week now. Americans of every ilk and heart are taking to the roads," said Old Man Dorne, as if that closed the door on the subject.

The storekeeper was about to explain his breakthrough in understanding race relations, but as he fumbled for expression, he realized that some key parts of the knowledge that he had acquired just minutes ago had slipped away. He could remember that word "fellowship," but for the life of him he couldn't gather up the ends of the argument that had given the word meaning. So he said nothing. He waited, mildly uncomfortable in a small grief, but confident that some other equally small event would occur to freshen his psyche.

Minutes later another one of the old-timers entered the store, his eyes shining with a recently found nugget of information.

"You'll never guess what I saw," he said. "Had rolled-up pants like a stork and was wading to beat the band along the roadside shore of Spofford Lake."

"I can guess," said Old Man Dorne.

Ike Jordan drove off in his mighty Cadillac and now that he knew he had been recognized, removed the bandage from his nose. He also removed his teeth—"my smile," he would call them, immensely vain—and placed them on the dashboard. The bandage was for the sake of strangers. It was a trick he had learned while serving time at the county farm. An old con man had told him, "Put a bandage on your nose, commit a crime, and all the witnesses will remember is the bandage." Not that Ike had any intention of committing a crime, at least not today. He just liked the idea of deception, and so frequently he put the bandage on. It made him feel hidden. It never occurred to him that by repeatedly wearing a bandage on your nose, eventually some people will get to know you by that mark, that the bandage could become an identification card as well as a mask. Ike Jordan was known by his friends as a smart man with a stupid streak and by his enemies as a stupid man with a few dangerous smarts. He could read the subtle tale on the face of a man who had more money in his pocket than ability to manage it and who was begging you to swindle him in order to relieve him of the burden of it; but he had no insight into his own meager abilities as a gambler or even his own foolish hunches, which time and again paid off even less than the law of averages should allow. He often drove with his teeth on the dashboard because they reminded him that he was a successful man.

He was taking this little excursion into the town of Darby for a couple of reasons. He had a pretty good idea that somewhere in this town he could find his half-brother Ollie. He wasn't going to demand that Ollie return the beer he had taken from him because that would show that he cared. Rather, he wanted merely to engage Ollie in conversation, to smile upon him, to humiliate him if possible, to show his own ascendancy. Normally, Ike would not dare take on Ollie, but he sensed now that his brother's power was on the wane. It was time for a challenge—family battle, Jordan style.

Another reason he had come to Darby was to scout town properties for possible burglaries. Ike Jordan was a proud burglar. He thought it the curse of his profession that you could get public acceptance for your talents only by getting caught. Sometimes he imagined that he had died and in the newspaper the next day there was a comment by a prominent public official, say the police chief in Keene, to the effect that Ike Jordan was one wing-dinger of a burglar. As it was, he was satisfied (most of the time) with the adoration of his young kin, whom he had taken on as apprentices in his craft. It was the craft that had spurred Ike Jordan into being a reader. He had realized early on that the newspaper was full of tips, and so he had taken his few years of education and enlarged upon them through study. He was not sorry. He found the obituary columns especially useful, for they provided the names of persons who would be sure to be away from their houses during funerals. He also read all the realty ads for hints on the value of items that might be in certain homes. All in all, Ike Jordan was one of the most careful, grateful readers of *The Keene Sentinel.*

Not that finding an empty place to burglarize took that much work. The skill came in finding the right place, and also in developing a system of selling one's wares. So it was that Ike got into the auction business. He fancied himself very honest in that business, although that wasn't exactly true. Occasionally he cheated a buyer on general principles. He never auctioned the goods he stole. He trucked them to an associate in Connecticut, where he was able to exchange them for goods stolen from other areas. Thanks to his profession as a burglar, he had acquired knowledge in antiques, art, architecture, history, etiquette, and even psychology, for he learned that people outside the Jordan kinship tended to judge their fellow men by appearances. Oh, he had his blind spots, but for the most part, he considered himself a pretty well-rounded guy.

He drove along the roads of Darby, sometimes concentrating, but more often just enjoying the nice day. He wasn't trying very hard to find Ollie. He only wanted to show himself that he was ready to take him on, if it came to that. He knew that Ollie might be at Howard Elman's house, but he didn't want any part of Elman. Nevertheless, he decided to take a ride past the Elman place to see what had been done since the fire there last spring. He found that the house had been removed, a new trailer was parked in its place. The change did not interest him, but the changes to the Swett house up the hill captured his attention. It was evident from the remodeling job that someone with means and flair had bought the property from Swett's heirs. He listed the house as a possible for burglary, one of a number that he filed away in his mind.

The property that intrigued him most was the widow Clapp's residence—a brick, colonial house with a granite foundation. He remembered reading the obituary of Osgood Clapp a while back. Osgood and Amy Clapp had moved into the house recently from Keene. But the item that he had filed away for future consideration was that Osgood Clapp had been a past president of the New Hampshire Antique Clock Association. The place must be jammed with clocks, he thought. Old clocks were wonderful items for burglary. They were easily moved, easily valued, easily disposed of. And they were beautiful. The idea of stealing the clocks stirred him. He took only a professional's dispassionate satisfaction in stealing purely utilitarian items, but it gave him great pleasure to take things of great beauty. Driving by, he saw that the house sat behind some maples that partly shielded it from the road. He resolved to learn more about the house and Mrs. Clapp. As he turned the Cadillac back toward the main highway, he realized he had some studying to do. He put his teeth back into his mouth, the bandage back on the nose. Now, I can think better, he thought.

The widow Clapp sat in the living room of her fine, old house, surrounded by clocks, her feet in a pan of warm water to soothe the hurt joints. She had disconnected her hearing aid and was listening to the waves crashing on the beach of her mind. Someday they will find my empty skull, she thought, and they will hold it to their ears and they will hear the ocean, as in a conch shell. More and more, she preferred the sound in her head to what she heard with her ears. What she heard was a gentle moan much like the sound at York Beach on a night sixty-five years ago when Osgood was courting her. It was a violent sound, yet restful, too, because you could depend on it and because it judged not. She used to like to listen to the chattering of her grandchildren, the ring of the telephone, the birds that woke her in the summer at five o'clock, even the damn television, which she associated with the sound of gunshots (Osgood Clapp loved westerns), inchoate music, and what she apprehended as the *er, er, erup* of David Brinkley, although the voice she heard might actually have belonged to Walter Cronkite or Harry Reasoner—any newscaster.

But things had changed for her, or the world had changed. Hard to tell which, and really she didn't care. Time, quite literally, was rushing by for her. It was as if the world were a movie and someone had speeded up the reel. Cars raced by her house; her family came to visit, scurried about like hungry mice, and was gone; television shows came on and before she could grasp the plot, the program had changed; she sat in her chair after tea, and before she knew it the sun was setting. She reminded herself now to keep an eye on the telephone. It had a light as well as a bell, and she could plug in her hearing aid to answer it when the light went on. Even with the hearing aid turned up high, the voice on the other end would be small and distorted. Every day her son Philbert—no, Raymond: Philbert was dead, must remember—called from Keene, sounding like Donald Duck, to inquire as to her health. The truth was the purpose of each call was an inquiry into her state of mind. He was getting ready to lock her up in an old folks home. "Must watch the telephone for the light," she said aloud. "Must prove . . ." She lost her train of thought. "Oh, yes, must prove competence." What did it matter to them whether she was competent or not? Crazy sense of duty, or maybe it was fear that the neighbors would talk about them, say they weren't meeting their duty. Well, that was saner. Worry the neighbors and eventually they'll bring you down: rule of life.

When Osgood was alive, she had hated to face her own old age, because his old age had been so repulsive to her. Now that he had passed away—how she liked that phrase, "pass away," like fall leaves in the wind—her attitude had changed. So what the aching joints, so what the high blood pressure, so what the dimmed senses, so what the longing to be touched? Old age had its compensations. Whereas before her mental world was cluttered with worry and imaginings in dull black and white or even just in words, now that world was as full of color and story as a wild dream. So what that trivial matters such as the name of the new grocer or the precise location of the aspirin seemed to escape the grasp of her mind? The important things, such as the time she ice-skated all day in the January of her twelfth year, came back to her time and again like a beloved movie to entertain and instruct her. If middle age was time to gather, old age was a time to dispose, so that one could see better the value of what remained. Old age was a transition period between this world and the next. They think I'm senile, she thought, but I'm already part ghost, and that's why they're scared of me. She sensed now that all the clocks in the house were striking five o'clock. That was impossible of course, since she had refused to rewind them after Osgood died. Still, she could hear them sounding, each and every one. It passed through her mind that Osgood was trying to reach her from the beyond. She considered that idea for a moment and found it good. She turned up her hearing aid. The clocks stopped. It was quiet in the house. There was only the sound of her own breathing. She noticed now that the water in the pan was tepid, her feet soft as overboiled potatoes. "My how time flies," she said, to hear her own voice.

After Ollie Jordan left the Witch, he immediately drove to Keene. He had a half-assed idea that to survive he must light out for the woods. He had a vague plan about hiding Willow from the Welfare Department by bringing him to a place he had discovered while hunting deer a few years back with Howard Elman. But at the moment survival was not a problem. He had food in his belly and money the Witch gave him in his pocket. The closer to Keene he drove the better he felt, and the better he felt the vaguer his plan became. Even when he arrived in Keene, he knew that it was wrong for him to be advertising himself in broad daylight. But jeeze, he felt so good. The charm the Witch had given him was working, the charm and money were making him carnival-crazy, he thought; and having identified the nature of his mood he set out to enjoy it. He parked his vehicle in the lot behind Miranda's Bar. He chained Willow to the steering wheel and locked the doors, although he left the windows open to keep the heat from broiling the boy. The short walk west on Roxbury Street from the parking lot to the bar was pleasant, although he knew that someone from the Welfare Department might leap upon him at any moment and take Willow away to a school for the mentally retarded. But at the moment, he was absolutely confident that he could handle such an eventuality. It was the charm, he thought. He entered Miranda's, looked dead on at the Greek behind the bar, and said, "bee-yah."

The bartender was startled. "I'm not open—too early," he said.

Ollie had seen the bartender a hundred times and knew his name to be George but nothing else about him. He saw that George recognized him, too.

"Well, whoopie-do—the door was open. I'm a paying customer, and I got money," Ollie said, and he unrolled the bills that the Witch had given him.

The bartender looked at the clock. "Ten twenty ay-crisely-em," he said. "The place opens at eleven, but I suppose that's what I get for keeping my door unlocked. Did you have a brand that you were interested in?"

"I'll take a Molson, if you got it," said Ollie, bragging about his money in the roundabout way of ordering expensive beer.

The bartender locked his front door, brought Ollie a beer, snapped on the television set, and started mopping the floor. Ollie took a swallow of beer and turned his attention to the TV. A children's program was on the air.

It seemed to him that he had seen this program before, but had never given it much thought. Now he homed in on it. His senses and reflexes were sharpened from food, from the Witch's touch, and the program was a universe for him to consider. After half an hour had passed (two and a half beers), Ollie began to shape in his own mind what the program meant. It was about all these creatures who lived in this Says-me Street. It was the strangest place he'd ever seen. The fellow he most admired on the program lived in a garbage can. He was the only one of the characters that understood that the world was a dangerous, unpleasant place. There was another creature, a giant bird, who appalled Ollie. The bird was so unnaturally huge, so ignorant of the obvious. Furthermore, it seemed unnatural that the other creatures on the program did not make fun of the bird. Not true to life, he thought. A couple of the smaller creatures, a Bert and an Ernie, reminded him of members of his own family. The Bert creature was practical-minded, but he was constantly frustrated by the Ernie creature, who had a knack of presenting foolish ideas in a sensible way. The Bert and the Ernie were like a married couple, he thought, like his Uncle Alvin and Aunt Leona. The Bert maintained a realistic grasp of circumstances, while the Ernie did not, yet in the end it was the Ernie who prevailed. True that life sometimes went like that, he thought, but it was downright immoral for television to glorify such disorder. At one point Ollie thought, Bert, don't take crap from Ernie—bat him one.

The make-believe creatures on the show, for all their defects, at least were somewhat believable. They showed certain human frailties. They even looked like people he knew. But the real people on the show were completely unreal to Ollie. They were always reasonable, and they were always smiling and dancing; they didn't argue, fight, or shout; they threw around a lot of unwarranted affection but seemed to have no sex drive. Maybe they just hide it, he thought. There were also black and white people, people of both sexes and of varying ages, all apparently getting along, and that, too, was unreal to Ollie Jordan. Throughout the story there were frequent interruptions by cartoon characters promoting the letter "v" and the number "6." It took Ollie a while to figure out that the whole purpose was educational, and this realization was accompanied by an unaccountable surge of anger.

As the show continued, it took on a vaguely menacing quality. At one point, the bird got stuck in a Volkswagen, its long neck and head protruding through the sun top. No one seemed to know what to do about the situation. The answer was clear to Ollie: cut open the goddamn car with a blow torch. It angered him that none of the creatures or people on the show could come up with that simple solution. Then his anger gave way to unease. There was something strange going on. Someone should know how to free that bird. It was as if they were all crazy, as if they were trying to make the people who were watching the show crazy as themselves. The only sane one on the show was the fellow who lived in the garbage can, and they were all trying to change him, make him one of their own, make him crazy. It struck him now that the people on the show and most of the creatures probably worked for the Welfare Department, and the show was their way of molding minds. The idea saddened him and made him fearful. He felt a great kinship for the fellow in the garbage can, but he doubted the fellow's ability to stand up to the forces around him. There were just too many people against him, too much cunning to overcome. Finally, he turned away from the television set. It was just too depressing. He finished his beer, but it did nothing for him. He felt menaced by the TV. He paid up and left. He was resentful. Says-me Street had robbed him of his good mood.

Donald's Junkyard

When Ollie got back to his truck, his nose told him that Willow had shit in his pants. He smacked the boy in the face and—as usual—immediately was sorry. "If I tie you up, how can you help it?" Ollie said, knowing that his tone would serve as an apology, knowing that Willow would understand apology no better than he understood the purpose of the blow. He cleaned the mess as best he could, rolling up Willow's trousers and underwear in a ball. Once again, he had a bareass son beside him. A sign? And, if so, of what? That he could not provide, as a good father must? Perhaps. The thought depressed him. He wondered what to do with Willow's dirtied clothes. They were evidence, he thought. If they were discovered by the Welfare Department they might be traced back to him. Ollie didn't bother to consider how such a trace might be done. The fact that the idea had occurred to him was enough to convince him that it had some merit. He tried to think about the problem, but got lost for a moment in an intrusive revery about a green place full of singing. He was jolted then by voices, two men talking on the street about land taxes. It seemed to Ollie they were conspiring against him, and he drove off in a small terror. Must get rid of the evidence, he thought.

He was frantic, and his mind was working with the fragments of thoughts, one upon the other. He believed for certain that he was being pursued, and yet he knew that he was not being pursued; he must get rid of the evidence of the dirtied clothes not so much to divert the pursuit as to rid himself of the feeling of pursuit. He drove until he found himself at Robin Hood Park in Keene. The water in the park pond was brown, with white lights tossed about on tiny waves. He took his bundle and got out of the truck, with the intention of weighing the bundle down with rocks and throwing it in the pond, but there were some kids fishing across the way. Ollie stood there, unsure now of what to do. He wondered vaguely whether the kids worked for the Welfare Department. He noticed now that Willow, although chained inside the truck, had rolled the window down and was waving to the kids. Must do something, Ollie told himself. About fifty feet away was a trash barrel, and so he decided to chuck the bundle in the barrel; but when he got to the barrel he could not do it. Ollie was a collector of trash, a dump rat, and all his instincts cried out for him to take away, not to deposit. He rummaged through the can and found a damaged kite, some brown paper bags, and a red crayon. He rescued these items and returned to the truck and drove off.

Calmer now, he pondered his goods: kite, bags, crayon, shitty pants. It seemed to him that, somehow, he had been commanded from on high to take them, that they held some meaning. He tried to think now, but fell back into his revery of the green place. It was the place up on the hill called Abare's Folly that he and Elman had found. A place as hidden and as beautiful as a great idea imprisoned in a wild mind. And the solution to the problem of the dirtied clothes came to him, as he knew it would. He wrapped the dirty pants in the brown paper bags, tied them with the string from the kite, wrote with the crayon "Welfare Department" on the package, and dropped it into the first mailbox he happened upon. The Welfare Department would find the pants anyway, let 'em get the stuff direct, he thought, and laughed to himself. "Willow," he said, "you ain't the only one with a good sense of humor." Willow did not answer. He was looking out the window. Looking perhaps for the boys who were fishing.

Ollie's good mood returned, if somewhat dimmed; his good sense exerted itself. He must have clothes for Willow, and for himself too, he realized, not just to cover Willow's bottom, but for warmth and even for style in the days to come. He headed for the Salvation Army Citadel on Roxbury Plaza.

Ollie liked the Salvation Army. He liked the spiffy uniforms of the soldiers for Christ. He liked the way the brigadiers, by maintaining a certain aloofness, allowed a man to keep his own aloofness intact even as he begged at their feet. He liked the lovely singing that came from their chapel, which he had never entered. The singing seemed to him to blend sadness and celebration, as if the singers were on the deck of a great, sinking ship giving their all before it slipped into the deep. He liked, in a harmless lecherous way that enriched his interior life, the pale ladies in blue who rang bells around Christmastime.

In the citadel there was a secondhand clothing store. Here Ollie came to buy summer outfits for himself and Willow. There were plenty of clothes to choose from. Members of the richer classes of the city discarded many of their clothes here, partly to assuage a vague guilt and partly because the citadel was in the middle of town while the dump was five miles out. It was the Witch long ago who had set certain standards of dress for the Jordan menfolk. She insisted that they wear suits in public, preferably dark wool suits. She wasn't particular about shirts, however, and as a result the summer uniform was a dark suit, felt hat, T-shirt, and shoes which ranged from boots to sneakers. In the winter, the T-shirt was replaced by a union suit, and the ensemble was covered by an overcoat and galoshes. In addition, the Witch liked men to have what she referred to as "a little ball room," and so she always bought trousers several sizes too big. Ollie normally held his up with suspenders, and Willow usually wore a rope belt. Ollie had contributed to the style that the Witch had wrought by devising a certain way of walking in public. He was young and vain then, and he walked with a slight goose step, holding the cuffs of the oversize suit jacket in his palms. He fancied he looked pretty dapper. He had long since lost the vanity of his youth, but the habit of his walk remained, and he had passed it down to his sons and to the kin who had come to live with him during the prosperous years by the Basketville sign. Ollie bought two suits each for himself and Willow, along with two huge canopylike overcoats, two pairs of pants, some under things, and a hat for himself. The total cost came to twenty-four dollars.

He returned to the truck and dressed Willow in some plaid slacks and a suit jacket. "Who says Willow Jordan ain't sharp?" Ollie asked, admiring his son, and off he drove, not headed for any place in particular.

Having discovered that his mood had improved, Ollie automatically set aside his mission to retire with Willow to the boondocks. That can wait, something in him said. It was a beautiful day, and he wanted to enjoy it. Why waste it with labor and thought? Still, he needed to start planning, he realized, and felt his spirits beginning to dampen. The clash of want and need made him irritable. He resisted an urge to cuff Willow in the face. The boy was hanging his head and both arms out the window. He seemed delirious with the joy of meeting the wind. Ollie reached for a beer. The single most impressive achievement of mankind, in Ollie Jordan's view, was the invention of beer. A man could think better with beer in his belly. Beer dulled one's aches, washed out the insides, provided nourishment, reduced the appetite during bad times, whetted it during good times. "Too good a day to waste with irritability," Ollie said aloud, knowing that Willow cared not.

They were moving down Main Street now, past the Central Square common with its great trees, statue of a Civil War hero, and park. The late morning light in the green of the grass seemed to bounce back into Ollie's face. It reminded him of how much he detested a lawn. He had nothing personal against grass, which like anything else would grow where it could. But a lawn was something else. A lawn was an example of the madness of mankind. It was crazy that anyone would want to plant a lawn, feed it to make it grow ever faster, and then cut it down routinely at great expense and labor. For a long time he thought there was something wrong with him, that he had failed to see some obvious advantage to the cultivation of short grass. After all, the richest people had the biggest lawns and the shortest grass, and rich people didn't get rich by being stupid. Thus, he had theorized that perhaps short grass was a source of nutrition or an intoxicant, but the theory didn't stand up to a test of boiled grass and beer and he had abandoned the idea. As the years passed, he realized that there was no mystery. There was no good reason for a lawn. It was merely a make-work thing for people who couldn't get out of the habit of work itself or of having work done for them. It was bad enough that the public nurtured their lawns in and around their abodes, but somehow he expected the city to know better.

Take Willow to the wild place now, a thought, which came like a voice, sounded inside him. He shook it off.

"Too fine a day to get balled up in serious thinking, eh, Willow?" he asked. Willow cut loose with rip-roaring laughter.

Ollie drove on aimlessly until he found himself at the gate of Donald's Junkyard. On impulse he decided to pay Donald a visit. He had no reason to make the visit except to pass some time.

Here was a vast pasture of derelict cars, put out amidst the startling green beauty of the New Hampshire hills, framed by stone walls built by the forefathers. Donald's Junkyard was an honored place in Jordan lore. It had begun under Donald the Elder as a pig farm. Slowly, through Donald the Elder's hobby of tinkering with machinery (in preference to caring for his animals), the place was transformed from a farm into a hospital and mortuary for machines, and finally into a business. When Donald the Elder died, the business fell to his eldest son, Donald the Younger.

Donald the Younger brought a new element to the business: a colorful personality. People from all over Cheshire County came from miles around to dicker with him—and to hear him swear. It was said that Donald Jordan could weather the paint on a church merely by speaking. He rarely used conventional curse words, preferring to brew his own in the cauldron of his mind. Ollie Jordan pretended, even to himself, to be unimpressed with Donald's swearing. There was no meaning behind it, no anger, no idea that set it forth, no goal that brought it home. "It's just show-off swearing," Ollie would say. The truth was that Ollie viewed Donald as a rival as top guide to mores for the Jordan clan.

As he pulled his truck into the yard, Ollie saw Adele's child playing in the dirt by the house and Fletch Jordan's pink and black Buick. Some of the kin who had lived with Ollie in his shacks under the Basketville sign had sought succor from Donald. Ollie understood, but it pained him to realize that he already had surrendered so much of his leadership. Someday he would find the means to regain his role.

Ollie chained Willow to himself and walked in search of Donald. He was easy to find. Ollie just followed the sound of his voice. Donald and his son, known as Donald Again, were in a shed pulling out the engine of a Ford Pinto with a rusty chain hoist.

"A man would have to have darned little pride to drive a car like that," Ollie said.

"Saint Bugger, bless my moon, if it ain't cousins Ollie and Willow come down off Fart Mountain from preaching the gospel to the good folk of I-91 to break wind with us junkyarders. Hello, Ollie. Say hello, Again, to your cousins."

" 'Lo," said Again. He had always been a quiet boy. Ollie distrusted him because he seemed contented with work.

That was the end of the greeting. The Donald Jordans continued their labors. Ollie unchained Willow, lit his pipe, and sucked on his beer. Willow sat himself among some junk parts in a corner and started stacking them in odd patterns, like a child playing with blocks. No Jordan was expected to shake hands, embrace, or greet a member of the family in any conventional way. Jordans passed a subtle eye signal among themselves as an invitation that they were willing to be tested in conversation. It was a signal that had grown out of generations of crowded living, and it was so much a part of Jordan manners that it was almost unconsciously delivered. Without the signal, Jordans ignored one another; sometimes they ignored one another for days.

"Willow was testifying as to his sense of humor," said Ollie, with deliberate dignity. You could not joke for long with Donald. Jokes were Donald's weapons. If you joked with him, he would soon gain ascendancy over you.

"Heard on the radio how Willow's bare ass humored the town of Darby. Did I laugh—thought I'd shit my pants," said Donald. He was a shade darker than most Jordans because the automobile grease had settled into his skin like a pigment. Like Ollie, he was a slim, hard man.

Ollie looked at Again for a hint of Donald's true mood. Again was almost grim. Why was he not smiling? He should be smiling. Again was his father's accomplice. Ollie probed.

"I daresay your business is booming," he said.

"I daresay my business is slow as a Frenchman trying to get a hard-on in hell," said Donald.

Again did not smile.

"I see you got a new garage—nice block building. Next I imagine you'll be advertising," said Ollie.

"I'll suck a pig's ass first," said Donald. "They tell me you was with the Witch last night. How is the old hag? Still gumming every old man in the county?"

"Still banging, I imagine," said Ollie. He mustn't let Donald take the offensive, mustn't show his sensitivity about the Witch.

After considering the matter, Ollie decided that the reason Again was not smiling was that the Donalds were fearful that

Ollie would ask for succor. After all, the Donalds were becoming wealthy; they were working regular hours; they had prestige outside the kinship; they had duties to the culture. He and Willow would be a reminder that they, the Donalds, had duties to the kinship, too. Armed with his suppositions, Ollie launched a new offensive on Donald the Younger.

"What would you say if I asked you for succor?" Ollie asked.

"I'm bound to give you succor," said Donald. There was no conviction in his voice. Ollie felt he had an advantage now, and he pressed it.

"And Willow?" he asked.

"Uh-huh," said Donald, wetting his lips with his tongue. Ollie could see that Donald wanted very much to signal an end to the conversation.

Ollie made as if to speak and then held off, deliberately holding Donald in a moment of anxiety before releasing him.

"I didn't come here for succor," he said. "Me and Willow will be on our way in a minute."

Donald's self-control snapped away from him. He realized that Ollie had been putting him to a test and that he had just barely passed.

"Damn your soul to a hell of barfing choirs—you can't go anywhere with him," Donald said, pointing at Willow.

Again nodded vigorously.

So that was it—they were afraid of Willow, Ollie thought.

"He's in the kinship same as him," said Ollie, pointing at Again. Ollie's voice had all the righteousness of a maiden aunt preaching on morals.

Donald the Younger stopped his work and put his hands together like a man praying; the hands looked like two complicated greasy-black gears about to mesh. Ollie challenged the gesture with a humorless smile of his black, jagged teeth.

"Ollie, the kinship ain't what it was," said Donald the Younger, with a tenderness so genuine and so enveloping that, in a second, Ollie felt himself plummet from the peak of his ascendancy.

"I'll say it ain't," said Ollie, righteous, cold, but the cunning gone out of him.

Donald immediately took advantage of his opponent. He pointed his finger at Willow, who by now had constructed a small castle of junk metal, and said, "Send his blasphemous ass up to Concord or Laconia. He ain't doing nothing for you, and he ain't doing nothing for this kinship—what's left of it."

Ollie realized he had been stupid and wrong to come here. Had he the means he might have apologized. As it was he pressed on, even as doing so sickened him.

"He is the kinship," said Ollie.

"Then you know what's wrong with it," said Donald.

Ollie experienced a brief moment of peculiar peace, like a man resigned to dying. The Welfare Department, he knew now, had taken his land and seduced his wife; those whom he had succored were scattered to the four winds; those who were obliged to give him succor regarded him as a menace. He and Willow were completely cut off now, from both the culture and the kinship. It was a situation that could only spell disaster, and yet there was that feeling of peace, as if—at last—he was getting what he really wanted, a chance for union with his divided self. "Come, Willow," he whispered, and the boy seemed to understand.

After Ollie and Willow had gone, the Donalds noticed for the first time the junk castle that Willow had built from the spare parts of automobiles. They found it so restful to behold that they left it alone, and each day thereafter as they entered the shed they would look at the work and take pleasure from it.

Ollie frittered away the remainder of the day. He knew that something in him had changed. He knew because he was afraid. He bought some more beer and drove around with Willow, the two of them stopping at various rest areas and parks, where great white pines loomed over them like great ideas. They would stay, Ollie sitting and drinking and Willow exulting in the nuggets of green trash barrels, until someone came or until Ollie felt pursued. During this time, it would have been logical for Ollie to be making plans, or at least to be reflecting on the nature of the changes that he knew were swirling within him. In fact, he spent most of the time wondering whether or not to buy hard liquor. Like his father before him—the father who, through some frightening alchemy, was but a shadow in his memory—Ollie had a weakness for hard liquor. He knew that if he succumbed to it, he would lose his son to the Welfare Department and himself to . . . to something horrible that once briefly he had experienced but forgotten and that remained in him as a sense of loneliness, of grief. "Still," he said, talking to himself but aloud at Willow, "the joy of straight juice might be worth the cost." The more he thought about the matter, the more beer he bought; and the more beer he drank, the more piss stops he made, until the gravity of the situation lightened and he made up his mind to buy a bottle of whiskey. It was six o'clock. The state liquor store was closed. Ollie was grateful. He was quite drunk, a condition he recognized by a dull sheen of green that seemed to him to rise up from the earth like a scent. He bought some hot dogs and potato chips, and he and Willow ate supper on a dirt road that thrust into Robin Hood Park. After the meal, Ollie and Willow lay in the back of the truck and went to sleep. In the middle of the night, Ollie woke out of a nightmare.

"Willow . . . Willow," he whispered. The boy did not stir. Ollie touched his face. It was cool. He lit a match and brought the light to Willow's face. The boy's eyes were open, and they were calm and full of wonder; they moved from the sky to the match, and instantly Ollie blew out the light. Ollie looked up into the sky. He could see a few branches sway slightly and he could feel the intense green of them, and he was cheered, almost giddy.

Niagara Falls Park

Ollie Jordan took his son Willow to a place far up on the side of a hill known on the geological survey maps as Prospect Hill but called Abare's Folly or just The Folly by the people of Darby. A logging company owned most of the hill, but had not touched the land in years. The slopes were undeveloped—and for good reason. Abare's Folly was a 1600-foot-high chunk of granite, with slopes too steep to accommodate anything but logging roads for skidders. The soil was sparse, the weather unpredictable and mean. Yet somehow dense stands of hemlocks and hardwoods took hold on the granite. The presence of trees didn't cheer up the place, but rather added gloom to inhospitality. Even hikers avoided the hill, mainly because the trees prevented views. Near the summit, where the trees grew like the wind-blown hair of women at a beach, the last logging road ended, blocked by granite outcroppings. "Willow, behind the ledges is heaven," Ollie said.

A relatively flat shelf of about five acres jutted out from the side of the hill. Here hemlocks grew with sugar maples, black birches, and white birches. Boulders of varying sizes with green mossy backs, resembling basking turtles, parked on the forest floor. There were also boulders of white and russet and ink blue, and a spring which gushed out of a crack in a ledge, flowed about twenty feet to fill a small pool, and then continued down for a date with Trout Brook far below, which continued on to the Connecticut River and the Atlantic Ocean. Here he and his son might find refuge, Ollie believed.

For the first week Ollie and Willow lolled. The weather was perfect, with warm sunny days and gentle breezes from the south in the tops of the trees. Nights were cool and there were few mosquitoes. Ollie had vague plans to build a shelter, but there seemed no need. They slept under a crude lean-to of maple saplings, which Ollie had cut with his Sears bow saw, and some clear plastic. They ate food out of cans that Ollie had brought along—hash, sardines, tuna fish, peas, soup. Once in a while Ollie boiled a potato in the one pot that he had. He had planned to ration the two cases of beer for a month; but at the rate he was drinking it, the beer would be gone soon. Ollie settled in a place that included a patch of sunlight through the trees for much of the day and that was dominated by a flat-top rock about six feet square and two feet off the ground. He named it the altar stone. There were plenty of dead branches on the lower parts of the hemlocks, and with these he built a fire on the stone. He spent nearly all his time sitting before the fire, watching and listening to the flames, drinking beer, smoking his pipe. On the fourth day, it struck him that he was happy. "This is it—no thinking, no doing," he said to Willow, who had found a comfortable place in the crook of a tree. He, too, was happy. Ollie had freed him from the chain. He figured he was taking a risk, but he believed that here Willow was free from the culture as the culture was free from him, and that furthermore, a creature should not be fettered here. Sometimes he listened to Willow babble to himself and was filled with love. It would not be so good if Willow made sense, he thought.

It was during the fourth night that the first disturbing event occurred. Ollie usually stayed up all night, watching the fire, returning to the shelter before dawn and sleeping off and on during the day. But one night he sat before the fire and something dark rose up out of the flames to encircle him. The thing was so black that the night was bright by comparison. A moment later, Ollie opened his eyes and saw that there were only a few coals on the altar stone. He had not been awake at all; he had dreamt the fire, dreamt the apparition. He walked the few feet to the plastic and sapling shelter. Willow was gone. And it was as if he were back in the dream, as if he himself, Ollie Jordan, were gone, too. This mind that reported to him the world, this bag of bones of a body that hauled him about, were not his. He lay down to make himself—itself— smaller. He wanted to cry out for the self that was out there in the forest, but he had a terrible fear that the voice that would speak would not be his own, that it would be the voice of the darkness that had come out of the fire. Finally, he said, "Willow?" There was no answer, but at least the voice that he heard was his own, and the feeling of strangeness in him began to fade. After a while, he noticed a difference in the night, not so much a lessening of the darkness as a softening. A few birds began to chatter. Dawn was coming. Weariness, the only mother that had ever brought him comfort, stroked him now, and he fell asleep in her arms. He woke in late morning. Willow lay beside him snoring. Had Willow really left? Was there something out there affecting their minds? It didn't matter. He was happy. But the questions continued to nag at him during much of the day. Finally, he concluded that the way to solve the problem, if there was a problem, was not to sleep at night until he heard the birds of dawn.

During this time Ollie often exercised his mind by asking questions that actually he felt no real need to answer. "What good is sense?" he asked Willow, who responded with a Bronx cheer. The sounds of the wind in the tops of the trees: Did these make sense? What of baby sounds? They made no sense and yet there wasn't an adult on the earth who couldn't be moved by the beauty of a baby cooing. Furthermore, as children imitated their elders, the beauty of the children's own utterances began to decline. Meanwhile, adults would imitate the sounds of their young ones—itchy-bitchy coo. Shit like that. The end result was that the children became adults, and the adults became fools. Having grappled with this idea and having finally subdued it, Ollie gave it voice.

"Willow," he said, "if I got something you want, and you take it, then I ain't got it no more. Everybody knows that. What they don't know is, you ain't got it either. Not only that, but the more you take from me, the less we both got."

Willow growled.

Ollie's most important task during the first week was to name the property. A number of possibilities came to mind, but none was satisfactory. "The Wild Place" was accurate but it had no oomph. Other names he considered included "Ollie's Secret Woods" and "Willow's Backyard," but these names made it seem as though he or Willow owned the place, and really neither had been here long enough to make such a claim. What was needed, Ollie decided, was a grand but familiar name. One day down by the spring, he looked at the water trickling from the ledge above, and the name of the wild place came to him: Niagara Falls Park. Later, for the purposes of conversation, he shortened the title to "The Park."

"Willow, The Park's got plenty of good dry firewood," he would say.

"Tow-hee, tow-hee," said Willow, as if to say, "Now here's the latest thing on your hit parade."

If the first six days on The Folly taught Ollie anything, it was that life, to be good, to be free, must be bare of duty, desire, involvement. He fancied he was becoming wise. He had vague notions of coming down off the hill to return in triumph to his clan, to preach to them the secrets of happiness. "Empty that mind," he'd say. "The trees—smell 'em. Sardines—eat 'em. Beer—drink it. The fire—watch it." And then it rained.

At first the rain was pleasant, coming as he napped in the afternoon, a pitter-patter in the trees like the sound of hamburger frying in a pan. He listened for a while with his eyes closed, and then he opened them. Willow stirred uneasily beside him. From his nest under the plastic tarp, Ollie watched the first drops kick the ashes on the altar stone. Moments later, the last of the fire went out. The rain increased. He could hear the wind building in the tops of the trees, until cold drafts worked their way under the open ends of the shelter where father and son lay. He reached for the one blanket he had, covering himself and Willow. A feeling of dread rolled over Ollie. It was worse than mere fear. It was like a realization hitting a dying man that he had lived his life all wrong.

It rained that day, that night, the next day, and the following night. Temperatures fell into the fifties. The ashes on the altar stone were washed away. The beer supply ran out. The matches got soaked and Ollie could not light his pipe. He hiked over the ledges to the truck in the hope of finding matches. He found none. But he did start the engine and warm himself by the heater. When he returned to the shelter, he discovered that Willow had gathered dozens of hemlock boughs and made a nest under the plastic. He was dry and comfortable, and Ollie was proud of him, but he had left no room for anyone but himself. So Ollie spent most of the time in the cab of the truck. The seat was not wide enough for him to stretch out on, and the floor shift jutted up into the middle of the vehicle, so that when he lay down it always seemed to be sticking into his gut or his back. He made frequent checks at the shelter and discovered that Willow was doing fine. Willow slept a great deal, and when he was awake he retreated into some private realm. He was accosted by neither cold nor hunger. He was doing what any animal does in a storm.

Ollie did not endure so well. He suffered from wet, cold, and dread. There were ways, he knew, to increase his comfort, but he felt powerless to act. Having been betrayed once by his instincts, he feared that to yield to any new idea was to leave himself open to further betrayal. In addition, he was withdrawing all at once from alcohol, tobacco, and caffeine. He found himself painfully and uselessly alert. He could not keep warm, even with the heater on in the truck. He was afraid of running the engine while he slept, because his cousins Merwin and Imelda Jordan had died of monoxide poisoning while parked at a drive-in theater. Remembering the incident reminded Ollie that these days you could see naked women in the movies. Progress, he thought. After that, he spent a lot of time thinking about naked women. In fact, that was about the only thing that made passing time in the rain bearable. But thinking about women made him terribly lonely, and he wished that Helen were here to give him succor. At dawn he went out into the rain to check on Willow. The boy slept all innocently, like a child. He reminded Ollie of the Witch herself during a moment long ago. Ollie worked his way into the nest until he was beside his son. "Room after all," he said. Willow touched his forehead and Ollie, sinking—at last—into a restful sleep, thought that perhaps it was he, Ollie Jordan, who was the son, and Willow the father. "New kinship," he whispered, and fell asleep.

When Ollie woke, the rain had stopped. Willow was already up, sitting twelve feet off the ground in a crook of a branch on a maple tree. He was eating. He had opened a can of Dinty Moore stew and was helping himself. The boy was contented. Ollie realized that Niagara Falls Park was a different place for Willow than for him. Willow could take on the mood of the weather, like any other animal. Given some time out here, some protection while he learned the ways of the forest, Willow might find The Park a good home. But he, Ollie, could not, for he was a man. There was no animal knowledge left inside of him. The week in the woods had taught him that to survive he must rely on his abilities as a man. He must scheme, build, dominate: He must think. He cupped his hands and said to Willow, as if sharing some great secret, "A man's nothing if he ain't a stinker and a thinker."

"Tow-hee," said Willow.

Ollie took inventory of his things, discovering that he could not possibly get by for another week, let alone the long haul. He was wet, cold, and hungry. Think, he shouted to himself.

And so he thought, and an idea came after about an hour. He gathered some birch bark and a couple of reasonably dry pine cones, soaked them with some gasoline that he got from the truck carburetor, put the ingredients in a hubcap, and set them on fire by crossing wires on the battery. This experiment was so successful that he nearly incinerated himself. The fire soon burned out, but still Ollie was thrilled by his own cleverness. Eventually, he figured that he could transport the fire in some sticks lashed together. He got a big blaze going on the altar stone, set his clothes up on branches to dry them, and started a smaller fire to boil water. Soon he was drinking hot coffee—the best that he'd ever had in his life. He lunched on tuna fish from the can and a couple of biscuits about to go bad. After the meal, he drank more coffee and smoked his pipe. Well, he thought, I'm happier than a pig in shit—if a little lonely. He was tempted to put aside the unpleasant memory of the storm. But he was wiser now, realizing that he must take only a morsel of contentment and get on with the business of survival. He studied Willow during the afternoon and concluded that he could leave the boy for a day or two and he would stay at The Park because that was where he wanted to be.

That afternoon he left for Keene, backing the truck a mile down the hill because there was no room to turn around. Even with four-wheel drive, the truck would not move on the logging roads once the snows fell in late fall. Keep thinking, Ollie said to himself. He stopped at the first store he saw and bought some beer.

Grant Us Peace

The City of Keene loomed strange and beautiful to Ollie Jordan. He saw the clock on the steeple of the First Congregational Church for the first time in a week. Ten minutes past three. Wonderful invention, the clock. He must salvage one for The Park, one with little arrows instead of numbers. He watched pretty women walking down the street. He liked the ones with the high-heeled shoes. He liked the way their calves bunched in the back. He crossed the street to Central Square and sat on a bench to rest. Here was an island surrounded by traffic. He watched the cars go by. What he enjoyed about them were the pretty colors. They were like big metal, rolling flowers.

Soon a small blind man, carrying a fiddle almost taller than himself, crossed the street to the square. He was accompanied by a pregnant woman with mischief in her green eyes. She was carrying a guitar. They sat upon the grass, and Ollie heard the woman sing, all at once sweet and strong so that he wanted to weep for something lost.

The TV speaks to Emily in her rocking chair.
The Secret Storm rages and then subsides.
A woman confesses how she rid the chafe
From her hands.
  Roses for Emily.
Emily's waiting for Love of Life to come on the screen.
The sun has wilted her plants,
And the leaves are in mourning.
The wind tips the rocker first forward then back
And blows through her thin, gray hair.
Outside, the cat yowls for the back door
To open itself.
  Roses for Emily.
She's waiting for Love of Life to come on the screen.
She always liked this room—the smell of the sofa
And sounds of the shade cord tapping on the window.
On the floor, years ago, played the Lieutenant boy
She lost in the war. On the lawn today, Mr. Robin bobs
For a worm, like a fine gentleman
Tipping his cap.
  Roses for Emily.
Emily's waiting for Love of Life to come on the screen.
The wind carries the fragrance of flowers inside,
To linger by her rocker, like an oarsman pausing
To watch the sea. The neighborhood is napping;
Children lie softly as fur. The rower dipping
His oar first in the water and then the sun,
The insistent cat, the flowers teasing the wind,
The robin and his great dignity; the children,
Even the woman with the chafed heart
Have what Emily had until 3 o'clock. The Secret Storm
Has ended and Love of Life comes on the screen.
  Roses for Emily, Roses for Emily, Roses.

The woman's voice left Ollie Jordan hungry for succor. He shut his eyes so that he could see better the women that he had loved. He drifted briefly. And then he was hearing an argument between two men. Ollie opened his eyes. One man had soft brown eyes and soft brown skin and lips the texture of fish flesh. He spoke fervently.

"The radiation from nuclear fallout has lowered the average IQ throughout the world. The more nuclear power plants are built, the greater the radiation in the atmosphere. It's sapping our brains, I tell you. I can feel it in myself sometimes, and I can see it in others . . ."

The other man, standing casually but stiff inside, a body at odds, smiled mirthlessly.

"You want us all to get leukemia to prove your point," he said. "If there's IQs going down here they belong to those that turned their backs on good food like meat, the flag, the good Lord. You can take your antinukes and . . ."

Ollie was annoyed. He didn't like an argument that was going no place, that, in truth, had much in common with the lovemaking of those who like to hurt and be hurt. He wanted them to go away. He wanted peace to think about the pregnant woman and her rose-petal voice. Pregnant women drew him. They brimmed at once with sex and sweetness. He thought about Helen, how serene she was during pregnancy, how ready—and how bitchy after the baby was born. He turned to catch sight of the woman with the guitar. She was gone; the blind man, too, was gone. He shut his eyes again.

He had met Helen Abrahms at the Cheshire Fair thirteen or fourteen years ago—he couldn't remember exactly. He was a young man then, but already the father of two children by two different women. His wife Iola (he called her Cousin Owl) had left him, running off with her baby—it was a healthy one, a good one—to a place of dreams called Reno, never to be seen again. Ollie had found temporary succor for himself and Willow with the Witch. Ollie was working at the tannery then, pulling skins, earning some money to get away. He went to the fair looking for adventure, as young men will. He had seen Helen standing at the wheel of fortune. She was lean, bony, but with flair to her hips. He breathed in the smell of her long brown hair—wood smoke, fried foods, the piss from babies, farm animals—and he knew she was of his own kind.

"You want to play the wheel?" he asked. "I'll pay."

"No," she said. "I've been too long without luck to think I can get it now. I just like to watch it go round and round. It don't matter to me where it stops."

"I never had no luck either," he had said. "Anyway, it don't matter at all: it's fixed." He had the confidence of a young man who believes everything he has overheard.

"That's better than what I got," she said. "Nothing I got is fixed. It's all broken."

For a moment he had thought that she was making fun of him, but then he had figured she had just misunderstood him. Now he realized that she had understood him all along and had used his idea to suit her own purpose, as women will with men. They had talked on. She knew his Uncle Jester, who was the half-brother of her Cousin Homer's Aunt Carlotta. He knew her half-sister Harriet Thatcher through her ex-husband Boynton Bigelow, who had served time in the state penitentiary with Ollie's Uncle Mortimer.

Ollie and Helen strolled about the fairgrounds until they happened onto a commotion. An enormous fat man wearing overalls and red suspenders had gotten into an enclosure of prize 4-H pigs, and with apparently amorous intent he was chasing a sow. He had the look of a man who has drunk himself into a state beyond stupor into a hot glaze of awareness. Moments later three policemen were in the pigpen, splashing about in the mud amidst the sounds of scared pigs.

"Man's got a mighty unusual sense of humor," said Ollie in admiration.

"Man's crazy and mean," said Helen, her voice low. She was shaking with fear and Ollie did not understand. Then it dawned on him that this was the man she had come with to the fair, her man.

He hustled her away from the area, buying two tickets for the evening's main attraction, an automobile demolition derby. Sitting high up in the grandstand, Ollie and Helen munched on shell peanuts, watched the cars collide below, listened to the wild music of revving engines and steel hitting steel, and talked. She had two children of her own, one still on the breast—sort of—even though it was two. Also she cared for a third one belonging to "him," which was how she identified her man. Ollie found out later the man's name was Pork Barrel Beecher. They exchanged more family information and then came to an unspoken but mutually understood agreement that Helen was to leave Pork Barrel and live with Ollie. Having accomplished that business, they relaxed, turning their attention to the demolition derby.

"It don't make no sense to me," she had said.

Ollie explained the winning techniques of the game. "You've got to keep moving, the more often backwards the better, so's they don't smash your front end and put your vehicle out of commission. If you're smart you don't get in the fray until the end when your neighbors are all bummed up. Him that still moves when all others is still is declared the winner and gets a case of oil."

"If the way to win is to lay back until the cows come home, why don't they all lay back?" she asked.

"Then there wouldn't be no demolition," he had said.

As the evening wore on, he saw that she had gained ascendancy over him. What surprised him was that he was glad.

The next day he had driven out to the Beecher place, a shack surrounded by some poplar trees that had overtaken a field. He could smell the cesspool kicking. Pork Barrel lay unconscious in the driveway. Helen had bailed him out of jail, brought him home, put more booze to him in the hope of knocking him out, and when that tactic had not worked entirely, had assisted him into the peaceful realm with the aid of an iron frying pan laid on top of his head. Ollie feared that Pork Barrel was dead, but the body was warm and perspiring and out of the mouth came occasional gurgles and squeaks. The mosquitoes were gorging themselves on the blood-alcohol mixture. "I'm for leaving him as is," Helen had said. But Ollie had pitied the body and sought at least to get it away from the mosquitoes. So, with the help of Helen and the kids, he was able to put Pork Barrel in a wheelbarrow, lay a two-inch plank along the front steps, and wheel the body into the shack. He remembered he had heard a soft noise that had made him think of dirt being thrown in a coffin hole. For just a second he had been gripped with a feeling of unaccountable terror, similar to what he later experienced that night of the dream at The Park. But the noise had only been the sound of Pork Barrel pissing in his sleep. Apparently, the motion of being transported had reminded the body that it was alive and had duties to perform. Ollie left Pork Barrel in the wheelbarrow, and took Helen and the kids away with him. That first night with Helen had been the most passionate of his life. What had heightened the sex for him was a fantasy of Pork Barrel dead. Even now the thought stirred him. Pork Barrel had not died. He had been arrested and jailed for almost killing his cousin Emile with a broken bottle. He had only served six months (because his victim was his cousin and not a stranger) and Ollie saw him now and again on the streets of Keene. The man did not seem to recognize him.

His life with Helen had been pretty good, Ollie thought. She was older than he was, and in the early years she treated him like a child, insisting he hold down a job and keep his drinking under control. They got on rather well. He realized now that it was only after he had taken command of his own destiny that their life together had begun to come apart.

Ollie began to walk the streets. Soon he heard himself humming the tune to "The Tennessee Waltz." He didn't know why the song came to mind, but there it was: a sadness. He figured if he walked enough he would bump into the woman with the guitar and the blind man. Perhaps he would follow them until they sang again.

In their years together, Helen had asked for little, had given little, had offered no explanations for her actions, and had required none concerning his own. In conjugal matters, she let him have his way as long as he was not drunk. In this manner, she modified his drinking habits so that instead of getting drunk from seven to midnight, he nipped from noon to bedtime, staying mildly inebriated for most of his waking hours, but rarely getting outright drunk. He was happy for the change in himself. Too much drink all at once made him feel strange, out of control. Yet, except in the morning when coffee would do, he required small amounts of drink in his system to feel stable. Without drink he was sick and dizzy, as if on a boat rocking in the sea.

Helen didn't seem to mind when he hit the kids, including those that were hers alone, but she was absolutely unreasonable about being struck herself. It seemed to him that her position was peculiar. Everyone he knew hit everyone else he knew. Occasionally, a tooth would pop loose, or there might be a serious accident, such as the time Mortimer Jordan had knocked his wife Amy Lou down the stairs and killed her, but that's what you got for living in second-floor apartments in the city. Usually little damage resulted from domestic battles. They certainly were less dangerous than automobile accidents. If you had a problem with people you lived with, and you hit them or they hit you, the hitting would solve the problem. Without hitting, the problem would remain and everybody concerned would feel bad. He had tried to argue this matter with Helen, explaining that he never hit to hurt her but just to relieve himself: "It ain't personal. It ain't to ruin you. Chickens peck each other. Cats fight. So do raccoons, dogs, and pigs. Every manner of critter hits his own kind. Act of love, I tell you." But she wouldn't listen. She merely repeated her longtime policy with him. If he so much as slapped her, she would murder him in his sleep. "You ain't natural—you're downright vicious," he had said. "Don't you hit me," she had responded.

There was no doubt that hitting loved ones was a family tradition within the kinship. As brother Ike was fond of repeating: "Women and children need to be beaten, women to keep them from becoming confused as to their position in life, children to teach them right from wrong." Right or wrong, it always had been done that way, Ollie thought. Any other way, right or wrong, meant a weakening of the kinship itself. Murder him in his sleep—the very idea. Who does she think she is? She was just being selfish. He shouldn't have let her set policy. He should have beat her anyway. If he had, chances are they'd still be together as a family. There was something in him—something in every man—that wanted to strike at women, children, anything helpless. There is no doubt about it, he thought, I was right and she was wrong.

Ollie reveled in a sense of justifiable outrage, but only briefly. Soon his loneliness got in the way. He found himself again thinking kindly of his woman. After all, what were a man and a woman but two sides of an argument? Divide the pair, and each was left shouting his position to the sky. "And the sky don't care," he heard himself say aloud, and the sound of his own voice brought him out of his thoughts.

He was standing in front of St. Bernard's Catholic Church in Keene. It was Saturday afternoon about four. People were entering the church. He couldn't understand it. He thought Catholics only went to church on Sunday. It offended him that most of them were so casually dressed. He was proud that he was wearing a suit, and he was glad that he had put on a fresh T-shirt before coming to Keene. He stood before the church steps, standing rigidly at attention, his hands holding the cuffs of his suit jacket. He figured he was showing them up. A young man in black came into view. He wore glasses and he had a frank stare that seemed to catch people, hold them, touch them, and release them. Now he was shaking his hands with people. "Good afternoon, Father," said a woman. The use of the word "father" cut into Ollie and opened him. He wanted to weep for all the terrible things he had done and that had been done by men everywhere. The man—the "father"—was coming toward him. He was extending his hand. Ollie was shaking it. It was all Ollie could do to keep from breaking into tears. "How are you today?" asked the father. "I'm new here," Ollie heard himself mumble. "Welcome to our church," said the father, and was gone, shaking other hands.

Ollie calmed down. The man's a priest, he said to himself. He knew a little bit about these things. He was not totally unfamiliar with religion, although the idea of God seemed strange to him. He was tired from walking. He decided to rest in the church. If somebody called the cops, he could produce the "father" who had said he was welcome.

It was the first time he could remember having been in a church. The air was different here. It magnified the importance of the simplest sounds—a whisper, a step, the rustle of ladies moving inside their clothes. Not a place to cut farts. The ceiling was extremely high—maybe three stories. There was no dividing line between wall and ceiling. The walls, decorated with colored glass windows of big fellows wearing long dresses, curved at the top until they were one with the ceiling. He felt as though he were standing under the belly of a great, protective bear on all fours. The people sat on heavy wooden benches with curved backs. It was as if they were at a ball game. He took a seat toward the rear because he did not want to draw attention to himself. He was comfortable with the place, despite the vague fear that the people might call the cops on him.

He wasn't exactly sure what was going to happen here. Some kind of ceremony. On the front wall was a figure of a man on a cross. This was Jesus Christ, Ollie knew. Christ was one of the guys from way back when, who shot off his mouth about the culture and got his comeuppance for it. Served him right, Ollie said to himself. What he didn't understand was how Christ had become a religion. He didn't seem to offer anything. Life's a bitch, religion said. But everybody knew that. What was strange to Ollie was that religion, having decided that life was a bitch, had come up with a reason for it: God done it. But instead of being angry at this God and seeking to bring him down, religion had said that God was good. It didn't make sense. Still, Ollie told himself not to draw too many conclusions. After all, he had not given much thought to religion, and now that he was in a church it was only fair that he kept an open mind. There might even be something for him here.

The ceremony began with the father that he had seen before coming out dressed up in a bright green costume with two boys with long black dresses and white tops. Everybody in the audience stood up, and Ollie was quick to follow. The father walked around arranging things and reading from a big book, while the boys fussed about with other duties. It was kind of hard to catch the meaning of the words of the father, but Ollie realized they were prayers. Mainly, the prayers told God what a great fellow he was and what cruds people were and would he please straighten them out. Maybe them, but not me, Ollie said, silently addressing this God, and he offered his own prayer: If you are what they say you are, then you done it, and don't put it on me.

Throughout the ceremony, the people were up and down. Now kneeling, now sitting, now standing. He figured they tried all these different positions to keep from getting bored, but he couldn't understand how they all knew when to get in the next position. He kept looking for a signal from the front, but he never caught on to it. After a short time, the father stopped fiddling around the table and gave a short speech into a microphone. Something about people overseas who didn't have enough to eat, and about how lucky we all were here in the USA. After he stepped down, some fellows came by with baskets and people put money in. Ollie wasn't sure what the admission fee was, but he put a nickel in the basket. Then the ceremony got serious. Some little bells rang, everybody knelt, and a hush fell over the audience. He marveled that the hush had been transmitted to him as though it were a thing that could be felt. The high ceiling in the church had something to do with the effect, he figured. The father was busy with something at the table. Ollie could see a container that looked like a metal beer mug and a tray holding a big white cookie. After praying over the cookie, the father raised it up in the air, and the bells rang some more. One of the boys was ringing the bells. The people in the audience bowed their heads. Ollie knew this was important stuff, but in what way was beyond him. Just when matters seemed about to peak, everybody took a break. The audience stood up, the father gave them all a big grin and said, "Peace and Christ be with you." And then a most remarkable thing happened. People started shaking hands with one another. A woman to the right of him offered her hand, and Ollie took it. "Peace and Christ be with you," she said. He returned the greeting: "Peace and Christ be with you," he said. Ollie got into the spirit of the thing, shaking hands with as many people as were within reach and exchanging that message: "Peace and Christ be with you." After the hubbub, everybody knelt and the ceremony became serious again. Finally, the father raised the cookie over his head and, with an emotion in his voice that Ollie couldn't quite identify, said, "Lamb of God, you take away the sins of the world, grant us peace." Moments later the father ate the cookie and drank the contents of the metal mug. Then most of the people walked to the front of the church, where the father gave them all a bite to eat from a metal mug—not the same one that he had drunk from. Presumably what they were eating were little cookies, but for what purpose was a mystery.

Ollie now had an idea of one of the charms of religion—the mystery. He tried now to make sense of one of those mysteries: Why the little white cookies? Something to do with food. He groped about in his knowledge of Christianity. A big picture came to mind. The Last Supper. It had been painted by an Italian. Christ and his buddies getting together for the last time. Having a meal and couple of beers probably. Could it be that the ceremony he was witnessing at the moment was a re-enactment of that meal long ago? His sense of logic told him that the answer to these questions had to be yes. The issue tumbled about in his mind until the church service ended when the father said to the audience, "May Christ's peace be with you." Christ or no Christ, there ain't no such thing as peace, Ollie thought.

He left the church skeptical of the purposes of Christianity, but—undeniably—soothed, too. There was something to religion. No doubt about it. He'd have to look into it when he had the time.

It was now almost five o'clock. He must start thinking, solving his problems at The Park—shelter and food. As he walked along, he tried to concentrate. Nothing came to mind. Why was it, he asked himself, that he could think just fine when he wasn't trying to think, but that when he had a problem to work on, he could not think at all? No matter. It was a pleasant day. Something would pop up. He bought a prepared sandwich at Romy's Market on Marlboro Street and he saw his cousin Tug Jordan sitting on the steps of the apartment house near the market. From the tone of his voice, Tug appeared to be having a heated discussion with someone concerning the Boston Red Sox. However, there was no one else in view. Tug would talk to anybody, including himself. Ollie drove off. He didn't mind being seen by his kin in Keene, but he didn't want any conversation. Oh, he would have liked to get some information as to the whereabouts of Helen and the kids, but in return he would be expected to provide some information about himself and Willow. He didn't want to do that. Once he told one relative where he and Willow had gone, the word would get around to all the kin. The Jordans enriched their lives with talk about each other. In fact, Ollie dearly missed the daily chit-chat that revealed who had the latest case of sugar diabetes, who had food stamps to trade, who had won twenty-five dollars in the state lottery, who was pregnant by whom. But he restrained himself from mixing with his kin because he still thought of himself as a man on the run from the Welfare Department. Indeed, the idea had become entwined with his sense of self-worth. He was convinced more than ever that his role in life was to keep Willow out of the hands of the Welfare Department. Already he could see signs of progress in Willow in his ability to adapt to the woods in a way that he had never been able to adapt to the culture. He was doing right by his son, he believed. The only question for Ollie was, Could he himself bear to continue this life—especially once winter came? He had no answer. He doubted his ability to sustain his own physical needs in The Park, let alone his son's, too. He told himself to think but the moment he gave himself that command, he rebelled against it.

He filled the truck with gas and bought some groceries and more beer. He knew he was running low on the money that the Witch had given him, but he didn't bother to count what he had left because he knew it would depress him. He remembered that Helen had a savings account with a couple hundred dollars in it, but he didn't know how to get at it. Besides, the banks were closed now. For the moment, it was best to drink a beer or two, drive around town a little bit, check things out.

All in all he liked Keene, he decided. He liked the way the big trees stood on a street corner like tall men standing in line at the liquor store, straight and untroubled. Forest trees grew one upon the other, twisted and battling, like drudges laboring on piece work at a tannery or a textile mill. City trees had health and dignity.

It was clouding up. The day was going to end in a shower. He drove to the Robin Hood Park pond. Here he had come as a boy to murder frogs. The kids called the pond "The Rez" for reasons that were mysterious to him, until somebody told him the place had been a reservoir years back. Now he sat in the cab of his truck, smoking his pipe, sipping his beer, watching the storm gather in the western sky over the city of Keene. It was one of those thunder storms that move with incredible swiftness across New Hampshire on a summer evening. For a minute or two the air was heavy and still. Then came the wind and rain. The temperature dropped thirty degrees. The dull rumblings of the thunder became sharp crackles. The lightning reminded him of his attempts at handwriting years ago in a school, and he was amused. For five minutes, there was a chaos about him that diminished to insignificance his own chaos, and he was at peace. God had said, "Get a load of this," and Ollie had responded, "That ain't bad." The sun came out. It was still raining lightly, but the air was clean. A rainbow formed. He thought immediately of the arch he had seen in the church. If only they could put the color in the church they'd have something, he thought. Why he might even start believing in God. "Grant us peace," he said aloud. Almost at the same time, a picture came into his mind that told him in just about every detail how he would build his home in Niagara Falls Park.

A
Deal

Ollie Jordan did not return to Niagara Falls Park that night. The stores were closed and therefore he could not shop for supplies, he told himself, although he knew that Grossman's was open. The truth was he wanted to celebrate his vision of the home he would build. It was a wondrous thing. He was proud of himself, and he was proud of the kinship. He decided to risk going to Miranda's. He might see someone there from the kinship, who almost certainly would learn from him where he and Willow had gone. But that possibility now did not seem so threatening. Indeed, it occurred to him that matters in general did not seem so threatening. His mood was lighter, freer. Why? he asked himself. And with the question posed, the answer took shape. He felt no sense of pursuit, either by the Welfare Department or by other darker forces. Why he was being left alone he did not know. Their own reasons, he thought; they'll be back by and by. In the meantime, he could take advantage. Have a beer in a public place. Enjoy the smells of the public. Breathe their breath.

He did not see one of his kin at Miranda's. Instead, he saw Howard Elman, who was the only man he was close to outside the kinship, who was indeed his only friend. He was a big man, with a pocked face and a nasty way of looking at people. He was the human equivalent of a bulldozer. He was the kind of man that shrewd men automatically measured and found dangerous because in a confrontation he would be the type to move ever forward. Elman was sitting at the bar when Ollie came into Miranda's. He did not offer his hand in greeting. He did not even rise. In the ten years they had been friends, the two men had never embraced. And yet there was an intimacy between them that each felt, although they would not think to speak of such a thing. They moved to a booth, sitting across from each other with a pitcher of draught beer and some potato chips. Ollie would put one in his mouth, soften it with a swig of beer, and chew it with his black teeth. Delicious. He felt larger, as if he were partaking of Elman's bulk. Elman loaded his glass with beer and then took a long drink from the pitcher itself. Ollie followed suit.

"Heavenly, ain't it?" said Elman.

"Just so," said Ollie. "I imagine that in heaven the beer is free, and the bartender is an angel that will tell you all the secrets."

"It doesn't matter, because you ain't going to heaven," Elman said.

"Just so," said Ollie, and he raised his glass to his lips, almost in the manner of a toast. Elman drank the rest of the pitcher and ordered another.

Ollie settled in. The business of catching up on each other's news was at hand. Ollie and Howard had a ritual for dispensing such news, as they had rituals for nearly every act in their relationship. The news would come in great gabby salvos. One man would start, talking in grave tones but off the top of his head, the truth being up to the other to interpret from the evidence presented. The idea was to exaggerate and talk on so that the other could not get a word in edgewise. However, each valued his drink more than the game, and thus the listener marked time until the speaker paused for a drink and then he would interrupt and launch his own salvo. Elman permitted Ollie to fire the first round by asking him a question.

"I heard you took off for the pucker brush. Is that so?" he asked.

"It's so all right," said Ollie. "That boy of mine and his sense of humor has got me into more crimey trouble. After we was evicted from the estate, most of my kin took off for parts unknown. Helen hauled the kids to Keene, and won't you know, moved in with the Welfare Department. Me and Willow knocked on Ike Jordan's door. 'Ike,' I says, 'hole me up, hole me up.' Well, you know what a horse's ass he is. Likes to do a man a favor so he can lord it over him. I couldn't stand it no more. 'Let's go, Willow,' I says. I figured I take the boy up to Canada, though I know deep down that ain't worth nothing, what with the spruce trees and the people there, as well as here, being black in the heart. Thinking about that turns me around, and, Howie, damned if I don't find myself driving up to the estate that I built, and they evicted me from and started me down this long, dark road. As my Uncle Remo used to say before he drowned in black waters, 'Don't love no whore, don't steal a shoe from a one-footed man, and don't go back to no old home.' Worst mistake of my life was going up there. Dozer wiped the Jordan mark clean off the face of the earth. Could of cried. Fact is I did. The tears just poured. But I never really had a chance to get properly aggrieved. I looks up and what do I see but Willow sitting on top the sign stark naked. 'What's this?' I says. 'Get your ass down.' Naturally, he ignores me. He just waves at the people on the highway. Next thing I know there's fifteen cops up there and a squad of little ladies from the Welfare Department promising Willow a blow job if only he'll come down—of his own free will, you know. Then they get to talking to me, saying how they're going to teach Willow to wipe his ass and how to say, 'Beg your pardon, ladies and gents, I just cut a fart.' Well, I wasn't going to put up with that, so I kind of wandered off. With the help of Ike's siphon hose (thank you, Lord, for making Ike a practical-minded thief), I load up a can with gas—high test, from one of the cop cars—and snake back by the sign on the steep side by the highway. Right under their noses, Howie! Willow's got 'em all entertained, so they're looking up. I douses the sign, touches a match and *foosh!*—up she goes. I wish I could of sat there and enjoyed the sight of all those state troopers with blackened faces, screaming, 'I'm blind, I'm blind,' and all those welfare ladies speechless for the first time in their lives. But you know how it is when you got work to do. I was watching Willow. He's no fool, and he scrambles down the sign before he gets hurt. I'm waiting at the bottom. 'Time to saddle up,' I say, and I hop on his shoulders. Off we go like the Lone Ranger and Silver. I can feel the wind in my face and I can hear the blind cops firing their Smith an' Wessons—*ksh, ksh, ksh*. I ride Willow maybe five miles through the pucker brush until we get to that big rock near the Boyle place where you can see Ascutney Mountain. 'Whoa, Willow, whoa,' I says. So we sit there on the rock, Willow catching his breath, and me smoking my pipe and watching the smoke from the sign burning up. We've been on the run ever since, staying in the woods up on The Folly. Terrible nice up there, though it's hard to make the few dollars a man needs to live on, what with the lords of that place being the bears and not caring about the minimum wage. Willow likes it just fine; but me, well, you know I need to shoot off my mouth from time to time, so I come into town to buy some smokes and see what's what . . ."

At this point, Ollie paused to take a drink, and Elman, seeing his chance to speak, began his own monologue.

"I know sure as God made hell on earth that you can live like an Indian with that crazy boy of yours as long as the weather stays kindly," Elman said, "but when the falling of the leaves comes, you're going to need shelter and foodstuffs, just like I did when I was unemployed back in the winter and I was forced to sell the better part of my land to that she-wolf neighbor of mine. You've got to stand up straight to the likes of her, I'll tell you. Turn your back, bend over to pull a weed, and she's delighted to tuck the hoe to you. Ollie, it's ones like her that's taken over these parts. You know their way: They tuck it to you, you tuck it to them, everybody tucks it to everybody else, until we all get along like farts at a bean supper. I'm not complaining, mind you. Mrs. Zoe Cutter made me see the light. It's not enough to be mean. You've got to be sly. This ain't a world for the pure heart, Ollie. I'm grateful to the she-wolf. She made a fox out of a bear. After we was burnt out—terrible thing, a fire—I kind of took stock, what with being kissed off by the lords of my shop, and my missus sick, my boy gone over the other side, and my little girl Heather sent off for schooling by the she-wolf. I went to work for myself. Howard Elman—businessman. Seems crazy, even to me. But it's so. Every day first thing in the Christly morning, me and old Cooty Patterson collect rubbish. You'd be surprised how much swill and old ju-ju beans people throw away every week. I got a dump truck, which I fixed into a honeywagon. Based on my good looks, they're going to give me credit at the bank for a new truck with a compactor body. Well, it ain't new, but I'll make it new. May have to take on some help pretty quick, too. Hard to find a good man who'll work for low pay twenty hours a week for a prick like me. I like to air out the back of the honeywagon now and again, and I like to imagine that Mrs. Cutter up on the hill gets a whiff, but I don't know. Course, I don't know nothing. Never did. Ask my smart boy, Freddy. He'll be glad to swear on the frigging Bible what an asshole his old man is . . ."

At that point, Howard Elman paused and took a long drink from the pitcher of beer. Ollie took over the conversation. They blabbed on for two more hours, getting ever more incoherent. Their conversation might have seemed like the pointless ramblings of drunks, but the fact is that Ollie Jordan and Howard Elman were making a deal. The two men conversed in a peculiar code, developed over the years without either ever admitting that that was what they were doing. It was as if they believed they were living under a totalitarian state, with agents and recording devices everywhere, and the only private conversation was through code; as if God's pleasure was like a dictator's, gathering the expressed aims of simple men as evidence for damnation. The code also preserved Ollie's and Howard's reluctance to ask a favor from a friend directly, and it added luster to their friendship, each feeling a sense of adventure in the presence of the other.

The two men had been making deals for years. They loaned each other machines, money, labor, but they never spoke of loans. What's more they both leaned toward complicated deals, meticulously negotiated but never acknowledged. Neither could have explained that the process included a recognition, in the small, nasty part of his brain, that really he had bested the other in the deal and, simultaneously, in the better part of his brain, that in truth a fair bargain indeed had been struck. The deal must meet each criterion, and furthermore the code was constantly being updated so that it took an hour of sideways conversation just to discover mutually what the rules were that day. In the end, Ollie Jordan agreed to work for Howard Elman three days a week until the first snow, when they would renegotiate the deal. Howard Elman agreed to pay Ollie Jordan what he could afford, day by day in cash.

Their deal consummated, Elman announced that he had to get a haircut, which of course was impossible at nine p.m. in Keene, N. H., and left. Ollie eased out of the door of Miranda's and flowed effortlessly down the steps onto the sidewalk. He felt like a canoe on a quietly moving river. It was getting dark, but there was something left of the sunset in the western sky over Keene, a small halo of golden-red light. It reminded Ollie of the church he had been in earlier and of the house he would build deep in the woods. It reminded him that the color green of the forest was a lonely color. "That's why they cut the trees down," he said, in a flash of insight, and his loneliness came upon him, all sweet and sad, the hardness taken out of it by the booze.

St. Pete's

Ollie slept that night in his truck. The next morning, as soon as the stores were open, he bought some rolls of heavy-duty clear plastic and returned to Niagara Falls Park. He recognized it as home by the smell of empty sardine cans "going ripe," as he would say, and by the rest of his litter on the forest floor. Willow was waiting for him.

He fetched his groceries, gave Willow half a dozen Sunbeam sugar doughnuts he had bought, and set to work making a fire on the altar stone to heat some water for coffee. Willow ate all the doughnuts, lay down in his nest, and fell asleep. He looked husky and healthy, if ragged, as he lay there, and Ollie thought, My God, he's actually gained weight out here. It struck Ollie that Willow must be going out into the night hunting down creatures to eat. The idea disgusted him, and he pushed the problem of Willow out of his mind. After all, he had work to do, a vision of home to be brought forth.

In his vision, Ollie saw a home of clear plastic held up by whippy maple saplings lashed together to make arches. The vision told Ollie that his home would resemble the church he had been in earlier, but if his mind had been clearer he would have seen that the structure would more closely resemble a Quonset hut. The vision itself was pretty, and it danced and changed and entertained him; but it wasn't until afternoon that he actually set to work to bring it forth. Nothing happened. The moment he started to think about the details—such as selecting the proper sized saplings to cut—the vision grew blurry. If he sat down and emptied his mind of thought, the clarity of the vision returned. He became very confused. He had to release the vision in order to make room in his mind to figure out how to bring it forth, but once he released it, there was nothing to bring forth.

The problem, he decided, was that the vision didn't like company. He tried to trick it. He strolled about, whistling, holding the vision on the front porch of his mind, and then he would casually pick up his bow saw and meander over to the grove of young hardwoods. But by the time he grasped the sapling in his hand to get the thickness of it, he would be wondering just what he was going to do with this young tree. Was the tree the right size? How would he join it with a brother to form an arch? How would he bend the arches? How would he put them up? Where? He didn't even have a site for his building. Come to think of it, he needed to clear a space, cut down big trees, take into account drainage. What would he do for a door? The details filled his mind, like mooching relatives filling a house. The vision went out the back door. He sat down again, leaned his back against a tree, lit his pipe, invited the vision to be his guest. In came the vision, out went the details, and he was right back where he started from. He did no work that day, or the next. By the third day, the vision had become vaguely menacing. Where before he had imagined himself inside his new home, the sunlight pouring through the plastic like a warm, shining rain, now the light in his mind grew hot and threatened to scorch him. *Silently burning, silently burning*, choirs sang in his mind. He realized he must bring forth the vision or be consumed by it.

Finally, on the fourth day, he contrived a fury and plunged into the saplings with his bow saw. He cut down dozens of trees, each about an inch and a half in diameter. He lopped branches and peeled off the bark. He laid out his work on the forest floor under the pines near the altar stone. He had no idea at this point just how he would use the poles. He knew only that they were necessary. After he had more than enough, he paused to take them in. They were lean and whippy and beautiful—cream-colored, like a woman's skin. He inhaled their fragrance, caressed them, and slept. When he woke, the vision was gone, but in its place was a modest, sensible idea of how he must build his house. He was sad. The vision had been so much better.

He paced in the land for an afternoon until he found a building site, not far from the altar stone, where the land was humped slightly; the rainwater would drain off. The place was dense with black birches, red maples, and red oaks, all between three and ten inches in diameter, and there was also a boulder about three feet high.

The next morning Ollie worked for Elman and negotiated to borrow a chainsaw and some other tools. He returned to Niagara Falls Park with the chainsaw and two dozen doughnuts. With the doughnuts he bribed Willow into clearing the trees from the house site and cutting the lengths into firewood. Willow stacked the wood in odd shapes, often changing the shapes until they met his purpose—whatever that was. Meanwhile, Ollie worked with an ax and pick to remove the stumps. The stumps could be removed easily by drilling holes in them and pouring kerosene in the holes every day for a week to soak and then setting them on fire, but that surely would get the attention of the Darby Fire Department. Chief Bell and his crew would come clanking up Abare's Folly in the four-wheel-drive Land-Rover Bell had convinced the town to buy. Right behind, curious, as if he were visiting a whorehouse, would be Constable Godfrey Perkins. Ollie could not risk a fire, and for once he overcame the urge to do things the easy way. He dug in with ax and pick, working all the daylight hours, getting so exhausted that he actually slept well at night. Willow finished his work in a day and a half, but it took Ollie three days to finish his. Ollie tried to get Willow to help him, but the boy refused to be bribed or bullied. Ollie was proud of him in a way. He's getting to be his own man, he thought. Well, maybe not a man. His own somebody, anyway. Willow did help Ollie push aside the stumps. Even after they had been moved off the house site, Willow tugged and pulled them and arranged them to suit his mysterious purposes. The stumps were often five feet across, brown, and dusty, with a thick headlike center, from which arms and legs twisted out. No doubt about it, thought Ollie: Below the earth under each tree is a creature with an idea.

After he had finished clearing his house site, Ollie basked in the feeling of a job well done. He decided he needed to reward himself, so he drank beer steadily for two days, taking time from sitting by the fire at the altar only to piss in the woods and to snack on sardines and crackers. Then he slept, waking uncharacteristically with a hangover, and so he did not work the next day. Gradually, he returned to his former, slovenly habits, staying up all night, sleeping during the day, finding excuses not to work on the house: He needed supplies and must drive to town; he owed Elman labor; he must tidy up the site some more; Willow's bottom needed cleaning; and so on. Then in the middle of a sultry night, while he was dozing as he sat cross-legged by his fire, the vision returned to him, more vivid and vague than ever. It seemed to him that his mind temporarily had grown sharper. He could see how men with visions could be driven to serve great causes, or evil causes, or causes that didn't matter. "A vision has got no sense of right and wrong," he said to Willow, who was not there.

Late that night came a violent thunderstorm, with lightning that lit up the sky. Out of his past, out of the lost time, he got a glimmer of a dark world suddenly made bright by a slap in the face and then gone dark again. Just as the rain broke, he ran for the shelter and scurried under. Moments later, Willow came out of the trees like some ape and joined him. He was shivering with fear. Ollie held him in his arms, noticing that his son's smell had changed, becoming sweeter yet more alien somehow. Ollie wondered whether he should wash him. He used to think that the smell of the kinship was in the blood and came through the pores of the skin, that it was as permanent as a curse. But now he was thinking that he might be wrong, that a man's smell might just come from the air of the place that he inhabited. The idea struck him as important, and he decided to ponder it. But the rain and the comfort of lying in someone's arms put him to sleep. He dreamed of naked men freezing in the arms of women made of ice.

He woke cold. The rain had wet his right side. Willow was gone. The vision was gone, too. In its place was a vague command to lash together two maple saplings with some nylon cord. He set to work. He braced the end of the pole in the crotch of a big tree, and bent the pole until he could brace the other end against another tree. He had created an arch under tension. He fastened another pole to the two sides of the arch about halfway up. He knew now exactly how he would build the house. He also knew that the vision would never return. He made sixteen arches, stood them sixteen inches on center, and lashed them together with poles placed perpendicular to them. He covered this framework with clear plastic, and he laid plastic on the earth. He now had a structure thirty feet long, open at the ends, with a high-arched ceiling. It was a great house, none like it anywhere, and it deserved a name. Looks like a church, he thought, and decided then and there to call his house St. Pete's.

"Hello, St. Pete," he said. The sound of his voice gave him a longing. He wished he could show off the place to Helen, or Elman—somebody. He took the good luck charm the Witch had given him and hung it from a string inside St. Pete's. Then he went down to the pool where he kept his beer. Summer was getting on, but the water was still cold. He brought three beers to the house site and sat away from it where he could take in its magnificence. It was, he thought, the greatest achievement of his life.

The Scarecrow

The Fourth of July started wrong for the storekeeper. First there was the fight with Gloria, and then there was the trouble with that Jordan character that kept him from seeing the parade.

That morning Gloria had taken his arm (she rarely touched him outside of relations), and she had said with concern: "The birds are eating the strawberries in the garden."

"Get nets," he had said.

"What do you mean—get nets?"

"Put nets over the strawberries and the birds won't get 'em," he had said.

"Where am I going to get nets on the Fourth of July?"

"Worry about it tomorrow, huh?"

"Thank you for your cooperation. Thank you very, very much."

He was stung by that uncalled-for second "very," and it provoked him into saying something he shouldn't have. "I'll pave it. That'll solve your problem."

"It would take Einstein to solve you," she had said.

They continued to argue until each knew it was time to back off and let the coldness come over the heat.

Back in Hazleton, Gloria had always wanted a garden, but they'd not had the room. The Flaggs' growing space, between the house-store and barn, had been a big selling point in getting Gloria to migrate here. But as things turned out, the garden became a strain on their relationship. In the Darby circles that Gloria moved in, skill in working the soil was a rung on the social ladder. Gloria felt that she was expected to maintain a garden up to standards. She resented him for not caring. He resented her for involving him. Once, just to kid her, he had suggested they pave the growing space for a store parking lot. Now all he had to do was mention that word "pave" and Gloria would get infuriated.

The storekeeper did not enjoy this battle with his wife. He wanted peace, but her preoccupation with the garden had jabbed a vague fear inside him. He wished he could explain it to her. He wanted to tell her that he loved the store and the house and the TV, with its great antenna sticking up from the roof, and he loved the indoor plants she moved from window to window, as though keeping them from getting bored, but that the outside here, the air, the sunlight, the brooding hills in the background disturbed him, made him homesick, not for Hazleton, but for a region in his mind that he had left. The plain fact was he did not feel completely settled in Darby. He dared not confess his unease to Gloria because he was afraid he would unleash certain doubts in her that would start them back on the road to Hazleton. So he stayed in the store as much as possible, and when Gloria hinted that she wanted him outside for some reason, such as working in the garden, he responded meanly, in the crazy hope that somehow she would apprehend his fear.

After the argument, the storekeeper experienced a rare attack of nerves. He watched as Gloria and the kids prepared for the Darby Independence Day parade. The kids played in the school band and Gloria would ride in Gregory Croteau's Cadillac as a member of the Darby Garden Club. The marchers were going to start at the fire station and proceed a short way to the town common, right past the store, and then to the school grounds for the beginning of the annual Darby Independence Day clambake. Just as his family was about to leave, the storekeeper announced that he intended to keep the store open during the parade because he expected a surge of business. Gloria knew immediately that this was a lie; he thought she would burst into tears. Back in Hazleton, where he had been the meat manager at a Weis supermarket, he had vowed he would never work on a holiday when he had his own store. He could see that Gloria believed that he was trying to make her feel bad by keeping the store open. How could he explain he only meant to relax for a while in the comfort of his store?

Later, he stood alone behind the counter trying to think of a way to make things right with Gloria, until he was distracted by events outside his window. Fire Chief Bell and other volunteer firemen were laying out parade markers on the road, as if no one knew the way. Constable Perkins was hanging around, but not doing any work, of course. The Bingham boy zoomed down the street on his bicycle, somehow balancing his drum on the handlebars. The storekeeper heard himself chuckle. All at once, he found himself keenly looking forward to watching the parade, even if it was only going to last about ninety seconds. A parade in a dinky little town—how strange and wonderful. They were going to march right by his store, his own kids included. He felt proud and patriotic. This is what makes America great, he thought, all aglow with insight. He left the counter and picked up one of the tiny American flags he'd been selling. He'd close the store, stand on the steps, and wave the flag at his kids. When Gloria approached in the Cadillac, he'd do something really dramatic. He'd blow her a kiss.

The storekeeper was holding the flag when Professor Hadly Blue entered the store. "Am I glad you're open. Can't live without the *Times,*" he said, and put a *New York Times* newspaper under his arm.

"Parade started?" asked the storekeeper.

"They were lining up when I walked by. A great scene. Diane Arbus would have loved it," said the professor, who put his money on the counter and left.

Arbus—the name didn't ring a bell with the storekeeper. But then again, he didn't know everybody in town. Not yet, anyway.

The sounds of the Darby Drum and Bugle Corps seeped into the store and excited the storekeeper. But before he could get to the door to turn his sign around to say "closed," another customer had come in.

"I'm about ready to close for the parade," said the storekeeper, but the man didn't seem to hear.

He had a stubble beard and greasy skin, and when he opened his mouth to speak, he revealed a mouth of black, decayed teeth. The storekeeper recognized the man as Ollie Jordan.

"Need some Black Label, a case, and a pack of Carter Hall tobacco," Jordan said.

The gossip in Darby was that Jordan and his idiot son were living in the hills, but nobody seemed to know exactly where, and no one cared enough to pursue the matter. The storekeeper had seen Jordan drive by the store in his funny looking truck, but he'd never stopped before. Apparently he'd been doing his shopping out of town and for this the storekeeper resented him.

"I don't have a whole case of Black Label in the cooler," said the storekeeper. "I'll have to go out back to get it."

"I can wait," said Jordan, "but I want the tobacco now. I run out."

The storekeeper could hear the parade getting closer. Godfrey Perkins was running the siren in his cop car. The thing to do was tell this Jordan fellow he'd get his beer after the parade and he'd darn well have to wait. But there was something about having the man in the store that dirtied up the storekeeper's vision of the parade. He wanted Jordan out of his store, pronto. Maybe he could discourage the man from buying. God, I must be soft in the head to turn away business, he thought and gave Jordan his tobacco.

"Beer in the back is warm—piss warm," the storekeeper said. "You come back after the parade, it'll be nice and cold."

"I can pay, I got money," Jordan said.

Oh, no, thought the storekeeper, I hit the guy where his pride lives. He thinks I think he wants credit.

"Parade's coming. I can hear the band—dee-dum," said the storekeeper, trying to plead with the tone of his voice.

"I got money. See, right here," Jordan said, laying a twenty-dollar bill on the counter.

The storekeeper took the bill and returned change for the beer and tobacco, laid his little flag to rest on the counter, and then jogged toward the rear of the store. If he got a move on, he could get back with the case just in time to watch the parade go by. He blundered into the back room without putting on the light, and the quick plunge into darkness made him believe he was going to lose his balance. He remembered now that in high school he was called "bird head" because his head was small, his neck long, his shoulders broad. "Those bastards," he whispered. He backed out of the room, snapped on the light, and went in again. He breathed hard. Harold Flagg, the previous storekeeper, had died of a heart attack—probably because of the demands of this damn store. The storekeeper grabbed the beer case and broke into a run, slowing to a quick walk once he got into the store. He didn't want Jordan to see him rush, although why in the world he should care was beyond him. Jordan was sitting on one of the straight-back chairs near the counter. He had lit his pipe and he looked content—the S.O.B. The storekeeper laid the beer at his feet, picked his flag off the counter, and quick-stepped to the front door. He stood on the steps as he had planned, flag in hand, and he could see the dregs of the parade in the distance—a couple of kids on bicycles, somebody's green Pinto automobile. The storekeeper waved his flag once and went back into the store. Ollie Jordan was just leaving.

"Parade passed me by," said the storekeeper.

"Why these people would want to walk on a hot road, when they could be drinking beer in the shade, I don't know," Jordan said.

"Ah-ba," was all the storekeeper could say. Not that it mattered. Jordan was walking away from him.

The storekeeper had just closed the store when Old Man Dorne drove by in his Buick, stopped, backed up, and said from the window in a voice that didn't sound quite right to the storekeeper, "Going to the clambake?"

"I guess so."

"Want a ride?"

"I guess so," said the storekeeper.

In the Buick, the storekeeper got a whiff of booze breath. That was odd. He didn't think Dorne was the type to drink in the daylight.

The storekeeper was comforted by this car. It had air-conditioning and therefore the windows were rolled up and the only sound was the reassuring doze of well-muffled machinery at work. Dorne didn't pull into the school parking lot, but stopped the car alongside the road. The storekeeper watched parade marchers mingling about. He didn't see Gloria and imagined that she was in the school preparing potato salad or something. He looked at his watch. It would be another hour before the feed started.

"Why am I always early for things I don't want to go to in the first place?" he said.

"Hard morning, eh?" Dorne said.

"It shows?"

"Little bit. Come on, let's go for a ride." And the old man drove off without waiting for an answer. Moments later, he reached under the seat and produced a paper bag. Inside was a bottle of Seagrams 7 whiskey. He handed the bottle to the storekeeper, who took a drink. The booze quickly settled him down. He felt like a high school boy again, driving around, seeing what's what.

The old man stayed on back roads, some of which the storekeeper had never been on before. There were roads that climbed into the gloom of deep forests, roads that followed streams through valleys, roads that came suddenly into open spaces with a big, blue sky hovering over green fields being mowed by black and white cows.

"Guernseys?" said the storekeeper.

"Holsteins," said Dorne.

The storekeeper saw pleasant but run-down wood-frame houses where machines and sheds and barns and garden plants and weeds and wild flowers and various grasses grew every which-a-way in harmony with the messy, disreputable forests that surrounded the homesteads; and he saw shacks and trailers where the messes had got out of hand; and he saw new houses, fancy and expensive, amidst brand-new lawns and huge septic-tank leaching fields that had been imposed bulldozerwise on the landscape. The scene left him wondering, Who do these people think they are? Country folk were either too rich or too poor.

The storekeeper got more and more relaxed. He found himself talking a mile a minute about what had happened that morning. Dorne laughed loud, a big roaring but sad laugh. There was no meanness in the laugh, and it made the store-keeper feel a kinship with the actors in the human comedy. Soon he, too, was brimming with mirth. "Don't life shake up the bladder?" the old man said and pulled the car off the road to a stop. The two men went tottering in the woods to take a piss. The storekeepr could smell pine needles.

When they came back, Dorne looked suddenly weary. He asked the storekeeper to drive.

"Tired?" asked the storekeeper.

"Sick," said Dorne.

They were traveling the road that skirted the steep ledgy hill known as Abare's Folly when Dorne pointed to dirt ruts disappearing into the trees. "I bet if you went there, you'd find your friend Ollie Jordan," he said. Impulsively, the store-keeper peeled off the blacktop and onto the dirt road. The car did bumps and grinds for about one hundred yards before the storekeeper realized he couldn't go any farther. Dorne was laughing again as the storekeeper backed up. "If you'd treated my Buick like this a month ago, I would've had you shot. But today I don't give a damn," Dorne said.

A shimmer of fear gripped the consciousness of the storekeeper. He darned near had had an accident. It was time to head back to Darby village.

"Don't think too bad about Ollie Jordan," Dorne said. "His kind are not like you and me."

"You know him well, do you?"

"I know him better than he knows me," Dorne said. "I knew his mumma way back when. Fact is, and I wouldn't have admitted this until recently—I got no shame left, you see; I'm free of it—fact is, I'm related distantly to the Jordan clan."

With that, the old man told a story about a relative of his who had made a living burning piles of wood for charcoal production, and how somebody had been incinerated in the pile. The storekeeper never did get the relationship between Dorne and the Jordans. But he was only half-listening; he was rerunning mentally a scene from a movie on television the other night called "The Birds."

They were almost in the village, coming up on Dorne's white colonial, when the storekeeper blurted out: "Where can I get nets?"

"You can't get nets on the Fourth of July," Dorne said.

"That's what I told Gloria. But, see, the birds don't know it's a holiday. Even if they did, they wouldn't be going to the barbecue when the strawberries are so cheap in Gloria's garden."

"You want to do something for your missus?" Dorne asked.

"I want her to take hold here, like in the garden," and the storekeeper wondered why the idea he wanted to express was so clear in his mind, yet so muddled in the speaking of it. But Dorne understood.

"You don't need nets. You need a scarecrow, and by golly if I can't make a scarecrow, seventy-eight years of sweet life come to this heart undeserving," Dorne said. He ordered the storekeeper to pull the Buick into his driveway.

The old man zig-zagged into the house, while the storekeeper waited in the car. He was getting edgy. He didn't like how the day was taking on a booze-yellow glow. He glanced at his watch. Dorne soon returned, carrying an armful of clothes, on top of which was a wide-brimmed, oddly shaped purple hat with a feather, like something out of a pirate movie. The storekeeper did not like this hat.

"You're not going to make a scarecrow from that suit?" he asked.

"I haven't worn it in the last twenty years, and I ain't going to wear it in the next twenty. This is not a burying suit, you see?" Dorne said, and chuckled. "Now let's go to your place."

Dorne found tools and lumber in the shed behind the store as if he'd been there before—and probably he had. Even though he was still under the influence, he was graceful and sure in his labors. He made a cross from 2-by-4s, cutting a wide groove in two pieces and joining them with a couple of nails. He had the storekeeper dig a hole in the garden, and then the two men planted the cross. The suit jacket hung pretty well on it, but the pants had to be fussied on with the help of another piece of wood and some coat hangers. Dorne made a head by stuffing a pillowcase with wood shavings from the shed, then tying it around the throat of the cross. The storekeeper was visited by intimations of strangulation. Dorne topped the scarecrow with the hat.

"Quite the hat," said the storekeeper, liking it less and less.

"I got that hat at the Tunbridge World's Fair back in—I won't say what year. I was a young feller and I thought the hoochie-coochie dancers would like me with that hat. I haven't put it on since. Better it graces the noggin of our friend here, Mr. Strawberry Savior."

"He doesn't have a face," said the storekeeper.

"The birds don't think you or I got any more face than him," Dorne said. "Besides, the hat will hide his face, I mean his lack of face."

Old Man Dorne was quite proud of himself. Much as the storekeeper disliked the hat, he realized that he had to accept it, that it was not proper for him to criticize it now. He experienced a surge of resentment at this perception. He made a mental note to replace the hat at some future date.

"This fellow will work for you twenty-four hours a day," Dorne said. "And he won't complain, not even about the weather, and he won't demand minimum wage."

It wasn't until the next morning at breakfast, while they were eating cereal with strawberries and maple syrup, and Gloria was in good humor as a result of the gift of the scarecrow, that the mystery of Dorne's behavior came clear to the storekeeper: The old-timer was dying.

A Night

August passed, September passed. It was disturbing to Ollie that he could not remember clearly certain incidents in the last two months, but he told himself that, on the whole, it had been a successful time. He had worked mornings three or four days a week with Elman on the trash route, and that had been all right. He was able to scrounge enough materials to furnish St. Pete's rather nicely and to board in the ends to include windows and a door (painted red). It was amazing the things people threw away—clothes, appliances, furniture, knick-knacks, not to mention glass containers, metal cans, and plastic holders of a thousand shapes and colors. And food! A man could live like a King of Arabia, just on the food his neighbors threw away. But what bothered him most was the tremendous amount of paper that people used—especially reading matter. People read too much. They read about everything. All over the world. It would come to no good. People would fill their minds with strange ugly things until they couldn't help being strange and ugly themselves. It could happen: a world gone mean and mad at once, as if all the eyes of mankind saw monsters everywhere in weather, in plants, in mirrors, in the faces of those most loved.

"Willow," he said, and the birds went silent as Ollie's voice carried through the night. Willow did not answer. Willow had gone somewhere, on his own personal errand. Ollie was getting cold. He shouldn't be out here. He should be inside getting warmed by his new wood stove, but he liked it by the altar stone. He liked the open fire and the solemn dignity of the stone itself. If God ever had something to say to him, it would be here. He rose, put two more sticks on the fire, and opened another beer. Somebody's got a plan, he thought. Even Elman was reading lately. He was taking a course, or some goddamn thing, and he would wear these little glasses, and he would sniff, as he held up a magazine: "Ollie, I want you to get a load of this," he would say, and he would read aloud some stupid-ass thing. Once he went on and on about somebody inventing a thing that would hold a million conversations.

"You don't believe that shit?" Ollie had asked.

"Course, I do," Elman had said.

"Just because they print it don't make it the truth," Ollie had said.

"Yah, yah, I know they lie, but that's only to screw somebody they want to screw," Elman said. "Those microwaves don't screw anybody. There's no reason to lie about a microwave. The difference between these educated people and the ignorant people is the educated ones don't lie unless they want to screw somebody. Now your ignoramus will lie to protect his pride or for sport . . ."

And on Elman would go. It was appalling. Somebody had taught Elman book reading, and every time he got on the subject he became a horse's ass. But, really, he had no complaints against Elman. He was a good boss, as well as a good friend. He was good company, too, and that's what Ollie needed after spending all those hours alone or with Willow, who had grown oddly powerful, not like a man but like a storm, or something godlike anyway.

"Willow?" he said. "Willow." Ollie hoped he'd return soon. Willow left every day at noon, sometimes not returning until late at night, sometimes not returning at all.

Ollie now was visited by a mental image of great pulsating hulks of metal and of plump, overturned chairs that were feminine somehow, suddenly bursting with their stuffing as though slashed by big knives, and of a dark-hatted slouching man, with pitted skin that resembled corroded aluminum. The man milled about menacingly like a whore killer on a whore street on a Saturday night, and Ollie could hear crows spreading evil tales in the fiery sky of the image. He knew that the picture in his mind was the distorted shape of a lost memory. He strained to identify it, failed, and then the image was forgotten, and he was thinking that he didn't like the way towns got rid of their trash these days.

It used to be that the fires in dumps simmered twenty-four hours a day and you could sneak in and pick it over for fascinating items. But now they buried the trash in layers, like a giant cake. Sanitary landfill. He didn't like it. Nothing to pick. Just layer upon layer.

"Umm," he said aloud. "Willow! Willow! Get your ass home."

The boy had done well. All right, he was getting mysterious and peculiar. But so what? All great men were mysterious and peculiar. The point was that Willow had developed, on his own, ways of survival. Thanks to Willow they had had a bountiful late summer. Ollie figured that the boy was raiding gardens at night, taking vegetables and returning with them to the park. He picked only the best and apparently he was very clever, for Ollie quizzed Elman closely about rumors around town of someone stealing from gardens. There were no such rumors. The boy had learned to move about without being seen. He never took more than he needed. Either the gardeners never missed portions of their harvest, or they put the blame on raccoons.

Willow never ate the food he brought home. In fact, unless Ollie brought home doughnuts or pies, he never ate at all in Ollie's presence. The idea that Willow was taking game somehow and feeding upon it both revolted Ollie and made him proud, but it wasn't the kind of thing he liked to think about so he pushed it around in his mind trying to hide it. The vegetables that Willow brought were beautiful things, and sometimes before he ate them Ollie would look at them through the sunlight fragmented by the trees and he would marvel at the work of God, God being another idea he was working on these days. He especially liked the ripe red tomatoes, some of which were big as grapefruit. Sometimes he ate them like apples, breaking into them with the black, jagged teeth, tasting the innards as they ran down his cheeks. They looked and felt like burst hearts. But most of the vegetables he cooked, boiling them into a gooey stew so that their individual identities vanished. In the stew he mixed sardines or Spam or hamburger or whatever he had that day. Sometimes he foraged for crayfish and frogs, for their legs. These meals brought him strength. He felt better now physically than he had in years.

Frosts had put an end to most of the garden vegetables, and lately all Willow brought were squash and pumpkins and occasional store-bought vegetables and fruit. Ollie couldn't imagine where he was stealing these from. He wished Willow would bring him meat, and he broached the subject, but Willow pretended not to understand. Ollie imagined that meat was sacred to Willow because it came from animals, which to Willow were his kin. If you thought about it, you'd have to come to the conclusion that all creatures were kin. The evidence was there: All creatures had flesh and blood; all creatures suffered and died. He figured that Willow had developed some religious ideas about the business of killing and eating animals, and that was why he refused to bring his father his game. It's easier for me, Ollie thought, I eat my meat from the can. It was hard to get religious about a can of sardines or Spam. But with that thought, he began to consider for the first time the idea of canned meat. How did they catch all those tiny sardines and how did they get them in the can? He imagined men with sailor hats and pea coats dragging the oceans with huge nets made of screened-door material, women with sweat on their brows and great sagging breasts working in a stupor with sharp knives cleaning the fish, and other women, more dainty and careful, packing the fish in cans and sealing them through some process beyond his imagination. The idea made sense, to a point—but what of Spam? It was meat, no doubt about that. Was there such an animal as Spam? If so, why had he not seen one on television? Of course, it could be they were small—can-sized creatures. Spam, ham, he thought. Hell, if a ham was a pig, maybe a Spam was a small pig, say the size of a football. You wouldn't need cowboys to herd them. They could live in rabbit pens or something. He found this explanation unsatisfactory and filed away the problem for future consideration.

"Willow! Willow Jordan come home."

He should put on a coat, but the coat was in St. Pete's and he didn't want to leave the fire. It would break his train of thought. He built up the fire instead. It was beautiful and ever-changing, it threw heat in his face, like a passion, and it warmed his spirit, but it had no arms to wrap around his shoulders. He was shivering. He wished now that he had a woman, not for sex, for a man could handle that chore himself, but for arms. "Oh, Witch," he whispered, and he hunkered down closer to the fire, turning his back upon it to warm the place that shivered between his shoulder blades. The cool of the evening fell upon his flushed face, and for a moment he had the sensation that he was feeling the touch of the night itself.

There was something out there that had interest in himself and in Willow. He didn't know what it was, but this much he knew: It had something to do with the darkness. He didn't feel threatened by it, not just yet. Only an idea, he cautioned himself. Mustn't go too far with it. Ideas of dark strangers were always dangerous: You don't believe in them and you don't believe them, and then you invite them in the house, and then you do believe in them, and they strip you for your things and kill you. Still, undeniably, this was an interesting idea to think about. He issued a mental challenge to the stranger that he did not believe in: Show your face to me some midnight.

For a moment he felt awesome, powerful, as though the weight of the altar stone had been transformed into energy for his own being. He felt as though he could lift that stone and hurl it into the stars. The feeling of power would pass quickly, he knew, so he gathered what he could of it for his mind, and expended it in a probe into the darkness, and he could see a shape squatting behind the trees, watching, and then the power was gone, and the shape was gone, and he was merely thinking now.

There might be, out there, he thought, a fellow from the Welfare Department spying. But if so, why hadn't this fellow called the cops and had him and Willow arrested? The answer was obvious: It was all in his imagination. Unless . . . unless. It was possible that the Welfare Department had plans for Willow that had something to do with his staying out here. Thus, they might station someone here to watch the place. But why just at night? Umm. Willow slept all morning, sometimes in trees, sometimes in his nest, sometimes in St. Pete's. But there was no reason to observe him then, nothing to be gained from him. Therefore, the fellow from the Welfare Department could take the days off. Have a few beers. The more Ollie thought about this explanation, the less satisfactory it became. After all, if the Welfare Department were on to him, they certainly could afford to have shifts of fellows watching him. He looked at the fire and then at the altar stone, attempting to draw from them their power, and he was seeing the dark shape. It was Willow huddled over another darker shape, as though plotting with his own shadow. Was it possible that Willow himself was in league with the Welfare Department, that he was meeting with them secretly at night?

"Oh, God," he said. "Willow, come home to Daddy."

He stood up. His back was burning from the fire, and his face was cold. He started to dance around in circles, trying to find the happy medium between heat and cold—warmth—because warmth was akin to arms. What he really wanted was arms. He tried to hug himself, but these arms—his own arms—seemed alien to him, alien even to flesh, as though they were wires, and he released himself. He wished he had some strong drink instead of just beer. He reached for the six-pack that he kept cloistered in a brown bag by his side, in a kind of absurd caution as though he were getting around a law against drinking in the woods. (It did not occur to him that if he were to get arrested it would be for littering, for the land here was covered with his empty beer bottles, cans of all kinds, but especially sardine cans, empty foam containers, and paper, paper everywhere—thrown by him to the ground, blown by the wind into trees, carried into small earthen caverns by curious rodents. Ollie noticed none of this work that he had done, although he was struck by the sense that Niagara Falls Park had become more comfy of late.) The brown bag was empty. Now he'd have to go into St. Pete's to get some more beer. He could put up with a little cold, but life in the night without beer was not worth living. Reluctantly, he went inside.

It was not that he disliked the place. In fact, he was altogether too comfortable in St. Pete's. That was the problem. Here with a small fire going in the stove he had salvaged, with his fanny settled into the easy chair he had salvaged, with his feet on the chopping block (Ollie split the firewood inside), with his drink and pipe in reach on the end table he had salvaged, with the portable radio (that he had salvaged) blaring, with the shelves he had made bursting with the knick-knacks he had salvaged that testified to his enormous competence, with thoughts of danger and evil seemingly unable to get rolling in the pleasantness of this place—here, he could fall asleep in the night.

But sleep in the night is what he did not want to do. It was not so much the nightmares that bothered him, because he remembered so little of their content even as he woke, but rather the feeling itself of waking out of the nightmare. It was a feeling that there was someone else in his mind. According to Ollie Jordan's law of personal survival, sleep must be fought off until the dawn's first light. He would sit there all night by his fire, drinking beer and thinking, and when the first few birds began to chirp moments before the darkness could be perceived as lifting, only then would Ollie return to St. Pete's, slide into the bed (salvaged), lay his head upon the pillow (salvaged), cover himself with blankets (salvaged), and sleep the gentle rest. He feared the coming of winter, not so much for the cold as for the longer nights, more chance for nightmares.

Sometimes he napped in the afternoon. He cautioned himself to waken before dark, but often he slept over and woke in a nightmare, which was bearable as long as it came in early evening, for Ollie Jordan had categorized the different darknesses of the night. Dusk, the first darkness, was not a dangerous darkness, but it was uncomfortable. During this time, the eyes of hunters opened. Sometimes, coming out of a dream, Ollie could see in his mind countless tiny lights that were the eyes of hunting creatures of all kinds. He would lie there terrified, not so much by the lights, for he knew they were only in his mind, but by the thought that when he opened his eyes the lights would still be there. He would open his eyes, and there would be no lights, just the dusk which was like the smell all around you of the breath of a man whom you cannot see who wants to injure you. This was a time for a quick drink, to ease the nerves. Much as Ollie was opposed to work, he had to admit that around dusk it was good to keep busy—split firewood, patch the roof, lay in leaves for insulation around the perimeter of St. Pete's, haul water. Once total darkness had replaced dusk, he would relax, sit and smoke his pipe, settle down to serious drinking, that is, measured drinking. This was a good darkness, this time between dusk and midnight, and his impulse was to drink hard in celebration of a good thing (the only way Ollie Jordan could imagine to celebrate a good thing was to drink), but generally he was cautious, because he knew that if he drank too much too soon, he might fall asleep and wake during the dangerous darkness, the time between midnight and dawn. Ollie had become convinced, through his recent experiences, that the true danger of the late darkness was that during those hours the barriers of time itself were weakened. Then spirits could move back and forth into past and future. The dead, or whatever was the name of the evil out there, had errands to do, errands that required living bodies to motor around their vaporous forms in this, a world of substance. He further speculated that certain bodies, through the porthole of the sleeping mind, could be influenced to do the work of the spirits, but only late at night when time could be bridged. A man could be haunted, even by his own ghost.

Still, he had mastered the knack of staying awake, he said to himself now, and it wouldn't hurt, really, to sit for a moment in the soft easy chair. The warmth of St. Pete's was settling into him. Watch out, he had said to himself. Don't get too warm. The warm man falls asleep. Well, he'd sit down just for a moment. Nice, nice, nice, nice—this chair. Ollie had salvaged it on one of his trips in the honeywagon with Elman. A dog had shit upon it and a certain Mrs. McGuirk had thrown it out. Ollie had brought the chair to St. Pete's and covered the offending stain with sheepskin (salvaged). The next day Mr. McGuirk asked Elman what the hell he had done with his chair, and Elman had said merely that he didn't have it. That was the end of it, for no man would want to challenge Elman's eyes, even one outraged at the loss of his easy chair. Ollie fetched beer now, which he kept in a cool spot in St. Pete's, and he lit his pipe and sat upon his chair. He smelled, or imagined he smelled—he wasn't sure which—the pooch that most certainly must have gotten his ass kicked after messing on this chair.

He missed his own dogs. He wished he had a dog. That would be his next project, he decided: Get a dog. Dogs were like men—such fools. Such sex lives. A bitch in heat will stand in one spot, as if ordered by a general. As for the males that came to her, it was the smell that brought them. The evidence had hit home once, years ago. He had owned a bitch hound, a wonderful animal on a rabbit track, useless at other times. He wanted to breed her with a weimaraner owned by his Uncle Cleo. Meanwhile, he had to keep her away from Rotten Ralph, an all-breed-no-breed mutt Helen had from her days with Pork Barrel and which she had refused to destroy. Rotten Ralph was a flop-eared, short-legged canine sex maniac. He had a good nose, the right disposition, and the courage to be a first-rate hunting dog, but he lacked the interest. All he wanted to do was chase bitches. In order to protect his prize hound—her name was Lillian—Ollie imprisoned her in an old pigpen. This was one of the best enclosures he had ever made, so good that it had kept a great pig, whose name was Everett P. Wilkes, from routing his way out through the earth beneath. If it could keep Everett from getting out, it could keep Rotten Ralph from getting in. Lillian spent her considerable free time lying on a wool blanket that Helen had gotten away from the Salvation Army. (These were the days before she had begun to come under the spell of the Welfare Department: good days, as Ollie remebered them.) Rotten Ralph dug, sniffed, and threw his body against the enclosure, but he could not get in. One day Cleo brought his weimaraner. He was long-legged, sinewy, and gray as a storm cloud. Ollie introduced him to Lillian. The two hit it off immediately, and Ollie and Cleo drank beer and watched the dogs mate. It was especially gratifying to Ollie to see a frustrated Rotten Ralph on the outside, pacing and whining and throwing himself at the enclosure. Several days later, Lillian stopped quivering and the stock-car whine of her voice changed pitch, and Ollie knew she was out of heat. He released her, and off she went on a run. Rotten Ralph showed no interest in her. Rotten Ralph entered the pigpen and attempted relations with Lillian's blanket. All this time, driven by a smell. It made a good story. Rotten Ralph getting what he deserved—nothing. Except that when the puppies were born, they were all flop-eared and short-legged.

Let's see, what was it he was thinking about? Dogs. Oh, yes, he must get a dog. A man needed a companion. A son wouldn't do. Even a good son, a normal son. The normal son sasses you back and breaks your heart. He knew the hurt that Elman carried over the desertion by education of his son Freddy. Not that the crazy son was any better than the normal son. The crazy son drew the blood out of you, drop by drop, like a mosquito with a limitless appetite. ("Willow," he said, but he only whispered the name.) As a boy Willow had been normal. Well—admit it—not normal. Crazy even then, and private. But affectionate in his own way. He would walk up to the women of the household—any woman for that matter, sometimes strangers—and stroke their heads. The trouble was he kept up the habit after he had passed his childhood. It was hopeless talking to him then, as now, but Ollie used to pretend that he understood. Patting the ladies is fine when you're a boy, he would say. Not so good after your manhood firms up. Scares the ladies. Got to learn to be sneaky with a woman. Steal a pat and steal a heart. Take a pat when the moment's right. Never beg a pat, or a woman will hate you. His advice was useless. No matter what he said, Willow could not, or would not, respond. Ollie didn't know what would be worse: to find out that Willow truly was an idiot and had never understood him and that everything he had said to him had been thrown down an empty well, or to find out that he had been right all along, that Willow was wise to him and to the world and had been mocking both. If that were to happen, Ollie knew he would fill with rage and he would beat his son for the pain he had brought him. *But then again, you beat him anyway*, a voice said inside him; *as to hurt, you and he are even.* Well, then, Ollie thought, maybe I won't beat him anymore. I'll save up all he owes me in hide, and when the moment's right I'll take it all off him at once.

He was getting angry, which was a good thing, for you could not fall asleep when you were angry. The trouble with anger was that it stole away from you in the middle of the battle it instigated and left you fearful. He could nurture the anger, or he could let it go early while he was still in command of it. Let it go, he said to himself. The fact was he wasn't really angry at Willow, or anyone, not even himself. He was angry because his mind chose to be angry, and he was hunting around for something to be angry at. Why, he thought, when a man gets in such a mood does he take it out on his loved ones? Beat the kids, beat his wife—if she let him. Umm. The answer that came to him was that a man would not risk the high cost of fighting an enemy unless there was profit in it. The cost that he expended beating a loved one was small by comparison to challenging another man and it achieved the purpose of relieving his anger. The fact was, he realized, that he—or any man— wanted a dog to pat it or to kick its ass, depending on his mood. God should have given men dogs instead of wives and kids. The world would be a better place under such an arrangement. His anger was slipping away now. He wished he could keep just enough of it to use as a barrier against . . . certain forces. Gone, the anger was gone, and in a second he felt hunted. Anger went out the door and terror came in. He rose from his chair and calmed at the moment of his standing. There was nothing here or out there to be terrified of. There was nothing for miles that wanted to devour or embrace him—unless a man's loneliness had shape and plan. He opened the door of St. Pete's and shouted, "Willow!"

Ollie could feel the deep weariness settle into him now. He mustn't return to his chair, or this time he would fall asleep. He put on his coat and went outside. It was quite cool, forty or forty-five degrees. The nights would come when he couldn't go outside, when it would be difficult enough to keep St. Pete's warm. He had enough food—well, almost enough. Firewood wasn't a problem, really. Willow had cut and stacked more than they could use. Ollie had split the green wood and left it in the sun to dry. It wasn't seasoned yet, but it would burn well enough when mixed with dry dead branches that were free for the taking from the thousands of trees that were his companions here in Niagara Falls Park. In fact, a green fire would last longer in the stove. Then again, a green fire was a smoky fire, and smoke from his chimney might draw attention. The Welfare Department might come to investigate. He didn't like that thought one bit. It disturbed a man's coziness. Still, he must face facts. They would see his smoke. They would come. He supposed he could burn a fire only during the dark hours, of which there were many more in the winter than during the rest of the year. That was the answer, but it was not a satisfactory one. Long hours in the cold, even daytime hours spent sleeping, were not good for a man's health. He was reminded of his half-sister Luella who, with her ridiculous husband, fell sick when nobody would sell them any oil to heat their apartment in Keene. Mr. Ridiculous wasn't working at the time, and anyway they didn't pay their bills when he was working. Luella died. Mr. Ridiculous went south.

What was it he was thinking about? Something about a dog. Oh, yes, he wanted one. Elman would know somebody with puppies. People who live in the town always know someone with puppies. Kittens were even more common. But he didn't want a goddamn cat. The only thing a cat was good for was finding out the most comfortable place in a room. You put a man in a room and he would sit in the chair that was provided even if it was in a draft, even if the chair was uncomfortable. Men, like dogs, endured. A cat would never put up with discomfort. A cat searched the premises for the softest place with the best air, and then laid claim to it. The best a man could do with a cat was to take a portion of its territory for his own comfort. He didn't want to bother Elman about getting a dog because Elman didn't like dogs. He didn't know why. It was puzzling. It used to be that Elman was quite the dog fancier, but he had changed. It was nothing he said or did, yet Ollie could tell from a word, an expression on his face, that Elman had developed a hatred of dogs. Maybe Cooty Patterson could find him a dog, but he didn't trust Cooty's judgment. The old man, out of instinct, would recommend the runt of a litter.

Ollie paced about the plastic confines of St. Pete's, pondering the problem of how to get a dog, not because he actually wanted a dog, but because it busied his mind. He was afraid to sit down because he knew he would fall asleep he was so tired. He didn't like pacing, but it was better than standing still. The trouble with being on your feet was that the beer didn't taste so good. You couldn't concentrate on the drink, and it sloshed around in your gut, which wasn't good for your health. Maybe he'd sit down just for a moment. He'd light a cigarette and hold it in the crook between his ring and middle finger, and if he dozed off the cigarette would burn his finger and wake him up. Somewhere in this house he had a pack of cigarettes (salvaged). He rummaged about, his purpose as much to admire his own taste and effort in the art of salvaging as to search for a cigarette.

Here were some child's toy blocks, a pile of girlie magazines ("One hand turns the pages,/The other drives the car,/Going down the highway of love/Hand in hand with my best friend . . ." Where had he heard that song?); here was a saltshaker (empty), some fish line, a flower pot full of bottle caps; here was an alarm clock, a bouquet of plastic flowers, a broken canoe paddle, assorted lamps and shades, a deflated football, a short knife crudely sharpened (it made him think of the betrayed sound pigs made when you stuck them in the throat). Let's see, what was he looking for? Oh, yes, a dog. But Ollie, he said to himself, you won't find a dog on your shelf. So it couldn't have been a dog. He wasn't so crazy or so drunk that he would search for a dog where he knew there would be no dog. Or was he? What difference did it make? There was no dog here. He could find no dog here. Whatever he had been looking for could keep. He sat down in his chair, stuffed his pipe with Carter Hall tobacco, and lit it, but a peculiarity in the familiar feeling of smoking made him realize that the pipe had something to do with the reason that he had been pacing about just minutes ago.

Was it possible that the Welfare Department had spiked his tobacco? It was a terrible thought for him. Even if such a suspicion could be proven, he would find it impossible to quit his pipe. When it came right down to it, his only two pleasures were drinking and smoking. They were enough, too. He wished for no others, could imagine no others that would satisfy him. He knew that some men could please themselves by watching television, or (like Elman these days) reading books and magazines, or playing cards, or dancing, or even generating certain useless types of motion, such as flying model airplanes or pushing tiny trains round and round a track. But none of these pastimes appealed to him. Ollie Jordan's idea of heaven was an unlimited supply of beer in a pleasant spot (the altar stone would do) and a corncob pipe that would never wear through, and angels that brought him tobacco.

Maybe the angels could help with sex now and again. Of course the wings could be a problem. He wondered briefly whether there really was a heaven, but that was too big an idea to consider, and he immediately let it go. Still, the idea of copulating with angels remained, and that was nice. Past copulations did not seem to register well in the memory. Perhaps that was because copulations at their moments did not seem to register in time. It was only the thought of future copulations that fired the imagination, stirred the loins. Time itself insisted on placing the quest for copulation on the horizon, to drive a man—or moose, any critter—to mate and pass on himself. Time was a strange thing.

He thought about the time in his life now missing in memory. Was it possible that one night long ago, a ghost had come into his dream and jerked him out of time, so that he hadn't forgotten that time at all but it had never happened? If time could be so traversed, then was it possible that someday the spirit would return him to the time he had missed? The idea of being jerked about in time seemed reasonable to Ollie, but why this was so was beyond him. He flirted with the notion, until it occurred to him that perhaps he was part of some important mission that someday would become clear. He thought of Willow. Someone had put him and Willow here and kept them together. Had to, else there was no sense to his life at all. It even was possible that whoever it was had recognized the dangers of the Welfare Department, as Ollie himself had, and that they were all fighting in the same army. Ollie thrilled to this idea. But a moment later, it struck him that the reverse was possible. The entire mess of his life and his son's had been established by the Welfare Department, or the evil force that guided that group, for a purpose that had nothing to do with them at all. It was possible that as men controlled the lives of certain rats in laboratories, so did creatures far superior to men control men's lives. This seemed more likely to Ollie than the previous idea, and he was depressed by it. The trouble with staying up all night was that you had too many thoughts, and it was difficult to know which were the good ones. Every man and every generation had different ideas on just about everything. How was one to know the truth? Even the simple pleasures, say the joy of watching a child make a funny face, or the warmth of alcohol coming into one's system, escaped a man's mind because as he felt them, he could not think about them, but could only recognize them after the fact through the distortion of his memory. All a man can know that is certain is his own hurt. But then again hurt was more likely than joy to be twisted by the memory into, say, a presumed lesson of life. He took a drink on the beer. It was like iron in his mouth. He drew pipe smoke deep into his lungs. The pleasure of these things emptied his mind of thoughts, and for a moment he was at peace. At the next moment he was on his feet. He had almost dozed.

"Thought you had me," he said aloud, and the voice was not his. He had dozed. Not long, but just enough for something to steal into his mind, if only for a second, for he was still whole, still himself. So they had spoken for him. So what? They hadn't taken over. He walked to the door and went outside.

"Willow," he shouted, and the voice was his own. "Willow, come home. This is your daddy speaking." There was a vague, indistinct answer, and he recognized his own, mournful echo. A close call. A few more minutes of sleep, and they might have had him.

A star was visible through a hole in the trees, but the moon had long since hidden its face. His fire on the altar stone had died, but there was still a mound of coals, like a bruise. He refreshed the fire, adding some dry pine sticks. He watched the smoke gather about the coals, and then the sticks burst into flames. It was crucial now that he not fall asleep. He fetched his portable radio (Ollie had salvaged it, and Elman had fixed it for him), and placed it on the altar stone to listen. He imagined that the reception was better on the rock. The late-night talk shows were in full swing. People complained about taxes, politicians, ideas of right and wrong; they harped about Puerto Ricans (whatever they were); they harped about Negroes (Ollie knew what Negroes were: men from jungles who were not found in New Hampshire because they couldn't stand the cold); Negroes harped about whites; everybody harped about everybody else; people told stories about being taken up into space ships, about miraculous healings, about strange and wonderful occurrences. One woman said she saw God. She was thinking about leaving her husband, who was hitting the bottle and her, too. God showed up one night while she was searching for her sleeping pills. He (the husband) used to hide them. He (God) appeared in the bathroom mirror and said, "Only believe in me and the wounds of your soul will be healed." He advised her to stick to her husband. The next day the husband quit drinking, and the man and the wife had been living happily ever since.

The story made Ollie sweetly sad and prompted him to make a solemn vow to quit drinking. He wished now he could weep, for purposes of cleansing, but of course he rarely wept—had no facility for it. In his mind's eye, he could see himself and Helen walking somewhere—where? Ah, the fairgrounds—and she was thanking him for rescuing her from the Welfare Department. Her voice was like mountain water—well no, not like water; more like ice-cold beer on a hot day. There was no sense in quitting drinking entirely, he was telling her, but rather a program of moderation was called for. He would sip beer to quench his thirst. She was nodding yes yes yes . . . And the sound on the radio suddenly had gone harsh, and his wonderful thought was fading, and he was angry. He wanted to hurt. He was glad Willow was not here, for if he were he would want to hurt him. He would hit and hit and hit. But this was good: You could not be sleepy and angry at the same time. He heard himself laugh. No, it wasn't himself. Crazy ghost inside. He got up and paced. He wanted to smash something. Step out, ghost, and take your medicine, he thought, but he dared not voice the thought for fear the voice would not be his own. Damn that Helen, he thought. Damn you, Witch. Damn all women. They were, at root, the problem. They nurtured the ghost that haunted a man. The woman's opening was the crack in time through which the ghosts entered our lives.

It was dark, and he wandered in his anger. He could not see his fire. The anger vanished and was replaced with panic. He must run away. Be still, he said to himself. Be still, else they'll find you. He stood absolutely still, and he could feel the sweat form on his brow from the strain. He wanted to wipe it away, but something told him to be still. He stood there for a long time, until he could hear his radio like a thing with a sick, raspy voice. He thought he could hear the voice say, *Save us, save us, save us,* and this calmed him even though he knew the words were from his own mind. He moved sideways a foot, and discovered that his view of the dying fire had been blocked by a large pine tree. He returned to the altar stone. He shut off the radio. He stood, relaxed now, while his fire went dark. He stood until he could feel, more than see, the first faint gray of dawn.

Then he said, "Willow, please come home," and he went inside and fell into a deep sleep on the bed that he had salvaged.

A Day

Ollie Jordan got up at his usual time, about noon. It was a work day, one of the three that he helped Elman with his trash collection route from 1:00 to 5:30 p.m. Elman and Cooty Patterson worked the morning round, but old Cooty was too frail to put in a full day. Ollie worked Monday, Wednesday, and Friday afternoons, and sometimes on Saturday mornings. Elman worked fifty hours a week hauling trash. At night, he struggled with his bookkeeping and with the home lessons that he told Ollie were going to lead him to a high school diploma. On weekends Elman could be found repairing his vehicles, which at the moment consisted of the honeywagon (the money-maker), a pickup truck (his fun vehicle), a ten-year-old Chrysler (to show the world he was Mr. Somebody, Ollie deduced), and a Pinto sedan (Elman said it was a girl friend for the Chrysler).

Ollie tried hard not to hold it against Elman that he was addicted to work. After all, work was only one of two flaws that Elman had, the other being clock-watching. Elman even worked when he was drinking. On Sundays, he could be found sitting on the floor of his shed, a beer at his side, a cigarette burning in the hubcap he used for an ashtray, and on the floor the parts of a machine that Ollie could not immediately identify. Ollie would be appalled by this sight. A man should drink quietly and with dignity. God had invented booze to help a man gather his thoughts. Ollie wanted to say to his friend, "Good God, man! How can you concentrate on your drinking while you are trying to fix an engine?" But Ollie reined himself in. He would not criticize Elman's ways, any more than Elman would criticize his ways: This was in the code of their friendship. Still, the realization of Elman's need to keep working, even as he drank his beer, left just a spot of tarnish on the enormous respect that Ollie felt for him.

Ollie viewed Elman's clock-watching as a less serious but more bothersome flaw. Elman was constantly concerned about getting to a certain place by such and such an hour. He didn't seem to understand that the place would be there no matter when you arrived, and if it wasn't there, why then it didn't make any difference at all. The worst of it was that Elman showed actual annoyance when Ollie was a little bit late for work, say half an hour. This flaw on Elman's part was the kind of thing that eventually could try their friendship, Ollie realized. On occasion he broached the subject with Elman in the hopes of making him see how unreasonable he was. When Elman had made some comment about having to get to the dump before it closed, Ollie had said, "The dump will be there by-and-by."

"How in the name of sweet Jesus am I supposed to do my route tomorrow if my truck is full up?" Elman had asked.

"Dump it in Mrs. McGuirk's woods," Ollie had said.

"Ain't you smart? I suppose I'd have to," Elman had said, but there was not the usual gruff friendliness in his voice. Ollie figured that Elman knew he had been out-reasoned and couldn't take the defeat. This would be understandable, but Ollie wasn't satisfied with his deduction. There was something else, some major difference between himself and Elman that had appeared during the summer. For a second he wondered about whether Elman had been tricked somehow into working for the Welfare Department, but he quickly dismissed that idea. It was just too hard to live with. Rather, he told himself that Elman was touchy in regards to matters having to do with time.

The situation bothered Ollie now, as he walked down to the stream to wash. He didn't like thinking about having to get some place "on time." He didn't like the idea of time being something you had to be on. You could be on a truck or a boat; you could get on somebody's back or his ass. He had even overheard one of Elman's trash customers, the professor feller at the college, mumble something about having troubles with "on we," and although Ollie didn't understand exactly what was intended, the professor's message of weariness was clear. But time just wasn't something you could get on. Who had invented that combination of words, "on time," and for what purpose? Ollie bet there was some evil intent somewhere. Maybe he could ask the professor. "Professor," he'd say, "you got your 'on we' and you got your 'on time,' so what I want to know is . . ." What did he want to know? He wouldn't think of approaching the professor for the answer to a question he didn't have. Maybe he could get the question from Elman, and then he could fork it over to the professor for the answer.

The water was cold in the tiny pool below the tiny falls that flowed from the stream that bubbled out of the granite about one hundred feet through the woods downhill from St. Pete's. It was so cold that on the first day he attempted to bathe in the pool, Ollie had been shocked as if bitten by millions of teeth, and it passed through his mind that the water was really liquid mica formed in the torture chambers of the granite that made up the body of Abare's Folly. He had jumped out, though he knew that the snarling beasts of one's imagination were no reason to be frightened. Since then he only dabbed a little water on his face upon rising. Once every couple of weeks he did build a fire by the pool and boil water for a sponge bath. He hadn't had a real bath since leaving Ike's place and he felt no poorer for the lack.

For a while during the summer, he would drag Willow

down to the pool, and once even risked taking him to the Connecticut River for a bath, but all the excitement sexually aroused Willow, and it made Ollie feel strange to see him in that state. As a result, he had decided to let the boy take care of himself. That decision made him sad and puzzled him, too, until he realized that he wanted very much to bathe Willow. Sometimes, in unguarded moments, he allowed himself the pleasure of the mental image of Willow stripped naked and swimming in the water. Later, the thought of such thoughts horrified him, and he worked at burying them in the caverns of the mind where things were forgotten. Willow thereafter took care of himself, and did a surprisingly good job. He was frequently scruffy from cavorting in the woods, but there was no old dirt caked in the creases of his skin, no faint glisten of smudged body oil, no earth texture to his face, no matted hair, no sign of those who wash not at all. In fact, on occasion Ollie could swear he smelled Ivory soap on the boy, but of course that was impossible. He fancied that Willow was clean, as the wild aninals were clean, that is, in spirit from the blessing of the forest itself and therefore—magically—clean in body, too. He imagined that even he himself was being cleansed by the forest. He continued the sponge baths out of a vague obligation to an old habit, but once winter came it would be too much trouble to bathe and he would quit the routine without regret. After all, bathing served no purpose other than to keep Mrs. McGuirk from talking about you, and since he didn't have any neighbors of her sort—no neighbors at all unless you counted the critters, the trees, the boulders—there was no reason to continue bathing. Still, he enjoyed the walk down to the pool after rising. He could swear he smelled the sun high up in the trees, and by taking the same route every morning, he got familiar with certain objects—a knot dripping jelly out of a wild cherry tree, the glitter of a boulder as the light hit it, some ferns that reminded him of pretty ladies at a square dance. These softened the hard ache of his loneliness.

He sat by the stream for a moment, listening to it as another man might listen to the news on the radio, and then he dipped his hand into the cold water, marveling at it for a moment before he splashed some on his face. Liquid mica. The water ran down his neck and he shivered once. He sat by the side of the pool for a moment and watched tiny sticks and leaves flow downstream. He had everything a man could ask for, except for peace of mind, and now he had even that. It was the morning itself that delivered peace, he thought. (Actually, it was past noon.) War battles, murders, horrible acts against the self, vicious acts against one's fellows—these might occur in the morning, but he bet they were never planned during the morning. The minds of creatures are naturally at peace in the morning, he thought. He should have some coffee and a bite to eat—he must remember to eat more—and be on his way to his job, but it was such a nice day. Maybe he'd just sit here for a while, thinking about how good the coffee would taste. Maybe he'd take a little nap afterward. Maybe he'd take one now. So pleasant here. The sun had touched a patch of pine needles and, just moments ago, had moved on. They were still warm, and he lay among them and shut his eyes. He lay between sleep and wakefulness for two of the most peaceful minutes of his life.

A moment later something told him to open his eyes. Willow was looking at him, his expression full of wonder and leashed strength.

"Damn your ass," Ollie said. "Where have you been? Can't you stay home, like a normal boy?"

It was his usual speech. It meant nothing. He expected Willow to grunt and go off. Instead, Willow smiled at him, like a baby who has just discovered a secret of nature, such as locomotion or the playfulness of light. He sat beside Ollie and put his head on his shoulder. Ollie put his arm around the boy and held him. It was one of those moments that Willow gave, always unexpected, and mysterious in their origin, and very precious to Ollie. The moments always came when he was in a good mood, as if Willow could sense it in him.

"Aren't you glad you came to Niagara Falls Park with your daddy? He's taking good care of you, you know. Look at St.

Pete's. You ever see a house so pretty for the money? You watch, it's all going to be nice here. You watch."

Willow purred. Ollie stroked his head. It was cool. Soon the cold weather would come, he thought, and Willow would need something to cover his head. At that moment, he decided upon a project for the day. He would salvage a hat for Willow. A moment later Willow was gone, and Ollie was opening his eyes again, wondering whether Willow actually had been there or whether he had dreamt him. Anyway it didn't matter. What mattered was the hat. He would get a hat. The thought made him chuckle. The very idea of a hat made him chuckle.

He returned to St. Pete's and heated water on the Coleman stove. He preferred to start the morning with a beer, but that interfered with his coffee need. Someday he'd have to quit coffee. It wasn't good for a man. He knew he should hunt up some food, but that seemed like a lot of trouble. Luckily, he stumbled upon a half-full can of tuna fish that had been opened yesterday and forgotten. He ate the contents, satisfied in his own mind that he had done the right thing for his health, and then he opened the front door to St. Pete's and absently tossed away the can. He checked the fire in the wood stove, not because it needed checking but because he liked the chore. The coals were still plenty hot and he tossed in a few dry sticks. He would let the fire go out during the day, because the sun would warm St. Pete's, and he'd rebuild the fire tonight.

The stove was a simple affair, made from a fifty-five-gallon oil drum. Elman had a welding torch, and one Sunday afternoon he converted the drum into a wood-burning heater. The door was from an oven in an electric stove that had stood in Elman's yard for years. Elman had even installed a baffle inside the stove. Ollie put the stove in because, for reasons vague even to himself, he didn't want anyone other than himself and Willow to step foot on the grounds of Niagara Falls Park. The stove pipe went up at a slight angle through a metal slot Ollie built, with great difficulty, in the roof of St. Pete's. The stove worked very well. It only required Ollie's care to keep St. Pete's warm. Of course it was possible that sparks could escape through the pipe, fall upon the curved plastic roof of St. Pete's, and burn the place down; but, well, he had other more important things to worry about. After all he had built St. Pete's once, and if it was destroyed he could build it again. The stove nestled in a cradle of rocks piled about three feet off the earth floor of St. Pete's. That was Elman's idea. He said that in the winter, a hot fire would heat the rocks in the evening and the rocks would continue to give off heat all night, keeping Ollie and Willow warm even though the fire might burn low in the stove. Although Ollie Jordan had been heating with wood for years, such ideas never occurred to him. Ollie went along with the idea because it was easy, but later he realized that keeping warmth in around the stove for long periods meant he could leave for a day and his beer wouldn't freeze. It was only then that he appreciated the idea of warm rocks.

After he finished his breakfast and coffee, he lit his pipe and took a short walk in his woods, looking for a good place for a toilet. He had considered installing an outhouse, but such places were stinky and unsanitary, and besides they were a lot of work to build. It was better to do such business Willow's way—the animals' way—that is, pick a new place every day, a scenic and private place that also possessed a certain—what should he call it?—a certain feeling of safety, that here for the moment one could not be attacked. After he finished his business, he headed back to St. Pete's, finding Willow dozing in the crook of one of his favorite trees. Another month and the weather would be much colder. Willow would need a hat then—no doubt. Must get a hat for the boy, Ollie said to himself. It was a big task. He'd have to inspect the trash he and Elman collected very carefully. After all, a hat was not a large object, and not commonly found in refuse. Of course, it was the kind of thing that people, out of habit, were apt to leave at the head of the heap. Still . . . still . . . hard work.

"God, you made this world a royal pain in the ass," he said, almost believing that he really was addressing a supreme being that was listening. Well, he'd go to work. God or no God, you gotta have money to buy your beer, he thought to himself. He felt good about making the decision. He felt as though he had made a sacrifice on behalf of world order, or something. As a result, it was only reasonable that he give himself a treat: He'd drink a beer on his way to Elman's. It was necessary for Ollie to justify the beer, because someone had told him, long ago, that the sign of an alcoholic was a man who drank before going to work, but of course a rule could be broken if a man did something to justify a treat. Around three p.m., when they reached Keene on the honeywagon route, Elman would want to stop for coffee, but Ollie knew it would be easy to get Elman to buy a six-pack instead. If Elman did not stop for beer, Ollie would start to get nervous. He didn't like going more than a couple of hours without a beer. To do so was to cheat himself, and the worst crime a man could commit was against his own self. It was best to drink steadily, as God intended. He didn't respect these guys who deliberately built a beer thirst and then drank their day's quota all at once. They were pigs—guys like Pork Barrel Beecher; they were ignorant. You had to drink with some responsibility. After he got out of work, he'd drive to Spofford, gather in the beauty of Spofford Lake with his eyes, and replenish his own stock of beer at Mort's Grocery. He didn't like to stop at the general store in Darby because he didn't want people in town to know that he was still around. The Welfare Department had informers everywhere. On the drive home, he'd drink a beer and eat a bag of potato chips. He liked the feeling of a chip softening in his mouth until he was ready to chew. When he got home, he'd play with Willow—provided Willow was home—and then maybe he'd do a little work. During the summer, when the days were long, he could risk a nap. But these days he dared only doze in a chair to get some rest before the coming of the night.

He left for work, noticing that some clouds were moving in from the west. Fall rain coming. Long rain. He was disturbed. The road that wound up The Folly to Niagara Falls Park was getting worse. During a couple of showers in the summer, water widened the gullies made by his truck's wheels and even washed out in a few places, so that he had to spend a whole day filling in the ruts. He could only patch this road so much. Every rain made the job harder. Once winter came, the road would be impassable. He'd have to park the truck at the bottom of the hill and walk down from the park. Kids might discover the truck and vandalize it, or worse, somebody might report seeing it to the Welfare Department. Even if he got away with leaving the truck parked at the bottom of the hill, there was the problem of hiking up the hill to Niagara Falls Park burdened with groceries and beer. How would he haul all that beer up the hill, through snow and ice and fierce, burning, blue wind? He'd have to get some kind of rucksack; maybe risk taking Willow with him to share the load. He couldn't imagine Elman tolerating Willow on the trash route.

The hopelessness of the situation crashed in upon him and he struggled with the problem in his mind. He could drink hard liquor. Booze accomplished the same purpose as beer, using less liquid. The idea suddenly thrilled him. He loved booze, but had avoided it because of the dangers it posed. Now there seemed to be an excuse to buy it. He could justify booze! His heart beat with anticipation. Slowly, as the truck bounced and slid down the dirt road, the thrill wore off. The booze could destroy him. He knew that. There was no doubt in his mind. In addition, there would be other problems besides lugging booze. He needed winter clothes for himself and Willow, especially boots. He should store some food for those days when the weather would be too bad to leave St. Pete's. How the hell was he going to store food? He remembered that in the old days the Witch kept her vegetables in a root cellar, but digging one of those was a lot of work. He was too busy for such a project. There were other chores that had to be done. The truck needed antifreeze, St. Pete's should be insulated somehow. These were important matters. They must be dealt with. But not now. Not now. Today's chore was to find a hat for Willow. He mustn't let himself get sidetracked. It was best to see a thing through before you took on another thing.

Ollie finished his beer in front of the Cutter place just up the road from Elman's. Using the hook shot he had perfected over the years, he tossed the empty bottle over the cab of the truck into the ditch to the right. He disapproved of throwing bottles on the road because they could cause flat tires. He pulled into Elman's yard and parked the truck on the grass behind the shed so it couldn't be seen from the road. There was only one sign of the fire that had destroyed Elman's house and barn—a huge pile of blackened rubble that had been arranged by a bulldozer, driven by Elman. To Ollie it looked like a church designed by the Devil, and it baffled him that Elman should build such an edifice. But of course it would have violated the code of their friendship for him to raise the subject, so he said nothing, waiting for Elman to explain it on his own. He never did, and to Ollie the result was one of those small, nagging mysteries that plagued a man in odd moments.

Ollie arrived only a few minutes late. He found Howard Elman in the kitchen of the trailer sipping on a coffee, his nose in the news magazine that he treated like a Bible. He was wearing his new spectacles, and he looked menacing to Ollie, like one of those fellows who come to your house and want you to repent. Elenore Elman as usual was not around. The question of where she was never came to Ollie Jordan's mind. The fact was Elenore was hiding in the bedroom, as she always did when Ollie showed up. He made her feel uneasy, as though by totally ignoring her he somehow reduced her essence. Besides, she found him ugly and sickly looking. She figured her life would be better if she just never laid eyes on him.

Elman slapped the magazine, like a man affectionately patting a horse on the rear. "Ollie, the way the world's going, I imagine somebody's going to blow it to smithereens in about thirty minutes," he said in the highfalutin tone he used only when he was going to talk about something he had been reading.

"I don't care," said Ollie.

"Nor I," said Elman, still highfalutin, peering over the glasses now at Ollie. "Before my studies, I never gave current events much thought. I see now I was better off in my ignorance. The more a man knows, the more he's got to worry about. Not that I've been worrying, mind you. It's just that if I was one to worry, I'd be worrying today about what was going to happen in the next thirty minutes. As it is, I know what's going to happen. Either nothing's going to happen, or they're going to blow us up."

"If they blow us up, might be a nice ride sailing along in the sky," said Ollie.

"Except you and I are both going to land right into the hottest spot in hell," said Elman.

Ollie nodded. Elman had a preoccupation with hell. He was always talking about dying and going to hell.

They left a minute later, Elman disappearing into the interior of the trailer. He could hear him shouting (Elman shouted sometimes, even when he was wearing his hearing aid), telling his missus that he and Ollie Jordan were going on the route. They'd make a run later at the Keene sanitary landfill, and he'd be back about quarter to six. For all the world, Ollie couldn't understand why Elman went into there every day to see her. After all, she knew where he was going, knew when he was coming back. What was the point of explaining it all? Oh well, it wasn't his business to criticize.

They left on the route, Elman behind the wheel, Ollie on the passenger side. Elman placed the glasses in a case (he claimed with pride that it was unbreakable), unbuttoned a pocket of his shirt, inserted the case, and rebuttoned the button; all the while he was starting the truck, shifting it into reverse, and backing it out of the yard.

Ollie blew his nose on his fingers and then daintily wiped them on his shirttail. The nose hurt him: It was beginning to act up again. From time to time during all of his adult life, Ollie's nose swelled, reddened, pulsated, and seemed to throw off heat. He had always had this problem, and he accepted it as one accepts any permanent burden.

He resisted the urge to tell Elman he was looking for a hat for Willow. Somehow, he thought he might jinx the search if he said anything. But the quest excited him, took away some of the dreariness of the work. He was very attentive to everything around him. You never could tell when you'd find what you wanted, or even something better. He lapsed into a fantasy of finding a hundred-dollar bill, but in the main stayed alert. They made several stops at houses, working their way toward Keene, but Ollie saw no hats or even cast-off materials that might be made into a hat. But he was patient. The scrounger must be watchful. He could not force events, but only recognize in them the elements that were important to him, like a crow circling above the world, waiting to eat leftovers from, say, a rabbit killed by a fisher cat.

They pulled into a place known to Ollie only as The Club. It had been built in the 1920s by rich people, who later had lost their money, Elman explained. The Cutter woman, Elmer's neighbor who had given him all the trouble, had bought it and turned it into a vacation spot for people from down-country. Beyond that, Ollie knew little about The Club, but he was grateful to its members for contributing a rich lode of refuse. Indeed, he had furnished parts of St. Pete's with some of The Club's castoffs, including a wicker chair with a ripped seat, a small rug that somebody had vomited on, and a supply of plastic cups and glasses, plastic utensils, and foam plates that was so steady that Ollie couldn't help being lulled into a belief that never again would he have to wash a dish. On the grounds was a big house that looked like something out of a movie about the Romans: dozens of shrubs with Marine haircuts, a lawn that went on and on for no apparent reason, some garages and fancy-painted sheds. Still, The Club was in the shadow of a big hill thick with forest, and Ollie felt that the trees were biding their time and one day would take over the place. When the weather had been warmer he watched women in short dresses playing tennis. He couldn't understand why anyone would want to get all tired out hitting a ball. He never did determine whether the idea was to hit the ball back and forth as many times as possible or to hit it so it couldn't be returned. Either way it made no sense. Sometimes after the play stopped temporarily, one of the players would shout the word "love" and a number. That was mysterious. The whole game was mysterious and therefore menacing. He asked Elman why he thought the game was played, and Elman said, "Exercise." But that didn't explain the short white dresses, the elaborate ceremony of it all. Ollie was finally able to dispatch this little problem from his mind by coming up with the conclusion that the game was part of a religious service, such as he had seen that day at the church in Keene.

He found the people at The Club interesting. A lot of them wore bathing suits, yet few of them spent much time in the pool. He had raised this issue also with Elman, who had said, "Sun-worshippers." Ollie had nodded, taking to heart that word "worship." The more he thought about it, the more sense it made: The entire place was devoted to religion. Now many of the minor puzzles about the place were cleared up. The young fellows and gals who waited on the tables on the patio were new in the religion. They had to wear little suits signifying their low status, and they had to wait on the others until . . . well, he didn't know what. Maybe until they did something holy. It seemed logical to him that hats would play a role in the observances of any religious group.

The more he thought about the matter, the more convinced he became that here somewhere at The Club there would be a hat. He imagined that in the past, probably, he had overlooked a number of hats in The Club's trash. After all, when you're not looking for something, you don't find it. He tried to call forth mental images from his memory of The Club in hopes of spotting a hat among them. This effort failed. The images were awash with the green of the lawn of the place, with the strutting behinds of a few of the women he had seen there, with a waiter walking like a duck, with two short white dresses filled with sun-burnt flesh playing at tennis amidst a blue sky that seemed about to fall. Still, he had worked himself up into a state whereby he was convinced that The Club's trash would be littered with discarded hats. Of course, he was wrong. The trash contained all the usual items—the foam plates and cups, slopped food as if drooled from the mouth of a great beast, various paper containers, cans, bottles, newspapers, and a few of what Ollie called "one-time onlys"—a broken plaster cast of a boat that apparently had served as a base for a lamp, a pair of sneakers that weren't at all in bad shape, leftover fish the maggots had got to already, and a box containing dozens of worn tennis balls. But no hats. Was someone playing a trick on him? No hats! Forget it, he told himself. Don't get upset. Concentrate on the business at hand—the trash. He forced himself to consider salvaging what he could. He inspected the items: the sneakers (too small), the boat (too ugly), the usuals (he had plenty in store). Finally, he left with a single tennis ball in his pocket, blurting out, "No hats!" Luckily Elman, who was always fiddling with his hearing aid, had it switched off when Ollie spoke.

Ollie felt betrayed. There was every reason in the world for him to believe that here he would find a hat. No hats! Disturbing. Was it possible that the Welfare Department was toying with him? He didn't like that idea one single bit. Face up to it, he said to himself. Got to be careful. If they knew he was looking for a hat, they most certainly knew a great deal more. They would know where he was living. But how? He hadn't even told Elman the specific location of St. Pete's. Willow! Somehow, they had got to Willow. Had to. No other way they could know enough about his movements to dog his footsteps like this. But how could they have gotten here so soon and removed the hats without disturbing the trash so he would notice? After all, he had just gotten the idea a little while ago. Jesus—dear, sweet Jesus—they were clever. It struck him that if there were a force that cunning, that evil, there must be some counterbalancing force with equal powers on the other hand, else They would have taken over long ago. Maybe They have taken over, he said to himself. Maybe he, Ollie Jordan, was the last one. But no. If They were that powerful, They could have taken him long ago. Therefore, there must be a force for good out there, aiding him. There is a God, he thought. Ollie Jordan's brain boiled with such thoughts for a while and then cooled. He didn't admit to himself that he was wrong, but he did admit it was possible that he had exaggerated the situation. It was getting on toward three o'clock, and he hadn't had beer in a while. Clearly, that was the problem. His mind had gotten away from him a little bit because he hadn't had any beer. But where were the hats?

When they were back in the truck, Elman turned his hearing aid back on, and Ollie said, "Howie, you didn't find no hats in that batch?"

"Nope. Looking for a hat?" he said.

"Maybe."

"What kind of a hat?"

Ollie looked at Elman very carefully. Elman was watching the road. He didn't seem to have an evil intent about him. Yet you had to be cautious.

"A hat for dancing," Ollie said, the words jumping out of his mouth unsummoned.

"A hat for dancing—goddamn," said Elman, giggling. "You want something for the boy, don't you? Something to make him say, 'Gee, wow!' Well, I know where there's such a hat."

"You don't say," said Ollie. He felt a dangerous surge of elation. He must rein it in, lest it gallop off with his good sense.

"The professor's got a hat like that for his prize student," said Elman and burst into laughter.

He explained that Dr. Hadly Blue of Southeast Vermont State College had a prize student who was a scarecrow in his backyard, upon whose head was a hat.

"You ought to know where the hat is," Elman said. "You've been there a million times. It's on the trash route."

Elman described the Blue place, a big, half-torn-apart Cape Cod house with an old about-to-die orchard, bordered by stone walls.

Ollie remembered the house but not the scarecrow. The idea that it had been there all along and that he never had noticed it bothered him. It was as if someone—something—had clouded his mind, deliberately kept the knowledge of the scarecrow from him.

As it turned out, there was good reason why he hadn't seen

the scarecrow. It was shadowed by an apple tree and could just be seen from the road. The only reason Elman must have noticed it was that he was soft for fruit trees and looked over every such tree with all the appreciation—and criticism—of a sportsman sizing up a shotgun.

The scarecrow hung on a cross of 2-by-4s. It wasn't too near the garden, and Ollie couldn't understand how it could scare birds from this spot, but he figured anybody who was a professor must know what he was doing. Ollie studied the scarecrow for a moment, seeing now something familiar about it. It resembled his Uncle Jake, known as Jake the snake, who had walked into the woods many years ago and hadn't been seen since. Maybe the professor had found Jake and hung him up to scare away the birds. The idea amused Ollie, and it occurred to him that being a scarecrow was pretty good work, if you could get it, the kind of work that Jake, who was lazy even by Jordan standards, had longed for all his life. Dr. Blue's scarecrow wore paint-stained blue jeans, a T-shirt, a gray tweed sports jacket with patches on the elbows, and red mittens. His head was made of a pillowcase stuffed with newspapers. Rain, wind, sunlight, and—for all Ollie knew—the moon had shaped his head and given it character, lumpy cheeks, and sagging jowls, but the same elements also had wiped away any remnant of eyes, nose, and mouth. That was Jake, all right. The head was in the shadow of a hat with a huge purple brim and yellow band out of which protruded white feathers. He had wanted something practical, something interesting, but warm for the winter, too. This was a summer hat. The winter wind might blow it off and the brim was so wide a snow storm would weigh down on a man's head. This was not a practical hat. This was a magnificent hat. This was a hat for dancing. Willow would rejoice in it, and it was better to rejoice than to be warm. Accordingly, Ollie decided that this was the hat he had to have for his son. The problem was how to obtain it. He supposed he'd have to sneak up in the night and snitch it. He didn't like such work. That was more up Ike's alley. He didn't much appreciate Ike Jordan as a man or as a relative, but he had to admit he was a good burglar. Ollie had little time to consider the problem, because after he dumped the professor's trash, Elman walked over to the scarecrow to look it over.

"Howie, you ain't going to take that hat in broad daylight, are you?" Ollie asked.

"Ollie, you've been hiding out too long," said Howard Elman. "I ain't going to take nothing. I'm going to ask the professor for it, and if he don't want to give it away, I'm going to try to dicker with him for it."

As they approached the house, they were arrested by a voice. A window was open in the house and Ollie could hear someone speaking in a peculiar kind of conversation. First it seemed as if the speaker were talking to someone else, and then he answered as if he were that someone else. The problem was compounded further by a quality of the voice, as if he were reciting words to a song. Very strange, thought Ollie, and he put himself on guard. Even though whoever was speaking had not heard them come to the door, there was something in his voice that said, "Do not interrupt," and so they stood there at the door for a moment and listened.

"We have Father Balthazar in his room, pacing, wondering why his God has gone," the voice said. "Finally, after an hour at his kneeler, he rises and scribbles in a fury in his secret journal:

> *Father, accept my sacrifice*
> *of these two pears.*
> *I will tie them in a loose bag*
> *to hang from this branch.*
> *They will turn soft and sweet*
> *changing gender as does a season.*

"Huh. Not bad. But do I really need the 'does'? Would Balthazar have brooded over the 'does'? Would you, Balthazar, you randy old curate, you?"

The question that Hadly Blue put to his fictional Balthazar struck home to Ollie Jordan. He didn't know who this Balthazar fellow was, or just what this bossy professor wanted of him, but he sided right away with Balthazar. Ollie was anxious to meet Balthazar. He imagined they'd get along. Maybe Balthazar hunted woodchucks or fixed radios or whittled charms—did something to pass the time while he was the professor's prisoner. Somehow Ollie knew that there was some kinship between himself and this Balthazar; in fact, he thought he could sense the presence of this being.

Howard Elman broke the spell between Ollie Jordan and Hadly Blue's fictional character by rapping loudly on the door.

Moments later they were ushered in by a slim, slouching man with helter-skelter brown hair. He was about thirty-five, and he was wearing blue jeans and sneakers, as if these might preserve an affinity he had with his youth.

"Yes?" he asked.

"Elman," said Elman.

There was a pause, and then the professor said, "Oh, of course, the trash man. Do I need to pay you or something? I'm a little busy. Composing, er, working."

Neither Elman nor Ollie caught the hint, and they walked into the house as if invited.

It was clear now to Ollie why the windows were open. Someone had cranked up the wood stove during the cool of the morning, and now the place was too hot. Ollie glanced into the front room, hoping to get a look at Balthazar. But there was no one in the room. He saw a wood stove and a desk piled with suspicious-looking papers. "Let's go in the kitchen," said Professor Blue. "I'm afraid the living room and my study are overly warm. I had this new stove installed, and I didn't realize how much heat it throws."

It seemed to Ollie that there was more to the situation than the professor's explanation. How was it that a professor, obviously an intelligent person, had overheated his house? He had also made it sound as though someone else had installed the stove, as if he didn't have the savvy—an obvious lie. Most important, what had happened to Balthazar? Was he here against his will? Had the professor hustled him upstairs, away from prying eyes? The answers to these questions were not forthcoming. There was something suspicious going on here.

They sat at the kitchen table. Ollie wished that he could go upstairs. He was quite certain that this fellow Bathazar was being held against his will. Meanwhile, Ollie could see that Elman was about ready to start dickering for the hat. He wished he'd hold off until they could find an excuse to go upstairs.

"What's upstairs?" Ollie asked.

The professor laughed, abrupt and squeaky, like one of those damn birds high up in the trees that Ollie often heard but never saw.

"Right now what's upstairs is a mess," the professor said. "All the plaster is down, swept into a rather impressive Monadnock in the front room. I've put insulation batts and plastic between the joists and rafters, and we're debating, battling might be a better word, over whether to put in Sheetrock or shiplap pine boards. I want the boards. She wants white walls. You know how these domestic arguments go."

Ollie figured Balthazar would be the subject of strife perhaps, the captive of one or the other. He thought of Helen and of the Witch, and of his own Willow.

Elman piped into the conversation. "My idea of hell is working with Sheetrock," he said. "Personally, I'd suggest paneling. Stuff's pretty, it's cheap, and it ain't much trouble to put up, provided you get a jig for your Skil saw. Hell, if you don't like the way it looks, you can always paint it."

Ollie realized that he didn't really want to rescue Balthazar. He had his own Balthazar in Willow. One Balthazar was enough. Maybe the professor worked for the Welfare Department and was using his Balthazar for mysterious and evil purposes. Maybe not. Either way, there was nothing he, Ollie Jordan, could do about the situation. In fact, if he admitted the truth, there was nothing he could do about anything; there was nothing anybody could do about anything. The best a man could do was find himself a hideout, furnish it, and live on.

Elman shifted in his chair. He was getting edgy, ready to

open discussion on the purpose of their visit. He spoke. "Ah, professor . . ."

"Hadly. Please call me Hadly," said the professor.

Howard Elman nearly blushed, like a child brought up to respect his elders suddenly called upon to act familiar. Except of course it hadn't always been so. Elman had been raised in foster homes. He was just now, in middle age, cultivating reverence for those he considered his betters, as if in a way they were kin he owed. This his friend Ollie Jordan could see, and he was struck with a peculiar grief. Soon he would lose Elman, too.

"Well, ah," continued Elman, struggling to manipulate his words so that he would not have to say either "professor" or "Hadly." "We, ah, have come here to, ah, negotiate the, ah, acquisition of your scarecrow's chapeau."

Where in the name of the crazy God who had invented this crazy world did Elman get all those words from? From the things he had been reading, the answer came to Ollie.

"I want the chapeau for my boy," said Ollie, and Elman grinned and nodded, and then both Ollie and Elman were nodding.

The professor seemed confused. "What?" he asked.

"The chapeau," repeated Ollie.

"The chapeau," repeated Elman.

After a pause, the professor said, "I have to admit that I really don't know what you're talking about."

Elman arose from his chair, and Ollie could see that Elman was back to his old self. He walked to the kitchen window, pointed outside, and said, "Professor, we're talking about the hat atop the head of that scarecrow. He don't need to scare no birds, because there ain't nothing left for them to steal that you can use. But we can use his hat, and we come to dicker for it."

The professor burst into laughter.

He had been laughing at them all along, thought Ollie.

"Doncha know," said the professor, breaking into an approximation of the local accent, "that I'd forgotten about it. I mean the garden was never mine. It was hers, my friend Kay's. I'm a January gardener. When the seed catalogues arrive in the winter, I make all the plans for the garden. I even read the *Mother Earth News* at that time of year. But with spring, I find the cold earth and the warm sun irreconcilable anomalies. To put it bluntly: I don't like outside work. I'd rather pull down plaster. Which, as you can see, is what I've been doing. As to the scarecrow, Kay put it up herself back in the early summer to buffalo the birds; whoops, there's a mixed metaphor. She got the hat from the storekeeper—you know, Joe Andarsky? His idea. Just gave it to her. No charge."

Both Ollie Jordan and Howard Elman were looking at the professor with concern, as though they expected him at any moment to have a fit.

"We considered the scarecrow and his, ah, chapeau, the ideal warrior. Keeps the barbarians at bay, kills no one," the professor said, pacing about the kitchen, giggling.

What bothered Ollie about the professor was that he had deep, mysterious ideas. As Willow was an idiot compared to himself, so he was an idiot compared to the professor. So it went, up through the chain of life to . . . where? God? Was it part of some master plan that he should get—or not get—that hat? He pondered the question for a moment, coming up with a pleasing answer to himself. If God—or whatever it was— wanted him to have the hat, he would have the hat. If God did not want him to have the hat, he would not get the hat. If God didn't care, if there was no God, it wouldn't matter whether he got the hat or not. None of the possibilities required a decision on his part. What would be would be, whether it be the hat or Balthazar or anything. His own role was to await events. The issue settled in his mind, Ollie now felt easier about the professor. The important thing now was either to get the hat or not to get the hat, but at any rate to act swiftly, for there was another important element cropping up in this situation: Ollie was feeling thirst for a beer.

As it turned out, there was little need to press the issue, for the professor gave them the hat, laughing all the while.

They were almost on the cutoff road to Keene when the mysterious Balthazar crept back into Ollie's mind.

"You think he's on the up-and-up, the professor?" Ollie asked.

"Eh?" said Elman, turning up his hearing aid. Ollie repeated the question.

"Don't know. Don't know's I give a damn, as long as he pays me first of the month," said Elman.

They drove on toward Keene. The clouds had backed off; it wasn't going to rain. The wild hallucination that is the turning of the fall leaves had passed, and now the leaves were falling. They were, Ollie thought, like ideas that were fine until tried, each one a grief. He could feel the harsh edge of his own intelligence slashing away somewhere in the tenderer parts of his mind, a signal that he needed a beer—and soon.

"Good to have a cold drink on a hot day," he said, realizing as he spoke that actually it was a cool day.

Back in the truck, even before Ollie took the first drink of beer, he felt calm. Ollie drank four beers; Elman drank two. It seemed to Ollie, as he reviewed his day's work and got ready to leave, that Elman gave him a funny look, as one might give a favored dog that had been hit by a car and would have to be put away; but the look vanished in a second, and Ollie forgot it. He had something else on his mind: the hat. It had become a major issue that needed to be mulled over. Exciting. Now he would have something to keep his mind busy during the long night to come at Niagara Falls Park. On the drive home, he deliberately did not look in the hat, smell it, inspect it with his fingers, or even think about it. He didn't want to spend his mental currency on it during the prosperity of day.

He arrived at St. Pete's and Willow had gone, although something of his smell lingered. He had been there only minutes earlier—or so Ollie imagined. Ollie bundled up in his overcoat and built a fire on the altar stone. He drank another beer while he heated a can of beans and a hot dog inside on the Coleman stove. He played the radio for a minute, hoping the talk on it would lift some of the loneliness from him, but the sounds seemed ugly and harsh to him, and he shut it off. The hat lay beside him on some pine needles. He set aside in his mind the idea of beer and took in the idea of a cup of coffee. Instant Nescafe. He heated water inside, made a cup of coffee in a foam cup—wonderful invention; he was grateful—and returned to his place by the altar stone. It was time to consider the matter of the hat. He glanced at it on the ground. It had seemed so purple, so rich on the head of the scarecrow. Now, even in the waning light of a fall day, he could see that it was faded, the band ready to fall off, the feather scraggly. Where had it really come from? Had the hat belonged to Balthazar? Umm. Was it possible that Balthazar had arranged to place the hat on the scarecrow as a sort of signal? Maybe. What signal, then? Think, Ollie said to himself. The hat was Mexican. No doubt about that. What did Mexican mean? Ollie searched his memory for his knowledge of Mexico. "Si senoir," he said aloud. The fire on the altar stone crackled, as if in approval. Ollie laughed. "The Cisco Kid," he said. "Hey, Pancho . . . hey, Cisco." Impulsively, Ollie snatched up the hat and plopped it on his head. It fit. He wished he had a mirror to see himself. He bet he looked pretty fancy. If Helen could see him now. This hat might even impress the Witch. Oh, don't fool yourself entirely, he said to himself. Maybe he ought to keep this hat for his own use. "Willow, you ungrateful bastard," he said aloud, and laughed royally. When he stopped, there was a sudden emptiness, and then he was hearing the fire sputter and gurgle, like a baby.

"Willow! Willow!" he shouted. There was no answer.

Ollie removed the hat and placed it on his lap. He took a swallow of coffee. His mind went blank for a moment, and then he was remembering the scarecrow. It reminded him, he realized now, of Christ hanging on the cross in the church in Keene. He imagined acres and acres of crops, dotted here and there with crosses with men hanging from them. Was that Christ's job as God and man: to scare away the devils so men might grow? He tried to make something of this puzzling image, but could not. Just a thing in his mind, he thought.

Ideas, pictures, memories, emotions popped up in your brain, and you tried to make sense of them, even when there was none to be made. You tried because you tried. The purpose was the trying. That lucky bastard, Willow, Ollie thought. Thinking don't mean nothing to him. All there is of him is want and do.

"Willow!"

Getting real dark out, he thought. I'll be crazy pretty soon. Got to stay awake. Drink the beer in the proper amounts. Keep the fire going.

Ollie now turned his attention to the hat. He felt it, rubbing his fingers into the cloth. With little effort, he punched a hole through it. Another. Oh, hat, all those summer days on the head of the scarecrow, bearing up under the sun and rain, has done you in. Oh, hat, there's nothing to you but the look of a hat. Methodically, Ollie ripped the hat up into little pieces, and then he threw them in the fire, with the band and feathers. The stuff burning had a bad smell. He wished he could cry, but of course he could not, and even if he could, it wouldn't have mattered.

"Willow!" he shouted. "Willow!"

Hadly and Kay

Hadly Blue knew it was going to be a bad day when his superego reminded him of the appalling condition of his desk at the college. On top of the heap was his notebook, full of Freudian trails of personae not worth tracking. Pick up the notebook and read, said his conscience. Hadly did as he was told, coming across some lines written by Balthazar, the main character in the novel he had been working on for ten years. He read aloud:

OCEAN BLUES IN PLENTY

Fears of scarcity seem like an ancient superstition.
Crowds shop instead of breaking windows.
Great rolls of time unravel. Only Darwin complains
that there is vengeance in a stool.
Philosophers favor memorial services for ideas over ideas.
A man named Edgar photographs poisoned fruit.
Darwin writhes. He has not found truth; truth has found him,

and he is awash in his own flogged flesh. Monarch butterflies
begin their journey south on I-91. Bits of flotsam
from a million human wrecks litter the seas. "The earth
has little use for our troubles," Darwin says, and drowns.
Finally, it happens—no more toilet paper.
Mankind up shit creek.

He tossed the notebook onto the cluttered desk and started
for class. Outside, two students were playing frisbee. Here was
a useful pastime; here one could achieve grace without implor-
ing a god for it. He had no idea what he was going to talk about
in class. He had invented the course, "The Murmurs and the
Paupers: Symbols in American Culture," as a jest at a commit-
tee meeting and the dean had taken him seriously. "The kid-
dos will love it," he had said. And they had, registering in
droves.

Without a smile, without a greeting, without a glance at any
of his students, he began to speak.

"The subject today is the secret sharers of Saturday morning. Let us begin with the Roadrunner and Wiley Coyote. I
presume that I do not have to explain that the Roadrunner is a
bird that lives somewhere in the American Southwest. The
Roadrunner looks like the offspring of an ostrich and a Reno
go-go dancer. The Roadrunner does not fly. Nor does the
Roadrunner walk. The Roadrunner runs. The Roadrunner's
vocabulary is limited to a single expletive, *"beep-beep."* The
Roadrunner does not feed, does not drink, does not speak, does
not feel, does not think, does not breed. The Roadrunner runs.
The Roadrunner is free. The gods have decided that the Roadrunner should continue to be, solely on the basis of her
being . . ."

Hadly stumbled on until he lost his train of thought. There
was a long silence that made him want to flee, and then he
continued.

"Let us now look at Wiley Coyote, the adversary of the
Roadrunner. Wiley is intelligent—if not wise—emotionally
complex, and physically repulsive. He is the ugly American.

Wiley is fixated on pursuing the Roadrunner, that is, in pursuing the American Dream. Being American in temperament, Wiley tries to catch the Roadrunner using mechanical contrivances. In fact, Wiley is a mechanical wizard of the Rube Goldberg variety. His machines are elaborate and interesting, but they don't work the way they are supposed to. Indeed, they seem to have minds of their own.

"What happens if Wiley catches the Roadrunner? The cartoon leads us to believe that Wiley will have the Roadrunner for a meal. But there are also vague sexual innuendoes. Wiley in his single-mindedness and the Roadrunner in her teasing often resemble courting creatures. One way or the other, if Wiley catches his prey he must consume her and die in a last communion. But of course he will not catch her. The myth will not allow him to. Ultimately, the purpose of the American Dream is to perpetuate the American Dream."

The sound of a doorknob turning distracted Blue and the class. Late student, he thought. It was bad form to chew out a student for something so trivial as being late, but today Hadly felt mean. When the door was half open, Hadly wheeled toward it and shouted, "As T.S. Eliot said, 'Time—time is the enzyme.'"

But it was not a late student who came in. It was the dean.

"Don't let me interrupt—I'll only stay a second," he said and sat down.

Dean Aimsley Jacobs had been at Southeast Vermont State College for a year, and during that time Hadly had the feeling that he resembled someone he knew. Now he realized who that someone was, the cartoon character Elmer Fudd.

"We will now turn our attention to one of the great archvillains of our culture—Elmer Fudd," said Hadly, thinking as he spoke: My God, how am I going to back that up? "As most of you know, Elmer Fudd is to Bugs Bunny what Wiley Coyote is to the Roadrunner. But there are differences. There is a kind of existential suffering in the coyote's life of frustration. It is as if he knows that the Roadrunner is an illusion that passes through tunnels painted on rock walls, knows that she is better than he is—his better half—but he goes on anyway in pursuit. There is no such redeeming quality in Elmer Fudd. Elmer is rich enough to afford to buy his food, and thus he does not need rabbit stew. Nor is Elmer driven, as is our coyote, by psychological forces in his pursuit of his game. Shooting rabbits is merely a hobby with Elmer.

"And, too, there are profound differences between Bugs and the Roadrunner. Bugs survives because he has keen wits. Bugs is a realistic ideal of what every American male aspires to. He's smart, without being intellectual; he's a master of one-upmanship; he is mentally stable and carefree; he has a good sense of humor; he has no guilt. In short, Bugs is Wiley Coyote after twelve years of classical psychoanalysis."

Hadly's mind went blank. He put his hands behind his back and paced, trying to gather his thoughts, any thoughts. Finally, unable to utter a single word, he went to the blackboard and started to draw. As if his hand were directed by some alien force, Hadly found himself completing a fair likeness of the head of the dean.

"There's our enemy, yours and mine," Hadly said. "Now is there anyone here who can tell me who or what Elmer Fudd symbolizes?"

"Is it the AMA, or Boeing?" guessed a student.

"Don't we wish," said Hadly.

The horror went on for Hadly. The class erupted into what he considered to be the lowest form of human interaction—the classroom discussion. When it was finally over, Hadly was spent. He had nothing more to say. But miraculously, the allotted hour had passed, and he only had to gesture toward the door to get the students to file out. Then the dean had his hand on his shoulder and he was saying, "Come to my office at once."

Well, thought Hadly, the ax is going to fall. His chance for tenure was effectively reduced to zero by his performance today. He felt almost relieved. Really, he didn't belong in teaching. What wounded him was that his students did not share his love for literature. He therefore felt tender, vulnerable to their indifference and armed himself in the usual way—by constructing defenses of cynicism, of parody, of seeming unconcern. He betrayed his beliefs to save his sensibilities. He wanted more than anything for someone to stop him from this burlesque of his own knowledge. Now, finally, the dean was going to do the job. "At last—" he said aloud, as he headed for the dean's office. By the time he reached the door he was calm, at peace with himself for the first time in weeks.

"Great stuff, Blue—congratulations," said the dean, as he grasped Hadly's hand and shook it like a war hero's.

"What? It was nothing. It was air." said Hadly, stunned.

"Brilliance and modesty, too," said the dean. "Admirable. But watch out. This is not an age for the modest. The modest get devoured. But no, don't listen to me. You're doing fine without old Aim. You just keep firing culture shots. They'll be heard 'round the world. Seriously," said the dean, taking a seat behind his walnut-top desk, folding his hands, "we're in a new era in the colleges, and you seem to have grasped the bull by the horns in midstream. The old Liberal Arts curriculum is out—defunct—dead—kaput—kung-fued by television and multi-media. These kids today, they don't care about Spenser and his fairy queens. Who does, really? Unless it's 40 percent of the population of Frisco, if you know what I mean."

The dean winked. Hadly found himself smiling.

"They need something that's relevant," the dean went on. "Between you and I, they need something that they think is relevant, else they'll register at somebody else's Podunk U, the bills won't get paid, and we'll all be teaching Am-Lit at Jefferson High some place in Indiana.

"The thing these professors don't understand is packaging. But, boy, you do. You're the best facilitator I've ever seen. You had those people eating culture out of the palm of your hand. What we need is more courses like yours. What say you package me a proposal for a curriculum based on Contemporary Culture? I'll write the grant.

"I'm sure—you sly, ambitious dog, you—that you know we're shopping around for a dean of curriculum development.

Why you've waited this long to apply, I don't know, but now's the time. Frankly, Blue, just between you and I, I want somebody in that job that I can get along with, somebody who thinks like me, somebody with vision, somebody, ultimately, who gets to the lunch bucket on the same wave length as me. Comprendy? Course you do . . ."

The rest of what the dean said was lost upon Hadly. It had struck him that if he were named a dean he wouldn't have to teach.

"I was thinking about applying, but I'd hate to leave the classroom." Hadly lied.

"Admirable. I know how you feel. How can you crank out the feedback if you don't get any input? I think we can arrange to let you keep a hand in the academic pie. You'll want to teach, maybe one course?"

Hadly arrived at the farmhouse about three o'clock. Kay was not home yet. It seemed to him, suddenly resentful, that she conspired not to be home when he had troubling things to say. She saved her sympathy for her work, which was terribly taxing, he had to admit. He struggled to hang on to his resentment, knowing that it was a shield for some anxiety waiting to sift down upon him. She was calculatingly sensitive, a classic liberal, pulling up mankind to proper philosophical heights by the hairs of the screaming poor, her capacity to love tied to altering genetic defects through social and psychological engineering. But he began to lose his grip on his resentment when he saw her jeans thrown over a chair. The moment she got home, she would tear off her skirt and put them on. On the hip pocket, she had sewn in red thread the word "Walrus." Sometimes she would whisper to him in the morning when she knew he was half asleep: "Walrus loves Hadly." He would find scraps of paper throughout the house that appeared to be messages to her muse: "Walrus will water her plants today!" "Walrus must buy toilet paper and Tab." Ultimately, his resentment of her was resentment of himself. The problem was he believed her to be superior to him. She had brain power; she had health; she had manageable emotions; she had big ideas for the species; she had beauty to match even wild creatures. If he resented her in any true sense, it was because she knew so much without reading. "When I get an urge to read I know it's time to do something," she would say, hardly realizing that as she spoke the words she was wounding his manhood, for his genitals were wired to his cerebral cortex. How could you explain something like that to a woman?

The solitude of the house was suddenly upon him. He wished she'd get home. He was not a man who knew how to fill free time. All he really liked to do in life was read, screw, drink, and chit-chat. But he had to prepare himself for these activities, and currently he had prepared himself for talk with Kay—and she was not here. What to do? At least in the old days he could smoke, but he had scared himself out of that habit. If Kay were here she would sew something, or sweep the floor, or make a long distance call—her only vice. Hadly looked out the window. Fall was declining into winter, as grimly dignified as a politician convicted for bribery. He turned on the radio, but reception on the public stations was not good. He settled for one of the Keene AM stations. "Dee-dum, dee-doo, dee-dum," he started humming, roughly in tune with that famous rock song, "Bamboo Eating Our Yard." In an age in which music appreciation had replaced godliness, Hadly could take music or leave it. But he played to the hilt the role of the music hater, because he noticed that it disturbed his friends. From their concern, their unease, somehow he extracted a feeling of power, a whisper's worth of influence to the ear of the mover of the universe.

He was considering, with loathing, putting up Sheetrock in the back room when he got the brilliant idea to take a tub bath, knowing it would trigger in him a desire to read. He sat reading in the tub, keeping the water hot with his big toe on the faucet, sipping claret from a wine glass that he had taken in a fit of familial kleptomania from his mother's dining room in Syracuse. For an hour and a half, he was at peace with his world.

Kay arrived home at five o'clock with the good-natured

outburst of a spring day. She opened the door to the bathroom, kissed her index finger, and flicked the kiss at him.

The serpent of a draft slithered in and wrapped its coils around Hadly's shoulders.

"Close the door," he said, annoyed with her, annoyed with himself for getting annoyed, annoyed on a secondary level at her for breaking into his easeful mood like the Gong Show coming on the air as you open a letter from a friend visiting Florence, Italy.

Predictably, she fanned the air with the door several times. He threw some water at her, and she shut the door and broke into giggles. Soon she changed into her jeans, she was barefoot, she had unbuttoned the top two buttons of her blouse, she had shaken out the tight, social-worker bun of her hair so that now it fell like water the color of pine boards turning gold. Instantly, his annoyance vanished. Meanwhile, hers came forth.

"Why don't you put the toilet seat down?" she asked, lowering both the seats and sitting.

"Why should I? What difference does it make?"

"It's just good household order, that's all."

"I can see it now," Hadly said, assuming the flip tone that made him master of his classroom. "Sir Thomas Crapper dating Emily Post: 'What you think, Miss Emily, of my new invention, the crapper?' says he. 'As the French say, wee or non keep it flushed; in good society, both seats down, sill voo pleh,' says she. 'Sill voo pleh, me arse,' says he."

"I wasn't talking about etiquette," Kay said. "I was talking about order."

"I'll keep the seat down, if you keep the door closed," he said.

They both laughed at the absurdity of this bargain that, because of their particular natures, could not be.

"How did it go today?" she asked.

"Pulled through," he said, indicating that he didn't want to talk about it, not now anyway.

She tweaked the hairs on his chest, took his glass, and returned with a refill. She had poured a Genesee ale for herself. He climbed out of the tub, allowed her to towel him dry, and they both knew what that would lead to.

Afterwards, Hadly sipped the wine, Kay pulled on the ale. They lay in bed together, each hungry, each lazy, each waiting for the other to cook dinner. Finally, it was time for one of them to make a move.

"How many hours did you work today?" asked Kay.

He wasn't going to fall into that trap. "Every single one of them so far. The day is never done for a teacher," he said with an exaggerated sigh. "There is always something to find out and someone ignorant to pass it along to. The only time I can really relax is when I hear the pot boiling on the stove, the cook whistling serenely."

"Real work?" she asked coldly.

"Four hours, but I had lots of angst," said Hadly.

"You thrive on angst," she said drily.

He felt a surge of rage. How dare she not take him seriously.

There followed a moment of silence in the room. Hadly was aware now of the sounds of wind outside, mindless in its music as debaters in their rhetoric. It couldn't last between Kay and himself, he thought. The invisible third person that the two of them created was too strong, too strange; it was like mercury—beautiful, rare, and you wanted to touch it, but if you tried to touch it, you could not touch it, for it would spatter. Someday they would do something ugly to each other. He tried to imagine something ugly, to prepare himself for that day.

"What would you do if I hit you?" he asked.

"I'd murder you in your sleep."

"Of course, you wouldn't. You'd bring me to court, squeeze my balls with the help of a feminist lawyer from Cambridge. Still, that's pretty good—murder me in my sleep—I like that."

"I got it from one of my clients. Helen Jordan?"

"Her former man, Ollie Jordan, was here, you know, with the trashman. Strange pair," Hadly said.

"Yes, so you told me. You gave them my scarecrow's hat," Kay said, making it clear with her tone that she hadn't forgiven Hadly for that transgression.

"Ollie Jordan—he used to beat Helen?" Hadly asked.

"Not with regularity," Kay said. "It seems she had another common-law husband before Ollie, and he used to beat her. When she took up with the Jordan creature she promised herself—and laid it right on the line to him—that if he ever hit her she would . . ."

"Murder him in his sleep."

"Why do you always interrupt me?" she asked.

"Because I love you."

"Well, I don't love you."

"Why are you always trying to wound me?" he asked.

"Because you won't answer my questions."

"I meant it—because I love you. You can always tell a couple when they've gone beyond the courting stage because they interrupt each other. It's a sign of stability in the relationship . . ."

"You mean 'he' interrupts 'her.' "

Hadly smiled at Kay, intending to indicate his triumph over her in the conversation, since she had just interrupted him, but he discovered that she was not looking at him, that she was lost in her anger. Here, too, he was dangerously close to failure, he thought.

He twisted and turned in the bed, keeping his back to her, hoping to capture her concern. He was successful.

"You had a bad day, didn't you?" she asked.

"Pretty crummy."

"What are you going to do now?"

"Get out of teaching."

"No, I mean right at this moment?" she asked.

"You don't care if I get out of teaching?"

"Maybe I'll care after I have something to eat."

She had won, maneuvered the situation so that he must cook supper. He went downstairs, put a pot of water on to boil, crumpled up some hamburg and onion, and started to brown them. He also opened one of Kay's ales. He liked to drink when he was cooking. It took the edge off his boredom. When the water was boiling, he added spaghetti to the pot. He used to add salt to the pot, used to add salt to everything, but not these days. Salt had replaced sugar "as the thing you like that can kill you that you can do without." So they had cut down on salt—for the while anyway. Modest denial with a health purpose: such was an acceptable middle-class form of low-grade suffering roughly equivalent as a glistening for the soul to kneeling on hard benches by the women of Spain. When the meat was browned, he added the Prima Salza, and lowered the heat to simmer. Now he could relax a bit before the meal was cooked. Oh, he should make a salad, but he could easily con Kay into that job. He would tell her that he didn't want any, and she would gather some greens from the refrigerator on the vague philosophical premise that a meal needed balance. In the universe, only the inner ear cries for balance, he would say. In the end, he would eat most of the greens. He stirred the spaghetti with a fork to separate the strands and then sat down in the living room with his briefcase to correct a few quizzes before dinner. But he didn't have the heart for the job. He sat there, abstracted for a moment, and then he was seeing in his mind's eye Ollie Jordan and his terrible mouth of black teeth, the man holding his prize, the hat that Kay had gotten from the storekeeper, a hat that apparently wandered from scarecrow's head to scarecrow's head. The image inspired him to write some lines on behalf of his fictional Balthazar:

> *The sea, in her gift for composition,*
> *Has made a place, if not a self,*
> *For that rock, that kelp.*
> *Thus I am unconcerned*
> *That my hat has blown away,*
> *That the gulls are laughing:*
> *"There is less of him than usual."*

He closed the notebook gently, like a priest his missal. "Oh, Kay, I love you," he said.

"What did you say?" she shouted from upstairs.

"I said, dinner is ready."

Winter

One December night, a cold, raw rain snuffed out Ollie's fire on the altar stone. Shivering, Ollie retired to St. Pete's. Willow arrived about midnight, smelling of soap, it seemed. Ollie slapped him, only once but very hard. "Where have you been?" he asked. Willow burst into tears. Not like him, Ollie thought. The animals do not cry over pain. The animals cry only over loss. The boy went to sleep in his nest near the stove, and Ollie sneaked over to his side and kissed him on the cheek. Willow did not wake. Not like the animals to sleep so soundly, Ollie thought.

Ollie Jordan was weary. Suspicion was dragging him down. He built up the fire in the wood stove and sat down in the easy chair. He lit his pipe and sipped a beer. Soon, the warmth from the stove came over him like a caress, and he dozed off. He dreamt that he had died. Sitting on a boulder was Howard Elman. "Here we are in white hell," Elman said.

At that moment, he woke. The gray light washed over him like an ocean wave and he heard himself cry out. In the next moment, he realized that it was morning and snowing out, that the plastic roof of St. Pete's had nearly collapsed with the weight of snow, that Willow was gone. Ollie bundled up in his winter clothes, but he could not find his mittens. It was all he could do to clean the snow from the roof, and at one point the plastic broke and the snow came into St. Pete's. His hands were numb by the time he had repaired the damage. He cast his eyes about for familiar objects and found them transformed. All the marks that he had left in the forest, the hundreds of bottles and cans and paper plates and foam cups and decayed food that had fed a horde of forest rodents were now covered with snow. Where before the altar stone seemed like a table around which men might chat and drink, now it resembled a jagged white anvil. He felt like a stranger here. He found the soft cups of Willow's footsteps. They went off on one of his regular trails and vanished. In the afternoon the snow stopped falling and the wind started blowing. Willow came home early that night wearing gloves and galoshes. The boy was a resourceful thief all right, but one day he was going to get caught. Ollie worried about him. He also worried about his beer. He had only a three-day supply. He stoked up the stove and moved the beer closer to it. That night the temperature dropped well below zero.

When dawn came, the air was still, and Ollie could hear the snow falling out of the trees, like dead men dropping from gallows out of a dream. He had it in his head that he could drive to town and get some supplies (beer and mittens). One look at the truck in the snow told him that was impossible. Even if the truck could battle its way down the hill through the drifts and the ice, it would never get back up again. It was stuck here until next June, after mud season. Still, he tried. The engine would not start. "Battery's pooped out, Willow," he said, even though Willow was gone. He lifted the hood and discovered that a dead battery was the least of the vehicle's problems. The engine block had split. He had never gotten around to adding antifreeze. He returned to St. Pete's dragging his feet through the snow. He was breathing hard and he was shaking. He warmed his hands by the wood stove, while cold drafts crept along the sweat on his back. It was blazing hot as he faced the stove and cold as loneliness when he turned away. He opened a beer, lit his pipe, and sat in the easy chair. As the alcohol took hold in his system, he began to feel curiously offended and yet grand, too. It was as if winter were a conspiracy against him alone.

He sat in the chair a long time, his mind searching about for the solution to a problem as yet undefined. It was not until he had finished three beers that he realized that something else besides the seasons had changed. His charm was gone. He knew in an instant that Willow had taken it for some secret purpose

"Willow," he said, addressing the woodstove, "you took my luck away," and he opened another beer.

Ollie Jordan dropped a nickel in the kettle. The Salvation Army bell ringer said thank you but never looked at him. He liked her cool professional air. He liked the writhing light of her eyes behind the thick glasses, and he liked the way the deep blue uniform made her pale skin resemble a bottle of booze. He wanted to warm himself by her. Now he heard the carolers singing at the bandstand on Central Square. He wondered whether God spoke to them. What did it matter? God speaks to all of us, at his bidding, of course. He laughed aloud for the street to hear. He was mocking them. He knew the joke. They'd find out. When they did, they'd remember that man in Keene. Not that he was fooling himself into believing they would remember *him*. But they would remember a man like him, a man laughing out of pain at what he knew, and they would not be laughing. Poor fools. They think God loves them. They'll find out. God doesn't love; God requires love. If you don't give God love, he turns into the Devil. God and the Devil are two minds of the same One.

The carolers stopped. Now he heard the traffic sounds, at once oddly menacing and reassuring, like the breathing of some sleeping enemy. He walked on. The cold of the city street was a nasty thing, he thought. The cold of the deep woods was softer. Just yesterday, he had heard God say, "Lie down in my cold and sleep." Or maybe that had been the Devil speaking. No matter. Same difference. The trouble with cities was they didn't know what to do with snow. They pushed it off the streets, carted it away as though it were something to be ashamed of, or let it lie there in long chunky rows to get dirtied up by farting motor vehicles. God did not mean snow to be moved except by his own forces of wind, rain, and sunshine. Ollie was singing now, "Hail, hail, the gang's all here, what the hell do we care? Do dum, dee dum. Hail, hail" . . . the song drifted away.

These moments of pursuit were not so bad anymore, he thought. They weren't good exactly, but tolerable. More than tolerable, actually. They were . . . fun. So much of his life these days was spent sitting, waiting. God did not speak to the man on the move. God spoke to him who stayed put. This was the lesson that Ollie had learned, isolated for days on end on Abare's Folly. The problem was God spoke so rarely. Ollie got lonely, he got tired, he got bored just waiting. Not that he would tell God that he was bored. God probably knew anyway, so why bring up the subject? God may know all, but he was busy like everybody else, what with all those stars out there full of beings grunting for attention, and he probably pushed the things he knew around in his almighty mind so that while he knew all, all his business didn't necessarily get his attention all at once. Of course it was in areas of mind temporarily unoccupied by God where the Devil could do his work. But the Devil, too, was overbusy—as evidenced by the unspeakable evil of the world—and, like God, he couldn't be everywhere there was an opportunity, either. Thus it was that most men, even ones such as himself who were marked both by God and the Devil, spent most of their lives waiting for God to speak and the Devil to act.

The latest pursuit had started early in the day, which was odd because usually the Devil preferred the night shift. Ollie had been studying Willow's tracks in the snow. He was certain that if the tracks could be read, Willow could be understood. So far Ollie had been unsuccessful, but there was something about the way the tracks paused here and there, turned back on themselves briefly, and then leaped back into the path—that is, into the appearance of purpose—that led Ollie to believe that Willow was mocking him. The pursuit came while he was on his knees examining some suspicious lumps of snow. It came as it always did these last couple of weeks, with a whisper, *out there.* He had never been able to figure out whether the whisper was a warning from God or merely incompetence in his pursuers. He knew from the start that the pursuers were agents from the Welfare Department, but it took several nights of deep head work to determine that his true enemy was the Devil himself, that the Welfare Department was just one small agency of the Devil.

The thing to do now was to remain calm. If he ran, they would hear his panic in the snow, for such was the way of the Devil's military men. On the other hand, if he pretended to be unaware, they would sweep over him because he was weaker than they. He must stay on the move constantly, keep out of the darkness, remain alert. He had made his way to the road, skirting St. Pete's to keep the pursuers away from his home. He was fairly certain that Willow was in cahoots with the Welfare Department, in fact that Willow had betrayed him, taken his charm. Still he worried about the boy. Although he could fear his son for what he had become, he could not hate him. Indeed, his love for him was greater than ever, if the wound from the loss of love from Willow was any evidence. When he got to the highway, Ollie relaxed. They wouldn't dare attack along a public road. Ollie figured he had the upper hand now. His plan was to keep moving, to stay in the light. He knew from experience that they would tire and call off the chase. Soon he was able to hitch a ride to Keene.

He hurried to Railroad Street, a fishhook-shaped lane that left Main Street and twisted onto Church Street, where Ollie had lived for several years as a boy. He headed for a great red brick building that once had been the Princess Shoe Company. Here the Witch had worked before she discovered she could make more money on her back than on her feet. Ollie could see himself now as a small boy standing outside the shop on a summer night waiting for her to get out of work, fearing that someone would make him go inside to face the heat, the noise, the smell that made him think of tortured flesh, the darkness even among the light, like a dream-curse, the slamming of metal parts that reminded him of the sex acts of adults that he had witnessed as a child, the *whirry, whirry, whirry* of great belts on spinning shafts that he believed then were the thinking parts of a huge evil being. Even then he had a mind that thought too much, a mind that recognized that there were evil forces moving across the earth sure as weather. But the shoe factory had changed. Somehow the evil had been driven from the building. In place of the shoe factory there now were small stores, crafts shops, and silent businesses. The smell of sweat and tormented leather was gone. The machines themselves were gone. It was so quiet in the building you could hear echoes and the padding of your own feet. Good had come to the Princess Shoe Company, he thought. And he looked for his main piece of evidence at the northwest corner of the building where now there was a state liquor store.

To Ollie this plain box of a room, white and blue with neon lights, was like a greenhouse with the bottles so many flowers blooming from the shelves. What he liked best was the color of booze, the soft, clear pools of vodka and gin, the browns of whiskey like morning light on tree bark, and the sweet reds, the silly greens, the medicinal yellows, and even the snobby pink of wines. He pushed aside in his mind his fear of pursuit and spent a good long time browsing in the liquor store, touching this bottle or that, marveling at the design of the labels, sighting through the liquid—long drink for the eyes.

Actually, he knew beforehand what he was going to buy—two quarts of Uncle Fred's Vodka. Ollie Jordan might like to admire, to dream, but when it came to getting his liquor he was a practical man. He might not know arithmetic too well, but he knew that the best buy in booze could be determined by a never-fail formula that included relationships of amount, proof, and price. Once he had said to his friend Howard Elman, before Elman had skipped to the other side, "Some stays and some goes, and all of it you got to respect like the mad daddy that beats your behind, but ain't none of it got the wherewithal of Uncle Fred." Elman had argued that he liked the taste of good bourbon, and Ollie had only smiled, as one smiles at a child. He knew that taste means nothing. If it was booze, it tasted good.

Ollie left the liquor store with a quart of Uncle Fred's Vodka in each of his overcoat pockets. He was now almost broke, and still he had not bought any food. Nor did he expect to have any more money soon. True, he could work a few days for Elman, but that would leave him open for attack from the Welfare Department. Elman was part-time evil, part-time crazy these days, and it was impossible to know when he'd snap. He didn't hold it against Elman. He didn't hold anything against anybody anymore. He had just recognized that the world of men was a battleground controlled by other beings. Most people were drawn into the struggle without their knowledge. They believed they were working for themselves, when actually they were unwitting soldiers of the Welfare Department. Others lived good lives under the blessing of God, but usually they were praying all wrong to begin with and were blessed only because of God's good graces, or perhaps his sense of humor. Hard to tell which. Ollie figured that his own advantage—and the reason he was being pursued—was that, in the purity of the forest, he had stumbled upon some basic truths that men were not supposed to know. He was a threat to the evil forces, and perhaps even to the good forces. He was himself a third force. If he could reclaim the loyalty of Willow the two of them might be able to wield some of that force. But as things stood now, Ollie felt like a halved man. Without Willow he was, literally, not quite all there. Indeed, without Willow, Ollie was not even certain of the nature of the force within him. Oh, they were so clever in getting to him through Willow. In a way, he should feel flattered. They had been trying to destroy him for years, most recently with the onslaught of winter demons, but he had always withstood them. Even now, in pursuit, he was confident of escape. Never mind that his hands shook, that they had sicced him with a fever. He had kept moving, and now that he had his booze, he would be free of them for a while. They would not have pursued him with such vigor if they didn't fear him. Of course in the end they would win. That was determined when they had gotten to Willow. Still . . . still . . . you never knew. Maybe he had a chance. Certainly, his new and daring use of booze had strengthened his mind.

All his life Ollie had been a beer drinker, afraid of falling victim to the perils of hard liquor. What a fool he had been. Winter had come and changed him, changed how he must live. Without a vehicle it was now a day's work just to get down and back up The Folly and hitchhike to and from Keene. It didn't make sense to go to town but twice a week. Climbing the hill was difficult enough carrying groceries, never mind two cases of beer. He knew. He had tried it. Impossible. Necessity had made him face reality. It was a peculiar feeling for him, and it had summoned the memory of a similar feeling from long ago, a million years, it seemed: He was with his daddy in a canoe, and he could hear a rushing noise that he thought was in his head, and his daddy had said, "Those are the rapids below"; or perhaps he, Ollie, was the daddy, and he had spoken the words to Willow. He didn't know. The memory was all broken up, as impossible to put together as a shattered bottle. He needn't have worried. Booze was good. In fact, he had discovered that a cocktail of booze and hard-winter loneliness opened the door to certain truths. He scoffed at beer now. Beer was for common folk and trolls, which in Ollie Jordan's mind was a derogatory word for an ordinary fisherman. You made a septic tank of yourself when you drank beer. The beer drinker was nothing but a mouth and a tired bladder. With beer, to get the proper effect, you had to drink constantly. The better way was with booze. But you could not drink booze as you drank beer, a little at a time all the time. It would make you alternately drunk and sick. Slow death. The way with booze was to lay off it for a few days, put up with the dreary passing of time, and then drink steadily for two days straight. The trick was to get past the drunken stage. You had to drink yourself sober. It was only then that you could see the true shape in the true light of the things inside your mind.

He meandered up Railroad Street, his hands in his overcoat pockets clutching the vodka bottles, like some outlaw of old enjoying the comfort of the guns in his belt. The problem now was to find a safe, comfortable place to drink. He figured he'd start at Miranda's. He'd order a draught beer, like any troll, and pull on the vodka during trips to the bathroom. "Hail, hail, the gang's all here . . ." he half-sang, half-mumbled, staggering down the street as if already under the influence of alcohol.

Ike Jordan was parking his new Dodge pickup in the city lot between Railroad Street and Roxbury Plaza when he heard the voice of his half-brother Ollie. He barely recognized the man. Ollie Jordan had grown gaunt and bent. The stubble of his beard was a dirty gray and brown. His overcoat was in tatters, and he hunched down inside it like a man hiding out from himself. At one point he removed his hat, inspected the insides, and returned it to his head. His hair resembled a nest constructed by a messy bird. He looked ten years older than the last time Ike had seen him, and it was evident from his complexion that he was sick. There was something comical, yet frightening, about his eyes, his movements. He looked like Harpo Marx with cancer. Ike Jordan thrilled. It was clear to him that Ollie had failed in his life, and from that failure Ike now found himself drawing strength. He decided to greet Ollie. He wouldn't demand his beer back, or anything like that. He would just make small talk, tell him about his new truck, about the vacation he and the missus planned to take to Bermuda, about his son enrolling at the technical school in Nashua. Not that Ollie would show any jealousy. He was too clever for that. But Ike figured his achievements would grow in the grubby earth of Ollie's mind and, Ike hoped, blossom into painful boils of envy. He got out of the truck, slamming the door. He decided now that, after all, he would demand the beer that Ollie had taken from him.

Just then Ollie turned toward him, and Ike was looking full into his face. The face shone in the sunlight like a knife blade; it was a terrifying, even murderous face. It was a face up from hell. Ike could not look upon it. A moment of panic swept over him. Had Ollie seen him? He didn't think so. The mind behind the face was preoccupied. The eyes were focused beyond him. Ike reached behind him, slowly opened the door of his pickup, slowly got back in, and slid his body down out of sight. He waited a couple of minutes and peeked over the window. He could just see Ollie walking up the alley between Goodnow's Department Store and Junie Blaisdell's Sport-O-Rama. Now that Ollie's back was to him, Ike felt his courage rejuvenating. Perhaps he would holler out to Ollie, call him on his crimes. But what if Ollie ignored him? What then? Chase after him? Ridiculous. Let it pass, he told himself. Swallow your pride. It was only beer he took from you. You've got more important things to consider. So he had. Ike Jordan was laying plans to burglarize the Clapp place in Darby.

At the alley, Ollie Jordan paused, listening for a moment for evidence of evil forces in the area, such as muffled voices or radio music. He heard only the automobile traffic behind the buildings. He uncapped Uncle Fred and drank. The booze went through his system like electricity, and he was hearing the traffic again. The noise, like breathing, reminded him of the sound of being in his mother's arms. The emotion, the gentleness of it, made him laugh cynically. "Almost got me there," he said to the Devil. Gentleness came from your mother, and he had never had a mother, had come out of the dirt like a weed, determined to grow, if undeserving.

He walked up through the lot beside Blaisdell's to Roxbury Street and turned left. It wasn't until he had reached the very steps of his favorite bar that he realized his pursuers had gotten here first. The yellow sign, rusting red at the edges, that said "Miranda's Bar" was gone. Miranda's itself was gone.

In place of the dirty window-front, with the broken statue of the half-naked Indian sitting on a stump and thinking, there was now a new store displaying peculiar objects—little wicker baskets, a hunk of cheese, fancy crockery, a stuffed doll that made him shudder when his eyes fell upon it. In the next moment, he could feel the perspiration coming out of his skin like slimy worms, the panic rising up right through the calm of the booze. He must think. He forced himself to think. Had they actually evicted Miranda's and moved in this strange business as a front to serve their evil purposes, or were they projecting false images into his mind again? He shut his eyes and opened them again. No change in the image. He touched the window glass and its solidness against his fingertips reassured him slightly. "Glass is glass. The same glass. Ah-hah," he said. He must go inside to investigate this place. Then again, they would know that he would want to go in. They would be waiting. He had to take the risk. He had to find out whether what he was seeing was what he was seeing or a projection. They would know that, too. He had to admire the cleverness of the construction of the predicament they had put him in. The plan was too good to come from the Welfare Department. It had to come directly from the Devil himself. He had to admire the old boy. He was damn clever, stimulating in his cleverness. When the mind of God split, the evil part that was the Devil made off with the sense of humor.

"You put the joke on old Ollie this time," he said. The edges of the things he saw shimmered from his anxiety, but his voice was steady, and he bravely headed into the store. Everything that was once known as Miranda's Café was gone, even the smell of piss and greasy dust. They had taken down the walls, building new ones of Sheetrock here and there, but in one place leaving bare the brick of the building itself. He took this architectural touch as a mockery of himself. He touched the brick. Real. He walked around, carefully imitating the slow-motion daffiness of a browsing customer so that he could touch everything. Everything appeared disturbingly real. He spotted a young woman stocking shelves. She had straight

blond hair, and the sleek but firm lines of a maturing red oak
tree. He should touch her to see if she was real, he said to
himself. That idea was foolishness. Of course she would be
real. The Devil always used real people as agents. It was much
easier to spread evil among a kind with the same kind. The
truth was, he wanted to touch her because he wanted to touch
her. Get that out of your mind, he said to himself. They
wanted him to touch her. The trap in this place was the
woman. That settled, he found himself a bit easier inside. But
don't relax, he said to himself. It was possible that there were
other traps besides the woman. He continued to pretend to
browse, seeing nothing really, his mind blank, waiting for
something to happen, as it must.

Finally, a thought leaped at him snarling: It was possible
that there had never been a Miranda's, that they had planted
that idea in his mind long ago, only to confuse him later. He
recognized this thought for what it was, another trap; only this
time he had been caught, for he knew that the doubt would
stay with him for days. Luckily, these confusion-traps did not
kill, although they could wear away your confidence in what is.
All right, all right, his wiser half said. You stood up to it, now
get out. Stay here longer and they'll get you. But he did not
leave. He had to know how the Devil had pulled off this stunt,
this transformation of businesses, this weapon of assault upon
his memory. He remembered now that he had never known
the true circumstances of his eviction from the property under
the great sign. Come to think of it he had rarely known any of
the circumstances of anything important that had ever happened to him. Had he invented Miranda's? Had his family life
with Helen ever existed, or had he always lived up there on
Abare's Folly, his idea of the past a dream? It was possible that
the Devil's biggest trick against him had been to rob him
entirely of memory at an early age, not just of the time that
obviously was lost but of all things past; but thanks to God, he
had constructed a past to keep from being crushed by the
loneliness of being a stranger in time. Why would the Devil
want to make him hurt so, and for that matter why would God

want to lift his hurt? Perhaps the answer was the hurt itself. For every hurt that the Devil could inflict, the Devil hurt less. Still, that didn't account for the apparent need for conquest in both God and the Devil. If he could judge from the assaults from the Devil that he had beaten back and the assists from God that he had accepted, he could say that they both had at heart the conquest of his soul—whatever that was. He wasn't sure. But "soul" was the closest word he had to whatever it was they wanted. He could not know any of these matters for certain. Indeed, it was possible that hurt, which was the issue as Ollie Jordan saw it, in truth was no more than a pimple on the ass of Ultimate Purpose. Ollie started to hum a private dirge, until the clerk-maiden was standing before him, glistening like a rock in the sunlight after a rain.

"May I help you?" she asked.

The clerk suddenly caught the nervous smell of the man who stood before her. He was bearded and disheveled, not like the men she knew who cultivated such a look, but the real thing: an old tomcat too weakened from battle to care for itself, too vain or stupid—too something—to know that he already was defeated. His eyes, also, shone like a cat's, squirming and strange—Christmas gone crazy. The next thing she knew he seemed about to fall toward her, as if he were fighting an impulse to touch her. She gave no ground, remaining still, unthinking, unfeeling, fascinated, like that split second when you realize you are about to crash the car; and then the movement toward her dissolved into a sort of half bow, and the man turned and left the store. She did not know whether to feel fright, revulsion, or pity. Minutes later she closed the store for the holiday.

They were after him now. He couldn't hear them or see them, but he could feel their presence. The thing to do now was to keep moving, staying in public areas until he could find a place where he might drink his booze unmolested. He returned to Central Square. The Salvation Army sister was gone, and in her place was a man in an overcoat. They had made the switch to confuse him. He was in grave danger. He needed a drink and he needed to remain in public; yet if he drank in public the police would put him in jail, and then the Welfare Department would come and take him away. A public men's room would do. The trouble was there were few such places left these days. They had even closed the toilets in city hall. Maybe people just didn't piss as much as in the old days. He supposed he could try the rest room in the new transportation center on Gilbo Avenue, but he had never been in there, and his good judgment told him to stay away. Strange people who rode buses great distances could be found in the transportation center, and who knows what sort of mischief they might be planning? The idea of traveling any other way but by automobile seemed vaguely communistic to him. Another problem was that if he went to any of these places he might be seen, reported, and the Welfare Department could catch him out of view of the public, for a public toilet could be private. Oh, this was difficult.

He'd have to risk sneaking off somewhere, hoping that he wouldn't be seen. He had a place in mind and headed for it. He walked south of Main Street, and turned left in an alley called Lamson Street. After half a block, he reached another alley that cut underneath the Latchis Theater. Here he found a comfortable, protected spot among some garbage pails. He paused for a moment, listening. The traffic sounds could be heard, and they were rather pleasant, muted by the brick fortress of the theater. He sensed that here, for a while at least, he would be safe.

He found a narrow opening between some crates and decided that here would be his nest. He rummaged about the garbage cans, coming up with a foam cup and a bonanza of newspapers. He lined the nest with the papers, sat down, rearranged the papers until his back and bottom fit in place, then covered his legs and lap with more papers. No one ever handled a newspaper more lovingly than Ollie Jordan that day. Soon he felt warm and secure, and, thinking that newspapers might just contain properties that protected one against the thoughts inserted in your mind by the Devil, he filled the cup with vodka. "Home," he said in a whisper, and sipped from the cup.

He was feeling good, and he was a little sad that his stay at this mental way station in his passage would be so brief. He didn't like what was down the path—drunkenness—the obstacle that he had to drink past before he achieved a new level of sobriety. He imagined that he was in a valley meadow in the summer as the butterflies escaped from their cocoons. He giggled with mirth. His mind began to shape cocoons of its own making. He pictured a cocoon of newspapers and foam cups, decorated with bottles of booze, until it took on the qualities of a Christmas tree. Inside was a sleeping human being.

Nudge him, wake him, said the voice, surfacing into his conscious from the depths of the lost years. The voice gathered strength, took hold of him, and dragged him down into a darkness. He was spinning, falling down the shaft of a well. He was going back in time. He hit the bottom of the well and there was a great splash rising up, like the spreading wings of a butterfly, and he had burst through the well into a different world. There in the cocoon was Willow, sleeping, gathering his colors. There was himself, a young Ollie, except that he resembled the grown Willow, and he had blazing eyes. There was the Witch, all in colors. And there was a man, slouching, with his face obscured by hazy light. This world had a pond and vegetation and a stone wall that snaked up into a black sky. The man was holding roses in the cups of his hands. "They are mine," he was saying, moving menacingly toward the cocoon, until his intent was clear: He wanted to steal the colors from within. And he, Ollie in Willow's body, was telling the man to keep away. Then there was a gap in time, and he and the man were dancing slowly toward the wall, the motion producing something in his stomach like car sickness. They fell. The man vanished, and Ollie was holding the roses, and the Witch was tugging at him, as if trying to wake him up. He said to her, "The roses are mine."

Ollie realized now that he was speaking aloud, and he

thought he could feel the vibrations of his voice amidst the garbage cans. He strained to remember something of the vision, and he was able to summon the image of a meadow and butterflies struggling to be free of cocoons, which reminded him now—quite suddenly and delightfully—of women wriggling out of tight clothes. And he was seeing women with butterfly wings flying off into the sky.

The sound of an automobile horn on Main Street plucked him from his thoughts, and a second later the vision was gone, forgotten, replaced by a vague yearning. What had he been thinking about? Something about the Witch and a dance. He tried to reach back into his mind and discovered his brain power had diminished, a sure sign he was getting drunk. He sipped from his cup, knowing the drunkenness would come swiftly now. He wanted to get it over with, get past it. He refilled his cup and downed most of it in one gulp. Moments later the cup in his hand duplicated itself. "Seeing double, double, double," he tried to sing, but couldn't think of any more words. "Double, double, double," he sang. There was some meaning here, and he labored to find it. "Double, double, double." He needed words to go with double. Um. Trouble. "Trouble, trouble, trouble . . . double, double, ble, drouble, rubble, ble, ble, ble, b,b,b, b b'bum, dee-do, bum, bum, bum-a-roodoo, dum-bum, bum-bum, do-deerodee, bum." Let's see now, what was he thinking about? Not that it made any difference, he admitted to himself. In his present state, he couldn't think about what he was thinking about anyway. He heard himself giggle. God, he was drunk. Fart drunk. He held the neck of the bottle and attempted to pour some vodka in the cup, but the bottle was empty. How drunk was he? An interesting problem to ponder. The fact that he could ask himself a question showed he was not totally drunk. He was where? Behind the Latchis Theater. The weather it was cold and dark. He was who? He was Ollie Jordan, daddy of Willow Jordan, idiot. "Willow," he breathed the word. "Willow, your daddy is shit-face."

Go to sleep, angels said. No sleep. Sleep and you wake up

cold. The door opens during sleep, and in comes the Devil. Keep drinking, drink to get sober. He opened the new bottle with some difficulty, fished around his newspapers for his cup, failed to find it, sulked for a moment, and drank from the bottle. The cup turned up when he stood to take a piss. It was lying between his legs. He bent for the cup, fell, and found himself looking toward the lights of the Keene Transportation Center. Here the buses came in from Boston and New York, and here working stiffs labored at second jobs as taxi drivers. But all Ollie saw were large shapes swaying amidst the Christmas lights, as if he were on a ship in a stormy sea and he was getting a glimpse of land.

He was walking on Main Street. Time had passed. It was ten p.m. by the clock on the big white church at the head of the square. He didn't know exactly how he'd left his nest and gotten to walking, but he knew he hadn't slept. Not strictly slept, that is. He had just passed from one state to another, in between which there was a period of forgetfulness. He knew he had tossed his cookies—indeed, there were still traces of vomit on his shoes. He knew that he had gotten past drunkenness. He was no longer seeing double. He was steady on his feet. He could think. Not that he was fooling himself into believing he was sober. He was not sober. He was outside it all, outside booze, the earth, even his own skin and bones. This body, this soiled man in a soiled suit (face it, he was never the snappy dresser he sometimes thought he was), this hunted face hiding all, scared behind whiskers, this constipated, shit-pile brain—these were not his. They were merely old parts from a junkyard that God had put together as a temporary vehicle of flesh until he was ready to take possession of his real self. Willow, he thought, and laughed aloud. God had given him Willow's body to live in, but something had gone wrong and he had never taken possession. Meanwhile, some poor spirit of an animal that he had learned to call Willow was inhabiting his own self. What a joke. Poor Willow, no wonder he was so screwed up. Wonder what he is? Maybe a cricket, or a god-damn hound. A hound? Wouldn't that be something: Willow a dog, a stubborn, lovable, dumb mongrel dog stuck, yes, stuck—as dogs get stuck in sex—in a human body, his, Ollie Jordan's own body. The idea delighted him. He wanted to laugh. He wanted to tell somebody, and he was speaking his mind: "The man I am ain't supposed to be in this bag of bones but in that one there, call him son, and the man in him ain't a man at all, but a stray mutt that strayed too far."

In the next moment, the sound of his own mad laughter snapped him out of his thoughts. He found he was standing in front of St. Bernard's Catholic Church. He looked back toward downtown Keene. The lights were like gunfire. He sensed that the Welfare Department was on to him. A few more minutes and they would be around him, crazy birds suddenly appearing out of a dark sky, crazy, starving birds pecking at his mind. He dug his hands deeply into the pockets of his overcoat, clutching the remaining bottle of vodka by the hard neck, and then he walked up the church stairs. He felt safe as soon as the door shut behind him. He was alone in the church. The only light came from burning candles whose flickering comforted him by reminding him of small boys whispering from a hiding place. The very air here was differ-ent, God's air. "Hush," it said. "Hush." Down front the Christ-man could be seen in shadow on his cross. The shadow shimmered like a fern in a gentle breeze. Ollie walked slowly about the aisles, looking for a place to rest. He rejected the idea of approaching the altar. The area seemed too holy for the likes of him. Besides, the Christ-man frightened him.

On one of the side altars he discovered a manger. There was a barn about two feet long, lined with straw. Inside were little statues of a man and woman in bathrobes, as in movies he had seen long ago at the drive-in theater. He studied the figures in the manger. The Christ-man looked a little old to be just born, but he supposed that was to be expected from the son of God, if that's what he was. People thought it was a pity that the Christ-man had been born in a barn, instead of a hospital, but

Ollie didn't see anything wrong with that. Lots of creatures were born in barns. Barns were pretty places, full of old wood beams intimate with one another, like so many fellows drinking together. Barns were comfortable places. You could put your feet up, scratch your ass, spit, holler, and nobody would think of complaining. Not like a hospital. No sir. In the hospital, they made you wait and behave like children in school, which to Ollie was another horrible place. Christ had known what he was doing getting born in a barn. He was no dummy. The couple in the bathrobes beside the child were the parents, Mary and what's-his-name. Ollie knew that Mary was regarded as a virgin by the worshipers here, and this idea seemed not only peculiar to him but lacking in purpose. He couldn't see how virginity could aid and abet worship. Oh, well, he supposed they knew something he didn't. It also struck Ollie as odd that the husband, what's-his-name, took on so little importance in the story. He admitted he didn't know that story well, hadn't paid much attention to the explanations, but it was clear that what's-his-name had brought up the Christ and then faded out of the picture. Never got credit. Well, that's the way it goes with the man of the house, he thought. He bet that Christ fellow gave what's-his-name an awful hard time. He knew what it was like trying to raise these special ones. Well, for what it was worth, what's-his-name had his warm regards.

In the barn with the Christ family were statues of three other men, standing together like three jacks in a poker hand. He remembered now: They were the three wise men, fellows who from the backs of camels tracked a star. Amazing. The whole thing, the fact of the birth in the barn and that it had been written about and remembered all this time—amazing. Of course there was no Welfare Department in those days. Good thing, too, or else there would have been no Jesus Christ. The three wise men were carrying fancy items for the baby that Ollie couldn't identify from the statues. A nice gesture, but pretty goddamn useless when you thought about it. What use would a baby, especially one that was half-god, have for a hunk of something from Mrs. McGuirk's parlor?

Outside the barn were sheep standing around, all looking kind of dumb and pleased with themselves, like folks playing bingo. Here and there knelt shepherds with bowed heads, except for one guy who was looking up at a gold star that Ollie could see was dangling from a wire. The wire reminded Ollie that this arrangement wasn't necessarily a true representation of the true facts, but merely someone's idea of what had happened. But, what the hell? It was an honest effort. What else could people do to reach the face of God, but try lots of different things?

Off to the side was a grandstand of candles in little red bottles just a bit bigger than booze shot glasses. He wanted to get a better look at the barn, so he pried one candle out, lit it, and held it inside the barn. One slip and he could ignite the straw and burn down the barn, maybe even the whole church. He toyed with this idea for a moment. He was half-thinking, half-mumbling now. "Well, God, what would you do if I burned down this church? I bet you wouldn't let the Devil take me, then. I bet you'd want my ass for all your own to kick from one end of heaven to the other. But don't you worry. I don't intend to burn down no church. I may be a lot of things, but I ain't no fire bug." He felt called upon now to perform some holy act, but he couldn't think of one. He asked himself what the good people did in a situation like this. The answer came to him: They knelt. So he knelt. It was an uncomfortable position, and it seemed foolish to him to attempt contact with God while you were uncomfortable. So he sat. Now, I suppose I ought to pray, he thought. "Well, God, here I am," he whispered, but could think of nothing more to say. Face it, he didn't know how to pray. So he remained sitting there on the floor of the side altar, his mind wandering where it would.

After a while, Ollie got bored. He found himself looking around the church. The ceiling was very high, which he supposed gave the place the feeling of busy air and which was probably a delight to God, who, if he was a fellow at all, would be a tall fellow. But Ollie couldn't justify a ceiling that high. It must be ungodly expensive to heat this place, he thought.

Also, he figured there would be a thriving colony of mice up there. For some reason, mice loved the high places of buildings. He remembered the "boodwar" shack he had built underneath the great sign. It was the third building that he and Helen had built, briefly providing them with privacy they had never had before and never would again, for soon Willow began to act up and it became clear that his place was at his father's side, even in sleep. (Ollie now realized that it was when Willow took a place on the floor beside their bed that he and Helen had begun to part as lovers. Perhaps even then Willow was the Devil's man, whispering tales of anger in their ears at night. Or was it the mice, chirping madness in the dark? Or was it the fibers from the insulating itself that had gotten into their systems?) Like most women, Helen complained constantly of being cold. She would say that one of the benefits of pregnancy was that it warmed the blood. She bitched about the house being too hot near the stove and too cold everywhere else, but then again she bitched about everything so that it was impossible for him to tell the important bitching from the sporting bitching. So he ignored her. He lived on the principle that if you could ignore a problem you should, that problems came and went with the inevitability of weather. Also, somehow, he couldn't get it into his head that she really hurt, that any woman could hurt. Evidence to the contrary was an act to get their way, which was fine with him as long as he didn't have to furnish the labor.

One day, God knows how, she learned about insulation. The next thing he knew she had a hammer in her hands and she was taking down the inside boards of their home, the boards he had salvaged from a chicken coop and painted white, and she was insisting that he go find insulation to put up. He complied because it was more trouble not to. Lo and behold, but didn't it make a difference! The house was warmer, less drafty, and they burned less wood. He had to hand it to her. He had to hand it to womanhood. Deep down, he knew they were more cunning than men, if less conjuring. What bothered him was that she couldn't just accept her ascendancy over him. She had to remind him constantly when she was right and he was wrong. She had a wonderful memory for the moments that he failed her. Of course, now that he thought about it, he had failed her a lot. He had failed everybody, and everybody had failed him. So it goes, from one generation to the other, he thought, everybody fails everybody else. She made a point of insisting he insulate the new bedroom shack, and that angered him because he had intended to insulate it all along. He built as he always did, without a plan, the structure taking shape as he salvaged what he could from this dump or that. He swapped a pistol and a snow tire with Ike for some good 2-by-8 western stock, which Ike must have taken from a job site, and it occurred to him in a comic way that he could hide the evidence and do some good for his house by using the 2-by-8s for rafters and insulating between them.

All went well for a month or so, but then Helen started complaining of hearing scratching noises on the roof. Soon he was hearing them, too. Mice, he had thought, late-night mice. Jordans usually didn't have mice in their homes, because so many half-starved cats lived with them. But the cats avoided these mice, as if the sound coming from above bore danger. Ollie set traps, and now and then caught a small, dirty-white mouse that had taken to its death a look of pure hate. Traps or no, the mice multiplied, every night scratching and squealing from the rising of the moon until an hour before dawn. It was Helen who first noticed that the mice were not on the roof but inside, between the rafters in the insulation. This new information bothered them in a peculair way: It made them distrust each other. He felt desperate to rid the place of the mice, and so he bought some poison. Helen refused to let him use it, saying he'd kill the kids. He wanted to hurt her then, not because she was right but because she made him realize that something in him wanted the kids dead more than the mice dead.

In a moment of fearful knowledge, it had struck him that the scratching of the mice was warring and the squealing was breeding, the two married in a single ceremony of survival.

Then came a strange odor that reminded him of dead animal, crotch, perfume, an old woman coughing up—all these things. Mysterious stains began appearing on the inside of the plastic against the insulation. He was having bad dreams, bad thoughts, bad feelings. He wanted to burn down the building and walk away, but he was paralyzed from doing anything at all. They were both paralyzed. They marched to their bedroom at night like prisoners obeying orders from a hidden warden who sent his commands to radio receivers grafted onto their brains. Sometimes when the breeding squeals of the mice reached a peak they themselves embraced, full of lust but meanly, like strangers copulating to spite other lovers.

One night Helen began to tease him as a child teases another child. This was not his woman. Someone had stolen her, and now was mocking him with this person. He hit her in the face with his open hand. And then everything was happening in slow motion. He had left his body and he was in the other room watching, judging, snickering over this fool who was stacking the dresser on top of the bed, then climbing like some clumsy monkey and ripping down the plastic and insulation. He could see Helen, her face buried in her hands like a kid who doesn't know any better playing peekaboo on Judgment Day; he could see mice raining from the rafters. The sight had reminded him of a vague memory he had of a story that the Witch told him when he was a boy, something about God punishing the wicked with a downpour of locusts, which he had taken to be grasshoppers or crickets and which upset him because these were among his favorite creatures and he didn't like the idea of them being used as a tool of divine justice. The mice soon vanished and were never seen or heard from again.

The rolls of insulation lying on the floor revealed a world—a network of tunnels and shelters constructed by the mice in the fiberglass quilt. There were caverns where seeds were stored for food; there were nursery stations where offspring sped from infancy to adulthood in a moon's age; there were toilets pressed against the rafters, now stained with mysterious markings in mouse urine. He lugged the insulation outside, laying the batts one upon the other until they made a monstrous hill. There the insulation stayed, untouched, surrendered to the weather.

It seemed to him now that he could hear mice overhead, scurrying about. Ah, he thought, church mice, agents of heaven, perhaps the souls of men and women who had screwed up and were sent back to repeat a former life closer to the bone of the earth. He listened. No, he wasn't hearing mice; he wasn't hearing anything except the air in here which spoke of the restlessness of God himself. He was reminded of his own loneliness. It nagged at him like a woman. He reached for his bottle, but only for the comfort of holding its hard neck. He would not drink until he found a place in the church that felt right.

He wandered. Against the walls were big pictures every eight or nine feet. Some light from outside came into the church through the stained-glass windows, but not enough to allow him to see the pictures clearly. He stood on a pew for a closer look, discovering that the figures in the pictures actually came out round from the flat surface like carvings, so that they could be touched, enjoyed, understood with the hands. It took him a while to realize that the pictures told the story of the death of Christ. Seeing was a strain, but touching was easy and it gave him great pleasure. He was, he thought, like a man who has devised a method to touch the characters on the TV screen. Slowly, he worked his way from picture to picture, fourteen in all. He could feel the fear and uselessness in the friends of Christ, the weeping of the women, the intoxication from shedding blood among the tormentors, the suffering and—yes—the conceit of the Christ-man himself. The tormentors were Romans, those villains of old he had seen in movies in the 1950s. The Romans were, let's see, olden-time versions of the soldiers of the Welfare Department.

He touched the Christ very carefully, discovering something unusual on his head. At first it seemed like some simple hat such as his cousin Toby Constant had worn before they sent him to Pleasant Street in Concord. But after testing the hat with the tips of his fingers, Ollie determined that it was made of something like barbed wire strung tightly around the skull, an instrument of torture. He pondered this evil. These Romans, they liked to hurt the head. So did the Welfare Department. However, there was a difference. The Romans only wanted to dish out some pain, probably just for the droolly fun of it. The Welfare Department wanted you as stove wood to keep stoked the fire in their own private corner of hell. They made hats so pretty you would *want* to put them on, and they put things in those hats—devices—which removed information from the mind, planted ideas and clouded memories. He figured that Christ had pulled a fast one on the Romans, getting himself killed all spectacularlike, knowing his death would serve as a kick in the ass for his followers, that for him to die was to live forever through them. Christ never could have pulled off that trick with the Welfare Department. They would not have allowed a public execution. They would have knocked him off in an alley somewhere, or more likely bribed him to save themselves the trouble, gotten him a cushy job in a liquor store or something. Through his fingertips, Ollie Jordan followed Christ up that long hill. The cross on his shoulders brought Christ down three times, and each time Ollie winced. "Don't go on," he whispered. "Make 'em lug you." But Christ did not listen. He continued onward and upward. It began to dawn on Ollie that Christ wanted to climb the hill, wanted the pain, wanted the abuse because at heart he had some damn fool idea that his pains would help make a better world. Sad how some people deluded themselves.

Temporarily having lost respect for Christ, Ollie found his curiosity turning toward the cross itself. It must have been made of wood. In those days, all they had for materials were rock, wood, wool, leather, and maybe some metal for spears, but not plastic or aluminum, or even shingles. The roofs must have leaked. Christ being a holier-than-thou fellow would have preferred a holier-than-thou wood for his cross, say, oak. Then again, he wouldn't have been able to lift an oak cross, let alone haul it from here to hell and back. But Christ was no ordinary man—had to give him that. Maybe he was knotty enough to carry an oak cross. Still, the Romans who hanged him on that cross thought he was ordinary, else why would they have hung him with two other fellows? It was doubtful they would have supplied a valuable wood such as oak or yellow birch for even the fanciest of criminals. It was more likely that they used a wood that was cheap and easy to carry, say pine or hemlock, so that the fellow put on a good show. Also, it was well known that they had nailed Christ's hands and feet. You could drive a spike through bone and flesh all right but it would be difficult to continue to nail on into solid oak, or any hardwood, without bending it. Of course you could drill some starter holes. But why bother just to hang a man dead on? A spike would drive nice and easy into pine. Furthermore, the fellow who had to drive those spikes in front of all those people would look good working with pine. He'd probably fix it so they had to use pine, knowing that the people in charge could be influenced in such matters where they knew little, cared not. All the evidence was on the side of pine, or at least some softwood.

Another question that popped into Ollie's head was whether the Romans finished the crosses with anything, some kind of varnish or stain, or whether they left the wood raw. Certainly, they would have to season the crosses because a green cross of any wood would be too heavy to carry. That raised some interesting questions. Was a cross used only once, perhaps buried with the man who had been hung on it? Or was a cross used over and over again until it just wore out? The latter idea excited Ollie. He could imagine nothing grander to look at than a cross that had been up and down countless hills, laid across the backs of countless Christs, the wood aged by the sun, stained with blood, sweat, tears, and dirt. If such a cross could know, it would know everything. No wonder these Christians hung their imitation crosses everywhere.

The cross was a story of a human pain revealed in the beauty of wood. The Romans must have put fellows in charge of the crosses—crosskeepers—men who picked the wood right from the tree, cut it down, shaped it, dried the wood so it did not split or check, and then fashioned two pieces in a cross with wooden dowels and glue. Course now and then a fellow would cheat, as workmen will out of anger or boredom or laziness, and join the pieces with a mahaunchous bolt. The crosskeeper would store his crosses in barns when not in use, keeping them away from moisture so the rot wouldn't get to them. Later, when the crosses were retired from active duty, the crosskeeper would buy his old crosses at auction from the state, or maybe steal them if he could, cut them up and make them into coffee tables, selling them to the rich who lived down-country, or whatever they called down-country in those days. He bet those crosses lived long lives, longer than the poor bastards who were hung upon them. He concluded that the Romans had been wise to use wood for their crosses and Christ had been equally wise to arrange to have himself die on one.

After Ollie Jordan had completed his round of the pictures, he figured he had a pretty good understanding of the way Christ died. Not a sweet death but a showy one, its meaning formed by the minds of the crowd. He had to admit, though, that there was something missing in his knowledge. He had the potatoes and vegetables, but not the meat. He tried to recall what he knew about Christianity. Not much, and what he had came no thanks to the Witch. She was full of weird powers and crazy ideas and spooky talk that might have passed for prayer, but that was just to get her way. In truth, she was as godless as a government man. Still, he had picked up a few things about Christianity. Christ had claimed that he had died for the sins of mankind. If that was so, why had mankind kept on sinning after Christ died? And if he had died for sins of the future as well as for sins of the past, wasn't he giving an excuse to those of the future to sin, so a Christian man could say, "If he died for my sins, why I better rack 'em up on the board so he can say he done his job"? Maybe Christ was just another disguise of the Devil. Maybe. Yet, there was something to the Christ business, and he wanted to know more. What it came down to was that Christ, if he truly had the power, could take Willow away from him so that he could be his own man or join him to Willow so that they were one. There was nothing else that could be done for the two of them, even by the son of God, which he doubted that Christ was.

Ollie heard the mice again, the mice that he knew were not there. He wondered whether the Welfare Department had found him here and now was working their evil on him. He couldn't imagine that they would dare enter the church, but it was possible they were sending invisible rays through the stained-glass window. It was possible they had arranged to have the windows installed for just that purpose. Yes, he was under attack. He could feel something like a wall of hate in the darkness. He must find a protected place. He must drink his booze.

He stumbled upon the oddest closet in the oddest place. It was in the rear of the church opposite a side aisle, at the other end of the manger. There was no door on the closet, just a heavy purple drape that ran to the floor. Inside the closet was a seat. How convenient. He fancied that God—Christ, somebody—had prepared this place for him. With the drapes drawn the closet was black as his own smile; the darkness unsettled him, for he could feel himself losing his sense of upside down and right side up. He went back to the front of the church to fetch a candle. He returned, sat upon his seat, and saw now that on each side of the little closet was a slide panel. He opened one to reveal a window covered with a screen. He poked his head outside through the drapes and discovered that the windows opened into two other tiny closets, both with their own draped doors. What could these windows be for? They did not open to the outdoors. Why would you want windows in a closet opening into other closets? Certainly not to let the light, for there was no light. Certainly not to keep out the black flies or the mosquitoes, for a Christian hardly would object to the small pains insects dished out. And then the answer came to him: rays. The windows were vents; the screens allowed air to come through but blocked the rays. The word "rays" had jumped to his mind, and he struggled to give it meaning: rays—"conjuring gases sent through windows by the Welfare Department." It was as if, having defined the word, he had sent it out into the world of actions. Perhaps the rays could penetrate doors also, but not apparently these purple drapes. He touched them—they felt like a woman. He sniffed them—they smelled like cave air. They must be very old, old as Christ's cross. As long as he kept the drapes drawn, he would be safe here. If the air went bad, he'd just open a window. The screens would keep out the rays. He tested the safety of this place by sitting still, allowing the barriers in his mind to slip down for just a moment, inviting attack. There was no attack. There could be no attack. He was protected here. He could drink in peace. He thanked God, uncapped his bottle of vodka, and enjoyed the burning of the throat.

The candle was burning low; the bottle was nearly empty—these were clocks, telling him that time had passed. Without clocks, nothing happens, he thought. It's quarter to two, we say; it's going on three-thirty, we say; it rained and now the sun is shining, we say; time must have passed for my face is uglier, we say. He was drunk again. Not really stinko. Just a little bit outside of sobriety. He suppressed an urge to sing. He wished Helen were here. She could sing pretty when the spirit moved her. She used to sing such songs as, "My Heart Is Pushing Up Daisies Since You Gunned Down Our Love," and "Where Home Used To Be They Put I-93." He liked music, especially fiddlers playing at a contredanse, but he didn't like the words to songs. Most went on and on about how so-and-so had got gypped, or shot, or lost his girl. Seemed like nobody in a song could do anything right. Still, he had liked listening when Helen sang, although he never told her so. He'd always held the idea that if you showed a woman you liked something about her, you were making it easier for her to hold something against you at some later date. Maybe he had been wrong in not telling her, wrong about a lot of things. Not that there was anything special about being wrong. Everyone he knew was wrong all the time about everything. Of course you ought to treat a woman right, but what was right? Nobody he knew knew. He remembered that the Witch one fine day told him all would be well in his next life. She had given him comfort then, but now he wanted to ask her, "How come with all that experience, thousands of years' worth in thousands of bodies, nobody ever learns anything?"

He was brooding on this matter when he heard a noise. The mice? In a few moments he realized that he was hearing someone rummaging about the church. He blew out his candle. The sounds were disturbingly familiar. They reminded him of Ike as a boy practicing his sneaking-up on poor old Toby Constant; they reminded him of Willow browsing at the town dump; they reminded him of his own mindless putterings. An unsettling idea came over him that in this closet somehow he had been thrust back in time and the sounds he was hearing were those of his own self an hour or so ago. He was swept simultaneously with the urge to rush out into the church and embrace that self or kill it. And then there was light creeping under the drapes. How bony and red his hands looked. Whoever was out there had put on some lights in the church. Was the Welfare Department coming to get him? Was his own ghost prowling about? Had they sent his own ghost to haunt him? He had to know who was out there. Carefully, he poked his head through the drapes. He saw the back of a man wearing a black garb that resembled a woman's dress, reaching almost to the floor. A priest, a goddamn priest. What else in God's name did he expect to find in a church? For the moment, he was relieved, but then it occurred to him that there was no good reason for even a priest to put the lights on in a church in the dead of night.

Ollie Jordan did not know it was Christmas Eve and that in half an hour midnight mass was scheduled to begin. People were filling the church. He could not see them, but he could hear them and feel them, the way you can feel a storm coming. Perhaps these were troops massing for an attack upon him. He thought about Christ, dragged and kicked and spat upon and wept over, in the end dying with his hands outstretched. He felt oddly comforted by this thought that came to him as though it were a memory of his own experience. He pulled the drapes aside and peeked again. The seats in the church bulged with the backs of kneeling Christians. They made him think of gorged largemouth bass. A few people were standing in the rear, all of them men, he noticed. Apparently, women were not allowed to stand. This made sense to him. He smelled booze on someone's breath. A kin. He wanted to pat the fellow on the back. A daring idea came to him: He might mingle with the people and not be discovered. He stepped out into the body of the church. The people were looking toward the front and no one noticed him. He was almost disappointed that he was not attacked. There seemed to be no interest in him whatsoever. He was insulted. It hurt him to think that they did not care. Their inattention made him feel dead, a ghost who hadn't caught on to the idea of otherworldliness. He wanted to speak, to slap one of these fellows on the shoulder and tell him: God plays cruel games. But he remained quiet. Something here enforced a silence.

The priest, accompanied by a couple of boys who might have been his nephews, came out dressed like a bird in mating feathers and began the ceremony. Ollie could not tell whether the priest was the same one who had turned on the lights earlier. He was short and fat and rosy-cheeked and white of tooth, and he muttered his holy words with an affectionate growl, a man not at all like himself; yet Ollie saw something of his own ways in certain movements of the priest, especially the way he motored about his altar. He wondered whether the souls of some men pirated parts from other souls. Had this priest found him out, stolen something from him, left him lame in a limbo whose numbness would set in only later? Perhaps a priest actually could sense the presence of his own soul and therefore could command it about; or maybe it was the other way around, the soul bossing the mind, a priest as much a robot of God as a soldier of the Welfare Department was a robot of the Devil. Ollie could not say for sure. He wasn't even sure whether there was such a thing as a soul. It was just somebody's word for the unexplainable craving in a man to touch the stars. The fact was he wasn't even sure whether he had ever had contact with his own soul. Unless it was his soul that was waging a war within him at this very moment. But no. He could not believe such a thing. The evil was *out there.*

Ollie Jordan watched the ceremony carefully. Things made more sense to him than they had the last time he had been in the church. The priest told the story of the holy family being refused admission at the local motel, and how Mary had to have her baby in a barn. Then the priest put the book down and gave the people a piece of his mind, telling them they ought to be goddamn grateful for what they had, and to get off their asses and help those less fortunate. Later a couple of fellows circulated among the crowd with baskets on the ends of poles and people put money into the baskets. Ollie gave a quarter. What the hell, it might not get him into heaven, but it wouldn't hurt either.

The bells rang and Ollie knew that it was time for the important part of the ceremony to begin. The priest said something about bread and wine and Christ's body and blood, and the people bowed their heads as one. Apparently, the body and blood business was very important, but damned if he could make any sense of it. A deep—almost menacing—quiet took hold in the church. It was, he thought, like being in a dark cave full of sleeping bats. Bells rang now and again, many thanks to one of the boys helping out the priest. A choir upstairs in a small balcony blasted out some hymns that even Ollie had heard before. Accompanying the singers was a moaning pipe organ. The choir gave him the willies, but the organ was pleasant enough. The people got up from their seats now and stood in line, while the priest and a couple of helpers handed out those little white wafers. He was tempted to try one. He could stand in line like anybody else, and it was clear by now that nobody here meant him any harm—if in fact they could see him. (He couldn't get it out of his mind that he was invisible.) But something stopped him, the same force that kept him quiet before. So he stood there, lulled by the shuffling sounds of the communicants of St. Bernard's Church approaching the rail. They all look so sleepy, he thought.

His mind started to wander. A vision of summer came to him, like a windowpane blown out of its casing by a hurricane. He could feel the warm air, could hear laughing and big talk over beer, could watch the acrobatic displays of Willow, could catch the smell of cooking, could enjoy children fooling around in trees, could stir to Helen humming. Good things. There had been some good things in his life. They couldn't take that from him. And then he was thinking about a certain day long ago. There were ducks on a pond, and a man swimming in his underwear way way out, maybe half a mile, and there was a woman on the shore and a boy, just old enough to be getting his chin whiskers, and the boy was lying beside the woman and he was breathing her in and out, as though she were the very air of his life. Then, as he knew it would, the scene faded and his mind started to empty. He felt freed from the bounds of earth. The stars drifted by. He floated in space, like a bather lolling in an inner tube on a quiet lake. Here there was no loneliness, no fear, in fact, no importance attached to existence and therefore no chores to do, the pleasure of marking the passing of time was enough.

When Ollie came out of his revery, the priest was wrapping up the ceremony. Ollie felt older, more worn. He remembered something the priest had said, something about a lamb and the shedding of blood. The idea seemed wrong, strange. He had seen no blood. He thought hard. Finally, he realized what a fool he had been. They had killed something up there on the altar, and he had not seen it. Right before his eyes: a death. And he had not seen it. They had shielded it. Things happening right under his nose. Evil things. They had bamboozled him. He could trust nothing, not even the actions reported by his eyes and ears and touch. Spinning. The world was spinning away. All at once, the booze caught up with him. The priest became two, the altar helpers four. One part of him went thisaway, the other part thataway. He heard strange noises—children wheezing, old men breathing like dying, gunshot deer, women hissing prayers in hopes of getting some enemy broken by heaven. For a moment he was afraid he would puke in the church. He staggered outside, almost falling down the concrete steps. He found a tree to hug and he threw up. They shed the blood because it is demanded, Ollie thought. He had the dry heaves and he was cold.

The Appointment

February: the third day of a thaw. Ollie had put too much wood on the fire earlier and now it was hot and stuffy inside the shelter, but he didn't care. He could hear the tiny rivulets of melting snow rolling off the boulders and the trees outside. He decided to take a nap, listen to the melting as he drifted off to sleep. He didn't mind the nightmares anymore. Once you recognized that everything was a nightmare, the fear was gone. Everything was gone; the difference between life and death, hate and love was no greater than the difference between one snowflake and another. He crawled from his place by the fire to Willow's nest. The boy lay there, his eyes open and frightened; he knew something was up. Ollie had hobbled him with a chain around his ankles. "Daddy wants to nap now," Ollie said. "Daddy wants to listen to the melting. You sleep, too." And he breathed in the smell of his son and crawled off. Willow was silent. Soon he shut his eyes. Perhaps he slept. Ollie lay in his own nest. He felt weaker than ever before. His fever raged and his body ached. It was a good thing that this was the appointed day or else he wouldn't have the strength to do the appointed chore. He shut his eyes. The image of the easy chair he had salvaged took shape in his mind. It was outside at this moment, covered with snow. He concentrated, and in a moment he had left his body and was outside, looking at St. Pete's. The wind had torn its plastic skin, the snow had caved in the roof, the wooden framework had fallen down. (Poor design, and Ollie knew it.) St. Pete's had been reduced to a crude tepeelike structure that Ollie had built by leaning a few poles against the stove pipe, covering them with layers of plastic, newspapers, and hemlock boughs, all sewed in a crazy quilt held together with clothesline rope (shoplifted) and granny knots (his very own). There was no door as such, just a flap. There were no windows. The sunshine filtered through from about ten a.m. to two p.m., leaving bits of wandering green light that reminded him of troublemaking insects, and then it was dark in St. Pete's. The floor was littered with clothes, newspapers, empty bottles, and dozens of items that Ollie had picked up: bird nests, pinecones, oddly shaped sticks, rocks with white in them, and junk from the sides of roads. Whatever use these things might have did not interest him. What pleased him was their unusual shapes, which made the pity in him well up inside when he touched them. It was difficult to walk around inside of St. Pete's without tripping in the mess, so he crawled.

His home was a dream gone bad, and it was Willow's fault. Not that the boy was to blame, not strictly—the Welfare Department was to blame. If he could just escape from this dying body that he was imprisoned in, he might yet do some good for himself and his kin. He would try soon. The day had come. He would take possession of his true self, held now by the Welfare Department, through the creature they had set up as his son. He had no son; he had instead a sorrow: He still loved Willow. He imagined that the Welfare Department had stolen a mind somewhere, a poor ghost—perhaps the ghost of a child—and stuck it inside the body that was rightfully his own because they knew they could command the mind inside and because they knew that he would feel the need to be near the body, not only because he believed it to be a son but because of something else—a kinship of self that was there but which they never expected him to discover, only long for—and thus they could keep an eye on him and destroy him when he weakened. But he had fooled them. He had exercised his mentality.

Ollie Jordan lay in his nest, half-asleep—that is, pretending to himself to be half-asleep—and he imagined himself rising on a current of warm air, up, up, far above the trees until St. Pete's below resembled just another boulder that a traveler from another planet might feel kindly toward; up, up, until all that remained of Abare's Folly was the purple of a forest viewed from far away; up, up, into the high-beam glare of the sun, right on past into the night and the stars. "How peaceful, Willow," he whispered. He started his return to earth, working on the sensation of tumbling until he actually could see the stars spinning away from him, and then the darkness of the earth. And on he went, for hours it seemed, although he knew it was only a moment in earth time, spinning from light to dark to light. Very pleasant. But then the idea went bad on him. He was falling toward a city all lit up. He was spinning from light to light; he could not tell true light from made light, up from down, earth from sky.

"Frankly, Willow, I'd sooner fall onto the rocks of Abare's Folly," Ollie said, surprising himself with the sound of his own voice.

The boy's eyes opened. It was possible that the eyes were little television cameras, the purpose of which was to transmit images of earth as entertainment to outer-world beings sitting in their easy chairs. I'll give 'em something to get excited about, Ollie thought, and he looked at Willow with a malicious smile that tried to convey something of his plan without giving it away. He wanted to show that they couldn't conquer him. No, that wasn't it. He knew they could—would—conquer him. They knew, and they knew he knew. Rather, he wanted to show that he could surprise them, that to the end his mind was fresh.

Ollie stood. It took him a while to get used to the sensation of being on his feet. He should have something to eat, but what the hell, he didn't want to eat. Then, deliberately, he spoke aloud in Willow's direction as if addressing an unseen listener over a microphone: "I don't want nothing." It was true—food held no meaning for him. Not that it mattered; there was little to eat at St. Pete's anyway. It was just that he desired to put his pleasure before God and the Devil in the manner of one making a choice, even though there was none to be made. Once, before he had wised up, he would have felt vaguely guilty about not eating, believing that it was a man's duty to keep his body strong. But now he knew that eating was a trick by the Welfare Department to cloud the mind. They poisoned the food to prevent you from seeing the shape of truth. He had learned that if you stopped eating, the hunger went away, the mind became clear—well, clear enough—the senses more acute, and the pathfinder began to see. So what that he was starving. He had no obligation to this body, this face. This was an old man's body with raw, wrinkled hands that shook all the time, with a beard gone gray overnight and the eyes of a rabid dog. He had seen those eyes staring at him from shop windows, from various pictures of the Devil that passed as mirrors to the common folk. This sick thing was not his body. His body was there, and he stumbled over to Willow and handled the strong arms, the thick, powerful neck.

He caught, then, the look of the boy's eyes, like drops of pond water kicking with life. Ollie embraced his son. For a moment, he was swimming with affection. Then he pulled away. This was no good. He was confusing in his own mind just what it was he loved. Himself, the boy, the two of them together, some third party—a stranger striding away—whom did he love? Who loved him? He was shaking again. He needed some booze to calm down. He reached for his vodka. There was almost an entire bottle left. He must not drink too much, else he'd be late for his appointment. He heard himself cackle at this joke between himself and whatever was out there advising him. He must drink just enough to remain steady. He took a nip; another. The magic worked fast, warming him with silk handkerchiefs and rabbit fur. So it went when you were hungry and sick—the booze was kindlier, quicker.

He could think now. Thinking was the only thing that he had ever been good at. He bet that if they gave out prizes at the Cheshire Fair for thinking he'd get one every year. The problem was, thinking was no good. You couldn't make a living at it; you could only suffer with it. The Devil had invented thinking. Still, he was a thinker. He had to think, sure as Mrs. McGuirk's dog pisseth against walls. He should think about the appointment, for there were certain details to be worked out, but he was afraid to, afraid of the sting, the confusion. The fact was he hadn't been able to consider the act itself until he had come up with that word "appointment." Other words seemingly more accurate—"sacrifice," which was what the church people called it; "killing," which was what it was, really—prevented him from thinking about the act at all. Not that he felt that making the appointment was wrong. It was absolutely right, commanded by God. He had learned how God worked—away from words. The sounds in his head—such as the whispers of the female voice, calling *Ollie, Ollie, be kind*—were mainly from the Devil, not even directly from the Devil, either, but from the clutter the Devil left in the mind even after he had departed, like bombs dropped from airplanes that did not go off but blew up years later for no apparent reason. No doubt about it—words were the invention of the Devil. The truth was obvious when you thought about the matter: Before man got ahold of words, he was doing as fine as any common critter. God did not speak. God was mute as Willow himself. God did not say, "Listen up. Got an idea how you can get yours and his, too." God powered a man like a battery, charging his arms, legs, eyes, mouth, sex organs—oh, yes, those especially—so that he acted on command, often against his so-called better judgment, afterwards feeling sick and confused. All those years he had beaten his dogs, beaten his children, beaten his women (when they had let him), he had felt ashamed, quivering in fear at what he thought then was a nameless evil driving him. Now he realized, it was not evil but good that charged a man, drove him to do what he must, and evil that left him ashamed. He had been right to give in to his impulses. God had meant him to beat his loved ones for reasons that he likely would never know, could never know. It didn't matter what he thought personally about plunging a knife into the chest of his own son. God would see to it that he kept the appointment. He merely would be doing God's bidding. He was blameless as a pig gobbling up the young of a nearby sow, his young. He wouldn't be able to help himself . . . help himself. He started to shake with the horror of what he planned to do. "Please, I don't want to keep no appointment," he whispered. God comforted Ollie by directing him toward his bottle of booze. Ollie drank and was calmed.

The boy was crying, mocking him probably, but maybe suffering, too, suffering to beat the band. Who could tell? How long had he been crying? Two minutes, two million years? Was Willow crying, or was Ollie hearing himself crying? It was all the same—he was beside himself with desperation. He'd always been beside himself. Ha, what a good joke! He laughed aloud mirthlessly, stirring Willow into a weak, imitative cackle. Or was it his own laugh that was weak, and Willow's reproduction of it merely accurate? The whole situation—idiot son and crazy father, both doomed—suddenly struck Ollie as worthy of some notice. If only there was someone here to see, to appreciate all this—this body and blood wreckage of St. Pete's. Willow cackled again. Ollie waited for God to compel him to slap the boy, but no command came. Maybe there was no God. Maybe there was no anything anywhere that cared for anything anywhere. Whatever—he was grateful that there was no alien force in him at the moment. He didn't want to hit anybody. There was no anger in him. No anything in him. Never had been really. If there was anything, he was sure of it now, it was the fact of his own emptiness. It was possible that there were people out there who had been filled like a warm mug with beauty, love, knowledge—even riches—and had remained warm and full, but he doubted it. The human soul required fullness but it was full of holes. You could fill a soul with good, but it was like water and drained out in five minutes. Hate, being like tar, stayed in the system longer and thus was greatly favored by the population, but eventually it too dribbled out and got hard to find toward the end. Now Harold Flagg—there was a man who could hate. Ollie had to admire him, even though he knew that he himself was the tar in Flagg's soul. Maybe by hating him, Flagg felt less empty. Maybe he had done more for Flagg than he had done for any other human being. At this point, Ollie formed his mouth into the silly "o" of a carp's feeding-suck and he rapped himself on the head with his knuckles so that he could hear the hollowness in himself. Willow did the same thing, and Ollie walked over to him and slapped his face.

It was warm in here, Ollie thought. He shucked his coat and went outside. The sun was huge in the sky, perfuming the air like a woman's breath—warm, inviting, false. It was a good day to be alive, if alive was what you wanted to be. He laughed aloud at that idea and the echo of the laugh returned. It was a scared but not unfriendly echo. It had more character than Willow's imitations. He liked the echo. He wished to converse with it, test it for wisdom, but he laughed no more, said nothing. The idea of talking to an echo not only was crazy, it was undignified. If God and the Devil—or whatever was out there—were going to scorn him they would do so because of his probably wrongheaded attempts at doing right or because of their own plans, not because he was a fool. Gods, devils, employees of the Welfare Department—what the hell was out there? He wished he knew for certain whose wicked ass to kick, if that could be done, and whose holy ass to kiss, if that's what it was all about. He had tried everything: thinking, drinking, praying, cursing, pissing in the snow at midnight under a horny moon. *Olllllie,* a familiar voice whispered in his head.

"Damn you, if you got something to say, say it," he said. But he knew the voice would not answer. It was a female voice, not like the Witch's, softer. It was even tender. And it had something of himself in it. Sometimes he imagined the voice belonged to the ghost of his mother, if he had a mother. The idea of a mother had become clouded in him. She was part of that time that was lost. No one spoke of her. He did not think of her, as if there was danger in such thought. Still, she came to him in dreams sometimes, leaving him fearful yet oddly rested . . . He was fooling himself. He knew he had a mother, even knew her. He chuckled at that one. He pushed the knowledge away . . . He didn't have a mother. He was an orphan. His mother was dead. His father was alive somewhere—of this he was certain. But so what? He would not know his father if he saw him, and his father would not know him. A longing made no difference, for they would never know each other. They were strangers for all time. What bothered him, made him jealous as a matter of fact, was that his father had gotten away, and he hadn't, being stuck here with an idiot son—if idiot he was. Ollie still had a vague doubt. The boy still might be a genius, ready to crawl out of the cocoon of St. Pete's and fly away. But no, but no. It would not happen. Could not. The fact was the boy was not a boy. The boy was himself. He, Ollie Jordan, was the boy. He was the boy. They were the same person, yet not the same person. They must be separated, they must be joined. Today.

"Nice day for it, hey, Willow?" he asked, wondering whether the boy heard inside St. Pete's. He must be getting hot in there. It was already warm as french fries outside. He took off his shirt, pausing before the sun as if before a mirror or an admirer, and walked down to the pool to bathe, knowing that the water was frozen. It was pleasant down there. He paused to listen to the stream gushing under the snow and ice. It was said these little streams joined rivers and went all the way to the ocean. And why? Why for no better reason than that God insisted that water flow downhill. Stupid reason. He listened some more, and then thought he sensed danger. Willow was getting away! His friends from the Welfare Department had gotten up here and were freeing him at this moment. He rushed back to St. Pete's. Willow was on the floor, still tied but wiggling.

"Your buddies in the Welfare Department seen me coming and got scared of my scorn, eh?" Ollie said.

He attempted to hoist Willow into a sitting position, but failed. He was so weak and the boy was so strong. Why was the boy so strong? Why did he allow himself to be chained and slapped?

"Why, Willow, why?" he asked and slapped the boy. And again. Ollie felt the blows himself, even as he inflicted them.

It was time. He couldn't delay any longer. A man must be on time for the important things. It was getting late in the afternoon. This must be done by daylight. He drank some more vodka, as much as he could get down. He gave the boy something to eat, all he had left, actually. But Willow refused to touch the food—the remains of a rabbit Ollie had trapped days ago and a can of sardines. He tried to eat the sardines himself, but they had frozen and thawed, frozen and thawed, and they smelled bad. The rabbit, unrecognizable in a stew, looked appetizing enough. Too appetizing. His suspicions were aroused. Somebody had put something bad in the stew. What did that matter? What could they have put in? Something to kill him? Something to drive him crazy?

"Ha, Willow," he said. "They can't hurt what's hurt to death already."

Time passed. He didn't know how much. He had blacked out. It was later in the day but the air was still warm. Too warm. Had they shipped Abare's Folly to the southland? Pure meanness—that was the mark of gods, or whatever was out there. The bastards, they controlled everything from the seasons of the year to the urges in a man. All you had that was your own were your thoughts. He looked up, seeing the same old sun. He looked down, seeing the altar stone. It was whisked clean of snow, the mica crystals on its pitted surface shining like the hardened tears of the earth herself. He saw that his hands were bleeding. Apparently, it was he who had scraped the snow and ice from the altar stone. He was reminded now that he had an appointment to keep. The job ahead was to get Willow on the stone and figure some painless way to take from him his blood. There was a butcher knife (salvaged) by the altar stone. Where was Willow?

"Willow," he heard his own voice calling. "Willow, where are you?" The voice was cunning, but weak. There was no answer. Ollie returned to St. Pete's. Willow was not there. He was chained and could not have gone far. Ollie walked around St. Pete's in a widening spiral. The warm air had loosened some of the crust on the snow and now and then one of his legs plunged through. It was hard for him to get his foot out and continue on. He was getting so weak. He probably never would have found Willow, except that he heard the chain rattling. Willow was in plain sight of St. Pete's high up his favorite maple tree. At this moment, the sap would be running. It would be sweet.

"Well, I'll be—that boy always did have a fine sense of humor," Ollie said in a whisper to himself. Then he shouted, "Willow, you get your ass down here."

". . . ass down here," answered the echo.

"Down here," Ollie said.

". . . here," the echo said.

Willow said nothing. He was standing on a branch and he was looking to the west. Ollie figured he could see the Connecticut River from his vantage point.

"Willow."

". . . low."

"If all you can do is trail after me, I don't want to hear from you no more," Ollie said, addressing the echo.

As for Willow, he was not in a conversing mood. After taking in the view, he settled back into a branch-seat near the center of the tree. Ollie stood back to watch, to behold. "Willow," he called, but did not expect an answer. The boy folded his arms, looking beyond, ignoring his father. Soon, he was standing again, making his way out on the limb. The sound of water moving everywhere on the hill and the jangle of chains high up in the tree mingled in Ollie's mind to make music. A bird flew out of Willow's hand and dived into the snow at Ollie's feet. The bird was Willow's right shoe. Seconds later the second shoe dived earthward. Then came the coat, shirt, undershirt, fluttering like great, dying moths. Willow struggled to get his trousers past the chain, discovered it could not be done, and gave up. He sat, his bare ass on a branch, pants hanging from his bound feet.

An hour or so passed, Ollie wasn't sure exactly. He had swooned for a moment, coming to in the snow. He pulled himself up to a sitting position, took a few breaths, and rose. It took all the strength he had left to pull some boughs from some young hemlocks and make a bed on top of the snow. He lay down, leaning his head against a tree. He knew now the boy had saved him from madness and murder, if not from doom.

The afternoon was wearing on, and yet the golden light that gave all objects their own halo seemed to deepen. Ollie could see what he had made and unmade these last few months. There was St. Pete's, a wonderful idea that had failed for lack of care, just as he himself was the failure of some tinkering god. There was no pain in this realization. It was enough for Ollie now merely to understand. The refuse he had strewn about St. Pete's, like grass seed, was beginning to poke up through the melting snow. He could see the altar stone, bare and solid. It reminded him of the Witch, lying with her arms upraised.

"It wasn't your fault, Witch, or his fault, or my fault," he said. "It was the fact that we didn't know any better. I forgot out of hurt. You must have hurt, too, and Daddy, too. All except Willow. Lucky Willow. Too dumb to hurt. Poor Willow. Too dumb to know."

Ollie could not tell now whether he was actually speaking or whether he was thinking only. But he knew that his mind was free from false ideas. He could see now into the deep past he had forgotten. He had done right to forget. To know, until this moment, would have killed him with torment. It was the booze that had brought on the evil, the booze and fear and jealousy and just plain stupidity.

"You knew all along, Witch, didn't you?" he said.

He would miss the fire on the altar stone. He would miss booze, even though that was the start and end of his troubles, of his life itself. He was sorry that he had never been able to listen properly to God; for he believed now, sure as he was dying, that there was a God, a God who cared for him and who was weeping for him now and whom he had let down and who would forgive him. He thanked God for making him see that a sacrifice of Willow was not necessary to make him see his own madness. He shut his eyes, and when he opened them he found that the altar stone had been moved and now lay before him, a bright burning fire on its belly. "Willow," he said, but his voice was only a whisper. He shut his eyes, and opened them in what seemed like a moment. There was moonlight through the trees. He shut his eyes, and opened them. The sun was high and bright. He could see Willow up on the branch. The boy was still, apparently at peace, as he was at peace. The wind, which before had been from the south, now came from the northwest. It must be very cold, he knew, and yet he felt warm and comfortable. The melting had stopped, and now the only sound was the wind clacking through the dry leaves of a beech tree. He shut his eyes, and opened them. His mother and father were dancing in the snow in front of him. They came to him and kissed him. He shut his eyes, and opened them, and it was night. He could see Willow high up, blue in the moonlight. "Willow," he said, and found that by uttering the boy's name, he could lighten the burden of his own flesh until he was floating in the air. "Willow," he said, and he was rising now. He thought about the butterfly that comes out of the cocoon and leaves the grimey earth forever. When he got to Willow, the boy reached out to him and said, "Father." Ollie took him into his arms, and they flew off.

The Charcoal Burners

When the storekeeper returned from the funeral of Old Man Dorne he felt a need to work in the open air, so he decided to chip ice from the hardtop in front of the store. There had been a few warm days and some rain, but although it was April the ground remained frozen and the trees were still bare of leaves. Cousin Richard had said that New Hampshire did not have a spring. Now the storekeeper knew what he meant. Winter hung on here. What the natives called spring was really winter, South Carolina-style.

Gloria hadn't gone to the funeral. She didn't like matters to do with death. That morning he had been putting on his tie in front of the bedroom mirror, which he rarely looked at and which revealed a certain slouch that he had believed was peculiar to his father, and he had blurted out, "Gloria, everybody has got to die. Death is as natural as . . . as, ah, . . ." And the door had slammed, and she was gone. When he went downstairs, she was doing the dishes. She had put on the radio and she was humming with the music. So he had gone to the funeral alone.

The ice chipper had come with the store, one of the many tools that the Flagg family had accumulated. It had a long handle and a flat blade. It was nice to use because you didn't have to bend over to operate it. No one had wept at Old Man Dorne's funeral. These Yankees are stingy with their feelings, he had thought. Then he realized no tears were called for. Dorne had had a good life. He had left shining likenesses of himself in the memories of those who had known him. There was no reason to weep for him. The storekeeper wished he could explain that to Gloria.

The ice chipper made pleasant sounds, much more congenial to the thinking man than the music Gloria liked to listen to. The funeral had attracted a large crowd of family, friends, and acquaintances like himself. All these people had the look of the county, the women with out-of-date hairdos, the men with work-dirt creased in their hands. The exceptions were the piece workers at the textile mills, who were pale, bent, but neat. "A good weaver learns to keep his web clean and in so doing, himself," Old Man Dorne had said.

A woman in the back row of the church caught the storekeeper's eye. There was something out of place about her. For one thing, she was alone. Unwritten law of the land: Ladies do not attend funerals alone. She had long, straight black hair, a few strands of white showing. Her face was coarse, hard, masklike, and yet there was something about her eyes that said, "Come along, sailor boy." She looked like an old whore, the kind that hangs around bars whose doors open directly onto the street. Here in Cheshire County—a semiretired pro? No, he didn't believe it.

The casket was closed. That disappointed the storekeeper. He wanted to see Dorne in death. Dead people looked serene, hinted that there really was such a thing as eternal peace. The dead soothed the fear of death. He wished somehow he could explain this idea to Gloria.

During the ceremony, the storekeeper tried to remember some of the stories Old Man Dorne had told on those mornings at the store, but none came to mind. He could not even remember clearly what the old man had looked like—the color of his eyes, the shape of his nose and mouth. He could hear that voice, though, slow-talking and soft, yet penetrating, too, so you didn't have to concentrate to listen. And now as the ice kicked up around his feet, the work-sounds of the ice chipper lulling his mind, the storekeeper again was hearing Old Man Dorne's voice . . .

"It wasn't always so that the trees were here. There's been times when they were cleared, and sheep grazed in fields—and not so long ago, either. I can recollect when there were fields even on The Folly, although not all the way to the top, of course. Even before, in days gone by, there were three times as many people in Darby as there are now. There even was industry, as you can see by the stone foundations and brick litter down by the falls of Trout Brook. Nonetheless, the farmer was king. When I say farmer, I don't mean just the harvesters of vegetables. I include the keepers of sheep, which roamed these rocky slopes. There were no commuters then because there was no place anyone would want to commute to. Keene was only a town amongst towns. The railroad made Keene the city in the county. But it wasn't the railroad that changed these hills. It was the steamboat.

"You laugh. How could the steamboat change the face of Darby, you ask? If my Granduncle Evvan was here, he'd explain it so you could all understand, as he explained it to me on his deathbed. 'Leave the room,' he said. 'A dark man is coming to get me, and I don't want you here when he arrives.' Course I didn't leave the room. I was a boy and curious, and I'd just as soon take my chances with the dark man if it meant I could hear a story.

"Uncle Evvan, he didn't really want me to leave either. He wanted to talk, uncommon for him. He had come to live with us when the arthritis got so bad he couldn't pour water into a cup. Those were the days when you took care of your own. Never mind that Granduncle Evvan was Evvan Jordan, and after he died we'd lie about owning up to him as a relative. Long as he was alive and couldn't do for himself, we—his own—did for him.

"It seems as if in his youth Uncle Evvan had been a helper to a charcoaler. See, back when Mr. Fulton invented the steamboat, he says you going to have to run these things on charcoal from hardwood trees. The forest that grew around here suddenly came into demand. A trade developed, as it will when there's demand. These fellows would cut the trees down and build these mound-type structures with the logs, maybe forty feet through and eighteen feet tall. I suppose they resembled domes. These were skill-made things, with passageways inside. The charcoaler would make a smoky fire in that green wood. I don't know exactly how—lost art, you know—but anyway the idea was to drive the moisture out of the wood and combust everything but the pure charcoal, which then could be shipped south to feed the appetite of the steamboat. Anyone who has tried to burn a pile of brush knows that any open fire is difficult to control. You can imagine the dangers involved for the charcoaler.

"Granduncle Evvan was not one of those babies born of woman. He came out of the belly of a fish in Nova Scotia, made his way here as a boy ('Got no memories before age twelve,' he claimed), and hooked up with this charcoaler. These characters weren't welcome, and you can see why. It was a depression time in these parts then. The charcoalers would contract with some land-poor old fart, cut down all the trees, leaving smoke in the air for days and stumps on the land for years. Nothing to show for the visit but a few dollars and scars, scars, scars.

"Think of these fellows coming into town, exhausted so they moved like sleepwalkers, their skin blackened from exposure to smoke, their very being smelling of fire. They must have been a fearsome sight. Granduncle Evvan on his deathbed, in the hoarse voice of a man strangling in his own cough-up, said it was the kind of life that broke a man's spirit or made him permanently mean. As he spoke, I'd have sworn that I saw the dark, greasy tan of a man whose skin was altered by years of exposure to heat—in short, a demon. Course that was just the imagination of a boy.

"Granduncle Evvan was pretty coherent until he got to the part about the accident. Somehow, one day—the wind had been blowing: bad sign—the fire in the mound roared up out of control and incinerated Granduncle Evvan's mentor. He staggered out of the mound, looking like a hunk of burnt toast, and then, for reasons unknown, he went back in. There were no remains. Granduncle Evvan hunted through the ashes for days, trying to find some evidence of a body. He found nothing. I guess he blamed himself for the fire, and maybe justly so. It was hard to tell, as he explained it, whose fault, if anyone's, the fire had been.

"The upshot of the charcoal burners is that with the forest denuded, another group came on their heels and created, from the stumpy land, rough pastures. Here they raised sheep. Out of the ugly, pocked hill came green meadows. The place was beautiful in a way that it had never been before, in a way that even the Indians could not have imagined. For this you can thank the steamboat. Then the market fell out on the sheep business during the bad times of 1890 and again in 1910. Over the years, the farmers started heading west. I imagined they dreamt of warm sunshine, soil without stones. Later still, along came rayon and the like, and the wool industry all but expired. Finally, somebody invented the big tractor, which was just dandy for the plains states, but useless on these rocky, slanted hills, thus furthering the advantage of the western farmer. More and more New Hampshire farmers left, and their pastures did what this land does best when left alone—grew trees. All that's left of the pasture life are the stone walls you see today in every woodland. Except for some sporadic logging, these forests have been untouched for seventy-five or eighty years, and this part of New Hampshire is wilder now than it has been since the Indians were here.

"Granduncle Evvan he saw all this, saw the forest that he had cut down grow back up. That day on his deathbed, he led me to the window, and he said, 'See in the woods, see that man in black? I'll be leaving with him by and by.' The next day Granduncle Evvan died. The upshot to me is that I believed it. I saw that man in black that day, I see him still on occasion. You won't catch this soul walking no woodsy paths."

The storekeeper came out of his reverie satiated by his memory of Old Man Dorne's tale. Odd, he thought, that even though Dorne was from the heart of the county, there was something of an outsider's wistfulness about him. Such had been the kinship between himself and the old man. The storekeeper realized now that he was slightly overwarmed by his labors. He looked up into the hills and beyond at the sun, and then to his feet. There was a pile of ice chips lying there, a streamlet forming from them on the blacktop. Perhaps spring had arrived. "Nice," he said aloud. A peculiar sense of optimism took hold in him. He got the crazy idea that one of these days everything everywhere was going to be fine. And then it struck him that he was settled down in Darby town at last. He rejoiced. Now he had something he could talk about with Gloria.

Where Willow Went

She could feel herself coming out of the fog. Always an exciting time. Brain power increased. Awareness quickened. Colors of the world brightened and shook. Memories came on like cooling thunderstorms on a hot August evening. She was seeing Osgood's canoe coming round from the point on the pond—that gawd-awful, bug-ridden pond. There he had built that terribly primitive shack that he insisted on calling a camp, which bothered her because it was uncharacteristically imprecise of him. The only neighbors were beavers that slapped their tails on the water, as if in criticism, and then vanished before you could answer. She must have loved Osgood mightily to put up with that place. Year after year, she had nothing to do but knit. At least she had the comfort of her own easy chair. No thanks to Osgood. He had tried to talk her into sitting on something he built out of birch sticks. "Rough it, Amy," he would say, as though he were Teddy Roosevelt. "You rough it," she would answer, and turn on the radio; and he would go off, paddling around on the water with his fishing pole, hooking countless tiny fish and occasionally shooting some poor creature that could only be eaten in a stew treated with tomato and oregano. "Osgood . . . Osgood . . ." She was speaking aloud now. She might be deaf, but she could feel the vibrations of her own speech. "Osgood, why this black pond covered with green scum? Why not a blue lake with neighbors that feed ducks?" The canoe was coming round the point. The fog was clearing. The canoe was empty. She shrieked. A moment later, Miss Bordeaux appeared in her room with the new night LPN. They were blathering away—about her, she imagined—and she was glad she could not hear them.

"Mrs. Clapp, I want you to meet our new night nurse," said Miss Bordeaux. Then, turning to address the new nurse: "She can't hear us. She's deaf as a footstool, but we try to act natural around her because this one can lose contact on you real fast. Poor soul. Lost her husband a while back. We're not sure at this point whether she's senile or just depressed. It's a quiet night. Why don't you give her a back rub—gentl'er down, so's she sleeps well and doesn't wake up the others."

Mrs. Clapp found herself shaking hands with a lanky, sallow-faced woman with a blank expression. Mrs. Clapp liked the face because it told no stories, requested no sympathies. She liked the hand that took hers because it was warm. So many of these girls they hired were cold-handed. She especially didn't like Miz Coburn, or Coldbuns, or something like that. You could see that she was revolted by old people, but she faked a big smile and babbled constantly and she was cold-handed. Mrs. Clapp had derived some pleasure from telling her to go boil her nose. This new LPN—if that's what she was—had good hands. She squirted the lotion in her palm—not like Miz Cummerbun who shot the stuff cold right onto your spine—and she rubbed deeply and firmly into the back, but with no rush. Mrs. Clapp liked this one, all right. She would be ignorant as a pickle, of course. All the good ones were. The smart ones really didn't like the work. They liked the idea of the work.

"A lot of these old people," said the widow Clapp, "a lot of these old people, a lot of these old people, a lot of these old people . . . they don't. Oh dear, forgot my lines, as Osgood used to say. He also used to say, 'Crimey—Amy, where'd you put my crimey blue suit coat?' It's hell being old. You don't remember where you are half the time, and you worry the other half where you went. It's like a fog. I don't mean like the never-never land of fog that the high school kids are in, day-dreaming and all about pretties. I mean fog where you understand that everything is out there but you can't remember what it is . . . Um. What is your name? I said, 'What is your name, nursee?' "

There was a pause in the kneading strokes of the woman. She must be speaking. The widow Clapp turned over on her side, and said, "Am I shouting?"

The nurse mumbled something, but her expression remained unchanging.

"I can't hear," said the widow Clapp. "You know I can't hear. They must have told you."

The woman nodded.

"Your name is what?" said the widow Clapp. "They told me, but I didn't get it. Say it clear. Don't mumble like some teenager, and I'll know it."

"My name is Helen Jordan."

"Helen, you do a good job. You know how to give a back rub. Some of these nurses don't know how to touch."

The widow Clapp turned her head into the pillow, and the back rub resumed.

"I imagine you've got children," said the widow Clapp, and she could sense Helen Jordan nodding. "Of course you do. I know in your touch. I have children, all grown and wishing I'd pass away. I guess I can't blame them. I've been hard to get along with since I lost my Osgood. I used to be sweet. He'd call me sweet Amy. I imagine your husband has got a nickname for you too."

Mrs. Clapp could feel a momentary stiffening in the fingers rubbing her back, and she immediately jumped to the conclusion that the Jordan woman, like herself, was widowed.

"I know, I know," said the widow Clapp. "These men exercise all the time, and they get all that fresh air, and then they die, leaving us alone. It's not alone that I minded, up until recently, that is. It's the not being able to do for yourself. These men do for you for so long, and then they die. You'd think the sons would do for you, too, but they don't. Husbands do everything and give nothing. Sons give everything and do nothing. You don't know about such because your boys aren't old enough. But you'll find that the little boy who picked the flowers for you but wouldn't clean the sink still won't. They're all the same. I'm not bitter. Just being realistic. In fact, I'm grateful, because in my old age, I was delivered a boy like a woman dreams of, at least an old woman of my turn of mind. You don't believe me. Nobody does. All for the best, I suppose."

Mrs. Clapp began to drift off. She was grateful that the new nurse did not stop her kneading, did not try some phony comforting routine. She did not want to be comforted. She wanted to be touched. The fog had cleared and she was seeing the boy in her mind, remembering that first day when he came to her. Soon the fog would return, and she would forget. She tried to concentrate on her memories. She felt like some desperate god who was losing the power to open flowers.

She had just put a Table Talk pie in the oven. A woman knew she was sliding into the pit when she stopped baking her own pies and started buying them. Nevertheless, you had to eat. She couldn't bear to eat pies cold out of the carton. She opened the box, threw it away, and popped the pie in the oven, as if she were baking it. Sometimes her mind wandered, and the pies stayed in too long and were burned, and she would think about the Devil. She had been looking out the back window at the garden. It was early summer, and the vegetables that the Shepard boy had helped her plant were taking hold—but so were the weeds. She was too weak to weed, too weak to harvest. Looking at the garden made her angry, but she courted the anger because anger was preferable to the alternative—fear.

"Nursee? Nursee? I didn't hear him or see him at first, but smelled him, the scent of him like evergreen boughs and young manhood mixed coming through the screen door. I went outside in the yard, not knowing what I would find, but quickened by that scent. Boy who sleeps in trees: That's where I saw him first—in the crook of the maple in the backyard, just as at home as a bird. I'd like to tell you that he was a nice-looking young fellow, on the lines of the Shepard boy, but he wasn't. He was homely as a dog bone, and you could tell he was retarded. I wasn't scared of him. I said to myself right then and there that I was too old to defend myself, and therefore there was nothing for me to do but make the best of the situation. Besides, I could see he had no evil intentions. You know how it goes, nursee: No mind, no malice. 'Down out of that tree,' I says, and like a good boy he did what he was told. I soon figured it was the aroma of the pie that brought him, so I gave him a piece, and he ate it, and I gave him some more, and he ate that. Pretty soon there was no more pie. I says, 'Well, you've got some appetite.' He grinned a yard wide, but I could see it wasn't what I said that tickled him but his gratitude over the pie. Five minutes later he was gone, darting up in the woods, removed just as quick as a kiss from a nephew. I called the store and ordered some more goodies. Next day, same hour, my boy shows up for his pie. This time he stayed longer and kept me company. We got along fine, the two of us. It didn't matter what I said to him, because he couldn't understand, and it didn't matter I couldn't hear because he had nothing on his mind to spout off about.

"I'd strongly promote the idea that a young couple not speak to each other—ever. A couple should not cackle, but couple. You know how it goes, nursee: He says you don't clean the toilet bowl regularly; you feel hurt and sprinkle the Ajax on his head; he says and you says and he says and you says. You both say too much, and you say it all wrong. Trust the hands, I say. Let the hands speak . . . The boy would take my hands in his and hold them to his cheek and shut his eyes. I don't think anybody ever touched that boy. I touched him often, sometimes for his sake, sometimes for mine, and sometimes to lead him to the chores. Oh yes, ma'am, I made him earn his pie. There's a little la-di-da in this old lady, but some practicality, too. If I can get work cheap out of a fellow, I will. I showed him how to weed the garden, and if he pulled a carrot instead of the witch grass, why I'd bat him in the ear. Hands across the head speak, too. He stayed at first only for the pie, and then I touched his cheek one day and he stayed on deep into the afternoon like young summer sol himself. He liked to show me things he found in the forest—clumps of leaves, old bird nests, twisted branches and stones. He loved the mica shining in the stones. He loved patterns of things. He was a good boy in that he brought home no crawlies.

"Osgood was obsessed with slimy creatures. He would take me down to the pond and show me green, living nets throbbing to be born. They were his idea of adventure and discovery. He had other habits I had a hard time forgiving, such as squirting the eggs of fish into a bowl of scrambled eggs, and then saying—optimisticlike—'Amy, I got a treat for you this morning that will knock your socks off.' As if a woman likes her socks tampered with at breakfast.

"The summer wore on. The boy stayed nights sometimes, sleeping in the tree. Fall came and the night chill settled in me in a different way than in past years. The cold stiffened spirit and body. The boy came out of the tree and slept in the house. He didn't like the house after dark. Something in there bothered him. Night dust, house lights, house darkness—I don't know what it was. But he didn't like where he came from either, so most nights he stayed with me, up at all hours like a cat, and napping through the day. He liked to sleep in the living room chair, so the sun through the window touched his face. His cheek was warm. His cheek warmed my hands. He never stayed more than three nights at a time, although I tried my best to keep him. I wanted to steal him from the people he belonged to, whoever they were. They did not love him. I loved him. I deserved him. He always came back at pie time and usually left after pie time. Often, he left with provisions, vegetables from the garden and even food from the fridge. I probably should have stopped him, but I could see he was taking the food to someone, someone perhaps even less able than himself. It was important to him that he did this turn. I let him take what he wanted; I even bought extra food so that he could take it away, but I did it for him, not for his secret someone.

"Fall wore into winter, and with each cold morning there was less of me. I was shriveling like an autumn leaf. One morning I went outdoors and noticed that the trees were bare. I ran inside in fear and hid under the kitchen table. I felt put upon by a terrible immensity. There was something going bad with the boy, too. Day by day, he grew more nervous, confused, and sad. It would take a hot, soapy bath to calm him. This old woman will say no more of that. He tried to tell me things with his hands. Someone was hurting him in some way. He got worse. I got worse. I must save him I thought—I cannot save myself—but no solution came to mind. I never had the experience of saving someone before.

"I knew our time together was going to end when he brought me this thing, a piece of carved wood the size of your hand. I thought he'd taken it from the Elks Club, or someplace like that, and frankly I was insulted. But he made me look at it closely, and I could see that it was too crude to be anything but personal. He was trying to tell me some tale with it, or he hoped that my having it perhaps would do something beneficial for him. I don't know. This was puzzling, confusing. This was not one of those gratifying displays of love. Around Christmas, the grandchildren and the great-grandchildren came from Keene. Louisa found the carving. I made her put it back on the shelf. After that I felt disagreeable. The chirpings of the children set me on edge. Even then, I think I knew that, as this carving was lost, so was I. Time passed. I forgot. Remembered. Forgot. The boy did not return. I bought pies. Off to the dump they'd go in Mr. Elman's truck. I hated the waste. One afternoon, my daughter-in-law took me to the clinic for a checkup. When we came back, we found the clock collection gone, the house burglarized. Before getting sick on the spot—in direct contradiction to the proclamations of that stupid doctor, I might add—I think I said, 'Osgood has taken his damn clocks.' It wasn't until they took me out the door on a stretcher-bed that I saw the pile of stones that the boy left, stacked round like a pie, his way of saying, 'Thank you, ma'am. Good-bye.' I reached up and grasped the arm of one of the fellows carrying the stretcher. He was shocked by my strength. 'The stones,' I said. 'The stones have been rained on and the ice is on them like a topping.' He looked at the stones, and said. 'Don't worry lady, we'll clean them.' Then they shoved me into the ambulance . . . Osgood, Osgood, the fog is descending . . . Bring the boat in; get off the pond. You will be lost. You will drown. Don't go, I have something to tell you."

"She's asleep. You put her to sleep," said Miss Bordeaux.

"She takes good to a back rub," said Helen Jordan.

"You like this work, don't you Helen?"

"I like the old people. They are so cute."

"Did Mrs. Clapp say anything?"

"She talked about this and that."

"No, I mean was she coherent?"

"She just talked on."

Miss Bordeaux could see now that her new night attendant did not understand the meaning of the word "coherent."

"Did she say anything you could understand? Did she make sense?"

"I don't know what she said. She talked to her pillow and I weren't listening."

"If you had been listening, could you have understood her?"

"If she was talking to me and she was making sense, why I would have understood her."

"Therefore," said Miss Bordeaux, "she was not coherent, or else you would have paid attention."

"I guess you'd say she wasn't coherent," said Helen Jordan, wondering what in the world difference it made.

Statues

It was Howard Elman who found the bodies of Ollie Jordan and his son Willow. Elman had watched Ollie head for destruction. It was as if Ollie believed he were strolling onto the grounds of a picnic sponsored by a sportsman's club, whereas Elman could see him walking to the edge of a cliff. Another man might have tried to do something for his friend, talk to him or trick him into going to see a counselor or try to turn him from the way of doom, but Elman was not such a man. In Elman's code of friendship, you did not interfere. So he watched as Ollie became less and less able. Elman gave him work, pay, and companionship, but he did not interfere. When Ollie failed to show up for work after that brief February thaw, Elman suspected trouble. He didn't like these spells of warm rain and happy sunshine in the middle of winter. He liked winter. Winter was something hard a man could get used to, unlike, say, rejection by someone you loved. (He thought of his son Freddy.) Every December, you would say to yourself, surely this year winter will kill me, and then you found it was really Christmas that was the pain in the ass, and you went out in the woods and shot snowshoe hares and realized just how goddamnly awesome the woods are without all those leaves and mosquitoes and black flies and hikers tromping from place to place for God knows what purpose. By March, you hated to see the spring come—until it came, and then you marveled that you had borne up under yet another winter, and you went fishing, making sure to stay in the wind so the black flies wouldn't have your ass for supper. But a thaw was not spring. A thaw was a lie.

Elman began his search for Ollie Jordan on a Sunday morning. He should have set out on Saturday, but that was a work day. Work came before everything with Elman. He outfitted himself with a rope, cigarettes, matches, hunting knife, and his .308 rifle. Howard Elman never went into the woods without being armed. It was a crisp morning, the sky blue, the temperature well below freezing, with a couple of inches of good tracking snow that had fallen during the night. The sun was bright and it did something exciting to the snow; Elman looked forward to the hike. After some study, he chose his pickup to drive, the most reliable—if least comfortable—in his current stable of vehicles. He headed for Abare's Folly. Ollie had a camp up there somewhere, although he had been careful not to divulge the exact location. Still, Elman had a pretty good idea of where he would find Ollie. There was a spot on that nasty, ledgy hill that was relatively flat and that caught the southern sun. Elman remembered how he and Ollie had stumbled upon it while hunting years earlier. The place wasn't exactly paradise, but compared to the rest of the terrain on that hill, it looked mighty inviting.

Elman hoped that he could drive up the logging road of The Folly, but he soon found that that was impossible. The thaw may have wiped the old snow from the valleys, but there was still plenty on the hill. Besides, the road itself was in terrible condition, probably just barely passable with a four-wheel drive vehicle in the dry season in the summer. Furthermore, someone—probably Ollie himself—had felled trees along the trail to make access impossible even by snowmobile. The only way up was to walk.

Elman was feeling vaguely uneasy. He was afraid that he would stumble upon Ollie, hale and hearty. Elman did not flinch at the possibilities of Ollie's wrath, and it did not disturb him greatly to violate Ollie's wish for privacy. However, he could not bear the thought that Ollie would think him merely nosey. Still, he walked on up the hill for about an hour before he came to Ollie Jordan's truck. Out of habit, he lifted the hood and looked at the engine, discovering quickly that the block was cracked. "Ollie," he said to the sky, "you stupid bastard. You didn't even have enough sense to put antifreeze in your radiator." The truck had gone as far as possible. The road ended here against some ledges rising above. It was years ago that Elman had been here, but he figured that the garden spot had to be just over the ledges. He climbed. When he reached the top, he got a glimpse of the Connecticut River valley far below, and for a moment he could imagine himself catching smallmouth bass on a warm summer night. Immediately below, Ollie's camp site was visible. Elman could just make out some sort of plastic, man-made object through the trees.

The moment he stepped down from the ledge, he felt a difference in the air. It was less windy, quieter, warmer; he could smell evergreens. There were no tracks in the snow, not even of mice or birds. The place had a kind of near-perfection about it, like an expensive shotgun that you could admire but didn't want to own because you might mar it. Whatever errors of God or man were here, they were covered with new snow. Elman wished he could glide above the surface of the land, so that he wouldn't disturb the snow with his footprints. A short way from the shelter he found firewood, covered with plastic and neatly stacked between trees: Willow's work. The boy might be an idiot, but he could do some things well, if he felt like it. Ollie never had the patience for neatness. He always threw his wood into a big pile without cover and complained when it got wet, as though it were somebody else's fault.

Beside the shelter was a table-shaped rock. Very pretty. Elman could see that the shelter once had been more elaborate, although it was difficult to tell just what the original layout was. What was left had no form, no stamp of individual mind. It was strictly shelter, as if made by an animal. Inside, Elman saw many of the items that he had helped Ollie Jordan gather. There was a clock, its face pointed toward the wall, empty cans of food lying about, a radio on the littered floor, and bits of junk everywhere. The place disturbed him. It was in such contrast with the outdoors: objects were not in their proper place, but strewn about like bones in the den of a beast; the air itself smelled sick inside the shelter. Elman was happy to get out of there.

He found Ollie and Willow beside a tree. The snow had covered the bodies, but Ollie's face was visible. The eyes were closed, the expression placid, the skin deep blue. Elman was gripped by what seemed to him a powerful realization: Snow was blue, pale blue. Water was blue and snow was one-twelfth water and therefore one-twelfth blue. Bits of sky fell with every rain, every snow. He wanted to say, "Ollie, thanks to you I now know that snow is blue." He whisked away the snow from the bodies with his cap. The boy was naked in his father's arms. They were half-sitting, half-reclining, as if on a chaise longue. They were both frozen solid, interwound so they could not be separated. Blue statues formed by some master craftsmen. They were beautiful.

Elman sat down on a log to smoke a cigarette. He didn't know what to do next. By law, he should walk down the mountain, call the cops, and lead them back up here. But he knew that Ollie hated the authorities and would not want his body or the body of his son in their hands. Elman imagined Godfrey Perkins, the town constable, spreading it all over Darby that Willow had been found bareass in his father's embrace. He would make a dirty thing of it. Howard Elman decided right then and there that whatever he was going to do, he wasn't going to turn these bodies in. He sat smoking, looking at the bodies, feeling oddly elated. He should be sorrowful or angry or revolted. As it was, he felt clean and bristling with life. The statues (he was thinking of them as statues) had put him in touch with his own life. They were, he thought, concentrated sky come to earth, and he could feel their power settle into his body. The things he saw were brighter, the smoke he drew into his lungs sharper, the quiet around him peaceful as a house after company has left. Elman basked in this mood until it began to slip away, and then he began to think, considering the bodies as a problem. He could not leave them here. Spring would come and soften the statues until they were again merely dead flesh, and dogs and wild animals would devour them. That was certainly a better fate than falling into the hands of Godfrey Perkins; but it was hardly desirable. Elman believed he had a mission to give these bodies a dignified resting place. He touched them. They were hard as stone, even the eyelids. It would be easier to move them one at a time, but difficult to chisel them free from one another without damaging them. He decided he would move them as one.

If Howard Elman was vain about anything, it was his ability to deal with mechanical problems, and he had no doubt that he could solve this one. He put his hands behind his back, like some brooding college professor, and paced in the snow. Without conscious thought, he then began to dismantle the shelter. He knew that he had solved the problem, but as yet the solution hadn't surfaced in his mind. When the idea finally burst forth, he smiled for the pleasure it gave him. He wrapped the bodies in plastic and rope from the shelter, and he fashioned a sled from its collapsed poles. He put the bodies on the sled, then paused a moment to admire his work. Even underneath the layers of plastic the beauty of the shape of the bodies interwound came through. Elman hitched a rope to the sled and tugged it. "Um, heavy," he said aloud. "But we'll get you on home, Ollie. Have no fear, Howie's here."

Howard Elman was a large and powerful man, but his burden was heavy and by the time he dragged the sled up over the ledges he was winded. After that, most of the going was downhill, and he knew he'd make it. Still, it was almost three hours before he got the bodies to his pickup truck. He levered the bodies, with sled, onto the bed of the pickup and covered them with a brown tarp. He headed for home, tired, hungry, thirsty for beer, and absolutely delighted with himself. He felt as if he had stolen some rare statues from evil forces and was bringing them to some fancy museum, which would show them off for the ages, with a plaque underneath that said, "Delivered by Howard Elman." But there was more to the feeling than just that. He was spiritually uplifted, joyous, full of wonder. He couldn't explain the feeling, even to himself, and he didn't try. He just enjoyed it.

When he got home, Elman walked into the house (he called it "the house," even though it was a trailer), and he said to Elenore, "Whoopie-do! Give me a beer."

"Get your own beer, you. You. You. What right . . ." and she could not go on, for her anger was in the way of her ability to bring form to her thoughts.

She was angry because he had been out a long time and she had worried, Elman knew. He searched around in his own mind for a means to apologize, but the best he could do was say, "I guess I'm late."

"I wish you'd call. You never call. You'd rather scare me," she said. "I don't want you to have a heart attack or get hit by a car." She said these things as if such misfortunes would be his own fault.

"I wasn't near no telephone—I was in the woods, er, hunting around," he said.

"Shooting dogs again," she said.

"Nope."

"For the life of me, I don't know why you men have to go out in the woods and shoot things."

"Crazy, crazy, crazy. We're all crazy," he said, and burst into laughter. There was such mirth in his voice, such mystery, that Elenore found it difficult to hang on to her righteous indignation.

"Well, you are in some kind of mood," she said.

"Indeed, I am."

"I imagine, then, you must have brought home some game. A rabbit? Are you going to clean me a rabbit?"

"In a manner of speaking, I brought home some game," Howard said, and laughed again.

He drank a couple of beers, and they ate supper—meatloaf with boiled potatoes and canned peas. Afterwards he said, "Elenore, that's the best meal I've ever had in my entire life."

Elenore ignored him. He always said his last meal was his best.

All that night, Howard Elman could not get over this giddy feeling. A man was not supposed to be this pleased. It was dangerous. It was the kind of thing that made you trust your fellow man—dangerous stuff.

"I tell you Elenore, happiness is as dangerous as misery," he said, right out of the blue as they were watching television.

"Then you're in trouble," she said.

Elenore didn't know what was happening, didn't care. Her husband's glorious mood was infecting her. At bed time, he took her hand. They both knew there was romance in the offing.

The next morning, Howard Elman stood outside looking at the bundle in the back of the pickup truck. Crazy, he thought. His friend Ollie was dead, and yet he couldn't help rejoicing.

"All these years, and it's only now that I realize the snow is blue," Elman said, addressing the bundle.

He lifted a corner of the tarp and looked at the bodies. The boy's face was buried in his father's bosom. Their arms were around each other.

Elman went back into the house. He didn't quite know what to do next. He couldn't leave the statues on the truck. Warm weather would come eventually and raise a stink with them, or some kid would be intrigued by the package in the bed of the truck and would steal it. This thought made Elman chuckle. He could rent freezer space at Horland's in Greenfield, Mass., perhaps visiting the statues from time to time, taking a peek at them and saying, "Hello—good-bye," which was as close as Elman could come to conjuring a prayer over the body of a friend. The freezer plan wouldn't work. Eventually, one of the employees would get curious and discover the statues. He sat in the living room of the mobile home with his coffee and some toast, and he watched part of a show on television that Elenore was following. It was on the educational channel, and he felt uplifted by that very fact. The fellow on the screen said that everything, from rocks to teardrops, was made of molecules, which he demonstrated with the help of models of little colored balls in clusters. "Chains of being," he called them. The idea of chains of being thrilled Elman and triggered something in his mind, and he was seeing Willow doing some stupid-ass thing and hearing Ollie saying, "My, what a sense of humor that boy has got," and his knowledge of the Jordans came together. In a moment, he understood the kind of love that had welded Ollie and Willow.

"Goddamn," he said.

"What is the matter with you?" Elenore asked.

"I got a secret," he said.

"Get it off your chest," she said.

"If I was to tell you, you'd wet your pants," Elman said, roaring with laughter.

"Tell," said Elenore.

"Nope."

"Not fair. If you got a secret, why tell me you got a secret and tease me? You should have shut up to begin with. But since you didn't, then tell."

"It ain't pretty," said Elman, getting serious now.

"Nothing you say is pretty. Tell."

Elman considered for a moment. He knew he couldn't keep the secret of the Jordans bottled up forever. So he told.

"That ain't a secret," Elenore said. "That knowledge is as common as dandelions."

"I know, I know. People say that, I know. But I know for sure. I tell you I know. I know it all now."

"Well, I didn't wet my pants," said Elenore, and she rose from her chair, limped toward her husband, and punched him on the shoulder.

Elman laughed and set her on his lap. "There's more to

tell," he said, and he spun his yarn about finding the bodies.

"You do what you want with Ollie and his boy, just get them out of here," she said. She should have been upset, but Howard's mood was so buoyant, it floated her somehow.

Howard Elman transferred the statues, still wrapped in plastic and a tarp, into his dump truck. It did not bother him that the corpse of a friend lay amidst trash, because Elman had no more ill feelings toward trash than an average person would have toward sawdust or earth itself. He left Cooty Patterson behind today, and set off on his trash route alone. As the morning wore on he realized the nature of his responsibility toward Ollie and Willow, and he knew where he was going to take them. He finished his work first. Work came before everything. He completed the Keene leg on his route by eleven a.m. Amazing that he could work faster alone than with Cooty. Actually, he needed Cooty—and Ollie when he was alive—to slow him, keep him from burning up his energy with work. The statues were now surrounded by piles of refuse. All his life, Ollie Jordan had been a dump rat, living off the discards of others. He must be happy now, Elman thought, and he headed the truck for Dubber, N. H.

The trailer where the old whore lived sat in a lonely spot by a swamp. The sky was huge here, and Elman took a moment to look at it. He thought of that color blue, which in concentrated form had settled into his friend. "Blue sky, I got your friend—your friend and mine," he said. The swamp itself was silver and blue with snow and patches of ice revealed by the wind. Here and there were coffee-colored stumps, decayed signs of a past age like signs of a business gone broke. In winter, it would be cold as iron here; in summer, hotter than a stray piece on a Friday night. Still, he liked the swamp, liked its isolation. He imagined that it would be a wonderful place to fool around in. The trailer was old, ugly, and small, and it tilted slightly to one side because the concrete blocks it sat on were sinking into the ground. There was some kind of hippie beads hanging in a window. He didn't have to knock because the woman came right to the door, opened it, stood there looking at him, and held her ground, making it clear he was to state his business but not come in. She was no spring chicken, but she had long, black hair and there was something undeniably alluring about her. He wanted to break the news to her kindly, but he never had the knack for kindliness, and he heard himself say next:

"I got your boys out here."

Estelle

If it hadn't been for Old Man Dorne's funeral, Estelle Jordan never would have recovered the Kinship Charm. She had known Dorne, as the Bible would say. He was a half-way decent man, even if he was a hypocrite. But they were all hypocrites. Hypocrisy rose and fell in a man just like his prick. She had learned to forgive hypocrisy—and all the other sins—when she realized how pathetic men were. She ranked Dorne as decent because he was not cruel and because he paid in cash, without quibbling. She went to a lot of funerals. She would say to herself that she should "pay her respects." In fact, respect had nothing to do with it. Estelle Jordan long ago had lost the very idea that human beings deserved respect. She liked funerals because there she could almost regain the feelings that she had lost so long ago. She would take on the emotional shimmer of widows and children, occasionally being able to draw from them just a hint of what true grief must be like. She had been so long without feelings, so hungry for feelings, that she was willing to settle for the worst, because they were the easiest to come by.

She hadn't bothered to bathe. Now if she were going to Hiram Lodge's funeral—which she hoped some day she would—she would bathe, because Lodge liked it clean, liked it neat, liked the room itself and even the bed neat and clean. Dorne wasn't like that. He was common stuff, liked it common. She sprayed on some Evening in Paris, which was what she called any cheap perfume. She dressed slowly in front of the mirror—black undies, black stockings, black dress, black veil. If she could not feel pleasure, at least she could remember what once pleasure had been like. She spent a long time looking at her breasts. Even at her age they were firm. She was glad that she had never allowed any of her children to feed from them. It angered her that nature seemed bent on destroying a woman's beauty with birthing, destroying beauty with beauty. Before she went to the funeral, she smoked a weed. Marijuana was the best she could do by way of capturing bliss.

After the funeral, Estelle had troubles with her car. She detoured to her son's place, Ike's White Elephant. Ike was not home, but Cousin Irv was, and he fixed the car. While Irv was working on the engine, she browsed about in the great warehouse where Ike stored the things he got, who knows where. Out of curiosity, she opened a big box marked "Connecticut," and there she found the Kinship Charm. She had no idea how it had gotten here. She doubted that Ollie had given it to his half-brother. The two didn't get along, and anyway the thing held no value for Ike, since its maker, Oliver, Ollie's father, was not Ike's father. Somehow, through sheer accident, Ike had acquired the charm and now planned to sell it. Well, it don't belong to him, it belongs to the heir, she thought, and she plucked it out and put it inside her dress against her bosom.

April: the weather had begun to warm. Growing time. Changing time. Love searching. The bodies must be buried. She telephoned Elman. She liked his type: blunt, not stupid, if stupidly loyal. He suggested a fitting burial, saying, "He'll love it—be enough picking for him for all eternity." Of course he was talking about Ollie, his friend. It didn't matter about

Willow because Willow had never had a self. She remembered that both Ollie and Willow had been hard to birth.

When she and Elman arrived at the landfill in the dump truck, Elman drove up beside the operator of a pay loader. The two men seemed to know each other.

"I got some bulky objects," said Elman.

"White goods?" asked the operator.

"Statues—they won't mash down too good," Elman said.

Estelle Jordan could see in her mind's eye now the bodies buried in refuse, the pay loader driving over them to pack them, then distributing dirt across the refuse until a layer was formed. She saw layer after layer, no beginning, no end. The universe itself.

"Statues?" asked the operator. "We don't get too many of those. What kind of statues?"

"Religious stuff. People praying. Saints—jeez, I don't know," said Elman.

"Who'd throw something like that away? It's disgusting," said the operator.

"You know how it goes," Elman said. "If a man makes it, eventually it's no good and winds up at the dump."

"Put 'em in that corner," said the operator, pointing. "There's a low spot there, and they'll sit comfortable; and you can dump the rest of your stuff on top, and the saints will be happy."

"As you say," said Elman, and drove off.

Elman started the dump on the truck, and Estelle Jordan could hear the hydraulic lifters underneath pushing the load. Elman motioned her out of the truck. She watched him guide the statues—she too was thinking of the bodies as statues—into a hollow of trash. Then he walked down to the statues and pulled back the tarp. A moment later he said, "Well, I got my last look," and he walked away.

Estelle Jordan did not know she wanted a private moment with Ollie and Willow until Elman had left to give her that moment. She was wearing boots but it was hard walking in all that trash. The place stank of garbage once she got down out of the wind. She looked at the face of Ollie, blue and oddly calm, certainly calmer than it had been in life. Willow's face was turned away from her, into the bosom of his father. That was best, she thought. She remembered the day Oliver died now and she envied Ollie's ability to forget that terrible moment. Of course, in the end, he had paid. Ollie was a good boy. She had not seduced him. He had not come after her. They had just fallen in together after drinking, as was the way with the kinship in those days.

It had been a warm summery day when Oliver died. She was playing outside with the baby, Willow. Ollie was there, too. He was just sixteen himself, just as she had been sixteen when Oliver had taken her out of a shack in Sullivan town. Ollie liked playing with the baby. He was, she thought, more like a mother than she was. Then Oliver had come on the scene, drunk as a skunk. After that it was unclear in her mind just what had happened. There was an argument. Oliver threatened the baby—he never liked the baby; he knew where it had come from. Or, perhaps, Ollie thought that he threatened the baby, for Ollie had been drinking too. She remembered that Oliver had said, "He's an idiot. He'd be better off dead." She didn't remember them as fighting exactly. Oliver had grabbed Ollie by the shoulders, as a drunken father will, and they began to turn and step lively, like dancers, until they fell and Ollie was bashing out his father's brains on the stone wall near the family shack. She told the cops Oliver had fallen from a ledge.

Then Ollie forgot, and she ceased to feel. For months Ollie walked around like a zombie, knowing not even his name. Then one day he said to her, "You're the Witch." He recovered his memory, but not all of it, not that part that would hurt. It was she who had the hurt, so much of it that she had nothing. The name "Witch" stuck with her. She realized that that's the way it was with men. They did evil, and then they blamed women. Ask Eve. Call me Witch: woman who cannot feel, she thought.

She removed the charm from the inside of her dress, looking at it for a moment before surrendering it. Oliver had made it as a gift for her. It was the closest he ever came to telling her he loved her. He could carve pretty well, but he needed a model to work from, and he used to get angry because the final product never looked exactly like the model. Still, she could not imagine how Ollie could have seen a butterfly in the carving. She saw no such butterfly. The charm was what it was, nothing more. Oliver had carved the charm by copying the label from a bottle of Four Roses whiskey. She tucked the charm into a nook between the faces of Ollie and Willow. "Good luck," she whispered. The day was getting warmer. She could feel the sun stroking her cheek. She could feel a breath of air sweep down into the hollow and cleanse it. It was spring air. She could feel it. She could feel a great welling up inside of her. These boys, as statues, had released her.

"My sons, my sons," she said, and wept.

THE PASSION
OF
ESTELLE JORDAN

1

A Voice

The Witch stepped out onto the second-story landing from her apartment in the auction barn, and lit her corncob pipe. Usually, she didn't smoke until the sun was falling over the hills, but at changes of seasons she might draw down half a bowl before lunch, not enough to get her stoned, just enough to put a halo of yellow around things. Another Jordan might have turned to the bottle, but not the Witch. She hated booze. It was sewage, running through the Jordan bloodlines like shit in a stream. With a wave of her hand she made as if to shoo the spring breeze as it caressed her skin. She didn't trust touch, even a touch from nature; every touch was a frisk, somebody wanting something. Not a house in sight—glad for that. Fields, trees, even the air—greening up. All of Darby, all of Tuckerman County—greening up. Oppressive. To distract herself from the green, she invited the toke to sharpen the sounds of the countryside: birds (yammering like cheapskates), the wind (ambling through the trees like a satisfied pickpocket), the highway (moaning as if the rub of tires hurt), and, finally, a tractor-trailer truck (swearing slowly through its gears). She watched it chug over the hill and then down onto the straightaway that ran past the auction barn. It picked up speed and vanished into new foliage. Its power sent a subtle trembling through her, and without thinking about it she ran her hands across her blouse and down to her hips, as she might when posing for a customer. ("I like a man with a bulge in his billfold," she would say.)

Her eyes swept back along the highway. The road and the sky were milky and yellow in the late-morning light. Everything else was green or becoming green. She sucked on her pipe. Her eye stopped roaming an instant before her mind registered a thought: something wrong, nature's makeup smudged. A gleam in the trees, a black-and-silvery gleam. What did it matter to her? She turned away and walked down the wooden staircase. It shuddered under her footfalls. Like everything else built by Jordan men, it was rickety, whacked together, barely functional.

Piled against the barn were discarded electric stoves and refrigerators. It had been a couple of years since her son Ike had died—shot to death by an unknown assailant—but his son Critter had yet to move everything out, even though he had closed down Ike's auction business. The Witch guessed the white goods would be there long after she was gone.

The four-wheel-drive Subaru she'd absconded with when old man Williamson died was the only car in the parking lot. The mud was drying out. Soon it would be dusty. She wished Critter would pave it. She decided to have a look at the garden before leaving. It hid behind some briars. Delphina Jordan, Critter's wife, had broken the soil here, raising tomatoes, peas, green beans, and summer squash. The Witch grew only one crop, marijuana. Old man Williamson, who had been opposed to her vice, nonetheless had advised her how to plant it. "You put the toke in the ground when you put the tomatoes in the ground, day after Memorial Day, when the danger of a killing frost has passed."

The sight of the garden, dark and moist, awaiting her hand, changed her inside, tore away the protective shield of her anger. She was all soft now—could be hurt. She had to resist an impulse to kneel in the dirt. She remembered a young, shabby girl, violated, weighed down with children, bone-weary from hours in a shoe shop. She could see that poor girl now, shaking, lonely, sick to her stomach from ugliness (although at the time she didn't know that's what it was that sickened the human heart: ugliness). She remembered the stink of the shop. It soaked her clothes, infiltrated the pores of her skin. The stink was a mixture of smells, the burnt smell of raw leather, the acid smell that was the ache of machines, the nauseating smell that was the toil of human bodies. She had turned to the factory to get away from whoring. Oliver had said, "Go ahead. Try some real work for a change." Six months later, defeated by the shoe shop, she went back to her profession. After that any physically demanding labor filled her with loathing and sadness. But when old man Williamson had introduced her to gardening, he had made the work seem like exercise or play, even worship, an activity to make a person affectionate, strong, whole. With Williamson's spirit in mind, she'd made all sorts of plans to raise vegetables when she moved into the auction barn. But when she'd felt the raw touch of the earth, all the work fears returned, so she planted only what she needed.

The Witch knew something was wrong from the moment her car pulled out of the long driveway of the auction barn onto the state road. She felt more than saw the flash of black and silver, the way she felt betrayal in a man's eyes in the split second before he raised his hand to strike her. It was the same black-and-silver gleam she'd seen in the woods from the landing, a black Trans Am, the kind young men drove. It had been waiting for her, and as soon as she had turned toward Tuckerman, it had jumped on her tail.

She drove on, watching in the rearview mirror. The Trans Am kept a distance, just far enough away so she could not see the face of the driver. She speeded up. The Trans Am speeded up. She slowed. The Trans Am slowed. She felt almost as if she controlled it, even while she understood it controlled her, since it was the Trans Am (her mind welded car to driver) that chose the measure of distance between them.

"What's your game, sonny?" She spoke as if the Trans Am could hear her; if he were close, she had no doubt she could wither him with a witch's look.

Had to be a kid. No grown man would own one of those cars; no grown man would follow an old whore. Some kid driving, following, maybe drinking, for sure thinking, thinking, jacking off to beat hell, she bet. She was mad. Not because she had anything against masturbation or against someone taking pleasure from thoughts about her. What angered her was not being compensated for that pleasure.

The Trans Am roared up until it was only a few feet from the rear bumper of the Subaru. She saw now in the rearview mirror that the driver was wearing a black mask. Before this had time to sink in, the Trans Am fell behind her a bit, accelerated, then passed her, its metal skin almost (it seemed) scraping her own skin. In a few seconds, it was gone, rocketing ahead at speeds she herself had never known.

Something happened then that she did not expect and could not have explained. Her anger passed, replaced by another feeling both familiar and alien, a tangle of premonition and memory, desire and terror. She twisted the car mirror so she could see her face. It was old. She looked at her hands on the steering wheel. They resembled bandages that needed changing. She imagined herself aging—next year, sixty, then seventy, eighty, ninety, a hundred, and beyond, each age presenting itself as a mental photograph until there was nothing but bones, cobwebs, and green dust, and suddenly she was young again, beautiful, soft, fresh. The images faded, while the feeling that brought them on drove deeper into her. She bit the side of her palm, to experience with her mouth the trembling of her hand.

On the outskirts of Tuckerman, she turned into a dirt drive almost as long as the one at the auction barn. At the end was a two-story wood-frame house that had been so many years without paint the clapboards were weathered as barn siding: her son Donald's place. In the yard was a single elm tree, dead, and some grass but no lawn as such, some brush but no bushes, nothing planted by a hand. The view from the house consisted in all directions of junked cars, parked on the undulating acreage as if by nature, that is, in no particular order, left not even by the whim of the fellows who parked them but by convenience with no respect or attention to an idea of order: this the Witch recognized as Jordan order.

Kin and kinship—no escape. She had kin everywhere in Tuckerman County and nowhere else. Nothing she could do about it. She was in the kinship; it was in her; she was here; it was here. No escape. But she did not want to escape. The kinship, bad as it was, was preferable to the common run. She accepted this proposition without question, out of habit, an idea as deeply ingrained in her as the will to breathe or dream.

When she got out of her car, she scanned the area hoping to catch sight of Donald, for she knew he wouldn't be in the house at this time of day. He'd probably be in the shop, a four-bay concrete-block garage where Donald and his crew of kin worked on cars. No women were allowed in the building, but there was always the possibility she might get a glimpse of him in the junkyard or walking to his tow truck.

Donald Jordan was known locally as Tuckerman County's most creative swearing man, a character, intelligent perhaps, but ignorant and backward. But to the Witch and to others in the Jordan clan Donald was a pillar in their community, level, stable, almost kindly in his rebuffing ways, somewhat shrewd in business dealings, a man with deep knowledge of the kinship, a man to respect. He was her only living child, and she was proud of him and proud of herself for having given him life. Yet Donald was also a sore on her soul that would never heal. She'd had Ollie at sixteen, Ike at seventeen, Donald ten months later when she was still seventeen. She was just a child herself, and she couldn't handle another baby. Oliver didn't want him—Donald wasn't his; only Ollie was his. The state took Donald away from her. He was raised first in foster homes and later by this kin or that, whoever would offer succor. Of her children, he was the least ill-made. The Witch suspected he had turned out well for the very reason that he had been kept away from her during his formative years. He didn't call her mother or by her name, Estelle; like any other Jordan, he called her Witch, and his coolness toward her was a constant punishment. It was a punishment she accepted as her due and without a whimper, except that she longed to tell him, "Think what you will of this old whore, but don't hate that poor girl that bore you; mourn for her." But of course she could never say such a thing, and he could never hear it even if she could say it.

She watched a small boy dash from the house, run around the tree, and then vanish into the wilderness of junk cars, there, presumably, to play. Moments later a woman called through the screened door of the back porch. "Rickey... Rickey? Rickeeeeee?... Time to go.... Right now.... Or else." It was a weak summons, full of concern but with no authority, and the boy did not respond to it.

The Witch recognized the voice of Noreen Cook, a distant cousin. In the sense that everyone in the kinship knew all about everyone else in the kinship, the Witch knew all about Noreen. She was among the lowest of the low in the clan: a woman who didn't work steady, two kids, no husband. Until now the Witch had never paid Noreen any attention, but her encounter with the Trans Am had triggered a change...in her ...the world...something...somebody. In Noreen's voice she heard a voice within a voice. She knew absolutely that the second voice (that she realized did not exist except in her imagination) would hold great importance for her, although it puzzled her why she should entertain such a strange thought. The odd suspicion dawned on her that Noreen possessed something that belonged to her.

They met on the porch. Noreen was frail without being bony, her skin fair without being washed out; her whiteness contrasted with the Witch's darkness; her hair was the color of dried grasses.

"I wish you'd cast a spell on that boy of mine, because mind he won't," Noreen said.

"Smack his face." The harshness in the Witch's tone made Noreen wince.

"I can't bear to lay a hand on him, and he knows it." Noreen quivered but did not move, like a dog that expects to be punished.

Noreen: wasting herself on ungrateful men, how stupid, how unconscious. It would be a pleasure to smack *her*. In the conjuring lens of her mind, the Witch watched herself raise her hand and bring it down against Noreen's prissy little mouth. So she was shocked by the sound of her own voice, soft and kind, and by the words she uttered: "Boys are hard to raise— they got no smarts."

Her expression, too, must have softened, because across Noreen's face spread the joy and courage of one forgiven by a superior.

"You have ahold of your life?" Noreen held up a tiny, doubled fist.

7

A flicker of anger flared in the Witch, and she slighted the question with a smirk. But Noreen took it as a smile of encouragement.

"I wish...I wish...I wish somebody would take hold of my life," Noreen said.

The Witch enveloped Noreen's fist with her own hands. *Squeeze her, squeeze the stupidity from her.* But she did not squeeze. She opened Noreen's fist, as if setting free a bird. With that, something passed between the Witch's anger and her kindness. Strange and incomprehensible it was, a mirror appearing out of nowhere, reflecting not a recognizable image but a slash of silver light; then, nothing.

Noreen sensed something of the strangeness in the Witch. "Gee," she said.

With no further talk the Witch and Noreen joined the other Jordan women in the kitchen—Donald's wife Tammy, her daughter-in-law Jayne, and Delphina Jordan, Critter's wife. As in all Jordan houses, children came and went, toddling on floors perpetually gritty.

The women sat around a big polyurethaned pine-board table, littered with coffee cups, dirty plates, two ashtrays almost overflowing, cereal boxes, a blow dryer, toys, a *People* magazine, last week's *TV Guide*, and other items. There was hardly room for an elbow. The Witch never noticed the clutter, but she was aware in an odd way, like a grief, of the cigarette-burn scars on the table and dents made by children.

The Witch took her place at the head of the table, where a chair had been left for her. Noreen sat off to the side in a straight-back chair against the wall.

"Rickey won't come in," Noreen announced her troubles.

"Kids—you have 'em to keep you sane, and then they drive you crazy," said Tammy, whom the Witch rated as good-natured with a brain capacity the size of a hedgehog's.

"Call one of those lazy men to fetch him." Delphina Jordan emphasized the word *lazy,* and pointed at the CB mike hanging from the wall.

Tammy and Jayne tittered in agreement. Noreen wasn't sure whether to take the suggestion seriously.

With her long, bleached-blond hair, her huge breasts, and her voluptuous body full with child, Delphina was an impressive sight. By Jordan standards, she was magnificent.

"Still waitressing?" Delphina addressed Noreen.

"I took the day off. Split shifts are killing me. On my feet all the time. I'd give anything for a job where I could get off my feet."

The Witch scorned Noreen with a laugh. If there was anyone who had made a living off her feet it was the Witch. All the women but Noreen shifted uncomfortably in their chairs. Noreen seemed about to say something, thought better of it, then stared blankly ahead, in protective, enforced semi-catatonia. The women picked up on the conversation they had been having before the Witch entered the room.

"Donald says to me, he says, 'Don't call the garage on the CB—it's for emergencies,'" Tammy reported. "I says to him, I says, 'Well, why our whole lives is an emergency.' He says to me, he says—"

"I'll call him and ask him the time of day." The Witch exercised her right to interrupt Tammy.

"I believe you would," Tammy lied.

The Witch was bluffing of course, and the other women, except perhaps for Noreen, knew she was bluffing, but none would call her on it.

The Witch's ascendancy within the clan was of a special kind. It was not based on her ability to provide succor, but on her character and on the life she'd lived. While no one talked to her about her past, she knew much of it was well-known in the kinship and much discussed behind her back. They could see in her what the kinship was, in all its terrible intimacy.

Little Ollie, the Witch's great-grandchild, ran to the Witch and demanded attention. She hoisted him up and without meaning to looked deeply into his eyes. They squirmed with the wormy markings of the Jordan clan. The child, aware now of the eyes of the Witch (his own eyes full of pain and experience in the kinship), let out a single scream, like an animal caught in a trap. The Witch put him down and Ollie ran to Delphina, his mother.

She called for a sweet, and Jayne responded by fishing out a half a doughnut from under the *TV Guide*. Delphina shoved it in Ollie's mouth, and the boy quieted, crawling under the table with his prize.

Everyone was silent for a moment, and then Delphina let out an exaggerated moan, to gather her audience. She patted her great tummy, and said, "I'll be glad when this son comes into the world, because for all the world I'm tiring of carrying him."

"How you know it's going to be a him?" the Witch asked.

"I just know."

"You just know how to make boys, do you?" The sarcasm in the Witch's tone elicited supporting laughter from Tammy and Jayne.

Delphina folded her arms and let them fall on her belly, a pose that said, "Okay, you win, Witch, but I'm still royalty."

She treats her pregnancy like it was money in the bank—and she's right to do so, thought the Witch. Delphina probably would have a dozen kids, and with the birth of each she would grow stronger. The Witch saw her as a rival.

Why do you worry about such things? the Witch asked herself. By the time Delphina has all those children and the ascendancy they'll bring her, you'll be long dead or locked up in the loony bin like Romaine. The Witch couldn't remember the last time she'd thought about her mother, and now without warning she appeared in her mind, heavy-bodied and raven-haired, washing the child Estelle's face in cold streamwater. Romaine, why couldn't you have had the courtesy to die like Daddy? *Maybe when she passes on she'll take the ache she left me with.*

Romaine Jordan was in Concord, only seventy miles from Darby. But the Witch hadn't seen her mother in thirty years. Nothing scared the collective minds of Jordans like mental illness, and when Romaine had been committed to the state mental hospital, she might as well have been banished from the kinship. No Jordan would think of visiting kin in an institution, out of fear for his own sanity and concern for his fellow Jordans: mental illness was catching and Jordans were susceptible.

The women jabbered on, the Witch giving them less and less of her attention. Finally, bored, she left them without excusing herself, walking to the back porch. The sun was warm on the unpainted wooden floor, and she could feel the heat reflect up under her skirt. The air against her face was still a little cool, and the contrast of temperatures excited her. She went outside and sat on the steps, looking out on the junk cars, seeing them, but taking no heed of them. She was there less than a minute when Noreen joined her.

The Witch fixed her with a glare, and Noreen winced slightly. Noreen spoke a word then the Witch rarely heard, her own name.

"Estelle—Estelle?" The second "Estelle" was a barely audible whisper. *Who calls me, speaking from Noreen's throat?*

Below, in the maze of derelict automobiles, was Donald's shop. The Witch pointed at it. "Down there," she said. "That's where you'll find your Rickey. When they can, boys play near men."

11

"Right now, I don't care—let him do what he wants. I'm sick of my children—they tire me; I'm sick of my feet—they hurt me; I'm sick of work, and I'm sick of never having no money." On the verge of tears, Noreen brushed away spits of blond hair that fell onto her forehead. It was the kind of gesture that warmed a man, the Witch noted.

She felt no pity for Noreen, but rather a kind of desire, not sexual exactly, but close to it. Noreen smelled faintly of her own sweat and perfume, and her skin had the newness of the spring's growth.

"So, you disturb me for advice," the Witch said.

"I need an income and some time to myself," Noreen said. "I've been thinking. Your business. Maybe you could show me, get me started."

"You want to become a whore." The Witch dragged out the word *whore*—"*ho-wahhhhh.*"

Noreen sat stock-still, halted by the sudden turn of the Witch's tone, hard and cruel.

The Witch went on, dropping her voice to a malicious hush. "There ain't a job in Tuckerman County would appeal to you, Noreen. You're lazy and horny; you figure why not take money for what you've been giving away. You look at me and you say to yourself, 'Now there's a woman's made a living on her back.'"

The Witch shifted her body so that it almost touched Noreen's. "But the world has changed, Noreen. It's not what it was when I started out, my skin soft and silky as the petal of a rose. In those days, single girls were shy to give it, and married ladies often served it cold. No man wants cold cuts for his main meal. So, they would come to me, hungry for something hot. But today good, stout fellows don't need to pay no whore. They get it for free and they get it hot. The leftovers is what you're going to get—fellows with problems, fellows who want to hurt you, or who got private ideas about sex that will make you want to go to church and ask, 'Why do You allow this?'"

"Allow?" Noreen mumbled the word.

"You have to understand," the Witch said, "this old whore makes her living on old boys she's known for years, fellows with troubles you're too young to understand, like sickness and dying and loss. They talk more than do; they need to talk it out, to talk it up. I know when to listen, when to speak, and when to take my teeth out."

"Old men?" Noreen said with loathing.

"Once they get past your petal-soft skin, Noreen, they're going to see you ain't worth pissing on."

Although her words were cruel, the Witch had dropped her voice to a whisper, almost kindly.

"Something 'else, Noreen. I've seen your boyfriends. You don't pick 'em too good. You think they hurt you now, just wait until they're paying for it. Your problem, Noreen, is you're dumb; you got no judgment; you got no experience. All you got is an idea to improve yourself and an itchy twat for talent. It's not enough today. Today you got to have an education or wisdom. You ain't never going to have either."

Noreen began to weep softly. "I know what you're saying," she said. "You're trying to save me."

The Witch drew away.

When she had finished crying, Noreen shouted, "Rickey! Rickey!" and miraculously the boy came running. Noreen smiled at the Witch in gratitude.

The Witch smiled inwardly. Noreen would have been tough competition. Men liked young stuff, especially young stuff as naturally dumb as Noreen. As a dog's hunger was excited by the smell of a rotting carcass, so was the lust of a man excited by "naturally dumb."

Noreen and the boy left hurriedly. The Witch watched them sputter off in a yellow Volkswagen bug.

The Witch lunched, gossiped, and played some with little Ollie. The child seemed to have forgotten that he had been frightened earlier by his great-grandmother's eyes. With no more than a "See-ya-later," she left at her usual time, around two. Jordans came and went with bare amenities. They rarely shook hands, rarely embraced, and never exchanged more than a word or two of greeting or farewell. Jordans appeared and disappeared from a scene. They reserved touch for important activities, such as sex and fighting; their ceremonies of succor and ascendancy passed among them invisible and unspoken, if not unfelt.

Outside, the Witch took a long look at the garage where Donald worked. The building was plain, unmarked, and unpainted, like a beaver lodge in its dismalness. On impulse, she began to walk toward the garage.

Of her children, Donald was the only one living and the only one who had risen above her in the kinship. He owned ascendancy over her not because she needed him for succor (she needed no one); not because she feared him (although she did and was happy to feel that fear); not because of the shame of having abandoned him (although the shame was there, like grinding sand on a pair of knees); but because she sought to protect him from herself. She had a feeling, not so clear that she could have explained it in words, that her love was a killing thing. There was a curious power latent in this idea, for if she should ever want ascendancy over Donald, it would be there for the taking. She had no such intention. She was content to surrender her ascendancy to him.

Three of the garage bays were open. She couldn't bring herself to go in. Donald had a rule: no women in the shop. So she stopped at the closed door, where she couldn't be seen by the men inside, and she listened. She heard metal clashing, compressors passing gas, engines revving, and screechings whose sources she could not identify. Sometimes the sounds

14

were tidier, tinklier—wrenches turning bolts into place, hammers pinging metal, air whistling as it left tires, fenders responding almost with a sexual *uh!* as they were hit by rubber mallets. She heard muffled discussions of the current job spiced with Donald's creative swearing. She heard no talk about people, events, sports, or movies. No music played because Donald banned radios from the shop.

No women, no impressions allowed from the outside—Donald's rules made perfect sense to the Witch. In his work life, which consisted of perhaps all but two hours of his every waking moment, Donald had narrowed the world to a dent.

The closed door suddenly roared open, sliding upward on its tracks, and the Witch stood revealed before the maw of the garage. She had an image of herself being run over by a car, but she did not move. Neither car nor man approached the door. It had opened for no reason that she could fathom. She could see men working now, but they were all busy and did not notice a woman standing in the bright light of the day, only one step from the inside of the shop.

She watched Donald inspect a piece of metal, turning it over and over in his hands. She understood. The knowledge of the mind was useless without the knowledge of the hands. At eye level beside him was a welding torch, a hose uncoiling from it. Because the torch hung from a wire the Witch could not see, it resembled a snake about to strike. She imagined herself reaching out, interwining with the snake, suffocating it in her bosom to prevent it from striking its fangs into the neck of her son.

Working on cars dirtied a normal man. Grease streaked his hands and face with black marks; grit got under his fingernails and over time wore into the folds of his skin. Eventually, even his sweat appeared soiled. Not Donald. He didn't look dirty; he looked reconstituted. Exposure to steel and the fallout of automotive lubricants had given his skin a permanent, metallic

15

sheen. He changed his blue overall jumpsuit so rarely it had ceased to resemble denim but rather some rare cloth—stiff, dark, slick as black light reflected off water. Standing perfectly still, his welder's mask tipped on top of his head, he might have been a model for a statue honoring the mechanics of America.

Shadow obscured his face; she wanted to see it before she left, assure herself that this was really Donald, her only living son. But she dared not step into the shop, dared not call out his name. She waited, stupefied as Noreen had been minutes ago. As Donald reached for the torch, it appeared to the Witch that it was the torch that had snapped at the hand, and now shook it. A light cut across her eyes. Fire spewed from Donald's hand; hand and fire became one. He turned toward her then, slowly, head bowed, as one asking for succor. She strained to see his face. But he flipped the welder's mask down, and it was as if he had no face, as if the flesh of him had petrified into the things he worked—metal, glass, rubber, plastic, petroleum. The torch cut into metal. The light whitened until it was blinding; sparks flew. She felt a surge of desire for the light. She reached out to touch it even as she backed away from the garage, heading for her car. In that moment, she recognized the voice she had heard in Noreen's voice; it was her own from years ago.

2

Mired

"Well?" Avalon Hillary turned to his wife, sitting in her rocking chair. She looked strange to him, no knitting in her lap, no cookbook, no newspaper. Nothing.

Melba smiled faintly at him. That was a surprise. Usually she'd sound off at him if he tried to butt into her thoughts.

"There's something about the way you're sitting—all loose," Avalon said. He was going to add "your hands unoccupied," but that was foolish.

"I'm just tired," she said.

He found himself uncomfortable, as if the air in the room were draining away. He wanted to say to Melba, "Wouldn't you like to just get away, suffer our old age in Florida or Arizona, anyplace but New Hampshire?" Instead he said, "I'm heading on out to dig that ditch."

"Maybe you could sit with me for a minute or two," she said.

"Melba, I've been trying to find the time to do this job for weeks now." It surprised him that he was sharp with her.

"Of course you have," she said.

These last words sat in Avalon's mind as he hurried outside into the bright spring sun. It wasn't what she had said that unsettled him somewhat, but the way she had said it, completely without sarcasm. Is that my gal? he asked himself. Something told him to rush back into the house, but he continued to walk on. He was a farmer, and work came before any urges a man might have. By the time he reached the backhoe, parked on the concrete slab at the lower edge of the barn, he had dispatched Melba from his thoughts and turned his attention to the job at hand.

Avalon, astride his backhoe—"like a goddamn Wild West cowpoke," he said to himself—began digging a drainage ditch in the field that unrolled from his house and barn like a wrinkled green carpet. He didn't really need to dig the ditch. The low spot had been there for generations of Hillary holsteins. When it rained they avoided it. No problem. But it had rankled him for years: unproductive land. And, too, he wanted an excuse to mount the backhoe—Yankee cowpoke, *eeyaha!* He shouted the exclamation in his mind. From the sitting height of the backhoe his fields seemed thicker, lusher, greener. And his girls (Avalon's nickname for his cows) seemed to pay him more attention when he had the backhoe to bulk out his pathetic human form. Ma-ooed in appreciation of his efforts to make them content, they did. Oh, sure. His daughter Julia now hogged into his thoughts. "They are not your girls, Daddy. They are cows—animals. Even if they were human, they still would not be your girls, because they are adults. They would be women. A cow is not a female person; a woman is not a girl." People these days twisted around the things you said into the goddamnedest knots.

Avalon did not dwell upon this thought, nor did he dwell upon his sense of exhilaration at driving the backhoe, the sudden apprehension of natural things upon his nostrils (the smell of the river through the fumes of the backhoe). Thoughts, emotions, memories zipped through his mind with the ease of his old Buick speeding on I-91 on the other side of the river. Not that Avalon Hillary was an insensitive or unreflective man. Quite the opposite. His wife Melba would say, "You do brood," and he would answer, "I do brood." It was just that Avalon

Hillary was of little importance to Avalon Hillary. What was important, what Avalon brooded about, was the farm.

It was acknowledged locally that the Hillary farm had for generations produced the best holstein herds in Tuckerman County. Yet Avalon took no pride in his standing among his peers. Rather, it was a burden to him. "Keeping up" was how Avalon put it to himself, keeping up with the legacy of his father and grandfather, keeping up with the demanding spirit of the farm itself. He, Avalon Hillary, was hardly a being unto himself. He was but one part of the farm, no more important than a cow or a shed or a tractor or a clod of earth. A cow made milk, a shed provided shelter, a tractor did work, a clod of earth grew feed, and a man schemed out the factors, the "work and worry." He did this not for himself, but for the farm. It seemed to Avalon that after sixty years he'd had not a rich life or a poor life, but no life at all, except insofar as his life was a cell in the greater life of the farm. A beast the farm was, wiggly with life and death, and yet unfeeling, unthinking; a blob, an idea; critical and judgmental by the fact alone of its being.

Thank God for Melba. She had warmed him, steadied him, and, most important, listened to him. He was a man other men looked up to, came to for help, or held at arm's length as a rival. He wasn't naturally chummy. He'd had plenty of work and worry, but no one of his own sex to sound off to. So he talked to Melba. Sometimes she said, "No, you shouldn't do that" (usually he ignored her advice); sometimes she heartily agreed with him (not often) and he swelled inside; sometimes she laughed in his face; sometimes she patted him as if he were a beloved dog; sometimes she never said a word. She had become his friend, his only friend. She had her own problems—the bad ticker, the children who seemed content to keep miles between themselves and the farm (they sensed it wanted to consume them), the sheer loneliness of a large,

19

empty house, secret hurts from a rough-and-tumble upbringing. He knew these things in her, and yet he could offer little
more than his presence for comfort. He could tell her his
problems, which of course were the problems of the farm, but
he could not listen to her problems. She understood a man
could not receive a burden while he unburdened himself, so
she bore up and kept a silence about her own troubles. He
knew her and he knew nothing about her. Face it—he'd failed
her. He wished somehow to make it up to her, to understand
her as she understood him, if not for justice's sake, for no
better reason than to satisfy his curiosity about her. Melba,
you know this poor soul—now tell me about thee. There was
only one way to accomplish this—get out from under the farm.
Then maybe he could pay her some attention.

But their chance had gone by. Some big business group had
approached him. Wanted to put up a shopping mall in his fields.
Asked him what he'd take for his acreage. He'd quoted a staggering sum. They said okay. The thought of the money had
ridden over the ghosts of his father and grandfather and over
the voice of the living, demanding farm. Nor, surprisingly, had
he felt any guilt about selling out. Merely relief. He'd done his
duty all those years, so he didn't owe the farm anything, and
there had been so much money involved the practical thing
to do was take it. If nothing else, Hillary men were practical-
minded. His father and grandfather would have done the same
thing, taken the money, although he suspected they would
have criticized him for doing so. Town politics had done him
in, that and bad luck. After a town vote had defeated a proposal
to rezone the land, the Magnus people had left and built their
mall in Tuckerman.

He was right back where he started, except dairy farming,
which had been difficult to begin with, now was agony for
him. He had put the place up for sale, but the legal heap

surrounding the mall issue had composted and composted, and the heat from it had scared off potential buyers. He had no choice but to continue draining udders for a market glutted with dairy products. Work and worry had become a crucifix across his shoulders. Yet he worked on, worried on—did his best for the farm. He knew no other way. There was something in him that could not stand to do badly. As long as it was his farm, he'd push, push, push, make it a grand farm. What sickened him most was that he had shifted some of the weight of the crucifix to Melba. Dear wife, I'm sorry, and I heartily promise to amend my life.

He had reached the low spot, the backhoe bucking and belching all the way. He stood up, straddling the metal seat, and perused the sitation. Not that he didn't know what he was going to do. He had mulled over this job many times, along with maybe six or seven thousand other jobs that should get done but didn't need to and that therefore probably wouldn't. The last thing he'd think about before drifting off to sleep at night would be how to do a particular job, particularly one that didn't have to get done, the had-to-be-dones being no bringers of sleep. But now that he was about to do the actual work, he'd give the land a long look. He was a cautious man, even while he was a daring one. (He brooded his way toward decision, never did anything rash, but he did like to experiment. Once, he'd volunteered his cows when a university fellow had come up with a plan to remove an embryo from a superior cow and place it in the uterus of an inferior cow. The practice was routine today, and because Avalon had got in on it early he had a leg up on other farmers locally. The supercow he'd produced was worth more than the rest of the herd put together.)

The low spot, in fact, was a high spot, but a hump of earth blocked water from running off. He'd carve a three-foot-deep trench through the hump for forty feet or so. He should start on the dry side, work his way through the hump, finally chew out the last dam of earth holding back ankle-deep water. He looked hard. My, how that low spot looked inviting. Saw grasses unfit for a civilized cow; useless reeds; the puddling up of water like the pursed lips of some Upper Darby grand lady; insects hanging around like lazy teenagers—the more he thought about the low spot, the more he took it personally; unproductive land! And the more he wanted to bring it into the functioning farm.

"Goddamn," he said, settling into his saddle, gunned the engine, and started forth, heading not for the high, dry side but for the low, wet side. He felt giddy as his ancestors must have felt burning off the forest to pasture the first cows in this valley.

There was a *splook!* as the backhoe chugged into the low spot. He knew in an instant something was wrong. He'd driven this old backhoe for fifteen years, and in all the places he had brought it, it had never made a noise like that. He peered over the side and looked at the earth. The cool water was clouding up. The tires had sunk a foot and a half into muck. He tried to shrug off the feeling of impending disaster. He raised the great arm of the backhoe and scooped out some earth. It was dark, peaty. Maybe he'd save some for Melba's garden. Looked like good stuff for flowerbeds.

The trouble came when he tried to drive forward. The huge rear wheels spun, kicking up enough mud to discourage General Patton. He let up on the gas, noticing the wheels had sunk in another foot.

He was suddenly furious, blindly so—like he'd never been in his life, it seemed to him. He jumped out of the saddle, landing feet first in the muck. It grabbed his work shoes. Icy water seeped in over the tops into his socks. "Goddamn, son-of-a-goddamn, g-d." His voice petered out. He was so angry he could not even cuss properly, so angry he did another stupid thing. He put his shoulder to one of the wheels. He knew even as he heaved no man could succeed at this. Still, he heaved and heaved, and goddamn the illogic of the act; he heaved some more.

The anger left him all at once with the realization he was exhausted, dizzy. A crunching sensation radiated across his chest. He fell back into the mud, landing on his bottom like some fool. Oh, Lord, he thought, I'm having a heart attack. Can't die here, sitting down like this. He got a glimpse of the saddle of the backhoe, and an image came to his mind of a cowboy breathing his last on the desert floor. Never saw the desert, never saw anything but this g-d farm. Don't count those two weeks in the Virgin Islands, Lord—that was vacation. Oh, Lord, if you get me out of this, I'll get out from under the farm. I promise. I'll take Melba to Spain or Fitchburg, Mass., wherever she wants to go. Oh, Lord, save this poor wreck for another day. What had always been in doubt, the existence of this presumed "Lord," now seemed cemented in reality. In the wisdom of dying was God. Oh, Lord, if you want me to die like this, in the g-d mud, okay. But frankly I don't feel ready to go. Semi-prepared for death, Avalon awaited his end.

He looked up at the seat of the backhoe. Did he want to die in the saddle, did he? He imagined himself struggling up to it, singing out his last words to humanity—*Eeyahh!* No, he'd never make it up there. He'd only keel over and fall back into the mud. Crawl—I'll crawl. He might make it out of this swamp, to the house, to die in Melba's arms.

A moment later, or maybe it was five minutes, Avalon felt a little better. His vision was no longer edged in yellow. His chest hurt less; he was breathing hard, but not as hard as before. He stood, wavered a bit, and took a step forward.

By the time he reached the house, he felt tired, really weary, and sore, but he was breathing normally, and his chest no longer hurt. He was now aware how muddied up he was. Would Melba laugh at him, take pity, scold him? He was almost amused, wondering what she would think of her husband in this disreputable state, when he found her, in her rocking chair, her skin blue, no pulse—gone to her heaven.

3

The Tremor
and the Trans Am

Toothless, Estelle Jordan slowly sipped orange juice, slowly chewed mushy oatmeal, slowly drank black coffee, her eyes attending to the portable television set on the kitchen table, but her mind far away from the *Today* show or *Good Morning America*, whatever was on. It didn't matter; the TV's only reason for being was to provide company. She divided her thoughts between practical matters (cleaning up after last night's customer) and memory (a young girl feeding on soft foods and the crust of her own humiliation).

Her natural teeth had begun to rot in her teen years. A few men had complained to Oliver about the ugliness in her mouth. She too had complained—about the dull ache of tooth decay. One evening Oliver had made her drink whiskey until she was blind drunk, and then he had pulled out all her teeth. Even through the haze of alcohol, the pain had been bright and clear. But there had been something else, the skim of an emotion riding on the pain, some mixture of fear and desire, a response to the dim realization that Oliver enjoyed inflicting the pain. Pain, pleasure, mouth, Oliver: it was inevitable she should take to oral sex, that it would become her specialty, her fame.

These days she owned a fine set of false teeth that looked perfect, if unreal. The Witch never thought of them as *her* teeth. They belonged to a second self, proud and stiff, who sold weed pots and dried grasses at the weekend flea market in the auction barn and who was called Estelle by her fellow vendors. The Witch wore the teeth like black lace, as a lie, a private joke—scorn on those who scorned her in their lust— and last night, as always, she had removed them to go to work.

Teeth told who you were. Jordan children grew up on sugar; Jordan children grew up without dental care. To a Jordan, a disfigured mouth was as normal and inevitable as a rusting rocker panel on a car victimized by salted roads. Never mind that the common run of Tuckerman County had healthy, cared-for teeth, and therefore a Jordan could be identified by his rotten teeth. Part of the measure of a Jordan in his own eyes was his difference from the common run, measure not by difference in quality or quantity but by difference alone.

After finishing her coffee, she washed the breakfast dishes along with a wineglass from last night's customer. He was one of her Mr. Boyntons. The meek ones paid well and they didn't hurt you and they didn't make outstanding demands, yet there was a time when she had despised them. The ones that roughed her up or gypped her earned from her a grand mash of awe and hate that, on occasion, sexually satisfied her. So, too, it went with most men, she thought. A woman gave her all, and she was a slut in the eyes of the man whom she had received; a woman withheld and whined, and, more likely than not, she'd get a marriage proposal. These days the Witch was grateful to the Mr. Boyntons and she kept her distance from the Olivers.

She tidied the kitchen, brought out the garbage, and dusted, using a pair of men's boxer shorts, size 42, her hand in the fly. She broomed the linoleum floor. She inspected the debris— lint, a gum wrapper, dirt (dirt? What was it anyway?), and the night's spores that fell in a constant rain from the dozens of hanging bunches of dried plants with which she decorated her apartment. Once, in the clutch of the toke, she had discovered the sound of the rain of spores. It was like the soft breathing of a child thinking.

There was zest in her approach to housekeeping, but the job never quite got done, the place never quite seemed picked up or clean. She abandoned tasks just short of completion.

A Jordan might have a personal idea of cleanliness and not violate the Jordan codes. A Jordan woman might or might not wash her hair, or a Jordan man might or might not wax his car. But the idea that a house should be clean and picked up made no more sense to a Jordan than it would have to a dog. It wasn't just that Jordans had no feel for cleanliness and orderliness; Jordans favored messiness. The land they occupied had so predisposed them. Jordans kept their houses, their yards, even their lives in very much the same way nature kept the woodlands of Tuckerman County. Dozens of varieties of trees grew wild, at random, competing for space and light, their growth dependent on weather, luck, and the benediction of the soil. It was a forest where the wind-twisted, the insect-ravaged, the sun-denied reached skyward with the straight, the healthy, the lovely.

After she finished with the kitchen, the Witch paused to admire her work. As usual, she felt something pressing in upon her enjoyment: an urge to disturb, to dirty up.

She put Lestoil and Comet in a bucket with some sponges and moved to the bathroom. She sponge-mopped the floor around the toilet. She could understand why men preferred to stand to piss, laziness and male vanity, but why was it that over a lifetime they never perfected their aim? In the sink was a trail of mouth-spoiled toothpaste she'd spit out, brushing her false teeth and rinsing her mouth having been the last business of the previous evening. She scrubbed the sink and rebrushed the teeth as part of the same action, as if sink and teeth were both bathroom fixtures. Her chores finished, she dabbed her face with a washcloth, and ran a comb through her hair. The moment she touched her face, moved toward adornment, she could feel the whore in herself.

Late in the morning, the Witch's grandson, Critter Jordan, paid her a visit. Critter was regular-featured, even handsome as Jordans went. He was ambitious and pushy, but not mean. The Witch liked him, and yet she reckoned it necessary to establish her ascendancy over him immediately, because he was not only her grandson but her landlord.

"You can come in, but the dog stays outside," she said while Critter was still on the landing and before he had a chance to speak.

"Stay—stay!" Critter commanded.

Crowbar, certain by his master's voice he was guilty of something but not of what, collapsed in a heap to await forgiveness.

The Witch didn't exactly invite Critter to sit at her dining table, but, rather, she stopped in front of it and he took a seat.

He'd probably ask for coffee, and she didn't want to bend to his demands, so she headed him off. "How many sugars you take in your coffee?" she asked.

He filled the air with fiddle-faddle talk until she poured the coffee, and then he began to back into his purpose for calling on her.

"Fine building, this old barn," he said.

"Uh-huh." The Witch wondered what was coming.

"Fact is, there's no profit in it," Critter said. He was all business after that, and the shift in his tone—cold, to the point—took the starch right out of her. The truth of her position in life came down on her. Her Witch's ascendancy was a flimsy thing, a veil. A man with property or money or a weapon could walk through it.

He didn't come out and say so, but the Witch gathered Critter wasn't satisfied with the weekend flea market. It didn't pay enough in rents. He left it for her to conclude he was doing the flea-market vendors a favor. He reminded the Witch he charged her no rent at all for her own flea-market space, where she sold dried plants in pots.

"I'm going to have to open a new business in the barn," Critter said.

"Uh-huh."

"Not sure what kind of business yet, but I come to see you, Witch, to offer you work, clerking, bookkeeping—whatever."

The Witch considered. She had some money saved up. If she worked part-time for Critter and he paid her medical insurance, she could retire. The old whore with no men calling— what an odd idea. If she threw in with Critter, she'd live by his succor; her ascendancy would pass to him.

"Work for kin—I think not," the Witch said. "Besides, I operate my own business."

"So you do," Critter said. He was on his feet now, on his way out. She could tell he'd never expected her to accept his offer. He'd been doing his Jordan duty toward her, warning her change was coming. At the same time, if she'd happened to go along with his plan, why he would have established ascendancy over her. As he most certainly expected, she'd turned him down, and now he could do whatever he pleased.

She watched him through the window, descending the stairs from the landing, the dog, happy now, bounding ahead of him. She watched them get into the van, roll out the driveway. As they disappeared up Route 21, she caught just a glimmer of black and silver between new leaves.

The Trans Am had followed her into Tuckerman three times since the first a week ago. She tingled at a thought of him: mask. She tried to understand the feeling he excited in her— rage and fear, but something else too. She'd had sex so early, so hard, she'd never known what it was like to be in love. Perhaps what she felt now was that feeling twisted by time. She searched about in her mind for a name for the feeling—

and found nothing but the feeling itself, uncomfortable, but irrefutably inviting.

She drove slowly out of the driveway, glancing in the Subaru's rearview mirror as it turned onto the highway. No gleam—and now he wasn't in sight. This disturbed her more than if he had jumped on her tail. All the way to Tuckerman she looked for him—and never saw him. The strange feeling subsided, replaced by the drizzle of common loss. When she arrived at Donald's place, everything seemed as it had been. She was the Jordan Witch, among her own.

"No Noreen today?" she inquired sardonically of Tammy, so as not to betray a tinge of disappointment. For some reason she wanted to see Noreen, smell her, be in proximity to her.

"Quit her job—on the loose," Tammy said.

What did Tammy mean by "on the loose"? The Witch probed. Tammy had meant nothing—neither Tammy nor any of the other women knew Noreen's plans. That made the Witch all the more suspicious. Had Noreen set up her own shop? Was Noreen recruiting her customers? Images flashed in the Witch's mind. She was slapping Noreen; she was embracing her. She was Noreen, being slapped, being embraced. Clutter of mind washed over the Witch like wreckage in a hurricane-driven sea. And then someone offered her toast, and that broke the spell. She was all right after that. As the afternoon wore on, she melded into the women at Tammy's house. When she left, the Witch was in an agreeable void, detached from memory, anticipating the drive back to Darby.

Country drives, she had come to realize, brought temporary cease-fires to the wars of the world and the wars of the self, but had little effect on her overall frame of mind. It was as if the pleasure in the drone of driving, in the contemplation of the countryside, simply sifted through her and was lost, so that when she arrived at her destination she was, so to speak, back where she started from and the wars resumed.

On the road, she marveled at the forest, leaning into the highway, or bordering a field, or seeming to be marching onto a row of houses, miles and miles of trees, wavering in the breezes or stiff and dignified in still air as old friends of the deceased paying their respects to the bereaved. Moody— the forest was moody. Oh, darling, I know how it is with you. All those creatures to born, to provide for, to shovel under.

She always noted the sky when she drove. It varied from day to day, season to season, but it wasn't the variations or even the beauty that made her take notice. It was the invitation to escape the earth. She lit her pipe and drew down the bowl like a thirsty deer at a pool. The road was a river. Her interest was not in the debris carried downstream, but in the tranquilizing rhythm of the flow.

I watch and listen, I lie in the mother's arms of my drug, I dive into myself and surface in memory: who is this? how lovely she is, I touch her, she falls, injured, she rises confused, all my fault my parents' hate, my mother, our mother, my father, our father, he drinking, hitting her from the drink, she getting back at him by sleeping around, you, I, thinking I did this, I made this bad thing happen between them, my fault, you hid in yourself as if love were a casket, you thought hard hard hard hard, figuring if I think hard about the way it should be, it will be, so let them hit me, hurt me, and my pain will make it right between them, so you invite them: hit me, and they oblige, and you understand nothing but that solution: to save heart you can't just suffer, you must suffer and die.

And the Trans Am was suddenly in her rearview mirror, and everything came together as that feeling, the twist of love, the feeling for which she had no name.

"Bastard—who bore you, the sky?" the Witch shouted into the rearview mirror.

Everything was pounding now, her heart, her womanhood,

the car, the colors—everything. She hadn't seen him come up on her. Had he been there all along?

"Who bore you?" she shouted again, the sound of her voice settling her somewhat.

She slowed the Subaru. The Trans Am slowed. She continued to slow until her car was only going fifteen miles an hour. The Trans Am kept the distance. A truck passed them, the *oooo-ahhhha* of its horn like the caw of some awful crow. She speeded up. The Trans Am speeded up. Soon the Subaru was going as fast it would.

She could see the auction barn up ahead, an approaching blur, the weathered siding seeming to anchor it to the ground, while the new, tan shingling on the hip roof pulled it into the building into the sky. She drove past it for a mile, then turned off the highway onto Center Darby Road, and turned off again, dropping onto River Road. She drove not by thought but by that feeling inside. The Trans Am kept the distance.

The land was different here, less rugged, less forested, rolling grassy with the river—farmland. She slowed again, the Trans Am slowed. Finally, she pulled to the side of the road beside a cow pasture of the Hillary farm. Stuck in some mud up slope in the field was a backhoe. The Trans Am sidled in behind her. She began to back up. The Trans Am backed, keeping the distance. She backed for a couple hundred yards until they were out of view of the backhoe and the pasture, and in the trees again. The Witch stepped out of her car but remained standing by the door with the engine running. The Trans Am idled, its mufflers growling. The feeling fell into the same key and rhythm as the Trans Am, as if feeling and engine were two instruments playing the same song despite the wishes of the musicians handling them. She had hoped to get a look at the mask, but the sun through the trees was on the windshield of the Trans Am and all she saw was a wavy bar of silver light. I'll stay here until death, she thought. I'll bluff him with time itself.

Minutes passed. She sensed she was winning the battle of nerves. Of course. She was the Witch—the Witch had an eye for this kind of work—look at the eye.

She thought she detected a stirring in the car. A moment later she was looking at a young man's body. He was wearing tight blue jeans, black boots, a black T-shirt, and the mask. She could see it clearly now, illuminated by a bar of light through the trees, black and shiny, clinging tightly to the features of the face, wrapping around the head like some terrible skin, two peepholes for seeing, a zipper where the mouth should be. He stood before her, a knife in his left hand, his readied prick in his right hand, knife hand still, other hand busy. The feeling fell into the rhythm of the hand. The name for the feeling formed in her mind now—the tremor; she had thus cornered the tremor; now it cornered her, increasing in intensity and power. The Trans Am ejaculated in less than a minute.

"You owe me fifty bucks!" the Witch shouted.

What happened next surprised the Witch, shocked her. The man screamed, a scream of hurt and rage ripping through mask. The tremor: he feels it too, she thought. And then she lost a moment in time. The Trans Am was gone, and she was alone, hearing birds sing, looking at the sunlight through the trees falling on the dull mat of the earth.

4

A Birth

Critter Jordan was tempted not to respond to his belt beeper when it began to sound. He was in the auction barn, drinking a beer, just sort of "inventorying," as his father would put it when he wanted to be alone. Critter liked the barn. Sometimes it seemed to him he could smell animals from long ago, cows and pigs and chickens, and he imagined he was a farmer and the animals were his: Critter's critters, feeding, mating, borning, dying—everything that people did, except simpler, quicker, with less fuss and no complaints. But he was no farmer, he knew that. He might like the idea of farming, but the idea of getting up early in the morning, why it made him sick even to contemplate.

The trouble with the barn was it didn't pay for man or beast. After his father was killed, Critter had liquidated the auction business, using the revenues to fix the roof and shore up the place so he could turn it into a weekend flea market. Even so, it failed to turn a profit. The rents he collected from the Witch and from the flea-market vendors barely covered the property taxes and expenses. He needed to make the space in the barn pay during weekdays.

The beeper continued to sound until he could no longer

ignore it. He strode outside to the van, where Crowbar, his all-breeds hound, waited. From the van, he called Delphina on the CB. "Van Man to home, Van Man to home."

"I don't feel so good." Delphina's voice crackled through the speaker.

Crowbar lay on the passenger-side seat, paws over ears. Certain noises on the CB drilled into his skull.

"Is this is it—calving time? Over," Critter said.

"Maybe it is, and maybe it ain't."

"Does it feel like the last one? Over."

"How should I know?" Annoyance with him issued from her voice. "All's I remember is I worked in the garden and it was the first day in months my lumbago didn't kick up."

"You call back when you're sure. Over," Critter said.

"Come home now! Ten-four!" shouted Delphina, and that was that.

Critter hung up the mike, started the engine of the van, checked his watch, and said to Crowbar, "Women got mean tempers."

They covered the three miles from the auction barn on Highway 21 to the house in Darby Depot in two minutes and fifty-two seconds. Critter announced the time as he barged through the rear door.

"My water just broke," Delphina said.

The front of her maternity blue jeans was dark with fluid. Critter turned his eyes away. "Why do babies always have to come at night?" he asked the dog.

Delphina called her doctor, and while still on the phone said to Critter, "Go upstairs and get the baby and my stuff. We have to go to the hospital."

She hung up and, without so much as a look back at Critter, she went to the bathroom. He stood for a moment, wondering why there was this distance between them. It hadn't been like this when Ollie was born. Delphina had had pains, and he had rushed her to the hospital and she had held his hand for dear life (young Ollie's dear life, their own dear lives that he had felt the blessing of in her fingertips). He heard the shower go on, and a picture sprang to his mind of tropical downpours, jungle trees, screaming monkeys, vines. For some reason he was aware of the newness of their house, the bare, white walls—the spaciousness. He realized then why he had never been comfortable here: no mess.

"We ought to buy some pictures to put on the walls," he said, but Delphina couldn't hear above the rushing water.

Upstairs, he lifted Ollie, his two-year-old, from his crib and lay his head against his shoulder. The boy was still asleep, but he instinctively nuzzled into the crook between his father's neck and collarbone. The feeling of the boy's soft, wet, sleeping mouth against bare skin took Critter off guard. He recoiled inwardly, as one awash in the bad breath of a stranger.

Downstairs again, Critter could see the outline of his wife's bottom wet-pressed into the seat of the chair she had been sitting on when her water broke. Where did the water come from? What did it mean—"break"? Was it really water, and if so what was the water for? And if it wasn't water, why, what was it? The sight and the questions troubled him. The less a man knew about the mysteries of womanhood—the period, birth, the change of life—the better off he was. He believed, as every Jordan man believed, firmly and devoutly, that "female knowledge" tainted a man, diminished him somehow.

"Let's go," Delphina said, and they went outside to the van for the fifteen-mile trip from Darby Depot to Tuckerman County Hospital.

Once they were on the road, Critter thought that by being cheerful he might reengage himself to his wife.

"I don't get it," he said, forcing a quizzical tone. "The last time you had a baby, you were having labor pains when your water broke and you were already in the hospital."

"Every baby comes different, they say," Delphina said.

Critter frowned. Women were supposed to know about born-ing, so why the "they say"? Nor did he care for the way she addressed him, as if she wished he'd shut up and leave her alone. He felt like a taxi driver instead of her husband.

Ollie, strapped in the harness the state required, began to cry in the back seat. Delphina ignored him. Critter watched in the rearview mirror as Crowbar licked the boy's face.

"Sit!" shouted Critter, and the dog cringed, expecting to be hit.

Critter removed his handkerchief from his hip pocket and gave it to Delphina. "Wipe the kid's face where the dog kissed him," he said.

"What in the world for?" Delphina asked.

"Never mind why, just do it." Critter's tone, the unexpected authority in it, stopped her cold. She wiped the boy's face. Critter felt steadier.

He brought her to the hospital, hung around a terrible long time (terrible because he had to watch Ollie) while she checked in. He signed some papers, and then drove Ollie to Donald's house. Tammy would take good care of the boy while Delphina was in the hospital. Critter fell into a brief rapture then, relief—freedom—at having ditched the kid. He returned to the hospital, leaving Crowbar in the van.

The nurses had parked Delphina in the birthing room. Things had changed since Critter had been here last. The walls were papered, the bed had a wood frame, maple furniture graced the place—an end table, a lamp, a magazine rack. The idea was to make mothers-to-be feel at home by placing them in a homey atmosphere. But the effect on Critter was the opposite of what was intended. He longed for a hospital atmosphere, cold and orderly and white and stinking of ether. Not that he liked hospital rooms, but he trusted in their safety; this, a mock-up of some common-run bedroom, felt unsafe. In addition, the affected casualness gave him the impression he was supposed to stick around, help out maybe. No way, José. Delphina had tried to get him to take the wachamacallit, LaMayonnaise classes, but he had flatly refused. A man helping a woman birth a child: it was an attack not only on his manhood, but on his Jordanhood.

Delphina sat up stiffly in the bed, filing her nails. Critter might have plopped down in the chair provided, but he decided to stand, the better to escape.

"I wish you'd have some pains," he said.

"I don't want pains—why should I want pains?" She snarled at him.

For a woman about to give birth, Delphina looked mighty comfortable, acted mighty grouchy.

"It's natural to have pains," Critter said.

"Birth pains hurt—don't you understand that?" Delphina said, and Critter did not hear the fear in her voice.

He found himself uncomfortable standing still, so he leaned first on one foot, then on the other, until he was sort of pacing in place. It angered him not that Delphina was irritable but that she was irritable on the verge of having a baby. It was a bad sign. Furthermore, under these circumstances, he couldn't argue back.

Somewhere along the line she realized how downcast he was, and she said, "Critter, I'm not mad at you. I'm mad at my mother, for dying on me, for not being here."

For a second, he understood then why he had married this strong-willed woman. He, too, had lost his mother. She'd run away when he was a baby.

"Delphina," he said. "You're it: you're *the* mother."

After a while, Delphina began to wiggle and squirm and moan, and the nurses poked at her and said things Critter didn't understand—"You're fully dilated"—and, finally, the doctor came in, grinning like a maniac. "Are you going to take pictures?" he asked Critter.

The doctor was crazy, and it struck him he ought to get Delphina out of there. The next thing he knew the wooden sides of the bed were removed, the furniture was shoved aside; a nurse pushed a button, and there was an *uh-uh-uh* sound as the bottom of the bed began to fall away; metal stirrups appeared. It was no bed; it was a birthing contraption. Critter backed toward the door. He'd meant to kiss Delphina good-bye, hold her hand, reassure her, and now he was slinking out like a coward. He wanted to apologize. But when he looked at her eyes, he saw apology was not only unnecessary but irrelevant. Delphina was deep into her mysteries. Critter got out.

He hung around in the hall while things happened to Delphina he wasn't aware of and didn't want to be aware of. Nurses came and went, never looking at him; he felt invisible. He went outside, walked the dog for a wee, then returned to the birthing room, but he dared not go in, dared not knock on the door. He went around the corner to the nurses' station, and asked, "Has my wife calved yet?" The nurse apparently wasn't too bright, because it took a moment for his question to sink in. "We'll let you know," she said.

Finally, tuckered out, he lay on a couch in the waiting room. He was awakened by the same nurse, who said a C-section was going to be performed on Mrs. Jordan. He thought no more of this than of a weather report on the radio, and promptly went back to sleep. Morning light opened his eyes. He arose and watched the dawn creep bloody red above the pines that bordered the hospital. He dozed on the couch off and on for another hour or so. It occurred to him he could have gone home and had a good night's sleep; it did not occur to him to check at the nurses' station on the condition of his wife.

He yawned, stretched out, and began to wander until he

found the cafeteria. He ate rather more heartily than he expected, wolfing down sausage and eggs, a doughnut, and coffee. He read a paper somebody had left on a chair and chatted with a guy waxing the floor.

"They keep these rooms clean," Critter said.

"If you work with the patients, they make you wash your hands after you go to the bathroom," the guy said.

Critter watched television in a lounge miles away (it seemed) from the birthing room. A feeling of unreality crept into him. Was he an inmate in a mental hospital? Was Delphina really here behind closed doors? Was there a Delphina?

He was on his feet now, walking fast, then running to the nurses' station.

"Has my wife calved yet?" he shouted.

"What?" The nurse frowned at him.

This was not the right nurse. Critter gathered his wits about him. "I'm Mr. Jordan, and I'd like to know what's going on with my wife."

"They've been looking for you," the nurse said.

"I had some eggs. Is she having the baby?"

"She's not having it—they're doing a C-section."

C-section—the word drew dark drapes across Critter's mind. He returned to the waiting room, picked up a news magazine, and, fascinated, read eight or nine pages before he realized nothing was sinking in. He stood, paced, gazed out the window and saw nothing.

Then the nurse called him.

The baby didn't seem to be his. It resembled an Eskimo. Ollie hadn't looked like this. Or had he? Critter couldn't remember.

They'd given Delphina something, and she was half here and half in never-never land.

"I tried it my way, but he didn't want to leave home, so they had to cut," Delphina said.

40

"Uh-huh," Critter said.

The nurse put the baby in his arms.

"You sure this one is mine?" he muttered.

"They're in such good shape after a cesarean," the nurse said. "They don't get banged up. They come out perfect."

She might as well have been speaking Arabic for all he understood.

"Boy or girl?" he asked.

"Most definitely a boy," the nurse said. "What are you going to name him?"

Critter glanced down at Delphina. He noticed her white Johnny gown, white sheets on the bed. At home they had yellow sheets and green sheets and rainbow-colored sheets, but no white sheets, and Delphina never wore white to bed.

"Del?" he called.

Delphina did not respond. She had fallen asleep.

"Dell is a nice name," the nurse said.

"No, Del is my wife's name," Critter said, still baffled by everything. "I was going to name him after me, Carlton, which is my real first name. See, we agreed if it was a boy, I'd name it. If it was a girl, she'd name it. But now I ain't so sure. I don't like the way he looks, yellow and squinty-eyed."

"That's the jaundice," the nurse said. "Nothing to worry about; most newborns do have a touch of jaundice."

"Johndiss—um. Johndiss Jordan," Critter said.

"You don't want to name a child after a disease," the nurse said.

Critter thought that over. She had a point, but he liked the way one *j* crept up on another. "All right then, Jorge. Jorge Jordan."

"A good name," the nurse said, cheer in her voice.

Like Jordans throughout Tuckerman County, Critter spoke with a thick, rural New Hampshire accent. When Critter said "Jorge" it sounded like "Jawj." Later, when he filled out the form for the birth certificate, he wrote the name the way he'd spoken it, J-a-w-j. In the clan, the boy would grow up as Jawj Jawd'n.

It wasn't until the next day when Delphina showed him her stitches that Critter understood about the C-section. Borning was a lot trickier enterprise than he'd ever imagined. He'd been right all along. It was nothing that anybody with any sense would get involved in. No wonder women developed peculiar ideas.

"I don't want more kids," he said to Delphina.

"Not for a while—I'll go along with that," she said.

"No more. Never. Understand?"

"I'll get some birth-control pills."

Somehow he hadn't expected her to say that, and he fell inside, as if he'd caught her in a lie. But he considered. He certainly wasn't about to wear safes, and the idea of more children was such a draining thing. So what else was there besides pills?

"You do that, you ask the doctor to give you some of those little pills." He couldn't bring himself to say the words *birth control*. His voice was sure, confident, yet inside he was oddly unsettled, as if he'd betrayed his wife, himself, the thing that made them one.

5

Estelle and the Witch

Although Aronson would touch her and in his own mind become intimate with her, she felt neither gratitude nor contempt for him, desire nor repugnance. She didn't even think of him as a man exactly, but as an idea—profit—made flesh. Yet at another level, the anticipation of his arrival quickened her blood. She was professional and cool, but also ready, hot, wide-awake—alive.

It was eight P.M., time to put on the whore's face. She'd wear black undergarments and purple stockings because Aronson, like most men, preferred his sex in mourning colors. It didn't make any difference to the Witch. When she was a young whore—soft, moist, pretty—she'd nonetheless had her failures with this fellow or that. She didn't listen, and that was a problem. (You listened not for his sake, since most men were too egotistical to imagine you weren't listening; you listened for your own sake, your education.) The main problem had been she sometimes wouldn't go along with the often peculiar, occasionally revolting fuss and rules a man insisted upon before the actual act itself. Eventually she learned preparations, fuss and rules, were as important as the sex. There was no right way or wrong way of sex, but only the way of the one who paid.

She buried her skirt and blouse in the hamper and, half one self, half another, stood before the bathroom sink and prepared to wash her hair. Right into her forties, people had looked at it with fear and awe. "So black," they said, and she would think, My black, no other black like it. When she brushed it, she saw gleamings of gold, brown, and red, colors of autumn.

Then a few years ago some silver hairs started coming in. She had been surprised. Somehow she'd always expected she'd pass on before the blackness of her hair. She'd pulled out the silver hairs, not because she found them unattractive but because every silver hair reminded her a black hair had been lost and made her think there was less of her. And maybe this was so. Her hair was her pride, not the Witch's pride but the pride of the deep-down dear self. The beauty of her hair, the softness of it, the flow of it was like verification that the dear self was beautiful, soft, liquid, no matter what time or man did to her body. She'd pulled silver hairs until it became impractical to do so. If she dyed her hair, the gleamings would be gone, what remained merely black—not even her black. Yet from the standpoint of her business, she had to admit gleamings meant nothing. Men saw color in great big panels to nail up; men saw black and they thought "whore," and men saw silver and they thought "old woman"; men did not see gleamings. Thus, since her hair was as much a part of her business as her person, the Witch in her favored dyeing it coal-black. But that other self, the dear self, Estelle, resisted. She saw gain as well as loss in the turning of her hair. While she might be less of the person she was, she was more the person she would be. Meanwhile, she needed gleamings. Gleamings were the energy source of magic carpets that carried women away from discouragement, depression, dislocation. But to the Witch, the turning of her hair signaled danger. The hair was not just turning, it was turning on her, like some old kinsman turning on you after years of building a grudge.

Estelle Jordan did not dye her hair; she bought a wig, keeping it in her closet in a box. Periodically she'd compare the wig with her own hair. Each time the wig seemed shinier, fuller. One day it would surpass her natural hair in beauty, and she would know it was time to pass on.

She ran water in the bathroom sink until it was short of too hot to stand, and then she let the water pour over her neck. She squeezed the shampoo gel into her hand and bent it into the wet hair. Since she washed it every day, her hair was never so much dirty as dusty. Therefore, she washed it without the violence needed to cleanse what was truly soiled. Great billowing clouds of suds pleased her hands and neck as well as her scalp. She rinsed, twirling hair in her fingers until the slipperiness went out of it.

She toweled gently, and retired to the chair in the living room from where she could watch the great sugar maple tree outside the window while she brushed her hair. The wind was coming up; the leaves on the tree seemed to tingle in the waning light. She could almost feel fluids coursing through the veins of each leaf. Deep in herself she brushed.

When her hair was dry and shiny and combed and she had enjoyed its gleamings, she stood before a full-length mirror in the living room. (She had installed the mirror to please her customers. Never mind that most of the business was conducted in the dark or in dim light, men expected mirrors in whoredom. One fellow had requested a mirror on the ceiling. "No thank you," she had said. "I don't care to look down on myself.") She peered into the mirror now and she couldn't quite believe her eyes. She had an image of herself as much younger, almost a girl—frightened, passionate, lost, and lovely, a bouquet of a person. What she saw was a woman with long, straight black hair streaked with silver, features too pronounced and strong to be considered dainty or even feminine, yet which were distinctly female and compelling. The skin was dark, glowing like a pine board that has been out in the sun. She had no makeup on, and wrinkles knifed cruelly into her eyes. The eyes themselves were boiling lava pools in which snakes writhed. She feared if she looked too deeply into those eyes she might fall into them and be consumed. Her body had filled out some, but it was still a good body. Barefoot, in white, she did not look like a whore, but like a patient in a doctor's waiting room. How plain, how homely you are, Estelle, in your white cotton underpants, she thought.

The living room served as the Witch's business office. Its most functional piece of furniture was a couch that opened into a bed. She did not sleep here, but on a smaller bed in a smaller room where customers were not allowed. With a pull of her hand she set loose the whore bed. The wonder of it: a couch that held a bed, a bed that held a couch. *A woman bears a child, the child consumes the woman that bore her and grows into that selfsame woman. The woman consumes the child that she has been and bears the child she will be, and so on, down through the ages.*

She stripped off her underwear and stood for a moment before the mirror. Her breasts were too large, too low slung to be fashionable these days, but she was proud of them; in their sensitivity and plenty, they had served man and child alike.

She put her hair up and took a short tub bath (Aronson liked it clean), and roughly toweled herself dry. The moment had arrived for work lace—black bra, purple stockings, black high-heeled shoes, garter belt, no underpants, the feast Aronson had ordered.

For some men she paraded in Queen of Sheba outfits, wild jungle stuff. To these fellows, sex was not exactly a human activity. They pretended they were animals, the better to forget they were men. Some liked her to dress in frilly undies and petticoats and play the scared virgin. She guessed these souls harbored secret desires to bed their sisters or daughters. Garter belts and stockings were especially popular among her clientele. She reckoned such rigs represented harnesses, harking

46

back perhaps to a time when men, lonely on the range, loved their beasts of burden as if they were women, later to return home to make the women they loved into beasts of burden.

She checked her outfit in the full-length mirror. "I wear black only for work and funerals," she said to the mirror. She didn't see her body now; she saw equipment to operate her business, and she scrutinized it as such. Did it look the way it was supposed to? Would it do the job it was designed for? What could be done to improve it? Too bad she couldn't get spare parts for it. The mirror told her the equipment was sufficient for the task at hand, at least as required by Aronson and her other old men. She was pleased, her pride the pride of the workman for his made thing.

She pulled the chair before the mirror. Beside her on an end table she placed a pan of water, a washcloth, a piece of kitchen sponge, and some tissue; on her lap was a makeup kit. It resembled an artist's paint box, with brushes, tubes, trays, and compartments for holding tins of colored powder. Staring, almost startled, into the mirror, as if seeing not herself but some creature from the beyond, she touched her face, gently at first, then more vigorously; she stroked it, kneaded it, hurt it to bring the blood to it. Soon she was seeing it: her face. Whatever changes she made, underneath would be this: skin only her hands had touched, a face only her eyes had seen.

She opened the makeup kit, and with that act her idea of self, the dear self, began to fog over. Her face would not be seen. It would disappear. What would be seen would be a mask. *I create a mask and call it a face. I am the Witch. I cannot be pleased, I cannot be injured; I can only be created, destroyed, and created again.* If she was marooned, alone, there would be no Witch because there would be no need for a witch. The Witch was the cosmetic over the true person, protecting the true person, destroying the true person. It's not just me—it's them out there. They make masks until they don't know who they are underneath. *I know who I am, I am the mask, I am the Witch.*

She scrubbed her face anew with the washcloth, to disturb the skin, open the pores, make them containers. When her face was dry and tingling she applied moisturizer with her fingertips, letting the cream soak in, feeling the soft caress of it, the pleasure heightened by the contrast of the still-felt discomfort of the scrubbing.

She thought about Oliver, her mother's brother, who had taken her from her family and ripped away her girlhood. Oliver would slap her for no reason sometimes, call her names, threaten to kill her as he wept with rage, then a few minutes later apologize, speak softly to her, stroke her throat as if it were a kitten's. And they would make love, if that's what it was. She'd swoon with security, warmth, comfort. Had she brought on the violent moments for the tender ones? She didn't know. One thing was certain: without violence there was no tenderness in Oliver.

She applied the makeup with the broken piece of sponge. She dabbed it in one of the trays of color, then patted it onto her skin, smoothing it with her index finger. When she finished the first application with the sponge, the skin was dull beige, unwholesome-looking and spooky, like a mummy's buried for a couple thousand years in sand and only recently revealed by the wind. Amused by this preface to a mask, the Witch imagined herself displaying it in public arenas: the whore parading herself half-made-up in a shoe store, a funeral parlor, a restaurant, posing at the bacon bits dish of the salad bar. Note this face. See? Not alive, not dead.

She powdered in red on her cheeks; she pasted on false eyelashes; she pressed in purple mascara. Mascara: she liked the word; it was a container for "mask" and "make," and the "ah" sound at the end pleased her ears because it seemed to have a female quality.

The last task was to enhance her mouth, make it resemble a vagina. She followed its contours with bright red lipstick, leaving it glossy as a plastic flower. Suddenly everything speeded up: her heartbeat, her thoughts, her very notion of time. *Shiny and dark is the dream. Look at my lips—they suck the dream. I am the fruit of the tree. Give a nickel and taste me. Plunge into me and drown, plunge into me and consume me and be consumed by me. Plunge into me, die, and live again.* She was finished, and she inspected her creation in the mirror. It pleased her. She was pure whore now, pure Witch, perfect conjurer. There was no sign of her face.

She didn't answer Aronson's knock. She parked herself in the chair, allowed a knee to show through the robe she'd thrown on, and said, "The door is open."

He was a small-boned, fair-skinned man, shallow in the chest but with a beer gut, big ears, shifty eyes behind glasses, and a mouth on the verge of motoring even when it was still. He wasn't very tall, but his arms were long and his joints knobby, so that he seemed to be all knees and elbows. He reminded her of a small hardwood tree after its leaves have fallen. She escorted him to the living room.

"I feel like candlelight tonight," he said.

"Ain't we the romantic one," the Witch said. Usually Aronson liked his sex by moonglow. She fetched a candle, and they went into the living room. She lit a match, melted some wax on the end table beside the whore's bed, and planted the butt of the candle in the puddle before lighting it. Aronson began to undress, humming a tune, "Swanee River." The candle cast huge shadows that made her thrill just a little.

"I like that—nice light burning so bright," Aronson said. He stripped as unselfconsciously as one preparing for a solitary bath.

She let the robe slip from her shoulders and fall to the floor.

49

She was rather proud of that gesture, but Aronson didn't notice. He was thinking, she could see, of the story he would tell while she gave him oral sex. And he was still humming.

She watched him in the candlelight, naked except for his shoes and socks, and the shoulder holster and gun. He owned a sporting-goods store, and gun shops (he said) were favorite targets of thieves, so he had a license to carry a pistol. The dark leather, the black straps that wound over his shoulder and around his chest, the gun itself—they gave Aronson's measly body distinction.

Customer and whore stood facing each another. She took his prick between thumb and forefinger and slid her tongue under the leather of the holster until it met metal. She liked the smell of the leather and gun oil, but the metal was cold and the taste unnatural. She let go of his prick, stepped back, and eyed the gun as if it were an important person.

"You pack that everywhere you go—weddings and funerals and on the can?" she asked.

"I'm comfortable with it. It's part of me."

"Would you use it?"

He liked that question, she could see. It gave him an excuse to pull the start-up cord to his motor mouth.

"If I had to I would," he said. "I was in the artillery in the war, and never shot a personal piece at another human being. But I think, pretty much, yah, I'd use deadly force if it was called for. Because you have to with these things. It's what they're for: dispatching. Once you make the decision to carry a gun, it has to be all the way."

They stood nose to nose now and he was feeling her up. He didn't like her to put her arms around him or anything like that. He liked her to stand stock-still, with her hands by her sides.

"You in the market for a sidearm?" he asked.

"Maybe," she said. "Some kid follows me in a car."

"Listen, everybody needs protection today, especially a woman, and especially a woman in your line of work." He knelt and began to nibble at her pubic hairs, but kept right on talking.

"Look at it this way," he said. "Mentally a woman can be tough—I'll grant that. But physically a woman, generally speaking, is not equal to a man. But if a woman carries iron on her person, the man is not equal to her. Suppose he also carries iron? Why, then, both parties are equally weighted, and both parties are equals, are they not? And isn't that what it's all about today—dead equality among the sexes? Right? Tell me I'm wrong."

"There's something in what you say," the Witch said.

Aronson withdrew from her and stood, wiping his mouth with the back of his hand. He paced in and out of the shadows, the white of his body like the belly of a fish. And then he pulled the gun. It took all the witchness in her to stand her ground.

"This is what you need, a double-action, .38-caliber revolver," Aronson said; he was becoming aroused. "Some of these gun dealers will try to sell a woman a .22, but unless you're good with it, it may or may not shut the door on some guy's intentions. Even if you hit the sweet spot, the guy can walk right through it and stick a knife between your ribs, and you won't have the satisfaction of seeing him die five minutes later. A .38 at close range will stop him in his tracks, first time you pull the trigger. The shock alone will knock him on his ass."

"How much?" asked the Witch.

"How about I take it out in trade?" Aronson was almost erect now.

"I'll think about it," the Witch said.

"Think about it and feel it." Aronson placed the gun in her hand. It was cold. She turned the gun over and over, feeling its ridges, its indentations, smelling its oil on her fingers.

"Cold—iron-cold." She gave the gun back to Aronson.

"Actually, it's steel," Aronson said.

The Witch ignored this technicality. "I've seen enough iron in my day," she said. "Iron can only draw the warmth from a woman, and a woman cold is no woman at all."

"What are you saying?"

"No deal."

Aronson sat on the edge of the bed, and the Witch knelt before him. The candlelight was like a wind blowing shadow waves that rippled across his loins. The Witch took her teeth out and went to work. Aronson sighed.

Afterward, Aronson said, "Candlelight is so pretty. Someday when I'm in the mood for something different, I'm going to watch you ride that candle."

"Specials cost more."

Aronson didn't like that comment. It returned him to the world, its despairing hardness. "Everybody's so greedy today," he said, and impulsively he blew out the candle and snapped on the light.

The sudden brilliance, the clarity it brought, startled them both. They saw each other as if for the first time, clearly and really, she with the loosening skin and pendulous breasts, he with the matted chest hairs and slabs of fat across his middle. Their eyes met, and turned away, shamed as adolescents who have gone too far with love. Aronson reached for his pants, the Witch for her robe, until all was as it had been before the light revealed them.

Aronson paid for his pleasure and left. The Witch listened through the open window to the night carrying the sounds of his footfalls and humming. "Way down upon the Swanee River"—she whisper-sang a line from the song.

The Witch stripped the sheets and pillowcases from the whore's bed and folded it back into a couch. In the bathroom, she washed the makeup from her face. Amazing that what was so colorful on the face was so dirty on the washcloth. She took off the Witch's black lace and put on fresh cotton underpants and a cotton nightgown. She could feel the Witch in herself give way. She could be hurt now, and yet that very knowledge, the shiver of fear it sent through her, made her feel more alive, more human and noble.

She breathed in the fragrance of her tiny bedroom—powders, roses in a glass vase (that made her think of a picture she'd seen of a naked child playing a flute), and an essence she recognized as belonging to her dear self, Estelle. The room was thick with bunches of dried grass, herbs, leaves, and weeds whose names she did not know. They were pinned to the walls, hung from the ceiling, and tacked to the furniture. Spores rained down in a deluge. She swept them up, marveling at their beauty, variety, and potential.

Then she sat on her bed, her hands in her lap. With her head bowed, she resembled one about to say her prayers. As it was, the room itself was her prayer, except she had no god to offer that prayer to.

Estelle's bed was small, a child's bed almost, a bed of olden times when people were smaller, or perhaps a bed made for one woman-sized person only, a bed of wood, dry and darkened by age, but softened too, yet still strong, and made with careful attention to detail and designed to be in harmony with itself, formed by gentle hands and an idea of order by, say, a man for his convalescent mother. It was a bed that held out no invitation for company, but neither did it scorn. It was simply a bed for one.

She lay down, curled on her side. She shut her eyes, knowing sleep would not come right away. Who would visit her tonight—one of her children, Romaine, a stranger? As she wondered, the image of Oliver appeared in her mind. She dipped into her memory and plucked out a few moments in time.

"You stepped out on me when I was gone." Oliver smiled mirthlessly at her.

"Why should I? You're so great in the sack, I was satisfied just thinking about it."

"You like to scorn a man." His voice was cold and she knew he was getting ready to strike her.

"You taught me about scorn."

Oliver had managed both her personal and professional life. It was a case of the blind adult leading the blind child. He was father to her, brother, lover, and business manager. He was at his worst when he felt the crush of love for her, for love opened his eyes to the evil he had done her. Full of love, he could no longer lie to himself. He'd want to flee, but he couldn't. As he had captured her, she had captured him. So he'd drink, and find something to blame her for. Usually, infidelity. For her part, she would make sure he had good grounds for his accusations. She was unfaithful to him for the very reason that he needed her to be unfaithful.

"You went out with Junior Joyle—I know, I was told," he said.

"I didn't do nothing."

He read the lie in her eyes, and the beating began.

She summoned the feelings of that beating: the shock (no fear, but a gulping, like being taken off-guard by unexpected bad news), the sting of a hand cracking across her face (not so bad), the spinning (horrible), the *uh!* of his breathing (that reminded her of herself in child labor), the nausea, and, finally, all the feelings turned inside out into a terrible tenderness.

And he was kissing her throat, forcing himself into her. It always ended that way, with lust.

Afterward, he wiped her brow with his fingertips and watched her weep softly.

Oliver might have consumed her in the bright fires of his violence, thus giving her what she'd wanted all along, and what—now, in her bed—she still wanted, a final plunge into light. The wrongness of their love, the mere bad luck of two people bad for each other, would have died with her. But they'd had a child, almost as if she'd meant to guarantee that the wrongness of their love would be carried into the future to create a greater wrong, as if she'd meant to perpetuate the kinship as she scarred it. Their son Ollie had murdered Oliver, bashing his head against a stone wall in a slow, boozy death dance, and thus had saved her from Oliver and saved his own son, Willow, by her, and she had lived on, but changed, Witch-born out of the ashes of her grief. And Ollie had died and Willow had died. It was said in the kinship that Ollie and Willow had merged into one creature and prowled the forest, but she knew better. She had seen them—blue jewels frozen by the touch of her mother love. And now the Witch herself was dying, consumed by her own conjuring. How could she, Estelle, live on? Estelle had no answer.

She could hear the wind picking up now, shushing against the maple tree beside the auction barn. Out West, Kansas or someplace, there were, it was said, great rolling fields of golden wheat, no trees in the way to break up the view, no hogback mountains to discourage the eye yearning to see far away, no twisting roads to remind one of bad memories, just miles and miles of wheat bending in the wind, the sound of the wind on that bended wheat (that she had heard only in her imagination) like a mother whispering to her child, "Hush, hush, hush," perhaps the sound of the wind startled now and then by a swoop of birds, up and over, then back into, the wheat. With this, the thought blossoming into an image, Estelle put herself to sleep.

6

Back-of-the-Barn
Adult Books 'n' Flicks

Headed east on his first trip to Boston, Critter proceeded under a false sense of security provided by his van. Driving it made him feel protected, smarter than the average Jordan, enclosed by a second skull. The presence of Crowbar also conspired to make him believe all was well. The dog was first-rate company, obedient, even-tempered, big, comforting to have around as a loaded gun.

"I wish Ike could see us now." Critter addressed the dog.

Crowbar, watching the highway from the passenger seat, nodded agreeably.

The fact was, Critter had mixed feelings about his father's ghost. He wished Ike really could see him now, a success in the business Ike had started; but he was also happy Ike was dead and buried. Ike had had a way of keeping him suspended between his boyhood and his Jordan manhood. With Ike's death, Critter had been overwhelmed not by grief but by relief. The hurt of his father's passing had been like the hurt of sunlight to the prisoner released from his dark cell.

Critter had put reins on Ike's untamed enterprises and corralled them. The first need had been to pay debts. Critter had solved this problem by liquidating Ike's auction business. It had been a pleasure to sell the things Ike had gathered over a lifetime, a pleasure to kiss the auctioneering life good-bye.

How sick it had made Critter to watch Ike deceive grieving widows for the spoils of a house suddenly too big, too full, how disturbing to transport from house to auction barn the belongings of the recently deceased, the smell of the dead man still alive in his things.

The second need had been to straighten out Ike's property holdings. If there was one lesson he'd learned from Ike it was how to gaff a crew, so he'd rounded him some kin and fixed the run-down houses Ike owned in Tuckerman and sold them off. That gave him a power in the kinship, endeared him to the bankers Ike had alienated, and gave him some capital to concentrate on his efforts in Darby Depot. He sold off some places, bought others. He paneled, painted, and raised rents. He converted village houses into apartment units. As he had said to Delphina, "So many people get divorced today, they need more places to live." He'd been right; the apartments were always full. He had half a hope that one day local people would refer to him as the Squire of Darby Depot, as they continued to refer to Reggie Salmon as the Squire of Upper Darby even though Salmon had died. At the moment, Critter was even-steven with the banks. Soon he might creep ahead. He envisioned the day he would be the first genuinely rich Jordan.

Critter had been able to gain control of Ike's estate because Ike had left no will and never bothered to marry Elvira, the woman he had lived with after Critter's mother had deserted the family. Critter had been Ike's only legitimate heir. On behalf of herself and her children by Ike, Elvira might have contested Critter's takeover and, Critter had heard, she had been so advised by a social worker. But she was not a woman of much iron (weak was how Ike preferred his loved ones), and Critter had averted trouble by offering her the succor of a house with free rent. Still, he worried some about his half-brothers, Andre and Alsace. He would have to keep his eye on them.

A car whizzed by and Critter caught a glimpse of a woman's blond hair. In his imagination, he quickly constructed a face and body to go with the hair. Here he dwelled for a few minutes, until the image, flimsy to begin with, fell apart into a mess of color and shapes, like a tissue blown out in a hard sneeze. He remembered, then, his mission: to Boston and the Combat Zone.

"Well, Crowbar, sometimes the bear puts his foot in the trap so he can show himself he can without springing it."

Crowbar yawned aloud.

Critter had remained faithful to Delphina. For one thing, if he cheated on Delphina he knew he would have to lie to her. Ike's power had been in his ability to lie, and therefore Critter was uneasy with deception, unless it was the offhand kind of lie you told for sport or in service of a dollar. Also, he was afraid of bringing home a social disease. Also, there was the nature of his sexuality, the keep of his private self. When he only thought about sex, he was frustrated; when he only did it, he was disappointed. In order to feel comfortable, whole, rounded—fulfilled by sex—he had to think about it and do it at the same time. The problem was he couldn't think about the woman he was doing it with while he was doing it with her. It didn't matter whether he was doing it with Del or somebody else, he would be thinking about yet another person. What he needed was not somebody else to bed down, but more somebody elses to think about bedding down.

"Mr. Bach in the Combat Zone will help us rectify this situation, eh, Crowbar?"

Crowbar gurgled, sounding like a dog practicing its growl.

Critter had devised a plan both to satisfy his private self and to make the auction barn pay. He would open an adult bookstore in the rear of the barn. The purpose of his trip to Boston was to complete a deal for books, magazines, films, and peepshow equipment.

58

His confidence held until the van came over a rise on Route 2. Below, fifteen or twenty miles away, loomed the cityscape squatting in pale, dirty reddish-yellow light, a jumble of buildings, bridges, and vague shapes that for all he knew might have been ships or dragons, but certainly not anything from the world as he understood it. The light itself, hazy from pollution, seemed strange and unearthly to him.

"It's like they blew up an A-bomb," he said.

Crowbar barked in concurrence.

The city was immense, imposing, unreal, as if a nightmare had flashed from his mind onto a giant drive-in movie screen. He dived into a burrow of memory: himself home in the backyard, smoking a cigarette, drinking a beer, casually tending to a steak on the grill, Ollie and Jawj playing but behaving and in sight, Del in the kitchen mooshing potatoes for a salad. That helped a little to file the edges of his panic, which he recognized as the ancient Jordan fear of leaving Tuckerman County. He had first sensed the panic in Ike (an acid smell from his body) and then in himself during trips he and his father made to Connecticut to fence certain stolen items. He couldn't say whether Ike passed down the feeling to him, or whether it was in him to begin with, like an allergy, ready to rub his nerves raw at every weak moment outside the county. He had thought he had outgrown the feeling. Now he was reminded a man never outgrows anything. Prod a man in the right place and you can bring to the surface his every thought, word, deed, and blood memory.

"The blue door beside the Silk Stocking Lounge in the Combat Zone." Those had been Mr. Bach's directions, and Critter had no doubt he'd find the Silk Stocking Lounge, but where was the Combat Zone? All he knew was it was the hootchy-kootchy district—bars, bright lights, sluts, guys playing pocket pool.

"Ike's in hell laughing at me." He whispered to himself so

the dog wouldn't hear the frailty in his voice, but Crowbar did hear—and cringed. Critter hadn't intended to hit Crowbar, but since the dog was asking for it, he obliged, smacking him on the ear. He felt better then, but not much. Here in Massachusetts he was no longer the successful young businessman from New Hampshire. He was just another Jordan hick, full of panic at having wandered too far beyond the borders of home.

Coming into the city, he was overwhelmed by the rows upon rows of dark, gloomy buildings, lacking not only yards but even space between them. Surely people didn't work or live in such forbidding environments. Increasing his anxiety were the roads, which went every which-a-way, and the traffic, which progressed in a distinctly hostile manner, as if every driver had a grudge against every other driver.

The buildings got higher and higher as he drove deeper and deeper into the city. Then there was the river. He hadn't expected a river. He saw sailing vessels, operated by people who hung their bottoms over the high sides of their crafts; he saw men oaring excessively long, skinny boats. Why? Why in the world would anyone want to row a boat when you could put a motor on it? Men and women jogged along the sidewalk by the river. Who were they? Where were they going? And why in the world was everybody and everything all bunched up? What was a city, if not topography gone mad?

It popped into his head that the joggers and the boaters and the motorists also were going to see Mr. Bach in the Combat Zone. Although he knew this notion to be unsound, it brought him a small comfort, and there for a few minutes he camped. He imagined a line winding for miles, people waiting, like himself, to purchase dirty books and films. Perhaps if he followed a car, any car, it might lead him to the Combat Zone, or if not there, at least somewhere. Somewhere was better than nowhere. A taxi passed him. Critter took this as a sign.

A taxi driver knew where he was going. He would follow the taxi. It would take him to the Combat Zone. An image came to mind from television: Louie, the short, stocky dispatcher on the program *Taxi*. Mr. Bach would resemble Louie, his headquarters like the taxi depot in the television show. Mr. Bach would be a dispatcher not for taxis but for UPS-style trucks lugging dirty books. Meanwhile, a voice drummed in his head, "Unsound idea, unsound idea, unsound idea."

The taxi turned off the four-lane road onto a regular city street, and although he knew better, Critter followed. Traffic slowed. They approached a great big park, a village common exaggerated to satisfy the vanity of a city. This was better, not so rush-rush. Soon the taxi turned onto another street, but Critter did not follow. He was beginning to come around in himself. He wasn't going to find Mr. Bach by motoring along the streets of Boston. This wasn't a two-road town or even a five-road town. This was a big city, *the* big city of New England. He was going to have to park the van and ask directions. He drove around the common twice, getting calmer and calmer. Maybe it was the green grass and the trees in the park, but soon he was himself again, confident, happy in the fact of who he was.

There was no place to pull over. All these people in Boston weren't headed for the Combat Zone, they were looking for a place to park. Just when the panic was on the verge of returning, Critter spotted a sign—PARK. Minutes later he found himself in a huge cellar, on the second tier of a downtown Boston parking garage. By the time his eyes got used to the gloom of the cellar, he'd climbed some cement stairs and he was outdoors again in the bright of the day, standing on green grass, on the common. He paused for a moment, concentrating on the feel of the soles of his feet, better to put him in touch with what he knew to be below. All those cars underfoot— amazing, incredible, mind-boggling.

Crowbar at his side, he began to walk along a wide footpath. He studied the faces of the people he passed. They all carried a certain look that detached them from other people. Critter knew the look well. After generations of living in crowded shacks and crowded apartment houses, every Jordan had mastered the ability to detach himself from the din of humanity and to project a look that said, I am pretending I am alone, don't tread on me. The difference was this was the first time Critter had seen the look on the faces of people out of doors.

He began to take in the offerings of the city—people of different colors, people dressed for weddings and people dressed in the only clothes they owned, gangs of youths, lone teenagers with mobile music boxes, daffy old women dragging plastic garbage bags, men with briefcases, men and women alike lonely as mountains, and a constant flow of pretty girls, who made him want to sing and dance but who also made him wistful because he would never see them again.

"Boston ain't so bad," he said.

Crowbar yawned an uh-huh.

He watched a cop standing on a street corner look up into the sky as if that was where he wished to be. Critter said, "Where's the Combat Zone?"

The cop frowned at Crowbar, and said, "Where in the Combat Zone do you want to go?"

"The Silk Stocking," Critter said.

It was only a short walk to the Combat Zone. Here fewer people strolled. The streets were dirtier, the red-brick buildings struck Critter as stunted. Although it was not yet noon, a few prostitutes prowled the streets. They looked like prostitutes to Critter because they wore miniskirts and mesh stockings. Guys walked with stiff necks. Here and there bums lurched. A man lay curled in an overcoat in an alleyway. Critter, curious, bent to look at his face. The man's eyes were glazed over from booze or drugs or illness, maybe all three, and he had a stubble of beard that seemed permanent. Except for the fact that the man was black, he looked for all the world like any Jordan down on his luck.

"Wonder who these fellas go to for succor?" Critter said aloud, and for once didn't care that Crowbar did not respond.

The place seemed almost familiar, as if he'd lived here in some previous lifetime. Critter felt right at home in the Combat Zone.

The Silk Stocking was inviting. Lettering on the walls promised girls totally nude. Critter was tempted to stop in for a drink, but he knew better than to get liquored up before doing business, nor did he want to leave Crowbar unattended on the street. So he swallowed his urges and knocked on a blue door.

Mr. Bach did not resemble Louie in the least. He was a tall, nervous man dressed in denim with slick black hair and a small gold earring. He sat at a big wooden desk stacked high with paperwork and dirty books. Critter eyed the books, Mr. Bach eyed Crowbar.

"Why do people keep these large dogs?" Mr. Bach said.

Critter made a mental note that Mr. Bach was the type to talk to you as if you weren't there. Before getting down to business, Critter figured he better do something to get some respect from Mr. Bach.

"Sit!" Critter shouted so loud that for a moment he thought Mr. Bach was going to draw a pistol. But he only flinched. Crowbar sat, tongue hanging out, and Critter knew he'd made his point with Mr. Bach.

"I deal in cash," Critter said.

"Well, well," Mr. Bach said.

They worked out the details, step by step. Critter liked the way Mr. Bach did business, cut-and-dried, no fooling around, no papers to sign, strictly cash-and-carry.

"You ship to me?" Critter asked.

"We can—customer's cost."

"How about I pick up the stock myself, periodically in my van?"

"Fine—no problem," Mr. Bach said. "Once a month, once every three months—whatever. The customer, him and me count everything together. One, two, three. They pay me, they load it. Everybody's happy."

"Suppose I run low, or there's something in particular I need."

"If they want some specialty items, telephone in the order, and we'll ship it."

"UPS?"

"Whatever."

Afterward, Mr. Bach didn't shake hands. That suited Critter fine.

The Witch was on the alert from the moment Critter arrived at the auction barn with kin, the four of them wearing carpenter aprons and carrying tools. Like people everywhere who lived in buildings owned by others, she associated workmen with trouble. Workmen meant change; change meant improvements, which meant higher rents; change meant expansion, which meant more folk in the building; change meant demolition, which meant eviction. They were going to do something to the barn, her home. The arrival of workmen loosed upon the Witch a score of memories of packing up, begging or borrowing a truck from kin (and the resulting loss of ascendancy); of tramping across the country to look at this or that swillhole for shelter, of becoming alternately excited and depressed by apartment ads in the newspaper, of feeling that peculiar and unique *whump* of air that only a door slammed in your face can produce, of being lied to and of having to lie—Yes, I'm married; my husband's at the shop at this very minute. No, we don't have no kids—wouldn't have 'em around. No, we don't have no pets—hate 'em. We like a neat place and quiet.

From the balcony of her apartment she watched her kins-men below in the barn—Critter, his teen-age half-brothers Andre and Alsace, their uncle Abenaki. She heard swear words from Critter, an exclamation of denial from Alsace, a cackle from Abenaki. Then laughter all around. They moved, and now the barn air carried their voices to her.

"I don't believe I've ever seen a carpenter's apron quite so distinguished," Critter teased Abenaki.

"'Distinguished'—Critter, you certainly have put some gravy in your vocabulary," mocked Andre.

"'Quite so dinstinguished.'" Alsace always tried to do his older brother one better, and always came out second best.

"It ain't distinguished, it's dirty—dirty with blood—and I love it," Abenaki said. He was short, brick-hard in the gut, bow-legged, and nimble. He lived in a shack in the woods, usually alone, but recently he had offered succor to Andre and Alsace. Abenaki was oddly vain. He wore the camouflage outfit of the bow hunter as a daily uniform. His dark hair fell to his shoulders. He never washed it but combed it frequently; it shined from its own oils. He trimmed his beard so it came to a point three inches below his chin.

"You shooting animals out of season again?" Andre pre-tended to scold Abenaki.

"I know what he done—I seen him," Alsace said.

Abenaki cuffed Alsace. The brothers laughed, except for Critter.

"Blood? You slaughter some game?" Critter needed to clear up in his mind the matter of the bloody apron.

"No slaughter, an operation. Castrated a pig. Took the mean-ness right out of him," Abenaki said.

"Tell brother Critter what you ate for supper that night," Andre said, and he and Alsace hee-hawed like mad fools.

"Tasty—tasty," Abenaki cackled.

"Let's get to work," Critter said.

The Witch eased down the steep wooden steps to the main floor of the barn. When Critter was alone, standing on a ladder, nails in his mouth, the Witch confronted him.

"Remodeling?" she prodded.

"Umm." He had seen her out of the corner of his eye, and been careful not to look in her direction.

"Coming along pretty good."

"Umm."

He was such a handsome fellow in his white overalls, a nice, big boy, full of pep and big ideas.

"Critter!" Her voice, charged with command, was not without affection.

"Umm."

"Get the metal out of your mouth. The Witch has something to say to you."

Critter spilled the nails into his palm. A few fell to the floor. The Witch picked them up, and handed them to Critter.

"This is my home," she said.

"I know."

The Witch folded her arms, and turned her head away from him. The gesture compelled Critter to tell her about his plans.

"An adult bookstore—what should I think about that?" the Witch said, and scorned Critter with a laugh.

"Don't think nothing about it. It don't concern you." Critter's feelings were hurt. That was a good sign. It showed Critter could be pushed and pulled this way or that.

"'Course it concerns me," the Witch said, deliberately sounding as if she were trying to explain something to a child. "What hours you plan to keep? You going to put lights on to bother these old eyes? You going to play loud music in the middle of the night? What kind of a crowd is an adult bookstore going to attract?"

"We'll be open three to eleven at night to start with. Except

66

Sunday—town's got an ordinance about business on Sunday. Can't do it unless you sell food."

"Oh, Critter, ain't you law-abiding." The Witch was enjoying herself.

"This establishment won't bother you none, Witch. It'll be around back, and you won't see no lights, and I got a little manager to take care of the place."

That got the Witch's attention. "What you mean—you have a little manager?"

"I thought I'd hire a woman," Critter said. "Men like to look at a skirt and, well..."

"And, well, you can get 'em cheap."

"That, too," Critter said, a little less on the defensive, a little more put out. "You could've had the job. I offered it to you. So, I had to go looking, but I hit it lucky. Noreen Cook is going to be my manager."

The Witch reeled inside as if socked in the stomach. "Noreen!" she shouted. "Noreen can't manage her period."

The work went on. Trucks rolled from the highway down the long dirt drive carrying sheets of plywood, lumber, gypsum board, window casings, wire, insulation. Sometimes materials arrived in huge cardboard boxes, and the mystery of what might be in them captured the Witch's imagination. Sex gadgets—they got sex gadgets in there, she thought. She had no clear picture in her mind what these might be, diddly-doos and such, but she could be pretty sure they were invented and manufactured by cunning Asians and beyond the ken of a poor country whore. She was curious and jealous and a little stirred.

Her apartment was at one end of the auction barn and the entry to the store was around the back of the barn, out of sight both from her landing and the highway. However, from her balcony on the inside of the barn, she could watch the men

67

frame in and, finally, panel off her view. The project reduced the space for the weekend flea market by a third, but that didn't matter much because there was still room enough for the dozen or so vendors. The Witch noted a back door connecting a storage room in the store with the interior of the barn.

The work went fast, ending with the implantation of a sign at the head of the driveway, a magnificent sign, the Witch had to admit. It was tall and stately, well lighted at night, with a drawing of a dancing girl in a G-string like one the Witch herself once wore at a private party, the lettering on the cream background in three tiers, the top and bottom tiers in black, the middle in red:

BACK-OF-THE-BARN
ADULT
BOOKS 'N' FLICKS

Next day the store opened. The Witch was on the lookout; she counted only five customers. But business picked up in the weeks that followed. Cars seemed to come and go willy-nilly. A fellow would drive hesitatingly into the lot early in the morning, and when he found the store unopen he'd peel out. What the Witch heard was not the sound of the car's tires but the sound of a man's anger, a sound that felt like an approaching argument with a loved one. She was at once repelled and attracted by the feeling. In the same way, the bookstore itself disturbed her while it freshened her. The bookstore was like the Trans Am in that it held out the possibility of terror; in terror, the experience of it, immersion in it, the Witch recognized a medium for transformation.

Noreen accepted the wooden pot of dried weeds the Witch brought her.

"For me? I don't believe it," she said. "Nobody brings me nothing. Did you get them in the mall?"

She was wearing a red dress, decorated in black across the front with the phrase BACK-OF-THE-BARN, the letters distorted somewhat as they snaked over her small breasts.

"I most generally swap for the pots, but the dried weeds I pick myself," the Witch said, while the thought in her mind was, The dear self picks those weeds.

"Weeds," Noreen said, as if searching for meaning by uttering the word.

"When the green goes out of a plant, and it gets brittle and creaks when the wind blows, that's when I pick it. Protect it, then, and it lasts forever. The green stuff is nothing, a trick that eventually rots, stinks, and disappears. The dry stuff is tough to find this time of year, for the green, but it's there and it lasts."

"Is that so?" Noreen said, in awe, uncomprehending. She put the pot on the cash register on the counter, which rested on a raised platform two steps above the floor of the bookstore. Noreen sat on a stool behind the register. The Witch remained standing on the main floor, content to be at the lower level.

"Do you put them in water?" Noreen asked.

She has a beautiful face that doesn't know anything, the Witch thought. Maybe that's why it's beautiful.

"You don't put anything that's dried in water," the Witch said, a hint of malice in her voice.

"I guess I knew that," Noreen said, ashamed, but not sure exactly why. "I thought maybe if you put them in water, the green would come back."

"If you had the wherewithal, Noreen, you'd stand and cheer and say, 'I'm for everything green and everybody happy,' wouldn't you, now?"

"I suppose I would," Noreen said, uncertain whether the Witch was mocking her or not.

The Witch turned abruptly away from Noreen. She pretended to stroll about, but she hardly saw the racks of magazines, the peep-show booths. She had retreated into herself. *Noreen is very clever, Noreen is trying to take advantage of me, Noreen is completely innocent, Noreen is the blush on an apple.* What to make of Noreen, what to make of herself contemplating Noreen—the Witch didn't know. All she had to guide her were her feelings: strong, compelling, confusing— half grief, half desire: the tremor.

"This place tire you?" the Witch asked, in an attempt to ground herself in the trivial.

"The hours are long, and I get lonely," Noreen said. "The men that come in here, they're not like people. They don't look at you or they look at you like... you know. But I'm not complaining. It's not so hard on your feet as waitressing, and there's long periods when I can just sit here and daydream. Who can complain about a job where you get paid for daydreaming? I try to keep busy. I sweep the floor and wipe the benches in the booths, and put the magazines back in the right place. But I don't fix projectors when they break. I give the customer his token back. Then I call Critter and he fixes the machines. He's here maybe five times a week. He does inventory and he tells me about his plans. Then it's not so lonely."

Having found in Noreen's words the triviality she sought, the Witch was disgusted, enraged by it; she felt betrayed.

"You had a hard life, a hard childhood?" The Witch pinned Noreen with her eyes.

"I don't like to think about it."

"You don't think about much, do you?"

"If I thought about my life, I'd probably kill myself." Noreen was near tears.

The Witch's anger with Noreen fizzled as quickly as it had flamed.

"You do well not to think." The Witch's voice was tender now. "Myself, I think too much; worse, you see, I conjure. I know the life you've had, because I've lived it: a womanhood awakened early and the men there to take advantage, shake their heads at one another and agree whatever happened was your fault. A boozehound for a father, a mother weighed down with other children, fear, and maybe health problems. Always choosing the wrong man, always laboring in the wrong ways to hold him because you don't know no better."

"I'm still here, I'm still alive." Noreen shook her tiny fist. She had dug down and found some strength.

The Witch saw the confusion in Noreen, her sadness, and through it all her power, which was her ability to endure suffering and in that suffering to rekindle the hope suffering had consumed. It was a power Noreen herself could not see, perhaps could not appreciate even if she could see it, for her own lack of... what was it? Intelligence? Wisdom? A Witch in her soul?

"What impresses me about you, Noreen, is you're good, you don't use people; you've managed to stay out of the whore's bed." The Witch resisted an impulse to take Noreen's hand, squeeze it, crush it.

Noreen was embarrassed on the Witch's behalf. "I'm not perfect," she said. "I talk dirty now and again."

"Oh, what's that? Nothing. Everybody talks dirty today—men, women, boys, girls, parrots. Girls walk down the street like sluts even when they aren't slutting. They dress like bimbos, smoke like pool-hall bums, say *shit* out loud, and scratch their asses in public."

"That's the way things are today," Noreen sighed, as one who had never experienced how things were yesterday and didn't, at bottom, care.

As she went on, the Witch found herself first on the side of sarcasm, now on the side of sincerity, never secure on either side. "Females have acquired all the disgusting habits of males," she said. "So what? From depot to hilltop, everybody sleeps around today. You sleep around, Noreen?"

Noreen blushed.

"Don't bother to answer," the Witch said.

"I don't sleep with somebody unless it's the real thing," Noreen said, trying to set the record straight, but the Witch ignored her, steaming along with her own train of thought. "Everybody sleeps for free today and everybody gives orals to everybody else. Makes life difficult for a professional woman, believe you me. Not that I'm criticizing progress."

Noreen now was aching to say something, and her ache gave her the courage to interrupt the Witch. She blurted out, "Love—you forgot love."

The Witch drifted out of the store, realizing in the brightness of the late-afternoon sun that her mind actually hadn't registered what her eyes had seen, the hundreds of books in the store, the pictured flesh, the peep-show booths. Even the image of Noreen was unclear, bright but shattered, as if recalled from long ago. And, too, it was as if she'd been talking not to Noreen but to a ghost. She conjured Noreen by two separate lights. She could truthfully say she wanted to save Noreen from a terrible evil, even if she couldn't define the nature of that evil; at the same time, she could truthfully say she herself was that evil—that if she destroyed Noreen, she would bring herself peace of mind. Yet Noreen the person meant nothing to her. Her feelings were not for Noreen but for that ghost.

7

The Old Farmer

The Witch, returning from tending her marijuana patch, heard the excited cries of her great-grandson Ollie. Up ahead she saw Critter and his entire family—wife, kids, dog, car. They were clustered about a giant snapping turtle that had wandered into the parking lot of the auction barn. The turtle had retreated into its dark green shell, while Critter crouched beside it with a stick. He teased the turtle by waving the stick before its hidden nose. In the background, Crowbar barked, Baby Jawj howled, the Caddy's radio played pop music, and Delphina whined like a stuck record: "Stop poking that poor creature—stop poking that poor creature—stop poking that poor creature."

"You watch your daddy," Critter bragged to little Ollie. Critter had worked the stick to the lip of entry into the shell.

Delphina spotted the Witch and said to her, "He won't stop poking that poor creature."

"What do you expect? He's a Jordan," the Witch said.

"Amen," Delphina said.

Ignoring the wailing baby cradled easily in one great arm, outfitted in nothing but a yellow bikini, the top stained by huge, leaking nursing breasts, her long bleached-blond hair falling to her shoulders, her white skin sun-pinked, Delphina was an impressive sight to the Witch.

"Going to the beach?" the Witch asked.

"No such luck. Going to sit under the garden hose. Him here"—she pointed at Critter—"he don't like the water."

With that, the Witch felt the power of the kinship. She too was frightened of water. While she had never been afraid of dying, she'd always been afraid of drowning.

The turtle lunged for Critter's stick, grasping it in its powerful jaws. Little Ollie whooped in ecstasy.

"That *poor creature* will take your arm off, Del," Critter said.

He and the turtle played tug-of-war until the stick broke and Critter went flying backward onto the seat of his pants. The turtle dropped the stick and retreated into itself. Delphina's disgust flip-flopped to mirth. Ollie whooped louder. Crowbar reared up on his hind legs like a bear and yelped in amusement. Critter frowned but only for a moment before he broke out into self-mocking laughter. Even Baby Jawj got into the mood, gurgling instead of yowling. All these sounds of happiness were accompanied by the music from the Caddy's radio. This, thought the Witch, is about as close as Jordans get to joy.

In a few minutes, the family motored off, leaving the Witch with only the turtle for company. In contrast to the din of moments ago, the quiet felt oppressive, like moist heat. The turtle was still, its head, feet, and tail drawn in. Without warning, anger surged through the Witch. She picked up the stick and jabbed at the turtle a couple of times. The turtle did not respond. Her fury, the stupidity of it, struck the Witch now. She threw down the stick and stormed off.

Like some cat that had been lying in wait for its prey, the Trans Am seemed to snarl and leap out of the woods. In a moment it was not five feet behind the Subaru. The image in the car mirror, the looming road ahead, the closeness of the interior of her own car—these perceptions twisted together in her mind, obscuring for a moment the protective witch in Estelle Jordan. How little her car seemed, how delicate, how foreign. And now she was picturing a girl pedaling a bicycle in heavy automobile traffic, the girl's pink underpants showing under a flowered dress. She knew that dress yet did not know it. As a child she had stared at it in a store window for weeks until one day it was gone. Forgotten for five decades, the memory of the dress returned bright, vivid, rich in detail, unattainable as love. And she was the Witch again.

They played this game at his convenience two or three times a week; she'd watched the leaves fill out on the trees, brighten through June like new tumors, then turn dull and dusty with the yellow July sun. Something had to change.

She speeded up, slowed, turned onto Center Darby Road, turned off at River Road, speeded up, slowed. She pulled off the road where she reached the place under the trees where the Trans Am had exposed himself to her. Today the forest seemed closer, darker, the air heavier, sweeter. Without consciously deciding anything, she jammed the accelerator pedal to the floor. The rear tires kicked dirt and she was back on the road again, the Trans Am on her tail. In a moment, she broke free from the forest. The sky spoke to her: See how immense I am. The sunlight made every thing distinct from every other thing, the bright-tar road distinct from the dull-dirt shoulder, a shallow ditch distinct from a barbed-wire fence, the wavy green field distinct from the flat white sky. Her eye meandered upslope about sixty yards to a dip of land where the backhoe lay in state, mired in mud to the axle, a rust bucket of magnificent proportion and shape. It resembled a defeated beast. And with that thought, she remembered her father, hoisting her onto his shoulders to watch her mother dance on the wooden floor of a meeting house, she'd forgotten in which town. The music that night, contredanse, played once again in her mind. It made her feel like a child safe from the pouring rain—oh, the tremor as music was almost unbearable.

The field crested, dipped, and ended at a stone wall and a border of trees. Beyond was the Connecticut River, not visible but felt, imposing and deliberate as the men who farmed along its banks.

She slowed her car and brought it to a halt on the shoulder. The Trans Am sped by, stopping ahead. The engines of the two cars idled, like the breathing of boxers between rounds. It occurred to her that she had inadvertently frustrated him, mocked him. There was no cover. He could not risk leaving the car fully masked for fear a passing motorist would spot him in his gawd-awful getup. She had him penned in his car, penned in his costume, penned in his warped mind. The Witch found herself amused.

She stepped out of the car and stood for a moment in the road—look at me, look at me. Cow-smell wound down upon her—rich, fragrant, fertile. The fence posts were pleasantly out of plumb and rotting at their bases. The black-white of the holstein cows clashed with the green of the fields. The cows, about twenty of them, stopped grazing and turned in stupefied attention toward her. They looked for all the world like people watching television.

She listened for the music of the river, hearing instead the traffic on I-91 west of the river in Vermont. The river might as well have dried up; the highway had become the river. There was no music in the sounds of the interstate, but a steadfast din that troubled her. It was like listening to the sound of yourself breathing all the time. It could drive you crazy. Maybe something like that had happened to Romaine.

She glanced at the Trans Am. He was watching her through his mirror. The gleam of the mouth zipper of the mask lacerated her eye. She tiptoed across the ditch (the ground was firm), lifted the top strand of the barbed wire where it had gone a little slack, and slipped under, taking it as a sign of encouragement to go on that she didn't catch her skirt. She headed for the backhoe for no better reason than it was there, impressive and upraised in a landscape that defined itself by being underfoot.

When she was halfway between the backhoe and the road, she turned and faced the Trans Am. He gunned the engine, startling her with the roar from the mufflers. This is dangerous, this is foolish, she thought. She should return to the relative safety of her car. But she remained still, immobilized by sunlight, by music—something. She bowed her head shyly, her hands awkwardly a-jitter at her sides, as if she were a child under the scrutiny of a greater power.

Her gesture of submission puffed the confidence of the Trans Am, stimulated him to act. The car backed slowly down the road until it was almost out of sight, then it stopped, huffing in place for a moment. The engine revved, its sound building from a throaty gurgle to an angry whine. She sensed the second when it was about to leap ahead, and she quickened in anticipation. At the noise of the popping of the clutch, she reached an imaginary hand inward to feel the tremor, as a lover reached outward for his partner. Smoke spat from the squealing tires, the rear end wiggled, the body bucked forward; the car laid a hundred yards of rubber on the road. Then, showing off brakes, the Trans Am came to a smooth stop. The car panted in place, shifted gears, revved, and backed slowly to the starting point. There it idled contentedly for a minute or two, preparing for the next run.

She listened to the engine, feeling her own satisfaction in its low doglike growl. She remembered herself on the front steps of a shack, listening to the highway, where teenage boys raced fast cars. The sense of sadness associated with the memory made her realize that what she was feeling now was an old woman's weak imitation of the thrill teenage girls feel when boys are showing off for them. She had never experienced the feeling in its pure form. Now, buried in the Witch's knowledge, the sensation vanished entirely, replaced by anger, betrayal, humiliation—emotions all too familiar. By the time the Trans Am finished his second run, the Witch was sickened by these feelings. The joke was on her.

"I'll get you," she whispered, threatening both the Trans Am and the dear self that had allowed this pain to surface.

The Witch threw her head up in defiance, raised her arm, and flipped out her middle finger.

The Trans Am, until now posturing triumphantly, stalled his engine. The Witch laughed. The Trans Am started with a screech, then quieted to a sullen idle. The Witch laughed louder and more theatrically so her scorn could not be mistaken. The Trans Am's engine sputtered and complained—*ernininininini*.

"Get your feelings hurt?" the Witch shouted.

The Trans Am revved belligerently, and the car began to move.

The Witch stopped laughing. Her greed for the pleasure of his hurt had made her careless; she had pushed him too far. The car glided along the narrow shoulder of the road, turned off where the ditch was broad and shallow, then ripped through the fence. It headed for her, bucking and squealing and murderous, determined for blood as any long-tormented animal suddenly uncaged. The cows scattered, as well as cows can; they could see the Trans Am meant business.

The Witch understood, almost sympathized—you receive an injury, you pay it back with interest.

The only possible refuge was the backhoe. She glanced up at it. Stiff and indifferent as a god it was, and too far away to run for. Someone young and lithe, such as Noreen, might make it, but not herself. If she ran, it would give the Trans Am pleasure to chase her down, and she was determined not to give away pleasure. Nonetheless, it took an act of will for her to stand this ground. As the Trans Am bore down on her, the Witch felt the colors grow brighter, her sense of time slow.

Oh, Lordy, don't leave no tire marks on this soul. Oliver, take my hand. Speak to me, instruct me. "Be nice, be scared; they like it when the girl acts a little scared. It makes them feel like men." Yes, Oliver, I will, yes, I will, yes. Whatever you say, Oliver. Only die. Do me a favor and die. Go back before they get you, Noreen. Fear is not the enemy, it's resignation, the signing over of your body to the whims of men and memory.

There was no need to jump. The Trans Am veered off at the last second, traveled downslope, crashed through the fence, and tore down the road. She couldn't tell whether the Trans Am had turned away because he had seen the tractor coming or whether he had another reason—recognition that without her his own tremor could not hold.

The Witch looked over the saggy-eyed man astride the tractor chugging toward her. Like the backhoe, man and tractor were old, out of style, worn, but well made, solid as monuments. She'd never met the man, never said a word to him, but there would be no need for introductions. She knew him and he would know her. Darby was that kind of town. You might not know everyone personally, but you knew everyone's story and they knew yours. The man would be Avalon Hillary, dairy farmer of great repute in Tuckerman County, owner of the soil under her feet. Hillary was a jowly, well-jawed man whose nose and eyes were too small for his face. The eyes were blue, wise but not cunning; the hands were rough as split firewood.

The tractor halted with a jerk as Hillary cut the engine. He shifted his considerable bulk in the saddle of the tractor and with a certain reining-in caution leaned forward to speak.

"You all right?" he asked.

"Still game."

"Who was that and what the hell was he up to?" Hillary was irate first, puzzled second.

"Kid hot-rodding, I imagine."

"He was lowering right for you," Hillary said, hoping, it seemed to the Witch, for an explanation.

"Just a kid showing off," the Witch said.

"Goddamn 'em—pardon my French—they destroy a good fence, tear tender sod, scare the dickens out of a lady and some innocent cows, and for what?"

"For fun."

"Oh, is that it? Vandalize, trespass, frighten—all for fun; for nothing, I say." Hillary talked slowly, in anger but without rancor. He shook his head as if hearing bad news.

At first the Witch thought he honestly believed fun was nothing, but then she realized he was mourning his own incapacity for fun. She understood such men, understood their weariness, fellows who had been go-getters all their lives and now found themselves unable to keep up to the standards they had set when they were thirty, fellows wondering whether to go on with revised standards or pack it in.

Then there was an awkward moment between them because he expected her to say something, and she kept a silence.

"You, ah, like these pastures, do you?" he said.

She translated this question as a polite inquiry into her presence on his property.

"I do like to walk fields. I smell the grass and look at the flowers," she said.

"My wife loved flowers. She'd put them in a vase in the parlor."

The Witch remembered now that Hillary was recently widowed. She placed a hand on her hip. It was one of her more subtle come-hither poses.

* * *

Disgust in his face, a boy of about five resisted the pull of his mother's hand, halted at Estelle's table of weeds and weed pots, and asked, "What are those things?"

The mother jerked the boy along. "Nothing," she said, studiously avoiding eye contact with Estelle.

Two hours had passed since the flea market had opened at eight, but Estelle had not made a sale. It didn't matter. She had never really been at peace with herself or the world, her soul hardly knew the meaning of the word, but she knew her feeling at this moment, this Saturday-morning feeling, was close to peace, standing over her table of dried weeds and pots, watching the world go by, not the Witch, nor the dear self, but in a sort of never-never land of being.

Piper, the old gaffer who sold even older tools from the table beside her own, had seen the boy and his mother. Estelle recognized the look on his face, true concern and true vanity; it meant he was going to give her some advice.

"Estelle." He called her as one drawing the attention of a waitress, sliding a few feet closer to her, but still staying in the territory defined by his table. Like most of the other vendors, he didn't know her primary source of income. He lived in Massachusetts, a retired telephone company toll test man who'd say, bitterly, "It used to be Mother Bell, don't you know?" He made the flea-market rounds through New England in the summer, Florida in the winter.

"What's cooking?" Estelle asked. She never bothered making real conversation with Piper; he was not one to listen to a woman. Or perhaps, in this position, between selves, she wasn't capable of real conversation. She didn't know, didn't care.

"Estelle, you should wise up and make a profit for yourself," he said. "Get into videotapes or Care Bears, candleholders— anything but weeds."

She batted her eyelashes at him.

He shook his head—poor, foolish woman.

For the flea market she dressed in a plain skirt and blouse, harnessed her breasts in a bra, put her hair up, and wore a minimum of makeup. Here she could mingle with folk other than kin and clients, put the Witch in a closet for a while. Most of the vendors were from out of town, retired people mainly, pursuing their hobbies and calling them businesses. What made them intimate was the barn and the unspoken knowledge they were all imposters in that this relaxed life they lived on the weekend had nothing to do with the real, for-keeps life of weekdays. They didn't know about the Jordan Witch. She was Estelle to them.

The vendors sat on folding wooden chairs parked behind their tables. They drank coffee, munched on doughnuts, deplored the price of heating oil, exchanged stories of medical catastrophes, related anecdotes regarding their grandchildren. They talked, not toward resolution but toward relief. It was familiar talk, familiarly spoken, reminding her of the chatter around Donald's kitchen table. But there was a difference. Here she felt no strain to keep up her ascendancy within the clan. Here she could pretend she was just another body among the common run. During the best of these times she felt oddly radiant.

But there were bad moments too, when her euphoria would be turned inside out. A sense of powerlessness would sweep over her, as if she'd suddenly been set down on some vast, treeless, windswept plain. This feeling was derived in part, she understood, from the way she was treated as Estelle. When they dealt with her, the men teased her or unconsciously bossed her around, while the women used her as a sponge to sop up their complaints. More often, because she had little to say, she was ignored. As Estelle purely, she had no anecdotes to relate, no opinions to put forth, no ability to cow an aggressor, no personality to command attention. In the worst of the moments at the flea market, when she was alone, ignored, she felt precisely as she had as a child—invisible.

A middle-aged couple, she with red hair, white roots, he with lips puckered for whistling but silent, approached her table. Like most of her customers, they didn't look at her but at her things. There was something in their concentration that spoke well to her of humanity, that gave her hope. Perhaps it was that in concentrating on things, they left their pride behind.

"How much?" The woman held up the pot, looking not at Estelle but at the pot as if the pot could speak. The man leaned away from the activity, body and soul.

Estelle's optimism vanished. They were going to be typical customers. They were going to dicker.

"Five dollars for that one," Estelle said.

"Give you a dollar for it," the woman said.

"Can't pay the rent for that—four dollars and you can walk away with it," Estelle said.

"Let's go," the man said. The woman acted as if he hadn't spoken; she frowned at the pot.

Once you introduce the idea of profit, Estelle thought, people displayed their bad side. She had to fight back the impulse to give the pot to the woman.

"I can let it go for three dollars and fifty cents," Estelle said.

"It's nothing but a piece of wood with a hole in it," the man said.

The woman deepened her frown.

"I can pick a piece of wood off the yard and drill it, and it won't cost nothing," the man said, and the Witch rising up in Estelle knew that the woman would buy the pot.

In the end, she paid two dollars.

Estelle listened while Piper and the widow Kringle, who sold needlework, jawed. Piper said it wasn't good for the country to have too many millionaires. A passionately held conviction this was, but he was having difficulty presenting his arguments so they made sense. Not that this mattered. The Kringle woman nodded in agreement to everything he said. When she spoke it was about her grandson in the Navy. He was stationed in Hawaii. Didn't like it—no change in the seasons. Piper uh-huhed her, then launched another attack on big money. So it went: nodding and uh-huhing and talk whose meaning came up short. Estelle was at turns drawn and repelled by the scene, as she was by one of those lie-about-life television dramas.

She was taking a walk, getting away from her table, when she bumped into Avalon Hillary at the front door. He smelled of cow and damp field grass. The smells made her feel good—solid, connected to something, she couldn't say what.

He greeted her with a grunt of recognition.

"Starting to rain out?" she asked.

"Yes and no," he said. "I mean the sky is gray, and there's moisture in the clouds, but there isn't enough of it finding its way to the ground to do any good."

"I should have known better than to ask a farmer about the weather," she said.

Hillary laughed at himself. "That's a farmer," he said. "Never satisfied with nature. Too much rain or not enough. I can't remember a day I couldn't have improved, given a divine hand."

"I don't normally see you at this flea market," she said.

"I don't normally frequent this flea market," he said.

"Is that so?" she said.

"I'm not bragging," he said, catching the slight taint of sarcasm in her voice. "It's just there's nothing here I want."

"Nothing but company."

"You guess right into a man's innards, don't you?" he said, returning the sarcasm she had presented him.

"I don't know about that," she said.

They were moving together now, strolling like a couple at an outing. She noted he was not looking at the goods on the tables but at the beams of the barn. Habit, she thought.

"I got sick of my house and my barn and my girls, the sameness maybe, and I hopped into my old Buick, said to myself, 'Avalon, why don't you go for a ride like you used to?' But I'm alone now and a ride is not the same thing as when you have somebody to talk to."

"You might listen to the radio," she teased.

"Radio music makes me suffer," he said with great exaggeration. Estelle said nothing, and the silence incited him to go on. "So I stopped here. Thought I'd look around. Impulse, I suppose."

"As you can see, not much to look at," Estelle said.

She fetched him a cup of coffee, and they talked some more. They meandered about the barn. He kept looking up at the beams.

"You know this barn?" she asked.

"More or less," he said. "Used to belong to one of the Flagg boys. When the new leg of the highway was built, it split the farm in two. Flagg didn't like the road, and he moved his house, actually trucked it away to the backside of his property. Left the barn to orphan. Left the land to orphan. Eventually sold the land. Then he sold the house. Then he sold himself out of the county. Ended up down south someplace. Town used to be full of Flaggs. Now none. Unless you count Mrs. McCurtin, who married out. . . . What's this door?"

"Leads to the dirty bookstore."

"Hooked up poorly, lock installed wrong—it shames this barn."

It took the Witch a moment before she realized he was not talking about the bookstore itself but about the workmanship that went into creating it.

"That's Critter," she said. Suddenly caught up in her Jordanness, she could feel the past of the kinship, serious and tragic, comical and foolish, everything the common run ex-

perienced, except more intense, more lasting for the imprint
it made in the soul. She measured, as if for the first time, her
correct distance from this old farmer, from Piper and the Kringle woman, from all manner of humanity outside the kinship—
a million miles.

"I suppose." Avalon frowned.

"You can't bear to see something poorly constructed."

"No, ma'am—I cannot."

He stayed awhile longer, then was gone. The Witch in her
reckoned it would be only a matter of time before he'd make
a date with her. She figured him for a once-a-week customer,
like any farmer, stingy but no crybaby; he'd probably like his
sex standard, but you could never tell with a man so she
reserved judgment.

Later, the afternoon winding to a close, Estelle found herself
restless, uneasy. She threw a plastic sheet over her table and
slunk out, not wanting to explain to the other vendors why
she'd closed early. Upstairs in her apartment, sitting by a window, she smoked a bowl of toke, conjuring on her loneliness:
it was like the sound and swirl of dipping oars.

Outside it was beginning to rain. A few leaves on the big
maple beside the barn had turned orange. Not real, she thought,
nothing more than bits of color in my eye. She saw the Trans
Am then. It pulled off the highway into the drive of the auction
barn. She left her apartment and walked around the corner to
the parking lot. She saw the car, but not the driver. He must
have gone into the bookstore. She stood in the rain, feeling its
coolness on her shoulders. The car, black and silvery in the
dull of the day, seemed poised to rocket off into the gloom. She
hadn't seen man or car since the incident in Hillary's field a
week ago. She wanted to touch the car, feel its smoothness,
but something kept her off.

Half an hour went by before a young man came out of the
porn shop, a paper bag under his arm. He wore a leather jacket,

tight blue jeans, and black boots. His blond hair was combed rakishly from front to back; his face was smooth-shaven, perfectly chiseled, lips full. She was amazed how handsome he was. She'd never seen a face so perfect.

He didn't notice her until he was in the car leaving the lot. He had plenty of room to get by her, but he stopped. Without expression, he stared at her for a long time. Then he nudged the car slowly past her. Its subdued roar was like the purr of a big cat. When it turned onto the highway, the engine revved, the tires squealed, and the Trans Am bolted forward.

Before setting out, Avalon dressed in his suit, just as if he were going to a town meeting, and he vacuumed the mats in the Buick for no better reason than that it gave him confidence. He had never expected to pay a visit to the town pump. The idea had come out of the blue. But now that he had made the decision, he felt thrilled, free, full of energy. It was as if all the fun he'd wanted to have as a young buck was now there for the taking—his due. God was saying, "Go to it, Avalon."

The car door closed with a satisfying *thunk!* and that told him his senses were unusually keen. By gosh, he felt downright optimistic. Once on the road, rolling, he didn't have to look to know he was flanked by his land. The response of the Buick to blacktop told him. Normally, without thinking, the farmer in him would glance at his fields, looking for a broken fence, somebody's dog free, a certain lean to the trees beyond that heralded bad weather. If he couldn't fix what was rent, he'd attempt to worry it whole. Not now. Not tonight. He gave potential problems not a whit of thought. Tonight the idea of land itself was sweet, a benediction uncorrupted by work and worry, productivity and practicality. Even the sight of the backhoe, stuck in the mud, swept him, not with guilt, but with love.

* * *

87

She could tell right away she was going to like him in bed. He was all business. No faky romantic stuff, no quirky rules to crank him up, no talk, no bragging, no whining, no complaints about the dim lighting or the bed or her hair in the way, no stupid questions—Does the price include a shower afterward?

He was a big man, especially through the middle. But his wasn't loose fat; it was good fat, the kind you live off of. He had shaved close and she was grateful for that. He explored her, as men will the first time, with eyes, hands, lips, nuzzling her like a gentle hound. He heated up quickly for an old fart, but seemed to reach a point where he wasn't sure what to try next.

"You know what I'm famous for," she said.

"Yah."

"Want some?"

"It's been on my mind."

She took his balls in her hand, squeezed them, and dived for his pride. He lay back, relaxed, and let her work. She wondered how far he'd want her to go. Just when she thought he was ready to finish, he touched her on the shoulder. She understood the signal, and rolled over on her back. He hopped on and rode off into his sunset.

Finished, he put his arm over his eyes.

"Bet you never had any of that at home," she said.

"Maybe, maybe not," he said.

She scoffed at his attempt to keep pure the memory of his wife, or whatever prompted his evasiveness.

"Don't laugh." He neither threatened, nor begged, only asked.

"I'll laugh as I please," she said.

"Pretty haughty, you are—and show-offy," he said.

"I got the skill. Shouldn't I show it off?"

"I imagine so."

"Tell the truth now—you loved a gobble."

"It's tart, I don't deny that. Sort of like they bring you a chair to get on the hoss. But mainly, ma'am, I like it from the saddle."

"Likes it standard," she mocked him.

"Likes it standard," he returned the mockery, and they both giggled like schoolchildren.

Time passed, she wasn't sure how much. They didn't speak, but listened to one another breathe. She felt him sigh as he watched her bring the nightie across her breasts and tie a bow in the ribbon that closed it. "Get your money's worth?" she asked.

"Goddamn if I can say. I haven't done this outside of matrimony enough to know how to rate it."

"It's as good as married love. Admit that."

"Close—goddamn close."

"Can't you tell an easy lie?"

He thought about the question for a moment. "You lie a lot, do you? I mean in your line of work."

"Lie all the time."

He *umph*ed disapprovingly.

"When something goes broke on your farm, you fix it?"

"Have to."

"Me too. In my profession, lying is a valuable tool. It fixes any number of broken-down old parts."

He looked at her closely to see if she was teasing. She made sure he couldn't read an answer on her face.

He turned modestly to one side of the bed and pulled up his trousers. The Witch put on her robe. She thought that was going to be that. But he hung around, looked around, searching for an excuse not to leave. She could have offered him a cup of tea, but she wanted to see how he'd handle the situation. He eyeballed her arrangements of dried grasses, and touched a bunch carefully.

"Don't you keep any live plants?"

"I like them this way, the water gone from them," she said.

"Living plants give you allergies?"

89

"I'm allergic to anything alive. Makes me sad."

He didn't know how to deal with that explanation.

"Some of them, the begonias, I think, used to make my wife sneeze," he said. "Cat fur, too. So we didn't have any cats in the house. We had barn cats. They harass the rodent population. Now that she's gone, I'm thinking, I'm tired of drowning kittens or giving them away—I figure I'll raise one."

"I used to keep cats, but they always died on me," she said. "They'd get run over or the coyotes would eat them."

"Goddamn coyotes. They're a brought-in creature, you understand. They were never here until the interstate highway was built. Some connection there. Don't know's I can say what it is. But it's there, I'm sure of it."

He wants to stay, so charge him for the time, the Witch thought. But of course she wouldn't. She wanted to see what he was about. He reminded her a little of old man Williamson, except he was confident where Williamson had been resigned. That was because he was a rich farmer. Williamson never had a pot to piss in, nothing but that trailer on Black Swamp. Resignation had come by way of necessity. Hillary had land— family land. He had animals and machinery and buildings and prestige and know-how and friends who powered the world of Tuckerman County. Of course he'd be confident. What she liked about him was that his confidence was not the know-it-all kind (she thought of Aronson). Hillary wouldn't even think he was confident. He would merely live his life with confidence.

"You take tea or coffee?" she offered.

She made some coffee, the no-caffeine kind, and they sat at the kitchen table. He told her about his wife dying suddenly, and no kids home anymore. His last daughter was in the military. What kind of world was it when a high-school girl could join the Army upon graduation? Mostly, he talked about his dissatisfaction with the farm. He wasn't asking her advice, not even faking he was asking, as some men might. He just wanted to run off at the mouth as a man can to a woman but not to another man.

"That backhoe is mired deep," he said. "Thought for a while it was going to drop all the way to China. But this is New Hampshire—it sunk in three feet and hit ledge. During Melba's funeral all I could think about was how I was going to get the backhoe out of the mud. I pretty much reasoned it out too. I was going to drive a pole in the ground, anchor the tractor to it, and then hook up the tractor winch to the backhoe. The first thing I did after the burial was hustle out to the field, still in my suit and good shoes. I took one look at the backhoe, and it all came back to me. I said, 'Goddamnit,' and bawled my head off. Crazy."

"I'll take a hard hurt over a long hurt anytime," Estelle said.

Avalon looked at her appraisingly, the same look he had used to inspect the dried grasses. "You look different at your kitchen table," he said. "I'm not sure what to call you. Mrs. Jordan, or what?"

"Some men like to make believe I don't have a name. I'm Hey-You. But you know what most of the local fellows call me."

"Witch."

"Well?"

He frowned.

"My name is Estelle."

"Estelle—good. That's a fine name." He had something to call her by and that seemed to satisfy him as well as the sex had. In the same way, it satisfied her.

"I like that name Avalon. How'd you come by it?" she asked.

"My mother wanted to call me Harry. But the menfolk in the family named me after my grandfather's best bull."

Estelle giggled.

"It sounds like a joke, but it was serious business to my father and grandfather. Naming me Avalon was their way of thanking God for giving the Hillarys that bull."

"God?"

"God."

"I don't believe in God," she said. "I believe in stars and clockwork, and that's about it."

"I believed in God and then I didn't, and now I do again. Yes, ma'am. I'm convinced there's a Supreme Being. I don't know's he's a Christian or a Hindu or a buffalo, but I know he's out there."

"How do you know God's a he?"

"Manner of speaking—you sound like my daughter Julia."

"I ain't going to spit in your eye. How do you know he's a he?" There was sport in her tone, and that perked him up for the challenge.

"Well, it wouldn't be a she—that's obvious. So it has to be a he. Process of elimination."

They broke out into laughter.

"I didn't know you were going to be a kidder," she said.

"I didn't know either. I didn't know I was going to have fun, besides, you know—it."

"It," said Estelle, speaking the pronoun with the Witch's contempt. "We do it, we get sick by it, we die by it, we weep by it, we continue the race by it. We do it and we do it, and we never learn nothing from it. Good ole it."

Such talk usually put men off, scared them, but Hillary only looked at her half in amusement, half in amazement.

"What do you want to do?" she asked. "Go another round? Play some cards?"

"Go another round—how I wish I had the energy," he said, and laughed into his empty coffee cup.

She refilled it. "I do hope there is a God—he, she, or it, I don't care," she said. "Just so's when I die, he, she, or it is eye-to-eye so I can give him a piece of my mind."

"He knows what he's doing." Avalon was serious now.

"If you were him, would you let go on what goes on and has been going on for thousands of years? You'd put an end to all this killing, this suffering, this stupidity." Estelle, too, was serious.

"You're saying that the average man or woman would do a better job as God than the one we got."

"Why, sure."

"You've got a feel for injustice, Estelle, but not for human nature," Avalon said. "You're not taking into account Original Sin or free will."

"Original Sin, free will—horseshit!"

"That's no argument."

"This is what happens when a man and a woman talk out a problem," Estelle said. "The woman calls a spade a spade, but she never gets her arguments down so's they line up one behind the other. Now a man can shoot half the people in New York City, and argue clean he done it for good reason—they were Reds, they ran drugs, whatever."

"That supports my original statement. God is a he." Avalon gave Estelle an I-gotcha smile.

"In that case, I'm happy to be on the downside," Estelle said.

That stopped him. He shook his head and smiled.

They talked on. When his cup was empty again, Estelle went into the living room and returned with the tie Avalon had left on the back of the chair. He took this gesture as it was meant, her signal for him to leave.

He stood, put on his coat, tucked the tie in the pocket of the coat, and made for the door. On the landing, he was suddenly awkward and formal. He was trying to find a way to thank her for the good time.

"It was all right," he said. "Not just 'it,' but the coffee."

"Instant and hot—that's how men like it," she said, ignoring his slight blush. "Why'd you put on a suit for it?" she asked.

"I own one suit. I put it on for weddings, funerals, and special occasions. Before I came here tonight, I brooded, wondering where to fit something like this in the scheme of things."

"You figured special occasion."

"Yah."

8

Critter in Upper Darby

Caddy-carried, Caddy-comforted, Critter Jordan and his wife Delphina sped into the hills of Upper Darby, headed for a party at the home of Roland and Sheila LaChance, Delphina's younger sister.

"No kids, no diapers, no dog—what a relief," Delphina said, squishing her big bottom into the plush seat of the Cadillac.

"Freedom—ain't it grand?" Critter said, although he wished she hadn't included Crowbar in her list.

He'd bought the five-year-old Cadillac from his Uncle Donald when finally he'd had a few extra collars in his pocket. The car served him on a couple of levels. It gave Delphina something to wheel around town in, and therefore got her off his back. More important, because it was a Cadillac it increased his ascendancy within the kinship. Never mind that he rarely drove it. The men in the clan understood that although Delphina might drive the car most of the time, it was Critter's car because only a man could possess a Cadillac since only a man knew what a Cadillac meant to a man. So went Jordan reasoning; Critter had no problems following it.

"We need to do something for ourselves once in a while," Delphina said.

Critter thought he heard a hint of forced contentment in her voice. He smiled to himself. He knew they'd be leaving the party around ten-thirty or so. Delphina would begin to miss her babies, find herself bored with adults, restless, and she would announce it was time to take her home.

Critter loved her, loved her dedication to their family. Family: that thing that had sprung up inside of, around, and between them that was not him or her or even themselves together, or even the two of them plus the kids, but something greater than the people involved.

"Family, once you're in it, you're in it—locked up," he whispered to himself.

"I wish you wouldn't mumble," Delphina said.

She was the core of the family. Without her, he and the boys would be nothing but drifters. He was proud of Delphina, proud of his children, proud of himself for making it as a family man. And yet marriage, family, business success, ascendancy within the clan, these great gains of his maturing years and the triumph and confidence they brought him were accompanied by a loss, like a grief, as if his dog had died. He saw no escape from this feeling. The farther he went in the direction he wished to go, the more distance he put between himself and something important he'd left behind.

"I'm happy but I'm not satisfied," he said.

"Are you going to be in one of your weird moods tonight?" Delphina said.

"I feel...I feel...I don't know. Alone," he said.

"You'll be all right—the people will be wall-to-wall at LaChances'." She talked to him the way she talked to their kids, and that made him want to hold her.

"I had a lousy upbringing," Critter said.

"Didn't we all," Delphina said, checking her face in the rearview mirror. He liked the way she smelled close up, like a bottle of perfume.

He'd been a lonely, confused boy, with a mother who had

abandoned him before he was old enough to know her and with a father who was self-centered and preoccupied with his own dramas in which his son was only a bit player. Critter had survived by thinking; mainly he thought about sex. But these days his mind was busied by practical thinking—fix, figure, buy, build, sell, swindle, borrow from Peter, pay Paul. There was much achievement but little fun in this. So he had mixed business and pleasure by opening the bookstore. It had stimulated him, but only for a while. He'd reached the point where he had to say a beaver is a beaver is a beaver. There must be more, he thought—"But what?"

"What do you mean, 'What?'" Delphina asked.

"Thinking out loud," Critter said.

"It's a wonder there was any noise at all," Delphina said.

My gosh, but she could be sarcastic.

They were off the blacktop now, the Caddy lazing over the dirt road that led into the Salmon Trust and the caretaker's house where the LaChances lived.

Delphina had gone along with the bookstore idea. She'd even work a shift or two to give Noreen some time off now and then. ("Anything for an excuse to get away from these kids," she said, but she didn't mean it.) He watched her finger through the raunchiest of the magazines and giggle. He told her not to take the plastic covers off them. It had troubled him that this good mother, this good wife, was herself so curious and forthright about sex. And it bothered him that in the bookstore Delphina could see what he saw; nothing of it was his own exclusively. The pleasure of his secret, sexual fantasy life was the secrecy as well as the fantasy. It loses something when you can't sneak it, he thought. A secret was to Critter's soul what a pizza was to his stomach.

The Caddy hit a bump, and Critter winced at the sound of the car's oil pan scraping gravel.

"You'd think they'd pave these roads," Critter said.

"'Course, you don't drive too fast," Delphina said.

Chance met them at the door. He was wearing blue jeans, ankle-top work shoes, a blue T-shirt and Soapy's old baseball cap. Critter reminded himself to call Soapy Sheila. Since she and Chance had got hooked up with the Upper Darby crowd, they'd become touchy about Sheila's old nickname.

He could hear Soapy playing the piano, and he watched Delphina slip away toward the sound of the music. Chance steered him toward a garbage can full of ice and beer. Chance took a Bass ale, Critter a Bud.

"Something you ought to know," Chance said, tugging unconsciously on his woodsman's beard.

Critter marveled at the transformation in him. Roland LaChance had come to Darby as a newspaper reporter, an outsider. But these days he talked like a native, dressed like a native, held forth on local issues. ("These out-of-staters come up here and they buy property and the first thing they do is post the land so's you can't hunt," he would complain. And what a joke that was, since hunting was not allowed on the trust lands of which he was the caretaker.) He had become more Darby than the homegrown stock.

"Shoot your wad," Critter said.

"There's a petition been started to shut down your bookstore," Chance said. "Mrs. Acheson is behind it. After they get a couple hundred people to sign, they're going to present the petition to the selectmen."

Critter eventually would take this news with the gravity it deserved, but for the moment it oddly buoyed him. A petition against him acknowledged he had become an important man in the affairs of Darby. He believed the real reason for the petition was people were jealous of him, and they didn't like someone from Darby Depot making a name for himself.

"Nothing they can do. I'm legal as trout in May," Critter said.

Chance seemed about to speak, thought better of it, turned, then struck up a conversation with a logger whose name Critter knew but had forgotten. They drifted away from him, until Critter found himself alone in the crowd.

He spotted one of the Butterworth girls filling a paper cup with wine. He sidled up to her, saying, "Tastes better when it's free, don't it?"

They chatted. He told her about the Caddy. She told him she was thinking about quitting college—funny name, Bad College. He told her he was a builder. She told him she had met a man who had built a birch-bark canoe. He fancied she fancied his looks. Some older woman called her name (was it Nestle?) and she slipped off through the crowd, and he waited for her to return, but an Upper Darby guy latched on to her, and Critter knew she'd be tied up for a while. He went after a beer.

He saw one of the Prell brats plant a wet kiss on the cheek of a woman with hair dyed pink. She laughed, cuffed the brat on the head; they parted. This, thought Critter, is what a party is all about: women, other men's women; cheap talk and cheap feels. He ached to express this thought, and he attached himself to a group of fellows talking about the pros and cons of the new mall in Tuckerman. Critter bided his time until there was a silence and he could interject his ideas about parties, but when the moment came he had forgotten what he was going to say. He was alone again.

He fetched a beer, slugging down half of it in a swallow. So the Acheson woman wanted to shut him down. Destroy his business. He imagined her blind drunk stumbling into the path of his oncoming Caddy. The violence of that thought, uncommon for him, suggested to Critter that the beer was taking hold.

"Feeling good," he said, but there was no one to attend to this remark.

Soapy stopped playing the piano, and someone cranked up the stereo and the party began to rock and roll.

Critter found the Butterworth girl and danced with her. But the song ended immediately after they started. She asked him to get her some wine. When he returned he couldn't find her. He drank her wine in a gulp, chasing it with his beer. He went in search of her again to explain the wonders of this new drink.

He bumped into Delphina. She was dancing with the logger. The next thing Critter knew Delphina was insisting he dance with her. So he did. It was kind of strange because the logger stayed on, the three of them dancing as if they were a couple. He and Delphina would make sweet love in the morning, provided, of course, he could wake before the baby did. They never made love directly after a party because he was always drunk and unfit for maritals, but later—*whooee!*

And he was alone again, the logger and Delphina somehow having danced to the other side of the room. He peeked at Delphina through the crowd, watching her swing her considerable ass around. It was as if she were someone else's wife.

Critter was on his sixth or maybe it was his eighth beer when he got sidetracked into the study. Here Chance and another man had set up a card table and they were playing chess. Critter recognized the second man as Hadly Blue, a professor at Tuckerman State College and the live-in lover of Persephone Salmon. Critter knew nothing about chess, but decided to watch for a while because Chance and Blue, in their concentration, hadn't noticed him, and he wondered how long he could stand not four feet away before they saw him.

"Check," Blue said.

Chance moved.

"Check," Blue said, moving a horse's head.

"Check yourself," Chance said, moving a tall piece with a crown.

Blue set his chin in his hands and went into a pout. "You put me in peril for my greediness," he said.

"That's chess, just like life," Chance said.

"Easier to beat you than life," Blue said.

Critter wished they'd hurry up and notice him, so he could leave. He wanted to dance.

Blue moved. "A little pressure for your queen," he said, smug now.

Chance immediately moved his tall piece the length of the board, and Critter could tell by the look in Blue's eye that his side was in trouble again.

"The queen transforms the pressure applied into her pleasure," Blue said.

"Yup." Chance was the cat that ate the canary.

"Why should the queen have so much power and king so little?" Blue said.

"Maybe chess was invented by an early feminist," Chance said.

"It is strange," Blue said, becoming animated. "Here's a game straight out of antiquity and yet the king is passive, an object of conquest, not the power but the lap of power, feminine, while the queen is active, a warrior—masculine. Kings behaving like queens, queens behaving like kings—something is amiss here, or perhaps a-Ms."

"Maybe king means kingdom—your move," Chance said.

"Maybe you guys ought to play checkers."

The gamesmen looked up at Critter. Like one four-eyed creature, he thought. Their education, the game, the queen-king stuff, the very world they came from, so different from the world of the kinship, united them. His personal tragedy struck him then. Outside the clan, he was lost.

"My father used to say I couldn't sneak up on the dead, but you can see how wrong he was—here I am," Critter said.

"Have a beer for yourself," Chance said.

Critter grinned—Ike's grin, a false thing; he could feel it contorting his face—and withdrew, not embarrassed exactly (he was too drunk to be embarrassed) but wary, an animal sensing a trap.

When he returned to the dance floor, he saw that Delphina was dancing with Garvin Prell, a lawyer and a member of the Upper Darby set. Critter was suddenly angry. He wanted to smash the man in the face, smash Delphina.

"I'm cutting in," he said.

"Cutting in." Prell groaned a laugh, and slipped into the crowd.

A slow song was on, and they waltzed, at times struggling to see who would steer whom which way, at times limp in one another's arms. Critter's anger passed, replaced by a feeling like fatigue; that is, he could say he was tired but he was also jittery. The people in the party seemed stupid and boring to him. They had nothing to say to him, he had nothing to say to them.

"Time to go home," he announced.

"It's only ten-thirty," Delphina said.

"I want to go home; I miss the babies," he said.

"You're drunk."

"I got something I want to tell you, something important. I want... I want... I want what I want."

"You've got the Cadillac," Delphina said, more puzzled than annoyed.

Delphina drove home. Critter rode in the back seat. He'd always wanted to ride in the back, like some rich guy being chauffeured. It amazed him what a smooth ride the Caddy gave. He imagined the Butterworth girl in the back seat with him. He wondered if she ever got her wine.

"Del?" he called.

"What?"

"Let's make like we weren't married and go parking."

"You really are drunk."

After she said that, he felt the distance between them widen. It was as if the Caddy were enormous, Delphina miles away. He sat there, not feeling bad exactly, but merely alone.

When they reached the blacktop, the Caddy made a whisper sound, like lovers cooing.

"Swing by the barn," he said.

"What in the world for?"

"I want to check on Noreen, make sure she isn't closing early on me," he said.

He didn't have to tell Del to wait in the car. She clutched the steering wheel impatiently. "Hurry up," she said.

"My sweetie." He meant to give her a little kiss, but as he spoke he was out of car, out of range.

"What?" she asked.

He didn't bother to answer, but weaved for the door to the bookstore.

Inside, he found Noreen, sitting on her stool behind the register, staring off into space.

"Hey-hey-hey," he called her, friendly like.

She almost fell off the stool with surprise, then giggled when she saw it was he who had startled her. By George, she was happy to see him.

"You may think I'm just a bad boss checking on his help at a late hour, but it's nothing like that." He was invigorated now. "It's just that the missus and I were—" He couldn't think of anything else to say.

"Oh, I don't mind you coming in. It gives me somebody to talk to," Noreen said.

"How's it been tonight—busy?"

"Earlier," Noreen said.

The red dress was a little loose on her. He wished it were tighter, but even so… "I thought I'd, ah, inspect the fire extinguisher. Town's down on us, looking for an excuse to lock our doors."

Believing Noreen was watching his every move, he took great pains to scrutinize the fire extinguisher. He put his hands behind his back. The fire extinguisher hung on a bracket on the wall. It was an old brass thing, left over from his father's reign of the auction barn, and he had no idea whether it would work.

"They can't get us on breaking no fire ordinance," he said.

"If they do, you'll figure something, Critter."

The sound of his name from her lips was like an embrace.

"Critter!" Delphina yelled from the Caddy.

On the remainder of the drive home, he savored the image of Noreen in her red dress, slightly off-balance as the sound of his voice reached her.

Noreen was an old story in the kinship, pregnant as a teenager, no husband, no education, her own parents divorced and disintegrated. She'd labored as an assembler in a factory, been laid off, collected welfare, clerked in a department store, been laid off, collected welfare, waitressed, left for personal reasons (feet), collected welfare, and so forth. She had lived with kin off and on, even though she much preferred having her own place. Even when she had work and cash, it was hard to find an apartment because landlords didn't like single women with children. Barely into her twenties, she'd gone through the hysterical stage, the anger stage, and the face-life stage, emerging a sort of zombie, stunned and impassive, as if someone had hit her between the eyes with a tire iron. She was kept from death and disintegration by the kinship, social service persons, her children, and luck. She was the perfect worker, beyond pain, beyond any idea of expectations. Critter knew all about this the way he knew the sky was blue on a sunny day, that is, unconsciously, without pity or sympathy, but also without contempt or condemnation, Noreen's plight part of the natural order of things. He'd hired her because he knew her type. He'd been right about her, too. Noreen did her job well.

He was proud of the way he had treated her. He hadn't laid a hand on her, hadn't made any indecent proposals, hadn't so much as copped a feel. He figured she must admire him for his restraint. Maybe not. People could be mighty ungrateful. Could be, too, she adored him. He mulled over this possibility. After what she had been through, Noreen would desire every man and no man. She'd give herself out of habit, probably even enjoy the actual nookie out of habit; then she'd wash her face and pop some bread in the toaster for the kids—habit. She'd be beyond desire, beyond love, beyond everything but habit. To give and not to get: that was what she was used to. He'd given her a job, hadn't smacked her or anything, hadn't made her do it with him, so she had good reason to be grateful— even to adore him. That was something to consider. A woman beyond love was not beyond adoration, in fact was subject to adoration. Religion proved that. If a woman adored you, she did what you asked without question. If a woman adored you, she was easy to satisfy, since your pleasure was her pleasure. If a woman adored you, she would do anything you asked and be a better person for the doing. There was only one way to discourage a woman who adored you and that was not to demand anything from her.

9

The Wig

The flea-market vendors were setting up their tables when Critter arrived with Selectman Crabb. The Witch didn't even have to look at Critter's agitated face to know something was wrong; the clipboard in the selectman's hand told her that. Paperwork was a weapon, sure as a gun.

They cruised the aisles in silence, Crabb stopping every now and then to write something down. After about fifteen minutes, they sat off in a corner at one of the tables. The Witch drifted over to eavesdrop. She knew men on men's business took no account of a woman.

"It's got the required number of fire extinguishers," Critter said.

"But it doesn't have a sprinkler system," Crabb said.

Arthur Crabb, like Avalon Hillary, was an aging valley farmer. In fact, he was Avalon's kin. The selectman's job was a hobby with him. He was known by townspeople to be pretty much on the up and up, as town officials went, and that made him easy or hard to deal with, depending.

"The bookstore has a sprinkler system, just like the ordinance says," Critter said. He was pleading with the old man, as a son will who knows he has no chance with his father.

"The ordinance states the system is required to cover the entire square footage open to public access."

"But the flea market's only open on Saturdays and Sundays," Critter said.

In the face of this irrelevant information, Crabb said nothing.

The silence seemed to incite Critter, alter the pitch of his anger from whining boy to injured man. "You people never enforced the ordinance before," he said.

"We had some complaints," Crabb said.

"I know the complainers—bunch of Upper Darby snobs." Critter stood, yanked by some invisible puppeteer. "My business is my business, and you can't shut me down as long as I meet the requirements of the ordinance."

"It's not the individual business but the parts of the building open to the public that have to meet the codes. Protect the public—that's the name of the game."

"You're telling me you can close my store just because these flea-market people don't have a sprinkler system?" Critter said.

Crabb rose slowly to his feet. He was fatigued but not intimidated by Critter's sort. "If there's a fire, it will burn the barn, not just the business that's offending the code," he said, paused, and added: "See the reasoning, do you?"

Critter moaned as if spat upon by a loved one. His mouth hardened up, his eyes widened, the worms inside them brightened. The Witch had seen that look before on a Jordan man; Critter was going to do something crazy.

He jumped on one of the tables and shouted, "Your attention please, your attention please." The urgency in his voice quieted the eighteen or twenty people in the barn. "Due to circumstances beyond our control, the flea market is hereby closed until further notice. Pack up your things and go home."

"But I paid for this space," Piper shouted.

"Yes, sir, you did," Critter shouted back, "and I'm going to give you a refund, not only for the week, but for the entire month. Come and stand in line now."

Puffed with self-importance and victory, Critter folded his

arms and faced the old selectman. "There—now you got no legal grounds to close my bookstore."

"Not today I don't," Crabb said.

After Critter had left and the vendors had finished their communal buzz (they whispered as if the barn were wired for sound), the Witch started bringing her things upstairs. She had stored her flea-market goods in the barn, and it felt strange to be moving them.

Why? The question, which she had no intention of addressing, seemed to form in the dusty air.

"You want some help lugging that stuff?" Piper asked.

"I can get it." She didn't want him to see the Witch's quarters.

He read something in her face, a fear, and he said, "This is not the end—there's other barns."

"Oh, sure," she said.

He left to load his pickup, then returned to say good-bye. He grasped her hand and shook it as if she were a man, an old buddy.

"Take it easy," he said.

She heard him on his way out, laughing sadly with the widow Kringle. Piper meant nothing to Estelle, and yet she couldn't bear to see him go. Piper, the other vendors, the flea market—these people, this thing, so outside her Witch self, brought her rest. Without them, there would be too much Witch in her. Like anything combustible, she risked being consumed in her own fire.

After she moved the last of her pots into the apartment, her rooms looked strange to her, not hers. She shoved things here and there, trying to regain a sense of familiarity, but everything she did seemed to make the place less her own. Finally she rose in fury, threw half the pots and weeds in the bedroom, and chucked the rest in the woodstove. The crackle of flames tripped in the tremor. She was okay now, righted by rage and desire.

She lit her pipe and went outside on her landing. The summer growth was so dense that she wouldn't have been able to see any sign of the Trans Am hidden in the woods, but anyway she sensed he wouldn't be out there. He followed her less and less these days, and when he did he kept a widened distance between them. He hadn't lost interest, she understood; he was biding his time, but for what purpose? The mystery frightened and excited her. What made her uncomfortable was waiting for him to act. She resolved to conjure on this problem, find a way to take the initiative in her dealings with the little monster. She stood, looking out over the hills for the longest time, but no ideas came to mind.

Later, restless, the toke high wearing off, she decided to drive to Tuckerman, buy some groceries.

Only a year ago, she might have stopped at Ancharsky's General Store in Center Darby Village, perhaps chatting with Joe, the proprietor, but lately she did all her shopping at the Magnus Mart in Tuckerman. She was never exactly comfortable there, and yet the place had an attraction for her. Maybe it was its immensity, not like a building, not like the outdoors, but like a world. You could rent a VCR movie, buy nylons, writing paper, or a prepared pizza as well as groceries. Maybe someday you could be born, grow, mate, give birth, and die in a Magnus Mart, without ever the bother of going outside. Unburdened by weather, sky, and earth, a body could curl up all peaceful, like a pear pyramided in a display, and just be.

She bought some apple sauce, a loaf of bread, margarine, fish on sale.

Her Subaru caught up to Noreen's VW just as the road dipped down on the straightaway in front of the barn. Moments later they were in the parking lot, walking to the bookstore.

"You follow close," Noreen said.

"I like it close," the Witch said.

Noreen was wearing her red work dress, but her hair wasn't combed, and her face was pale.

"Look at you, aren't you a disgrace," the Witch said.

Noreen blushed and her words poured out apologetically. "I'm late for everything, I can't help it—it's just the way I am—and so I have to rush rush rush in case Critter calls to check on me. I throw my dress on and put my makeup on soon's I open for business."

"Something for yourself on somebody's else's time—it's better that way," the Witch said.

Noreen fumbled with the key to the front door. Finally, the lock yielded and they went inside.

The place was unfinished, and likely would remain so, in keeping with Jordan fashion—just enough. Critter had nailed down wooden panels on the wavy barn floor, and that was that. There was no finish floor, no carpet, no linoleum. The gypsumboard walls were nailed up but left unspackled and unpainted. A few panels were missing in the false ceiling. Magazine racks were made of construction-grade lumber crudely whacked together and unfinished. The peep-show booths were raw plywood. In contrast to this background, the main counter consisted of a finely made oak and glass display case. The Witch recognized it as one of Ike's most favored pieces. He had spent almost a year of his spare time refinishing it. Now his son was using the case to show off dildos, penis rings, and inflatable dolls.

Noreen locked the front door behind her, then went into the back room to put on her makeup. The Witch followed. The room was crowded with stacks of magazines and boxes. The Witch saw a fire extinguisher on a wall, the door that led to the barn proper, a straw broom (rarely used from the looks of the place), a calendar (unmounted, showing the wrong month), a toilet, and a sink.

Noreen stood before the sink, over which was a doorless cabinet attached crookedly to the wall and holding a wicker bag, some Tampax, soap, and a toothbrush, its bristles badly mashed, ugly. Then the Witch saw a razor. The idea that Noreen kept something handy to cut with sent a shiver through her. She picked up the razor and removed the blade.

"What are you doing?" Noreen said, giggling with fright.

The Witch ran the blade lightly across her own wrist, not drawing blood but inscribing a pink-white line.

"You shave your legs with this?" the Witch said.

Noreen nodded.

"Relax, Noreen," the Witch said, and put the blade back in the razor.

"It scares me—it reminds me of my abortion." Noreen began to apply her makeup.

"You don't take any care, you just slop the stuff on," the Witch said.

"I don't like the bother. If I could afford it, I'd go to the beauty parlor every day and let somebody else make me beautiful."

"I knew a girl like you once—lazy, oh, so lazy." The Witch snatched a tin of powder from Noreen's hand. "I'll do your face. Start by washing it."

After Noreen was clean, the Witch led her, half-bullied, half-hypnotized, to the main room of the store. She sat Noreen on the stool in front of the register.

Fishing around for makeup in the wicker bag, the Witch found Noreen's birth-control pills.

"They screw up my period, but it's better than getting pregnant," Noreen said.

"I liked being pregnant," the Witch said.

"I can't remember if I liked it or not, I just was, and probably I didn't like it because I tend to forget things that give me grief," Noreen said.

The flesh of Noreen's face felt soft yet firm to the Witch's fingertips.

"I remember after the second one was born, I said, no more," Noreen said. "I took the pill, and then, well, it just sort of slipped my mind to take one every day. Wouldn't you know it, I was pregnant again. I cried and cried. My social worker says, 'Maybe you should consider an abortion.' One thing led to another."

"During my glory years, we had neither pill nor abortion doctors. You had the baby, or you learned to rid your body of it yourself. Today it's nothing. You go into the doctor's office, and there's a nurse and magazines to read while you wait."

"I didn't mind the operation—it was the hangover afterward that felt bad."

"I know," the Witch said.

Neither woman spoke for a minute, then Noreen said, "To be honest, I wanted my first baby, wanted it bad. After that, I wanted to die."

"I also," the Witch said.

Noreen shut her eyes. The Witch could feel her relax under her fingers. In the hum of the neon lights she began to hear the drone of insects on a summer night from long ago, and the Witch in her dozed for a moment and her dear self spoke: "When I was a girl, my mother's love, her hands brushing my hair—and then one day she wronged me, not even sure how exactly."

"If you found out you'd feel better." Noreen talked as one repeating wisdom garnered from television.

"If I found out, I'd feel something I don't feel now. But better? I don't know," Estelle said.

After she finished putting makeup on Noreen's face, the

Witch stepped back to admire her work. It didn't look right.

"Lipstick's too pink, and we have to do something about that hair," the Witch said. "There's no shine to it, no body—it's scaggy."

"I didn't have a chance to wash it this morning."

"Or yesterday morning, or the morning before that."

"What difference does it make? Nobody notices."

"It makes every difference. A woman's hair is every bit of pride she has."

Noreen blinked with incomprehension.

It wasn't only that Noreen's hair was dirty, it was the wrong color, the Witch thought.

"You get on with your work. I'll be back," the Witch said.

She returned to her apartment and walked straight for the closet off the living room. She was excited, as if she'd learned someone had hidden a treasure among her own things. From deep in the back of the closet she pulled out an old hatbox. She blew off the dust and opened it. Inside was the wig she had placed there when her hair started to turn gray. She stood before the full-length mirror, holding the wig beside her. The wig was a little longer than her own hair, and the individual strands were straighter, darker, shinier. She put the wig on her head, and it was as if she had been injected with a drug that made her younger and more vigorous.

When the Witch entered the porn shop, pausing at the door, Noreen said, "What do you have in your hands, a black cat?"

Like an aborigine showing off a shrunken head, the Witch held out the wig with one hand.

Noreen giggled.

The Witch put the wig on Noreen's head. Then she wiped Noreen's mouth and held her own nighttime lipstick before Noreen.

"It's so red it's blue," Noreen said.

The Witch painted Noreen's lips, letting the color spill over

113

slightly to fill out the corners of Noreen's mouth. The Witch stepped back for an inspection. Satisfied, she removed Noreen's pocket mirror from the wicker bag and handed it to her. Noreen giggled at the image.

"I never liked my hair," Noreen addressed the mirror. "Another dirty blonde. So I dyed it real blond, like Hollywood. But it was such a hassle to keep. Always battling the roots. Gave it up. I never imagined black. I mean, like never. Now here it is—black. It's so...so different."

"It's getting late," the Witch said.

"Yah, time to open the store, go to work." Noreen returned the mirror to the bag.

"I'll make you up from time to time." The Witch patted Noreen's wigged head, and left the bookstore.

Outside in the parking lot of the barn, the Witch stared at the sun. The brightness hurt her eyes. She reached a hand upward, as if to touch the light. She felt like a drowning child reaching through the surface of the water for the rescuing hand of her mother.

While Noreen had been admiring herself in the mirror, the Witch had been staring at Noreen, as if Noreen herself had been the mirror, and the Witch had seen her own self from years ago. Now, under the hot sun, she was remembering another summer afternoon, the last hours of that girl, in a crowded shack, waiting for something, not sure exactly what.

Before Romaine spoke, Estelle recognized a change in her mother's eyes. They were far away.

"Your Uncle Oliver is visiting," Romaine said, not looking directly at her. "Wash all over. My brother likes folks to be washed."

She made Estelle clean up, change her clothes, put on a dress and shoes.

Then abruptly, Isaac, her father, took her on his lap, as he hadn't in years, it seemed. He told her a long rambling story that she did not understand, the way he used to before the booze took him over. They both laughed, Estelle because she felt the little girl in herself and was protected by that feeling.

Romaine brought Isaac a bottle, and he turned his attention to it.

She felt not anticipation at Oliver's impending arrival or apprehension at the change in her mother or anguish at her father's drinking, but oppressive closeness, the closeness of the shack, the closeness of the forest outside, like a sentence from a judge: confinement for life.

She watched from a window as a big car drove into the yard. It was like a ship from the sea; it promised her escape while it suggested dangers.

Oliver touched her hair almost absentmindedly so that she wasn't afraid. He said to Romaine, "I'll take her for a ride in my new car. These young ones like a nice, big car." His face was sharp, his body lean, and she liked the way he smelled, not boozy (she had it in her head that all men would smell of drink like Isaac and his brothers); he smelled of flowers (she hadn't yet learned about after-shave lotion).

"Have a drink?" Isaac thrust the bottle in front of Oliver. Oliver took a pull and gave the bottle back to Isaac.

"Go! Get away!" Romaine shrieked at Isaac, cuffing him with the flat of her hand. Isaac slunk off and lay on the couch. A moment later she could hear him snuffling. The sound caught her attention because she had never heard it before. It was when she realized the snuffling was a form of weeping that she also understood what was going to happen to her.

Romaine and Oliver crouched at the kitchen table, talking. She listened from the rocker by the window. She could make out some of their whisper-misted words.

"Not ready, not ready," Romaine said.

"I have eyes to see. She is ready."

"Her shape, yes."

"The spring has arrived in her," Oliver said. "See her skin, flushed—ready."

"Estelle!" her mother called from far away. Estelle rose from the rocker and rushed to her mother. Romaine kissed her cheek, brushed her hair away, and pushed her off.

"See how she clings to me. She clings. Even to him." Romaine pointed at the S of Isaac on the couch.

"She's spoilt, then," Oliver said.

"None of us been spoilt. We never had nothing. To be spoilt, you have to begin with something to spoil. We never had nothing," Romaine said.

"See how she waits, how she knows. Now I ask you, Romaine, I ask you."

She watched as Romaine moved farther and farther away. It was as if her mother's soul had departed from its body, embarking on a long journey into the stars.

"As you say—spoilt." Romaine's voice was flat.

"I will unspoil her," Oliver said.

Soon she didn't even try to listen, but immersed herself in the feeling, the incredible intensity of it, like hands on her body: the closeness.

Finally, Oliver turned to her and said, "I bet you never been in a new car."

She shook her head no.

"I bet you'd like to ride in a new car."

"Can I go for a ride?" She cried out, because Romaine was so far away.

"You see, she's eager," Oliver addressed Romaine.

"She is and she isn't. She's always been of two minds," Romaine said.

"Should I go?" she asked Romaine.

"It's a new car," Romaine said.

"Get in." Oliver took her arm.

She thought, Romaine is not here, Romaine is gone. She summoned her. "Romaine!"

"Go with him." Romaine's voice came from the great out there.

"Daddy!" she called.

Her father, who often lay passed out on the couch, now lay pretending to be passed out. She could tell by the sounds of his breathing, quick and shallow instead of slow and deep.

She liked the way the car rode, quiet and smooth.

Oliver didn't say where they were going. That made her feel as if she would never return to the shack, as if the big car was setting her free from shacks and boredom and anguish, taking her to something new and bright and tinkling, and on the other side of the world.

"Don't be a stranger now." Oliver reached over from the driver's side and pulled her close to him. At the urging of his hand, she lay her head on his shoulder.

"Isn't that better?" he said.

"I can't see too good."

"Okay." He released her.

She ooched up so she could see the road, but kept her head cocked at the same angle as when it leaned against his shoulder. Trees and telephone poles whizzed by. One, two, three . . . she lost count of the poles when she began to feel carsick. But soon she settled in, voluntarily close to Oliver, although not actually touching him.

"A car this big is a lot of push and shove to keep up," Oliver said. "Take you the morning to wash and wax her. Worth it, though. Protects the body. I like a shine you can see your face in."

She listened less to the words than to the voice, its sharpness, the way it sliced off words and held them out to her, like pieces of neatly cut meat.

"How far west you been, Estelle?"

North—she pictured the North Pole. South—she pictured a Florida orange. West—no picture came to mind; she couldn't think.

"Which way is that?" she asked.

He chuckled, enjoying her confusion. "Toward Vermont," he said.

"I been to Rutland," she said.

He laughed, a laugh that nicked her.

"I been to California, and I'll take you there someday," he said. "Once you've seen it, you'll never want to come back to Tuckerman County. It's big—grand. They got tree stumps big enough to put your momma's shack on. Once you've crossed the Golden Gate Bridge, you'll feel privileged forever."

She pictured the Golden Gate Bridge. The thought of it, the goldness her imagination endowed it with, made her believe Oliver would care for her, that he could do anything by truing it with his carving-knife voice.

As for the car, it was freedom itself—escape from shacks, from the messy New Hampshire forest pressing in, from the very smother of the kinship. The car would fly them to California.

He drove to the flood-control dam outside of Tuckerman. They watched the sun set over the water. He gave her wine to drink. Just enough. The wine was the color of the sunset, and it tasted like the sunset. He reached over and brushed against her, and she thought, Now it's going to happen, but all he did was roll down the window on her side so she could have a better view. The smell of him—male flowers—grew stronger. It wasn't until the colors of the sky merged and cre-

118

ated the night and a few stars were visible that he touched her.

And that was the end of the tenderness in him. He went at her like a dog.

It wasn't the loss of virginity that had been ruinous (she never valued it); it was the lies, the promises, the empty words, the betrayals—the car that, as it turned out, he didn't own, the fact that he had never been to California; but mainly it was Romaine, who for some reason had given her over to her brother. But why?

"Why?" the Witch whispered to the sky.

A week after the Witch made up Noreen, Critter paid a call to the bookstore around eleven P.M., closing time. The next night when the Witch heard his van pull into the drive, she decided to find out for herself what was going on. Already stoned, she restuffed her corncob pipe with toke and crammed it into one of the cups of her black lace bra. Like a battery, the still-warm pipe bowl against her breast charged her with energy. She crept down the stairs leading from her balcony into the maw of the barn. The only illumination was from the light that streamed through the half-open door of her apartment. The light distorted familiar objects, transformed them, it seemed, so their meaning lay not in their physical being but in their shadows; the shadows were feathers to the touch as she felt her way.

She bumped into one of the wooden posts that held up the barn. She put her arms around it, embracing it, exploring it, as she might the torso of a new lover. So much the hands knew. Hardness, softness, sharpness, bluntness, a thousand textures. The eyes taught the mind, but the hands taught the heart. The post was perhaps ten inches square, hand-hewn, its roughness filed by years. Time smoothed a thing, time rounded a thing until finally the thing was something else.

When she found the door that led to the storage room of the porn shop, she allowed her hand to linger on the knob. It was cool, yielding, curvaceous; she would have sworn she felt the smell of metal in her palm. She turned the knob gently, and pushed until she felt the muted click of the bolt meet resistance. She slipped her nail file in the crack. The bolt gave way to the subtle pressure and the door opened. She stepped inside and quietly shut the door behind her.

She tripped into another world. The air of the barn had been light, cooling, restless; but the air in the back room was heavy, suffocating. The smells were young and simple—printer's ink, paper, piss. They made her realize how much older and more complex were the smells of the barn itself, consisting as they did of something of dust and sweat and varnish and mildew from the stuffing of chairs that retained the essence of the beer-swilling men who had lounged in them before thousands of television programs; and, too, the barn smelled after all these years of cow. She waited the longest time, hoping her eyes would get used to the dark. But they never did; the darkness was total, almost solid.

She groped about, touching smooth paper, rougher cardboard, feeling the grimy floor through the soles of her feet until she found the door that led into the bookstore. She opened it a crack. Light flew into her face like a hurled stone.

Critter and Noreen stood on the platform behind the store counter.

"Don't worry—nothing to worry over." Critter's voice was saturated with plan. He held Noreen in his arms; the Witch could see the backs of his hands on the shoulders of the red dress.

"I'm not worried—I'm afraid," Noreen said.

"Oh, shit, not that." He grinned as one before a child telling a tall story.

"Someone followed me again last night."

"What kind of car?" Critter humored her. He enjoyed her insecurity. It helped steam him up. Yet the Witch could see he wasn't the kind of man to hit a woman, and for that reason alone she believed it was Critter, not Noreen, who was vulnerable to a sudden reversal of the situation, he who might be struck down at any moment.

"A shiny car—black, I think."

"You've got to do better than that, Noreen. What make car— Ford, Chevy, what? You get the plate number? Was it the same car as before?"

"I don't know—I'm just scared."

Critter stroked her neck. Noreen baits her trap with her own fear, the Witch thought.

"You're tired and jittery when you leave, so you imagine every car that gets on your tail is following you," Critter said.

"No, I'm being followed."

"Okay, you're being followed." Critter's hands fell from Noreen's shoulders to her waist, then to the tops of her buttocks.

"Critter, you keep right behind me when I leave. Promise."

"Sure." He was concentrating on his pleasure.

"Every night. Promise."

Critter stopped fondling Noreen. "Not every night," he said. "I have a home life, I have things to do."

"Promise—please."

"It's nothing. It's the late hour. It'll be all right." Critter tried to sound reassuring, kindly, but failed. His own father Ike, the Witch's son, never had the gift for kindness. Critter had it, but had not the means for expressing it.

Noreen trembled, and her fear rippled outward, to Critter, to the Witch. So the Trans Am was following Noreen. He'd get her, too, like he'd never get the Witch, she thought. The Witch trembled, half with Noreen's fear, half with her own desire.

121

"Tell you what," Critter said. "I'll put a CB in your VW. You get in any kind of trouble, call the Van Man."

"A CB." Noreen cooed; it was a proclamation of victory. "I'll need a handle."

"Red Dress," Critter said, and as if by magic, the dress fell from Noreen's shoulders. She stood in panties and bra, no stockings; the black wig, long and flowing, made her face look small. Critter leaned into her, kissing her throat, reaching around behind and unhooking her bra. Noreen cooed again.

She sounds like some disgusting pigeon, the Witch thought. She was jealous of the quality of that coo. It came natural, you couldn't fake it. Worth money it was.

Critter stepped back and said something. The Witch heard only the word *model*.

Noreen slipped off her underpants.

Critter left the Witch's view for a moment, returning naked except for his shoes and socks, and a camera dangling from a strap around his neck. Noreen struck a pose. Critter took a couple of pictures, the afterbursts of the flash lingering menacingly in the Witch's mind. Critter pressed himself against Noreen, pressed her against the counter. In their passion, they appeared to be fighting. Critter withdrew; he couldn't make up his mind whether to take pictures or make love. In the end, he did both poorly. Noreen behaved as one learning to swim, all awkward and frenzied.

Afterward, Noreen put on her dress, sat upon her stool, and she and Critter drank bottles of beer in silence, not even looking at one another. Critter downed his beer and began making advances at Noreen again.

"I'm not finished," she said.

"The beer can wait—I can't." Critter began to pull the dress over Noreen's head.

"You'll rip it," Noreen said.

"I paid for it, I can dang well do with it what I please."

"But you gave it to me. You said it was mine."

Critter released Noreen and threw up his hands. "I get that stuff at home. I don't need it in my place of business."

"Promise to buy me a new dress if you rip this one." Noreen bowed her head, as one surrendering herself.

Oh, what a cunning one you are, thought the Witch.

"I'll buy you a new one anyway." Critter yanked the dress over Noreen's head. It did not rip.

Noreen cooed. Critter took some more pictures and did it to her again. Better this time. The Witch wondered why they hadn't gotten a mattress to put on the floor. Perhaps the difficulty and discomfort of the position—in part standing, in part seated, but never reclining—made the act seem not like sex but some combination of fantasy and penance, misconduct pardoning itself.

When they finished they rushed to get their clothes on; they resembled comedians in a silent movie. On their way out, Noreen said, "You're going to follow me home now."

"Most of the way."

"And the CB—when do I get that?"

"I'll install it first thing next week."

"And my new dress?"

"What?"

"You promised."

When they'd left and the Witch was alone, the scene with Critter and Noreen began to twist about in her mind. There was a moment when she wasn't certain who had been out there. Herself? Was the man a stranger? Then the images came clear again, and she could see them—a man and a woman, struggling.

10

Supercow

"What goodies do we have here?" Avalon Hillary reached into a brown paper bag Estelle had brought.

"Home cooking," Estelle said.

"Oh, sure. That's why it says Magnus Mart on the plastic wrap."

"I'll take it back and you can eat one of your cows."

"The sandwich will do, the sandwich will do." Avalon bit into the Italian grinder, rolling his eyes in imitation ecstasy.

They were sitting at Avalon's kitchen table, the weary old farmer and the weary old whore. He was almost never in the house, but he had installed an answering machine on his telephone, and when Estelle wanted to visit she'd leave a message: "Something to satisfy your appetite 'round six o'clock." She always bought the same thing—a grinder, an apple, a pint of cranberry juice. He never complained, and he never offered to pay her back; she liked that. They'd talk for an hour or half the night, depending on whether she had a customer later.

"Wonderful grinder. And an apple fit for a king," Avalon said, the usual mock "whoopee-doo" in his tone.

He took a large bite out of the grinder, holding the apple in the other hand, as if for balance. Then he put the grinder down and chomped into the apple.

"You've mighty good teeth for an old poop," Estelle said.

"Must be the milk my mother made me drink." He held up the apple, the bite out of it glistening with moisture that rippled Estelle with a small fright. "If I had to do it over again, I never would have involved myself in the family dairy business. I would have sold the herd the day my father died and planted some of those Granny Smith apple trees. Be a millionaire today and there'd be no cowshit under my shoes."

Estelle popped the top from the juice bottle, tore a paper towel from the rack over the sink, and tucked it into the throat of his shirt. He smelled of the outdoors. Avalon worked all day, worked alone, so when she arrived it was natural he would want to ramble. Estelle was content to listen.

"Today I eat at all hours, when I goddamn please, thank you." He took another bite of the grinder, following it with a swallow of juice. "But I used to eat three meals a day, big meals, too, at six o'clock, twelve o'clock, and again at six o'clock at night. At five of the hour I'd drool for my feed. Six, twelve, six—magic numbers for the stomach, a way of life. If I missed a meal, I'd be grouchy for a week."

"You fool," Estelle said, joking, one friend to another.

He shook the juice bottle at her and, pretending to be cross, said, "Why do you buy this stuff? It goes right through me."

"At your age, things go through too fast or linger too long," Estelle said.

Avalon chuckled. "Actually, I think I'm better off this way, going skimpy on the food. Better for health—I think. I don't know. Truth is, after all these years of trying to figure, I figure I don't know a goddamn thing. It was Melba had the where-withal in this household, pure instinctive knowledge of life."

Estelle turned her eyes away, signaling she didn't like him mentioning the name of his late wife. She didn't mind his frequent reminiscences regarding her green thumb or her housekeeping skills or her all-superior way of handling door-to-door salesmen, as long as he kept a distance between his living self and the deceased one, referring to her as "she" or "the wife." But when he used her name—Melba—Estelle could feel herself grow sick with dull anger and loneliness. The fact was she wasn't used to her affection for Avalon. Didn't have a word for it. *Like* and *respect* weren't strong enough; *love*—no it couldn't be love; it must be some kind of feeling she couldn't identify because it was new to her, because a man like Avalon was new to her. He was no Williamson needing an escort to the grave, no Oliver abducting a partner for hell, no Aronson hiring a whore for his dreams. He was a man, a real, bona fide man.

Later, after he'd eaten and drunk most of the decaf coffee she'd made, a worried look came across his face. She thought she knew what troubled him. They'd been seen together. People were talking. Farmer Hillary was keeping company with the Jordan Witch. She wondered whether he worried more that she tainted his good name or the memory of his dear wife.

"You look tired," she said.

"Tired of this farm."

So, she'd been wrong. He wasn't worried about his whore; he was worried about his property. Important things first.

"Well?" she said, knowing he'd want to talk.

"No doubt about it, I'm through with farming," he said. "This place is full of ghosts. I mount my tractor and I see my father falling from it, dislocating his shoulder; I turn a clod of earth and I feel the hand of my grandfather on the ash shovel grip he carved. I watch the sun set over the trees in the west, and I see my children staring daggers at me because they hated the work and worry of this place. Yet the land holds me. Mainly, I like the grass, like to cut it, smell it, watch it in the sunshine. It's the farm I need to get rid of, the goddamn cows. I got this nutty idea when the cows go the ghosts will pasture out."

"So?"

"So, I'm going to hold a cow auction, Estelle. Besides the land, the cows are the only thing of value here. House is tired, barn swaybacked, tools worn. But these cows, especially my Bess—top girl in this county—have some oomph in the marketplace."

"You got one special cow?" Estelle was suddenly suspicious.

"Bess is my supercow, worth more than all my milkers put together, plus you, and me, and a congressman. Sometimes I think I'm prouder of Bess than of my own children."

"Grateful for what you've done for her, is she?"

"Now don't be smart with me." He spoke with loving condescension. "I'll say this: I bred her into being and I raised her right. And she lives pretty good today, gets the best of feed and medical care and never worries about heaven, hell, or oblivion. Goddamned but if in her own way she isn't grateful. Unlike my children, she doesn't give me any back talk and she pays her way, and I can sell her, which you can't do with your kids and still save your soul."

"I don't see how you can call a cow 'super'; she's only meat on the hoof." There was something wrong, but Estelle wasn't sure what it was. Perhaps it was Avalon's attitude, a certain twist in logic. Bess was his supreme accomplishment. Now he had to cast her off, sell her because the price she fetched would measure the accomplishment. She thought of Oliver and how he would be angry and hurt if a customer wouldn't meet his price for her.

Avalon smiled wryly. "I believe you're jealous."

"Not jealous—amazed. Amazed a member of the male kind shows such a high regard for a member of the female kind. It's just that—"

"—that you don't get it."

"You're teasing me again."

"I suppose I am." He showed his fine teeth. My, he was

smug. He knew she knew he had a little secret and that she wanted to know it. As men will with a woman, he toyed with her by withholding the knowledge.

But, the Witch's cunning rising in her, Estelle folded her arms over her breasts and waited close-mouthed for him to make the next move. The gesture and the tactic of silence caught him off-guard. She'd remembered him saying his wife used to cross her arms and clam up.

"You come by Tuesday, around nine o'clock in the morning," he said. "Serviceman will be here, and we'll show you what makes Bess a supercow."

"Suppose I don't care," Estelle said.

"Come by anyway and keep an old farmer company." Avalon's voice turned suddenly gentle, the smart-aleckiness gone from it.

He took her to his bed then and slowly and by degrees she roused him and made love to him. No money exchanged hands. Love itself was the payment.

He let his contentment run its course before he allowed that worried look to return to his face. She understood. Like any practical-minded man, he shelved a worry during a meal, during love-making, during the gloom of another worry.

"Okay, what is it?" she said.

He began to speak, caught himself, and prepared to start anew. She guessed he was going to say she could read his mind like Melba used to, but she was wrong, had been wrong from the start about what had been troubling him.

"Estelle, I got a pretty good idea who almost ran you down that day in my field," he said.

Stay away, stay away—she thought for a moment she had uttered these words, but apparently she must have just looked at him quizzically, because he talked on as if answering a question.

"I wasn't going to mention it because I was afraid it would

upset you," he said, "but it's best you know, and maybe be a little upset, so's you keep your guard up. I've been on the lookout for that black car around town ever since that day. I've seen it four or five times. Knew I would. To find a fella does his thinking and mischief in his car, keep your eye on the road. I recognized the driver, Upper Darby stock. They've got six or eight or maybe twenty black sheep up there on the hill where the Salmons, the Prells, and the Butterworths live—they specialize in black sheep—and this fellow's one of them, pure pewter black sheep."

The Witch didn't want to listen. She didn't want to hear that the Trans Am was human, belonging to time and place. She wanted him on the road and in her mind, just as she wanted Noreen Cook before her like a mirror of the past, the two of them ripples of her tremor.

"When I spotted him I garnered as much on my own," Avalon continued. "Then I talked to Mrs. McCurtin, who was only too happy to fill me in on the details. Kid's name is Dan or Don or Dane, something like that. His mother is Natalie Acheson. Runs the boutique in the barn over there at the old Swett place?"

The Witch nodded, imitating Estelle's intentness for Avalon's words.

Avalon was fooled and went on with his tale. "Seems as if Mrs. Acheson used to be married to one of the Butterworths and they had this one boy. The marriage soured, the father left to live in San Francisco or some other such place at the other edge of the continent, and the mother remarried the Acheson man. The boy lived here, lived there, spent a lot of himself in private schools. Nobody really wanted him, I suppose. Eventually, he ran off, lived on the streets, or so the story goes. Of recent, he got into some kind of trouble, bad trouble. Mrs. McCurtin says probably drugs, but I could tell she was just speculating. Anyway—bad trouble. He's on probation, that much is known. Sounds to me, Estelle, like this is a nasty young man. I advise you to keep your distance from that car, and if he gives you even a horn honk, call Constable Perkins."

"You say the car you saw was black," the Witch said.

"Black as one of my holsteins is black and white."

"The car that almost ran me over was blue."

"No, Estelle, it was black."

The Witch shook her head gravely. "Blue," she said.

"Blue, you say. Why I must be getting old not to know black from blue." Avalon grinned, glint of steel in his eye. He was beginning to see the Witch.

In her Witch's knowledge, Estelle Jordan knew the car was black, knew her lie and its purpose, to protect the Trans Am. She reveled in the lie. In the sadness of the lie resided the dear self.

"In a bruise, sometimes you can't tell black from blue," she said.

"Do you think my face is okay?" Noreen said, looking up with cow eyes, as the Witch rubbed dark purple mascara with her little finger in a crescent under one of those eyes.

"Your face is your own until I touch it, and then it's mine." The Witch's answer was sharp. The question had disturbed her, not because she couldn't deal with it, but because it suggested to her that Noreen was a person, with opinions, feelings, thoughts, questions. Noreen was not a person, Noreen was not even real, Noreen was a reflection.

"You scare me but I like it—you're like a movie," Noreen said. "Is that why they call you 'Witch'—because you scare people?"

Estelle remembered the day her son Ollie had named her Witch. The sky was flat but restless, like the surface of a pond. She could see rows of stones. She didn't believe that farmers had made those rock walls; Indians did for religious reasons long forgotten. Blood seeped from the stones. And then her mind was back in the present. The storeroom of the porn shop, where nearly every day she made up Noreen's face, was dreary, disheartening in its ugliness. How ugliness wore away at the soul.

"It's a long story. It makes me sad to tell it." The Witch let her hands linger over Noreen's face, as if its beauty in her fingertips could decorate the room.

"But you wouldn't be anything else but what you are—the Witch: famous?" Noreen sought reassurance.

Estelle laughed darkly and privately, like a child hearing confirmation that wolves lurked in closets of her house.

Noreen looked up. "I know you don't really like me," she said. "Why do you make me up? Why do you do this for me, Estelle?"

Noreen's use of her name, sudden and unexpected, pierced the Witch like a musical note.

"I don't do it for you, I do it for me," she said. "Why do you put up with the abuse I heap upon you?"

"I don't know." Noreen waited for an answer to the question the Witch had posed to her. The Witch's answer would be *the* answer.

"You like my hands on you. Admit you like my hands," the Witch said.

"I like to be pampered. Nothing wrong with that," Noreen said, growing content under the Witch's familiar scorn.

"Shut your eyes now, relax, get some rest before you go to work."

Noreen looked into the Witch's eyes, seeing bright little eels in them. Soon she shut her own eyes, and fell pleasantly into a half-doze.

"How do you feel?" Estelle asked.

"I don't know—like, like I'm cozy, hiding."

"Like a lamb—you feel like a lamb."

"Yes, I feel like a lamb." Noreen drifted off.

She has no real being, the Witch thought. She becomes whatever people say, whatever they want. All she gets out of it are things. But there is no she; there is no Noreen.

After Noreen and Critter had closed the porn shop, the Witch stole into the storeroom, made her way to the main showroom and snapped on the overhead lights.

Her eyes were drawn to the magazine racks. So much color on shiny paper glistening like hardened sweat, all in service of making private parts public, every sex act she'd ever heard of and then some, women with men, women with women, men with men, women and men alone, women with objects, women with animals, twosomes, threesomes, foursomes, and -somes so many the organs got in each other's way, all the races integrated, pretty people and homely people, even a magazine devoted to fat ladies. She figured they'd have to pay the models double, once for the picture-taking, once for the sex. I bet these girls make a good living, she thought. An image flashed in her mind of a used-car lot, pennants slapping in the breeze, old boozer standing around with a cigar in his mouth— she was too old. Double pay, immortalized on film—not for her; she'd missed out. When she was young, she'd had a terrific body and nobody had actually appreciated it. She herself hadn't even realized the glory of it until it was past its prime. Men had looked her over and taken the goodies, but they'd never taken the time to appreciate what was there, never perused at their leisure, as today they might peruse one of these magazines. Another image: ruins of a temple shown in the *National Geographic* magazine. Of course she was as good as ever in her trade, maybe better because of the gum-it skill. But you couldn't show a toothless old woman in pictures and put the idea over. She looked again at the magazines in their racks, now seeing Noreens everywhere. Hundreds of Noreens, firmly

boobed, long-legged, toothed, eager, dumb—oh, so dumb—
or so smart they could fake oh-so-dumb.

Running off the main room was a short, dimly lit corridor
with peep-show booths on each side. She opened the door to
a booth. It was no more than five feet long, three feet wide;
there was a bench against the back wall and a white panel on
the inside face of the door. Apparently you sat on the bench
and looked at the panel where dirty movies were shown, and
upon which men had written crudely of their yearnings. Her
eye took in pictures of penises and vaginas, telephone numbers, lines of verse, messages. Perhaps some men came here
not to view the peep shows but to sit upon the benches and
contemplate what was writ, then to offer their own words. Was
this what men scared of flesh did in place of touch—write of
their desires? Some of the messages pleaded, some joked, some
screamed in anger. So many men had their peckers hooked
netherwise to their feelings of rage; anger and sex were different strokes of the same piston.

Something like a parking meter hung on a wall inside the
booth. This, she realized, was the thing you put the tokens in
to play the movie. The Witch rummaged around behind the
counter, looking for tokens. The cash drawer was on the floor,
shoved under the counter, the big bills gone. She found a
console box for a burglar alarm, wires sticking out of it. Critter
had had the foresight to bug the place but not the fortitude to
follow through with the work.

She spotted a cardboard shoe box on a shelf in the cabinet;
inside was a stack of nude photographs of Noreen. She seemed
frailer in the pictures than in the flesh, thighs scrawny, breasts
pubescent, smiling shyly, her face too small for the black wig
that covered her natural hair. In love with the camera, a girl's
harmless crush. The tremor thumped like a beating heart inside the Witch.

Hanging on a peg behind the counter were some keys. The

Witch returned to the booth she'd been in before; eventually, she felt the yielding of lock to key tremble through her fingertips. Tokens spilled out. She put one in the slot and settled in on the bench.

The movie began with no credits, no titles. Four men and a woman sat around a card table in a room furnished cheap and new; a motel room, as later the Witch figured out. The men were pool-hall wise, pool-hall sexy, the woman all too familiar—young flesh, old spirit, soft body, hard face, thick hair, thin hands. The movie was in color, no sound but the *hiss-click* of the projector. This suited the Witch. She didn't care to listen to a bunch of grunts and groans. The sounds of sex had always struck her as flotsam to the act itself. She was reassured by the noise of the film projector. It suggested that no matter what people did, no matter their pleasure or pain, the machinery of the universe ground on unawares, uncaring, but also uncritical.

The woman won all the chips on the table, laughed and left. Good for her. The screen went dark. The Witch put another token in. The men discovered they had been gypped, although how was not made clear. That troubled the Witch. Perhaps the woman hadn't cheated the men after all. Perhaps she didn't deserve whatever was going to happen to her. It was like watching a tragedy develop on television. She was both entertained and horrified; she had to know the end. The men abducted the girl. A gang bang followed. Rough stuff. Sucky-fucky. Cornholing. But no ending. The men shot their wads and the movie stopped, the fate of the card cheat unknown. The cost had been eight tokens.

The Witch shut her eyes and she could see and feel a shower of color from the movie rain down upon her.... Did they kill you? Or only scorn you with sex? Maybe you escaped. Maybe you killed them. The uncertainty, the fact that the uncertainty would never be resolved, made the Witch think about Romaine. Why did you surrender me to Oliver that day? Was it only because I was a nuisance or a burden?

She drifted around the porn shop like one on a rudderless ship, playing the peep shows, reel after reel, over and over again, so that eventually time and memory lost their meaning for her. She immersed herself in the sex acts of the movies; she became part of them. Perhaps she was not here, but in there, in the movie, and this old whore's body was make-believe. It didn't matter. There was no fear in her, no anger. She dived through time: *You'll never make it without my help, Noreen. Critter might lead you home tonight or tomorrow night and the night after that. But there will come a night when you'll be alone, and he'll be there, in the woods, parked, ready. He'll have you and he'll kill you, and I'll have you and I'll kill you.*

She returned to the booth with the movie of the woman at the card table. She put a token in, another, another. And she was seeing kin dancing to fiddle music on the wooden floor of a town hall. Which town? She reached out for a hand, reaching for her mother in a crowd, and the image vanished and she was looking at the porn movie. For the dozenth time the men caught the girl who had deceived them; for the dozenth time the mystery of the girl's fate scourged the Witch.

Exhausted, back in her apartment, the Witch washed and scrubbed the makeup from her face. She brushed her hair, dressed in a flannel nightgown, retired to the little bed in the far room, and lay down to sleep. A few images from the porn shop lingered in her mind, but they were like far-distant memories, vivid but removed from this dear self.

The sky was overcast the day Estelle headed for Avalon's barn and an encounter with his supercow. It felt like rain. In the auction barn's parking lot, Estelle watched the giant snapping turtle in some grass. Its head fully extended, neck stretched out, the turtle seemed to be reaching for the warmth of a sun determined to remain hidden, the crooked edges of its mouth like a cruel grin.

"What do you want?" Estelle called, as if to a wandering boy. The turtle did not respond.

When Estelle reached the Hillary Farm, the sky was even darker, lower, then when she'd left.

Avalon wore his usual work gear—blue denim overalls, blue cotton shirt, John Deere cap, and the black rubber boots he called shitkickers. And yet he had a gleam in his eye, like a man dressed up and slickered down for stepping out on the town.

They strolled into the barn together. Instantly, the barn air chilled her. The interior was cold, raw, dark, a triumph of gloom over the outside weather itself. In the auction barn, the smell of the past was weak, corrupted. Here it was strong, pure, no different today from a century ago. Nothing was new; metal was pitted or rusted, wood weathered and cracked. Even the spiderwebs seemed ancient. Like Avalon with his sloping shoulders, wide hips, and jowly jaws, the barn appeared to sag from the weight of its own presence over time.

"This place makes me feel uncomfortable, unwelcome," she said.

"It's because you're not a cow," Avalon said.

She confronted him. "You invited me here to watch you breed your Bess, didn't you?"

"In a manner of speaking."

"I know the act. It's not much different among animals than people, and I've had experience."

"This one time, Estelle, you are wrong—far, far wrong. Among farm animals the act is nowhere like natural. What

136

you're going to see this morning is science having knowledge of nature at her most serious moment. I'm speaking biblically now." There was no hint of the usual humor in his voice.

They descended into the guts of the building. This, she thought, is a place that has never seen strong light. Furthermore, she guessed her skirt at this moment had brought in more color than anything else over the history of the barn.

"There's my Bess." Avalon pointed to a cow tightly confined in a stall.

Something about the way he said "Bess" disturbed Estelle. It was the "my." The "my" took away from the identity of the cow. It occurred to her then that Bess was no name at all. A wise man wouldn't recognize a personality in a creature he planned to kill or use for commercial gain. The name Bess must have been a joke, mere man's play. Every cow was Bess. Estelle felt a slap of humiliation on behalf of Bess.

Someone hollered, but the air of the barn distorted the shout so the words were garbled. A shiver of danger ran along Estelle's spine.

Avalon recognized her fright. "Nothing to be worried about, old girl. Only the serviceman, nervous because I wasn't at the door to meet him. Wait here." He ambled off.

Alone, Estelle studied Bess. In the restricted area of her stall, she seemed immense, both burdened and exalted by her own bulk. She munched absentmindedly on some hay, neither contented nor concerned, but resigned, reminding Estelle of scores of Jordan kin, especially women, souls who had struggled to figure out this much: that they were incapable of understanding what their lives were all about.

Avalon returned in a few minutes with the serviceman. He was a thin fellow with a shoe-box face and a black mustache the size and shape of a bow tie. He was dressed in white coveralls, stained along the thighs with some kind of yellowish stuff that wouldn't come out in a wash. He never looked at Estelle, nor did Avalon introduce them. She was not part of the business at hand, and therefore she did not exist. Estelle stepped back and brought her hands to her face, to feel the reality of her physical being.

Avalon threw a rope around the cow's neck and jerked her hard, to get her started out of the barn. He led her down a long corridor, Estelle and the serviceman following. The wooden floor of the barn shuddered under Bess's footfalls. Estelle caught the serviceman sneaking a looksee at her. This made her feel as if she'd won something from him.

Although the day was cloudy and dark, the light outside, by comparison with the barn's, seemed brilliant, a gray glare. The serviceman threw up a hand before his eyes. Bess blinked, then bellowed. Estelle resisted the urge to run back into the barn. Only Avalon had anticipated the change in light, and he greeted it with a smile.

Avalon tied Bess to a stake driven into the ground, and the two men circled her, sizing her up. Estelle stayed back, standing in tallish grass; she could feel a moist coolness on her bare legs.

The serviceman said something she didn't catch. He talked fast with an accent she wasn't familiar with. She gathered he wanted to get the job over with, had more important things to do. Avalon taunted him by taking his time.

"She won't complain," Avalon said. He took Bess's huge face in his hands, looked into her brown, watery eyes like a hypnotist, then released her and whacked her on the neck with a blow that would have felled a man. Estelle understood this passed as a pat to a cow, but the roughness disturbed her. Men were always looking for an excuse to whack something, even in displays of affection.

"She wasn't too steady last time—tried to kick me." The serviceman fiddled with his equipment, a wood-grain metal unit with dials on it from which protruded a coiled hose; its silvery nozzle seemed poised to strike.

"You rushed her, my boy," Avalon taunted. "You can't rush these old girls, and you have to show 'em a kind hand."

"You always say that, Mr. Hillary," the serviceman said.

"My girls." Avalon spoke ironically.

The serviceman chuckled nervously, then shut down signs of emotion on his face. He put on eyeglasses and pulled clear plastic gloves over his hands, holding them up to the weather, like a doctor before an operation. He appeared very intellectual now, very impressive. Estelle sensed a change in the situation. The serviceman was no longer under Avalon's thumb; the serviceman had become the boss.

"Hold her steady," he commanded. The hose seemed to uncoil of its own will, the nozzle taking a position in the plastic-gloved hand of the serviceman.

"Hang on, Bess, we're going to delve into your future," Avalon said. He half draped himself over Bess's neck.

Nozzle and hand disappeared inside of Bess. The serviceman rummaged about in Bess's uterus, at one point shouting to Avalon, "Hold her! Hold her!"

Bess heaved and sighed, and stomped a foot heavily as if to the beat of music. The hose slipped out for a second.

"Bastard!" the serviceman grumbled.

"Steady, steady as she goes. Going to be okay, girl." Avalon reassured Bess, but to Estelle's ear there was a coldness about him, or perhaps a remoteness, at any rate a lack of recognition of Bess as something alive, as being anything more than a tractor or that cadaver of a backhoe in his field. Estelle wanted to shout, "Can't you treat her like she's human?" But of course that was stupid. So she stood there, stunned and helpless, not knowing why she felt like a witness to a crime.

Intense but cautious, the serviceman busied himself inside Bess. He was, thought Estelle, like a small boy poking a hole in the ground with a stick, imagining that inside is a snake. When he was done, he had sucked out the deepest, richest ore of Bess's femaleness.

Avalon grabbed some plastic gloves, slipped them on, dipped his hands into the creamy mucus, and held it before Estelle. His face was flushed with pride or victory or ecstasy, something, some man-thing she could not fathom.

"There, look," he said in bragging tones. "Isn't it a miracle? Eight, ten, maybe twelve fertilized eggs. Too small to see, but there. A miracle of being and science. Understand now why this Bess is a supercow? What we have here is a daughter of science, business, and God. You understand, Estelle?" The heat of his emotion radiated outward.

"Those eggs won't grow right outside their mother's belly," Estelle said.

"She doesn't quite get it." Avalon addressed the serviceman.

Calm, detached, the serviceman explained, "For years we extracted semen from the best bulls and bred cows with it. But the best milkers drop only so many calves. Suppose we bred only the best milk-producing cows with the best bulls? Now we can do that. We take a cow like Mr. Hillary's here and we give her drugs to divide her eggs and bring her into heat. Then we artificially inseminate her with the sperm of a prize bull. What we did today was flush the fertilized eggs from her uterus. They'll be surgically implanted in the wombs of lesser cows. This grand milk-producer here will never have to carry to term."

"We can make this Bess breed five, ten, twenty, fifty, a hundred or more of her own kind," Avalon said. "You see now why we call her a supercow?"

Estelle looked at Bess. The cow was munching grass, oblivious to what had just happened to her. Estelle looked at the sky. It was starting to clear up. Calves would be born. Sons and daughters, mothers and fathers—far away from one another, motherhood immaterial.

11

Romaine

Before leaving for Concord, Estelle worried, uncharacteristically, about what to wear and how to groom herself, finally settling on a navy-blue dress with white ruffles at the throat, pantyhose, and low-heeled shoes. The time she spent combing her hair seemed drawn out as if she were stoned, and she took even more pleasure than usual in the act, not knowing exactly why, until she remembered her mother used to comb her hair. And yet her memories of childhood were so confused that perhaps it hadn't been Romaine. It might have been one of her aunts or one of the women she called aunts who really weren't relations, or perhaps no one brushed her hair, her memory mere wishful thinking petrified into the appearance of fact by time. In the Jordan kinship, women had babies too early or too late, with so little knowledge of or respect for common family traditions that who was mother and who was daughter often became blurred even in the minds of the women themselves; to very young children, all women were mother and none was mother.

In Tuckerman she stopped at Donald's, bringing the Subaru to the garage to be checked over for the drive.

After Donald finished working on the car, he met her outside for a moment, silent but watching her, his signal he could be spoken to.

"I'm going up to Concord to pay a call on your grandmother Romaine," Estelle said.

Donald took a step backward as if her perfume offended him.

"Fan belt was loose, so I tightened her; freshened your anti-freeze, too." The sun, reflecting off the metallic sheen of Donald's skin, lacerated her eye.

"My, oh, my, I haven't seen her in years." She forced the words.

He made no sign he understood her urgency but he did speak civilly to her.

"They say cars aren't built like they used to be, and they aren't," he said. "They're built better. Especially the engines ... electronic ignitions ... no points to set ... change the oil when you feel like it, though I can't say I recommend that. Anyway, don't worry about this old pig from across the seas. It's engineered better than you and me and all the rest of the Jordans in Tuckerman County."

And he showed her his back and strode away.

Before setting out, the Witch bought roses for Romaine but also for her own comfort. She wanted something soft to look at, something soft to smell, something soft to contrast with the metal and glass of the car.

On the road, she imagined cutting her finger on a thorn of a rose bush, and the fragrance from the flowers healed the wound.

The hospital reminded her of the Tuckerman textile mills and shoe shops of decades ago—grim red-brick buildings three and four stories high, at once (it seemed) solid and permanent yet coming apart from the moment they opened. She looked for dazed souls walking the brick pathways; saw none. It didn't dawn on her that two thirds of the buildings were shut down. Rather, she experienced the emptiness of the place as an emptiness in her. A minibus pulled up and half a dozen people got out with the driver, a young woman in tan pants and a sweat-shirt. The fact that the driver was a woman, the fact that a woman was in charge, the fact that her dress was casual shocked Estelle. She'd expected all the staff people to wear white uniforms. Before the group disappeared into a building, she was startled by a laugh from one of the patients, startled because the laugh rang with mirth, not madness. Something was wrong. She would have been relieved to hear a howl or a shriek. She sensed she was approaching one of those moments in human life when a belief, so ingrained that it is part of the personality of a person, is proved wrong, dead wrong, wrong from the start.

At the reception desk, she had a panicky moment when the clerk had difficulty finding her mother's name in the files. Finally, she was directed to the geriatrics building. Clutching the bouquet of roses, she made her way down a long hall in the main building. The tile floor was dull and worn from the tramping of countless feet, and yet she saw no people.

Outside, she watched pigeons roost in crannies behind barred windows.

She stopped a bearded man getting into a jalopy that would have made a Jordan teenager proud.

"You work here?" she asked.

"Attendant," the man said.

It occurred to her he might be an escaped patient, stealing a car. The Witch in her searched his eyes for a lie. His eyes said, "I'm tired, I want to go home."

"Where are the crazy people?" she asked.

"Walking the streets," the man said with a faint grin that lightly mocked her question. "Drugs keep them out of the hospitals, that and these new laws."

"Laws?" What could law have to do with mind? she wondered.

143

"The laws say even if you're crazy the state can't lock you up unless you're dangerous to others or to your own person. People have lost jobs over those laws."

The man drove off, leaving Estelle to mull over whether it was her duty to sound the alarm that a possible mental patient was on the loose.

Unless you're dangerous—the words racketed about in her mind. As far as any Jordan was concerned, everyone was dangerous to everyone else. If danger was the issue, everyone should be locked up. But that wasn't the issue. The issue was crazy people. The reason they were locked up wasn't because they were dangerous or not dangerous but because they were crazy. She could go no further in thinking the matter through, for she had only her Jordan logic to guide her.

Once inside the geriatrics building, she announced herself to a white-uniformed nurse stationed at the reception desk. The woman was about her own age, built like a log skidder, with a scowl that could run a nylon.

"Mrs. Jordan is in Room 202, second floor," the nurse said coldly.

"Do you know my mother?" Estelle asked.

"I've been here twenty-five years, so, yes, I know her, quite well," the nurse said.

Estelle said nothing. She could see now that the nurse had something to say.

"You'd be Estelle," the nurse said.

Estelle returned a bare nod.

"She said if any of her kin came, you'd be the one."

"Is she coherent?"

"Hard to answer that question," the nurse said. "There was a long time that she wasn't coherent, and then she was again. She could have walked out of here ten years ago. She wouldn't leave. This had become her home. Nobody wanted her out there. And something else—she was afraid. She had about—oh, I don't know—four or five years of coherence. Today, well, I couldn't say where she is."

"And the future?"

"Bedridden from physical ailments. As for her mental illness, you should speak to the doctor."

"But you know what he'll say."

"You're some years too late. She's in her grave, and used to it." The nurse turned her back on Estelle.

On the walk to her mother's room, Estelle heard moans, a scream, a cackle, the whispers of professional people. She saw gaping mouths, bustling help in hospital whites, high-and-mighty doctors in sport jackets, and, being wheeled down the corridor, a woman with a withered jaw and only whites for eyes. These sights and sounds, along with the big nurse's guard-dog personality, oddly cheered Estelle. She thought, Ah, this is more like it; the grim expected put her mind at ease.

The unexpected returned when she saw Romaine in bed looking out the window. She had carried a picture in her mind of her mother: a big-bodied woman with long black hair, awkward but forceful in her movements. What she saw now was a frail old woman, thin and dry as the stalks of weeds Estelle picked.

She reached for a word of love inside herself and, finding none, held out the flowers.

The old woman slowly removed her gaze from the window and thrust it nervously toward her daughter, as one attempting to menace a physically superior opponent with a puny weapon.

"Roses," Estelle said.

Romaine made no move to accept the flowers. Whatever Romaine was seeing, it was not, strictly, these flowers, another person, this room. Romaine took in the things around her as if they were images on a television screen rather than the evidence of real life. Her eyes roamed from the plain white Johnny gown on her body to the view outdoors (a pine tree, dirty buildings, sky), to the flowers in the hand of her daughter, and finally to Estelle herself.

Her mother's gaze felt like the hand of a spirit passing through her body. Estelle dropped the flowers on the bed, and this act seemed to shake Romaine from her imaginings and moor her to the moment. Something that might have been recognition broke out on her face. Estelle experienced a brief benediction, warmth, as from a light; this—was this the radiance of a mother's love?

"Mother?" The word came hard to Estelle's lips.

The old woman took the longest time to speak. "Estelle? Estelle, can it be you?" she asked, sounding fascinated, yet skeptical too, as if addressing her own echo rising from the depths of a well.

Her mother's voice, unlike the rest of her, had not changed. It was still strung too high, it was still an instrument for digging at her daughter's innards. When she was a girl, most of the time she heard her mother's voice she'd felt fatigued, as if robbed of energy. That same feeling came back now.

"Yes, I'm Estelle."

Romaine turned again toward the window, and spoke as if to someone sitting on the sill, although there was nothing there but bird droppings. "Which one is she? My own Estelle or the other one?"

It was an accusation, delivered in exactly the same tone and with exactly the same quality of mystery that Romaine had used to befuddle her as a child, and Estelle knew no more how to answer it now than she had then.

"I am Estelle," she said.

Romaine paused, and then, as if she had received advice from her invisible counselor, asked slyly, "What has happened to your skin, and around your eyes?"

146

Estelle ran her fingers along the contours of her face. It felt dry, papery; only the bones beneath seemed to have abided over time.

"You're old—my Estelle is not old," Romaine proclaimed like a judge passing sentence.

"Oh, Mommy."

Romaine broke into tears. "Leave me alone. Go away, don't torment me like this."

Estelle tried to understand. Her mother didn't know who she was. Her memory of her was frozen in time.

"It's been so many years, Mommy. I've changed, you've changed. I know I should have come to see you, but..."

Romaine abruptly stopped crying, and pointed a finger at her daughter. "But, dear one, you do come daily to see me. Somebody comes. They say I'm crazy, I make you up, you're a hallucination. We have them on this floor, all the time in the middle of the night, horrible sounds and colors out of nowhere, like an awful pus. But not always—not always. Sometimes what I think I see, I really do see. You. Who are you?"

"I'm Estelle—real—touch me."

"I don't want to; I won't." Romaine buried her face in her hands, and Estelle thought she would weep again. Instead, she peeked at her through the spaces between her fingers like a two-year-old playing a game. "Tell Mommy the truth now. Which Estelle are you?"

Estelle backed a step away from the bed. She was beginning to understand. In her madness and loneliness, Romaine had invented two versions of her eldest daughter, a Witch and a dear self. This was Jordan womanhood: she, the Witch, was a distorted reflection of Romaine; Romaine herself was a distorted reflection of some female figure from the past; and so forth, down through the kinship.

"I am your Estelle," she said.

147

"I don't believe you—you're the other one." Romaine folded her thin arms and sulked.

"Remember, you used to take me with you to pick blueberries. You carried a pail made from a coffee tin. You used to say, 'The poorer the soil, the better the berries.'"

"Oh, how could you know that? We climbed over the granite, you barefoot. No men to beat us, no poverty to wear us down, no kinship—we were free." Romaine immersed herself in the hurt of the memory. "I can't bear this," she said, and turned toward the window.

Estelle knew at that moment that she should have distracted Romaine, kept her away from the hallucination, but something held her back. Finally, she said, "Look at me, Mother," but it was too late.

"Why should it matter which one visits? Whether she brings love or trades in love? It's all the same. Ha-ha-ha-ha!" Romaine's voice, one second sane, in the next mad with laughter, frightened Estelle.

"Mommy," she called, and reached out her hand.

Romaine brushed it away, as if it were an insect, her attention still on the imaginary figure outside the window. "A woman must have love, no matter if it be from the Devil," she said.

"The other Estelle, why does she haunt you?" The Witch was beginning to understand.

"How could it be any other way? I got rid of her."

"That day when Oliver took Estelle away, the other Estelle, took her away in a big car, that was the day, wasn't it?"

Romaine recoiled, not from the question but from the hallucination in the window.

"Tell me," the Witch whispered.

"I sold her," Romaine whispered to the window and then cackled.

She took Romaine roughly by the arm and twisted her toward her so she could look in her eyes. Bits of color in them squirmed like demons in hell. "You sold your daughter to your brother?" she said.

"Not my daughter—the other Estelle. I saved my own Estelle by ridding myself of the other one."

"How much did she fetch?"

"A hundred dollars. Big money in those days." Romaine sounded wistful; she missed the money.

"Knowing Oliver, I bet he offered less," the Witch said. "What took all that time before we went off in the car was the dickering. Isn't that so?"

Romaine pulled away. "How could you know about Oliver? My own Estelle did not know Oliver."

The Witch faced Romaine, and said, "I am the other Estelle."

Back at the front desk, the veteran nurse was on her feet. She'd heard Romaine shriek before. Even now, after all these years, the horror of it troubled her like bad news.

On the return trip to Tuckerman County, the Witch fell into a hole of forgetfulness. She knew, of course, she had visited her mother, knew now what had happened that day Oliver had plucked her from the family shack—"I sold her." And yet she didn't think about any of this as revelation, as instruction, or even as painful information about her past. It seemed trivial. Nothing to get upset about.

It had been a mistake to visit Romaine in the first place, a mistake that she, the Witch, hadn't been responsible for. Mysterious forces had steered her to Concord. Accordingly, what had happened in Corcord was false, a mix-up best put aside. That crazy old woman in the mental hospital was not her mother. Her mother, the woman with the strong hands who had combed her hair, taken her blueberry picking, fended off the menfolk from her, had passed on.

When she returned to Darby that afternoon it had begun to rain; the air was getting colder. Taking in the view from her landing, she felt the seasons change. Soon the green of summer would be gone completely from the hills, the bright colors of fall would vanish. The hills were dark and dreary, merging with the clouds. The north wind blew. The sick don't die in the winter, she thought. They hang on through the cold and snow; suffering itself keeps them alive. When spring comes, and the first warming rays of the sun like loving hands touch their brows, then they die. She longed for the lavender winter sky. She would do Noreen's face today.

Noreen stared up into the diffused glare of the neon lights of the porn shop. Knees together, sitting on the stool behind the counter in her red dress, her right hand reaching upward, with the Witch hovering over her like some mad scientist, Noreen said, "I feel as though I could touch the light."

"It's the toke—it dredges a soul," the Witch said. "You want to touch the light—it means you want to lose yourself in it."

The Witch took a pull on the pipe, inhaling the smoke deep into her lungs, held, and exhaled. She handed the pipe to Noreen, who mirrored the Witch's ritual with the unconscious, slightly askew facility of a child mimicking its elders.

"I never liked pot before," Noreen said. "It always made me feel kind of like—I don't know—I just couldn't enjoy it. But I feel good now, like—I don't know—all shimmery."

She doesn't know what she thinks, what she feels, or who she is, the Witch thought.

"That stuff you smoke from the streets comes from anyplace and it's cut with all manner of disgusting matter—it never smokes the same; your system never gets used to it," the Witch said. "And because it's from someplace else, it makes you a stranger in your own house. But this toke, this is the Witch's homegrown. Good New Hampshire marijuana. It grows from our local wood's soil. You light it, you set free the color of the fall leaves, the taste of the maple sap and the smell of sweet birch. It's got granite in it, too—solid stuff."

She remembered Isaac's lecturing her on the countryside, as if her father truly were an expert and not just a drunk. "There's two kinds of stone rows run through these hills. There's the tight boundary walls the settlers laid up, and then there's wider rows, aiming north; Indians built those for reasons of the spirit, long time before the settlers."

"This pot makes the sound of the rain louder, hurts some— don't you just hate the rain, Estelle?" Noreen shut her eyes, enjoying the touch of the Witch's hands on her face.

"A fall rain is a depressing thing, no doubt," the Witch said. She applied color to the face, puttying over the natural peach glow of it, masking the very thing that moved her. She could hardly bear the sight of the face. She desired at once to tear it to pieces and to weep for its beauty, its goodness, for something beyond her understanding.

After a silence, Noreen said, "Suppose you liked someone and they liked you but they didn't buy you the dress they promised you, and you wanted a VCR, would it be out of line to ask that person to buy you one, if that person could afford it, of course, sort of like to give him the opportunity to show how he really and completely feels about you?"

"You're talking about a product for sale and the price is a VCR," the Witch said.

"No, no," Noreen said. "I'm talking about appreciation; I'm talking about love."

"Appreciation is not worth a VCR, and love is, well . . . gone." The Witch did not know what to say next. The word *love* had taken her off guard.

"Wouldn't you give a VCR to someone you loved if they wanted it and if you could afford it?" Noreen asked. "He forgot about the dress. But he did get me the CB."

The Witch did not speak. In the silence that followed, Noreen's eyes tripped away from the light, toward some private realm. "I wish, I wish, I wish, I wish." Her words were barely audible.

Where she is now, I too have been, the Witch thought.

"Noreen, are you in love?" The Witch's question snapped Noreen back to the moment.

"I don't know," Noreen said. "When I think I'm in love, it kind of hurts, or maybe I just know it's going to hurt when it's over. Because of me. What I am. With me it's always going to be over, and it's always going to hurt. All I know for sure is I love my children. But the other kind of love, in-love love, like between a man and a woman, I don't know. I do know if I'm not in love, it's like I'm nowhere inside. You, Witch, have you ever been in love?"

"I trade in love," the Witch said. "When you take up pretend love, you hurt at first, then the hurt goes away and you're numb. Soon you realize that right from the start pretend love and real love are the same thing, a trick to keep people breeding. Think about it: you can get as pregnant with pretend love as with real love. In the long run, it doesn't matter how you went about it, as long as you did it, and even that doesn't matter, because even if you don't breed, somebody else will."

Noreen gulped as one shown horrible pictures, subjected to horrible sounds.

"Come on, Noreen, I know you've felt the numbness—no love, but no hurt either." The Witch scraped Noreen with her voice.

"Maybe you're right, maybe I can't feel true love anymore and maybe it doesn't matter anyway," Noreen said. "But I have to keep trying. I need love, real, true love, hurt and all. Do you think somebody will ever truly and forever love me?"

Noreen's passion and sincerity pecked at the heart of the Witch like the beak of a vulture.

At this point, the conversation was interrupted by a banging on the front door of the bookstore.

"A customer—I'm late again opening up." Noreen jumped nimbly from the stool, grabbed the black wig and arranged it on her head.

"Let him stew," the Witch said.

"If Critter finds out, he'll give me holy hell," Noreen said. She skipped over to the entry and pulled the shade up over the window of the door. Through the distorted glass, the Witch recognized the face of the handsome young driver of the Trans Am.

After Noreen let him in, he put a five-dollar bill on the counter and said, "Tokens." She took the money and counted out twenty tokens. The Trans Am kept his hands at his sides so that Noreen put the tokens on the counter for him to take instead of putting them in his hand. Thus, the transaction did not include touch. He wore crisp new blue jeans, a black leather jacket, black boots. From pierced ears hung earrings shaped liked daggers. His blond hair, combed rakishly against the sides of his head, was like water falling from a height. The Witch shifted about, tossed her hair back with a hand, trying to get him to look at her, but his eyes never left Noreen; they roamed along her throat, down to her breasts.

"Noreen." The Witch spoke so the Trans Am could hear the sound of her voice, but he turned for the peep-show booths, and it was as if she did not exist.

"Did I do something?" Noreen was bullied by the Witch's tone.

"Know him?" the Witch whispered now and glanced in the direction of the peep shows.

"Comes in once in a while," Noreen said.

"I bet you'd like to have something like that?"

"I don't know," Noreen grimaced. "I don't like to think about the fellows that come in here. They kind of give me the creeps.

Most of them don't look at you. That one looks you over. I don't like to think about it."

"You're alone here, and there's all this sex leaping out of pages, don't that make you stop and think from time to time?" The Witch wanted to see fear on Noreen's face.

"I don't pay any attention." Noreen stood stiffly, like a child shoved into a corner by an adult.

"You look scared to me."

"You're nice to me and then you pick on me. I don't understand you, Estelle." Noreen was on the verge of tears.

"It'll be all right. I was only teasing," the Witch soothed. She grabbed the broom behind the counter and handed it to Noreen. "Do a little work and you'll feel better."

Noreen left the counter and began to sweep the floor.

The Witch wanted to ask Noreen whether the Trans Am looked at her with more intensity when she wore makeup and the black wig, but of course she knew Noreen could not deal with such a question. While Noreen was busy, the Witch reached under the counter in the shoebox and took one of the girlie pictures Critter had taken of Noreen. Then she said goodbye and left the store. She wasn't exactly sure what she was going to do next; she knew only that she must make contact today with the Trans Am.

She stood outside in the rain by the car. Save for Noreen's Bug, it was the only vehicle in the lot. It had been raining forever, it seemed, and the ground was sopping underfoot. The field grass, which had been so bright and new in midsummer, now was worn, drab, dying. The surrounding forest dripping with rain imprisoned the barn. She could feel no wind, but she could see a nervous fog skitter here and there. Her mind went into a sort of doze. She was aware of everything around her, could have reacted to anyone calling her name. Yet she could not feel the rain, and no thoughts, no memories, no images sprang forth to trouble her; she was empty, insubstantial, a ghost, and almost blissful in her ghostliness.

She didn't know how long she was in the rain, but she was soaked to the skin when the Trans Am came out of the porn shop. He strode toward her, now visible, now obscured by the fog. At moments, it was as if he were walking away from her, but the ground between them was closing, crushing in upon itself, and they were coming together in spite of themselves.

She blocked his way. He looked around. He was going to hit her, she could see, and he wanted to make sure no one would catch him at it. She reached into her bra and handed him the pictures of Noreen. He stepped back, looking at them. The Witch removed her teeth, took off her blouse and bra and flung them aside. Stripped to the waist, her pendulous breasts hanging down, nipples erect, she knelt in the mud beside the car.

The Trans Am knew without hesitation what she was offering. He undid his fly; he was already erect when she went to work on him. He didn't make a sound; he didn't touch her, keeping his hands by his sides. She tried to cup his buttocks in her own hands, but he cuffed them down. If her face brushed his stomach, he pulled away. All he wanted was her mouth. He finished in less than a minute. Then, without a word or a gesture, with no acknowledgment whatever that she existed, he got into his car and drove off, spattering muddy water upon her.

The Witch remained kneeling in the soggy earth, rubbing her nipples between thumb and forefinger, touching herself below with her other hand, marrying tremor to orgasm.

12

The Auction

Hadly Blue was surprised by the size of the crowd at the Hillary dairy barn.

"Strange that so many people have turned out for this, when it's doubtful anything will be sold they can use," he said to Persephone Salmon. "I mean Selectman Crabb makes some sense—he's a farmer—but the Jordans? The LaChances? the Achesons? Who among them is going to buy a milk cow?"

"They're here for the same reason we are—theater," Persephone said.

The auction had already started when they arrived. Two men would parade a cow in view, the auctioneer (a fellow with a felt hat and red suspenders) would describe the animal in a language alien to Blue, and the bidding would start. There were perhaps a hundred people standing around or sitting on folding chairs brought in for the occasion, but there were only a dozen or so buyers of bovines. Avalon Hillary sat stiffly in a chair beside the auctioneer. It took Hadly a moment to realize why the farmer looked strange to him. He had exchanged his usual uniform of blue denim overalls for a suit and tie. It was an out-of-date suit, and Hillary seemed uncomfortable in it; the tie was poorly knotted. No one else in the barn wore a suit. Hadly wondered why Hillary had bothered to dress up.

Hadly spotted Critter Jordan and his wife. They had set up

a little bar and were selling coffee and doughnuts from the Dunkin' Donuts shop in Tuckerman. The sight triggered Hadley's craving for caffeine along with a hunger for sugar and fat. Yet while he wanted a doughnut he also wanted, by all means, to keep his distance from Critter. Jordan was unlettered if not illiterate, seedy and sneaky, yet oddly likable, at turns intimidating and pathetic, like the hound that followed him everywhere. He stood too close to you when he talked, his breath was bad, and his teeth were worse. He didn't have the built-in social gyroscope of most people. Yet this handicap freed him to speak his mind, while better minds were fettered to convention and etiquette. He was the kind of man who by sheer accident could make a fool of you.

Meanwhile, Critter and Delphina had made twenty-eight dollars thus far selling coffee and doughnuts. Critter was relaxed and pleased with himself until he caught the eye of Professor Hadly Blue. He admired Blue, called him Professor Had or Doc. But there was something mysterious, strange, disturbing about him. Once, Critter had recited to him the only poetic lines he knew, *"Roses are red, violets are blue, If I had a face like you, I'd join a zoo."* Professor Had had blinked, then grinned like a maniac. People with too much education were uncomfortable to have around because you couldn't know what they were thinking, any more than Crowbar here, dozing at his feet, could know what his master was thinking. Why'd Professor Had come to this auction? To laugh at us hicks? Critter kicked Crowbar.

"What he do?" Delphina asked.

"Nothing," Critter said. "I let him have it on general principles. You suppose Professor Had over there will be buying a cow?"

"He's already wangled himself some mighty impressive stock in the widow Salmon," Delphina said.

They giggled together.

Of recent, Critter and his wife were getting along. Why, it had gotten so he found himself preferring her company to the company of male kin. The idea that a man could be friends with his wife was strange to him, and he was a little afraid of it. Yet it felt so good, so sweet. Was this what life was about: love for children, friendship with your woman, sex life half in bed, half in your head? Critter sighed, half in contentment and half in fear, thinking about Noreen.

Delphina had to know something was up, and yet she hadn't said anything, hadn't hinted around, hadn't done anything but be his friend, the mother of his children, the queen of his domain. He wished he could talk to her about it, explain to her that he loved her and that he was happy with her, that Noreen actually solidified their marriage. How could you say to a wife, "This piece I got on the side takes the restlessness out of me, and so now I'm not cranky, and I'm happy to be a family man. If she goes, you'll suffer."

"Want a doughnut?" he asked.

"Already had three," Delphina said.

"I can remember when I was a kid, I'd dream about doughnuts." Critter saw those doughnuts now, parading from his memory past the front porch of his consciousness: jelly doughnuts with round smiling faces, marching on chorus-girl legs with mesh stockings. His father would buy the doughnuts at Doris's Bakery in Tuckerman. (It had closed down only recently.)

"Crullers, or what?" Delphina asked.

"Jellies, big fat ones, oozing sticky red jelly," Critter said.

"Nobody's perfect," Delphina said. Then she added, "Critter, I was going to wait, but there's something I've been meaning to talk to you about."

More than the words themselves, the shift in her tone set off a fire bell in Critter's mind. *Ding-dong!* She knows! Here it comes—the crack of doom.

"I was talking to Noreen Cook the other day." Delphina's eyes narrowed. My gosh, Critter thought, how strong, mean, and unforgiving a woman can be.

He'd deny everything. Noreen Cook, that scrawny bitch— think better of me than that. No, that was no good. He'd say it only happened once—a one-shot deal. That wouldn't work. He'd say it was Noreen's fault, she put him up to it. No, that was too low, even for him. Still, a man had to do what he had to do. It didn't matter what he said, Delphina would never believe him. He'd have to tell the truth, admit his guilt. I done it, I was wrong, I'll never do it again, I love you more than anything else in the world, more than Crowbar, more than my van, more than the kids. I promise, I promise, I promise. He was beginning to feel an odd sense of relief creeping into his anxiety. Delphina would forgive him. He could be himself again. Wouldn't have to live a lie. Everything was going to be all right.

"So what?" Critter said.

Delphina did not respond. She was distracted by some activity toward the front. Critter peered into the barn gloom, which was cut only slightly by a string of temporary lights.

"Look at her, ain't she something to be behold," Delphina said. Critter's eyes came to rest on a cow. He recognized the beast. He'd worked briefly a few years back for farmer Hillary and this was his super breeder. They were getting ready to auction her off. He wondered vaguely whether Delphina was going to bid on the cow. In fact, however, Delphina had not noticed the cow. Her admiring eyes were for Natalie Acheson, one of the rich ladies of Upper Darby.

"She smells like all the rest," Critter said, wondering whether to be grateful to the cow for staying his execution or whether he should press Delphina for her accusations and get them over with.

"Oh, no," Delphina tittered. "She wears special perfume they get from New York or India or someplace like that. I know, I smelled her."

"A high-class cow is still a cow," Critter said.

Delphina poked Critter in the side. "Sometimes, you are about the funniest man I know."

He wanted then to tell Delphina the one about the hunter who was bit by a snake in the privates. Hunter named Reb was taking a leak when a big snake bit him you know where. His friend Rab ran twelve miles to town for help, but Doc Jones (maybe he'd call him Doc Blue in the story) was busy delivering Mrs. MacIntosh's baby. "Reb's been bit by a snake," says Rab. "What manner of snake?" Doc Blue asks. "Black snake with a red stripe," Rab says. "You've got to suck out the poison," Doc says. "And if I don't?" Rab asks. "Then Reb will surely die," Doc says. So Rab runs the twelve miles back to his fallen friend. Over hill and dale, through swamp and forest he goes. He arrives, and Reb is barely breathing. He whispers to Rab, "What did the doc say? What did he say?" Rab answers, "He says you're going to die." Surely, this joke would put Delphina in a good mood. As Critter was mulling over this possibility, he listened to himself blurt out, "I can't stand the suspense any longer. What's your problem with Noreen?"

"It's not with Noreen, it's with you," Delphina said, and her eyes narrowed again. "I heard at Tammy's that you put a CB in Noreen's car. You never did that for me."

"Is that all you want—a CB?"

"In the Caddy,'" Delphina said. "This may not be important to you, but it's important to me."

As Delphina's words sunk in, Critter spontaneously leaped to his feet and laughed aloud. A second later he was surprised to find himself eyeball-to-eyeball with Hadly Blue.

"What's up, Doc?" he shouted with glee. He swept up a doughnut and stuck it under Blue's nose. "Here you go, Doc— for you, free."

"No, thank you; no, thank you; no, thank you," Blue said, moving off, vanishing into the crowd.

The noise level in the barn fell then, and the attention of Critter and Delphina turned toward the auction block. What had quieted the spectators was the bidding on Hillary's supercow. It was sky-high—out of sight. When it was over, someone began to clap. Others followed. Soon everyone was cheering. The cow got a standing ovation.

Critter watched the old farmer remove his tie and let out a whoop, like from an old Western movie. Critter could see there was more to Hillary's elation than just the money, but what it was he did not know, only that Hillary had something at this moment he didn't have, and likely never would.

It was two days after Avalon's cow auction that the Witch again made contact with the Trans Am. She met him outside in the parking lot of the auction barn.

"Do me," he said.

"Not now," she said.

"Here—now," he said.

"Later, when it's dark. On the road, while you're driving fast. I want to be in the car, and I want it to be going fast, a hundred miles an hour."

He considered, staring off into the gray sky.

"I'll bet you never got your rocks off at a hundred miles an hour," she said.

"These country roads are no good for that. We'll cross over onto the interstate. I'll punch it past a hundred, way past, and you can do me." He spoke, she could see, as though her suggestion had been part of his plans all along. She noted this attempt at deception, the fact that she hadn't been deceived, as a weakness. I'm smarter than he is, she thought.

The moon was up when she met him on the highway. She slid into the seat beside him. The engine growled, tires squealed, and they were launched. The Trans Am lounged on Route 21 five miles below the speed limit. They were fifteen minutes away from I-91.

The anticipation of speed and sex stirred the tremor in her. She teased herself with it, bent inward to it, then extended herself outward from it, so she could almost see her breath deepen, as if she were watching the emotions of a woman about to dive into the sea from the top of a cliff. She was, she thought, in love with the Trans Am, even while she understood that this affirmation spat in the face of love. She could not feel love; he could not feel love; together, they could not feel as lovers. They could not make love; they could only mock love; theirs was a death mask of love.

Now they were crossing the bridge over the Connecticut River. Free of the partial arch of trees, the road opened for a moment to the sky. Moonlight seemed to seep into the car. The Witch looked down into the river. Crooked lines of light traced the shore. The light defined the river; the light said, "The river is alive, dark, and serious in its business as a pumping heart."

The Witch turned her eyes to the Trans Am. The moonlight was a blue-white stocking pulled over his features. Like a huge and terrible cat, he seemed at once about to doze off and to spring to action. The light could say nothing about him. He obscured the light.

In a minute after crossing the bridge, they reached the interstate and the Trans Am headed north. He turned off the cassette player and said, "Listen." He wanted her to hear the sounds of the gathering speed of the automobile.

As it went faster and faster, her connections with the familiar parted like colored threads fluttering in some magical, wind-blown light. The highway rose into the sky, the Trans Am with it. For a few minutes, they didn't speak or touch or look at one another. Even the sound of their breath was lost in the moan of speed. Perhaps at this moment they *were* lovers. She felt about him as she used to feel about small wooden objects Oliver used to carve—crude heads, animals, crests, sometimes only shapes. In them he had left his softness, the softness that held her in bondage to him as sure as the hardness did. She would hold the carvings to her bosom in order to bring herself the comfort Oliver the man no longer brought, while at the same time she would entertain herself with visions of burning them. In the conflict of these two emotions, she could feel her womanhood divide in two.

The Trans Am reached into her blouse and squeezed her breasts, gently at first, then more violently. He squeezed until she whimpered a little with pain, then he released her. He's got a nose for death and no conscience, she thought. He says to himself, If I want it, it must be good; if I don't, it's no good. He's simple and unwholesome—he's what I want, what I need. She unzipped his jacket and pants, exposing a V of bare flesh from throat to crotch. She kissed his chest and ran her hands over his body.

She enjoyed his physique under her fingertips. It reminded her of the car itself—smooth and hard. His chest was almost hairless, and there was a hint of baby fat on his hips and under his chin. She guessed that as a boy he'd been chubby, matured late, almost overnight becoming a roaring man, and his idea of himself hadn't quite caught up to the fact of his body. The blond curly hairs rose from between his legs like field grass. She liked the Johnny-jump-up quality of his pecker, so different from the crank-jobs of her old men. (She lingered for a moment over a thought of aging sailors hoisting anchor.)

"Take your teeth out," the Trans Am said.

She did as she was told, then lay the side of her face against his shoulder and watched the road. She could feel the tenseness in him, which was the tenseness of the metal of the car under the stress of speed. They passed a pickup truck pulling a horse trailer. There was something about it, blinking and blurring, that puzzled and disoriented her until she realized she was traveling faster than she ever had in her life, seeing the world as never before.

The Trans Am glanced at her. His eyes were bright but impersonal. He ran a hand across her forehead, down the back of her neck; he stroked her palms. He was trying to feel signs of fear in her; fear was like food to him and he was hungry. But there was no fear in her. Her skin was dry as dead grasses.

He grabbed her by the hair, shook her head for a moment, then shoved it down to his loins. The darkness, the moistness, the vibrations of the car meeting air, the tires burning on the highway: these sensations interwound like snakes with the tremor. When it seemed as if the car would shake apart from the speed, he came.

They drove on, plunging northward at a hundred and thirty miles an hour. When the Trans Am wasn't looking, the Witch returned the teeth to her mouth.

"I feel like a beer," the Trans Am said.

"What do you drink?" she asked.

"Molson Golden Ale—nothing else," he said.

"Canadian stuff."

The Trans Am said nothing.

"Let's go to Canada, get the real thing," the Witch said.

"Canada—you're crazy." He smiled, as one scorning a fool. And yet they would head for Canada, she knew. He had no imagination, she could see; he could be steered here and there, and never quite realize it.

They didn't slow until they approached the border. Signs warned them they were leaving the United States. The Witch didn't exactly believe them. She knew of course there was such a place as Canada. She knew some basic geography. The world was round, covered mainly with water. There were continents; there were countries, zillions of them, populated by zillions of people, many of them who had no shoes to wear or who were communists. Yet while she knew all this to be more or less true, something in her didn't believe her knowledge. Something in her said the physical universe was limited to Tuckerman County. Everyplace else was a dream, a hallucination. A real place, insofar as it had meaning to her, had somehow to be linked with the county. She could believe in New Hampshire and almost believe in Massachusetts, Vermont, even Maine, because these places seemed like an extension of Tuckerman County. Connecticut, New York, states farther west and south dissolved into a mist of geographical knowledge, newscasts, hearsay. Canada hardly seemed on the same planet. Yet here they were: Canada.

When they crossed the actual borderline, she didn't so much expect things to look different—an ocean, strange buildings, men on horseback—but rather that she would feel different. Outside of herself, thrilled perhaps. But for the moment she felt the same as before. She was who she was, Canada was what it was, like Vermont, which was what it was, like Tuckerman County. The Witch was disappointed.

Up ahead, lights flashed in warning or welcome. Hard to tell which. A few seconds later, a sign glowered—and they were slowing to be checked at a border stop. This was more like it, this was foreign. A guard in uniform, hands behind his back, peered into the car as he addressed the Trans Am.

"What is your nation of citizenship?" he asked.

"USA," the Trans Am said after hesitating.

"New Hampshire," the Witch said.

"What is your purpose in visiting Canada?" the guard asked.

"Vacation," the Trans Am said.

"What will be the length of your stay?"

"Two weeks," the Trans Am said.

The guard waved them on.

He spoke with a Frenchy accent. The Witch liked that, not knowing why.

The Trans Am was pleased with the lies he had told, the Witch could see. He was the type that was more comfortable with falsehood than truth. Like herself, he knew a truth, even a seemingly harmless truth, exposed the teller of it. It was always best to lie when you could get away with it.

I-91 became Route 55, the highway marker decorated with a picture of a maple leaf. This, the Witch could see, had something to do with Canada as an idea, although for the life of her she couldn't nail down the exact meaning. What was so great about maple leaves, and what could they have to do with an entire country? Road signs were written in French and English, and this too didn't make sense to her. Why couldn't these people settle on one language? If you spoke two languages, which language did you think in? This one or that one? Both? Were you a different person in French than you were in English?

"Ain't you glad you don't talk French," she spoke aloud to herself.

"I do speak French. They made you learn it in one of the schools I was sent to," the Trans Am said.

Confusion of language: maybe that was his problem, the Witch thought.

"You went to a lot of schools?" she said.

"I ran away from most of them. One day they didn't catch me."

"On his own in the cruel world," the Witch said.

"I did all right. Did some dealings." His face didn't reveal the lie, but his hands did. They tightened on the steering wheel. In the future, she wouldn't tease him unless deliberately to provoke him.

A boy loose on the streets, men on the lookout for such

boys—his story was clear to the Witch. He was like her, a whore—wounded, dangerous, itchy for revenge.

They turned off the highway at the first good-size town, Magog. The stores had closed, so no Molson. Before the Trans Am could work up an anger, the Witch spotted twinkling lights that signaled a tavern.

It seemed to the Witch that the bar was more colorful, more cheerful, more refined than the bars she was accustomed to. Otherwise it was simply a bar—men full of har-har-har, a pool table, the bartender a woman, a young floozy wearing tight pants.

"Molson Golden Ale," ordered the Trans Am.

"Canada Dry ginger ale," ordered the Witch.

The Trans Am sampled the brew, then took a long drink. She watched him eye the floozy's rear end. He smacked his lips. Moist, they seemed vaginal to the Witch.

"You like that?" The Witch pointed to the floozy with her eyes.

"I'd like to beat her ass," he said.

"On the drive back, when I'm taking care of you, think about it." The Witch put her hand on his thigh.

"It's a good car—old, but solid and well cared for. I'll guarantee that, since I did the caring," Avalon said, as he opened the passenger door for Estelle. Since the cow auction, he was more restless than ever but also happier, almost giddy. He was on the brink of big changes, she could see.

They eased out onto River Road, rolling easily. Never drove over fifty with a woman in the car, he'd said. Estelle felt herself fall into a calm. She imagined she'd learned to swim and lay floating on her back on a warm lake, watching clouds frolic as if the sky were a big stage.

"This car is the only mechanical contrivance I ever babied," Avalon said. "I rust-proofed the body every two years, and just this spring I had it repainted. Goddamn acid rain raises hell with a finish nowadays. Whitewall tires—nothing but the best for this old girl. I've changed the oil with the rise of every moon since I bought her—new, zero miles on her, virgin. I won't say the year. And she's only got thirty-five original thousand miles on her."

He wasn't the kind of man who could say right out that he liked a woman. He found it easier to express his affection by talking about a thing. So Estelle listened, as one dreamily contemplating an admirer sing her praises. Never mind that he was talking about the car. She knew the affection was for her, and she was pleased.

"Fact is," he went on, "I don't have any actual necessity for this vehicle. As my father was fond of saying, 'A farmer can tell himself he needs a pickup truck, and the Lord will forgive him for browning the truth a little.' But a car? A big car at that? Noooo. A car is an out-and-out sin of luxury in a world weighed down with poverty. That's why I love it so."

They crossed the Connecticut River. Estelle could feel the emptiness between the bridge and river. He was taking her to dinner in Vermont. He wasn't ashamed to be seen in public with her, just uneasy about the situation. Perhaps this was because it wasn't the town he wanted to shock, so much as the ghosts of his ancestors. As far as the town was concerned, he didn't want the people to think anything about him one way or the other. So he was more comfortable hiding her from their eyes.

"Why don't you turn that farm of yours into a used-car lot?" she suggested.

"You think I have an aptitude for salesmanship, do you?" He was amused.

"Oh, you're full of that stuff you shovel to make the grass grow."

168

Avalon chuckled. "Sell cars," he said, tickled by the logic of the idea, so near to yet so distant from the Hillary heart. "You're quite a kidder, Estelle. Quite a kidder. Instead of cows grazing in the field, we'll park cars in them. Instead of a barn, we'll have a garage. Instead of cowshit under my shoes, I'll have ... well, I don't know—new shoes."

Before the auction he'd complained constantly about the work load of the farm. Now, after the stock had been sold and taken away, he complained the other way. Time on his hands, nothing to do, a feeling of strangeness, especially when he looked at the land—empty. So he pestered her with his presence. They took rides; they went out to eat; anything to get away from the farm and do something. She loved his company, maybe even loved the man himself. She didn't know. It seemed to her that one of the rules for a long life of the spirit was: Be grateful for a feeling but don't trust it. But what did you do when you weren't sure what the feeling was?

"If I've learned anything it's that I've carried a chip on my shoulder against my father and grandfather, and I suppose I sold the herd to spite the past, but darned if I could go so far as to asphalt the fields and park cars on them," he said.

"Sell it—everything," Estelle said.

"I don't want to sell. I'll tell you, Estelle, I like grass. I like to watch it grow, I like to watch the butterflies spring from it—though I admit I cut down on the population by mowing the cocoons as I mowed for hay. You understand, the farm always came first."

"Uh-huh."

In her mind's eye, Estelle could see a white house with lots of shelves where you set down weed pots of wood and pottery, earthen objects, containers for ribbons and all sorts of interesting things, a library of books packed with pressed flowers and leaves.

There was a pause. He was thinking about her *uh-huh*. "You don't like your grass green," he said.

"I like it dried, as you know," she said.

"I never met a woman like you—don't like growing things. The women I've known..."

"Farm women—what do you expect?"

"Uh-huh," he mimicked her, and they both laughed.

His car *was* solid, she thought. It was like a bunker. But bunkers never worked. The enemy went around, or tossed grenades through the windows, or the people inside went nuts from their own company.

"Pitiable," she said, after a pause, speaking a thought.

"Who—old farmers?"

"The human race."

"Work, worry, breed, die," Avalon said, and they tasted the sweetness of a moment of shared philosophy.

They arrived at the restaurant, the Fife and Drum. She'd always wondered what a fife was, but it had never occurred to her to seek out the answer. It was one of those trivial questions that pester a mind over a lifetime without that mind ever putting it to rest.

"Before we go in, I got something for you." Avalon's voice was suddenly gruff. "I was going to wait until I brought you home, but if I don't get this over with now, it'll ruin my supper."

He opened the trunk of the Buick. The inside was spotless save for a brown paper bag. He opened the bag and peeked in.

"You keep this," he said, so gruff now he would have sounded angry to a passerby.

She took the bag and looked inside. There was a potted plant in it.

"My wife kept plants like some people keep fish or *National Geographic* magazines," he said. "When she died, I gave 'em all away. Too much bother they were. Well, this one escapes me. It was in the bathroom on the windowsill behind the curtain. I'd never noticed. Who knows how many years it had been there. When I finally discovered it, it was almost dried out to death. Well, I been taking care of it and I don't much like the work. So I'm giving it to you. Put it in the trash for all I care. It isn't worth anything. It's not the plant I'm giving, it's a piece of my past."

So this is love, Estelle thought. He offers, she accepts. Afterward, she has, he has not. She watches it grow, he searches for what he lost. From this, things are made, wars instigated, babies born. The race is preserved, held together by a vague and probably false idea of the past.

Avalon stepped back, seeing a change in her eyes.

Estelle understood the gift of the plant. It was his first move in courtship. Soon he'd be asking her to change her address to River Road. He'd say, as old man Williamson had said, "A lot of people our age live together—never mind the matrimony." He was asking for comfort. Ferrying old men to the grave: it was her lot in life. No denying the pattern over the years. No denying that if she moved in with him, he'd die, and afterward she'd feel an odd sense of victory. Triumph would replace what had passed as love.

"I don't want it," she said, handing him the bag.

He looked at her, to make sure she had understood the purpose behind his act. "I thought you were my girl," he said.

She said nothing. When he looked again into her eyes, he saw the Witch's brew in them.

"You got things to do, have you?" he said.

"In a manner of speaking," she said.

"Well, why don't you do them and get back to me?"

"Because you won't want me then," the Witch said.

"Oh, come on."

"Only reason you want me now is to piss on the graves of your fathers," she said. "But never mind, when this is done, I doubt I'll want you."

Avalon laughed bitterly, ironically. He knew this was the end of them. "Can't you tell an easy lie?" he said.

"If I have to," the Witch said.

13

Preparations for the Shedding of Blood

As usual, they eased west on Route 21, the cassette player blaring, then rocketed north on the interstate. They said little; they were from different worlds, had nothing to talk about. And anyway he didn't like her to talk, didn't like talk in general, or silence, or peaceful-type music; he wouldn't abide anything that disturbed his pleasure, a union of music, motion, and metal, produced, she understood, by the car, by the leather he wore against his skin, by the knife strapped to his leg, and by a lowly old whore.

One thing that attracted her to him was that he was the opposite of a Jordan. His teeth were beautiful, straight, white, cared for. His clothes seemed perpetually new. He was always clean and clean-shaven. He had money, yet he seemed to hold no job. He gave the impression money came his way, so there was little reason to give it any thought. His valuables consisted of his car, his anger, and his erection—a thing, a feeling, a force. He had never mentioned his name or where he lived or who his loved ones were. The very idea of loved ones was alien to him. She knew who he was, of course, a Butterworth from Upper Darby, living with his mother, Mrs. Acheson, yet she refused to think of him as a person; he remained the Trans Am to her.

When the car began to shake with speed, seemed on the

verge of disintegration, she removed her teeth and placed them discreetly on the seat beside her so he would not see them. She bent to him, then, laboring at her·craft. Afterward, they would stop at a convenience market and buy some Canadian ale. They'd come back to Darby along the river, the old road, traveling slowly, he drinking, she smoking her pipe: it was only then she'd wish he'd turn down the loud music and say something.

It took only a minute or so before she sensed his entire body begin to stiffen—even his blood went rigid. She anticipated his orgasm, a cry like a lost boy's. A moment later, she tasted the first warm jet of semen.

But at the same time, she was startled by a screeching sound coming from the car itself. Her mind flashed back to the day off River Road, when the Trans Am had shrieked in anger and pain. I was right, she thought now, a man and his machine become a third thing. A split second later, the Trans Am's foot hit the brake. The Witch felt herself thrown forward, jamming her shoulder against the dashboard pad. The Trans Am grabbed her hair and pulled her to a seated position beside him.

"Fuzz Buster went off! Speed trap ahead!" He shouted in anger.

The Witch reached for her teeth. They were gone, apparently sent flying by the sudden deceleration of the car.

The Trans Am shut off the radar warning device and continued to brake rhythmically, easing off at fifty-five as they passed a state trooper car parked behind some trees on the median strip.

"Ruined my cum! Ruined it!" The Trans Am shook his fist at her, as if it had been her fault. For a moment, the Witch thought he would burst into tears.

Like a panicked blind woman, the Witch continued to feel along the seat beside her for her teeth, finally finding them in the crack between seat and door. Usually she slipped them back into her mouth with great secrecy and care. But she was frantic now, and she shoved them in just as the Trans Am returned his eyes to hers. In his eyes she saw her tremor flame up, die, and from the ashes flame up again, all new and strange, then flicker and go out, extinguished by an unfelt wind. She sifted through the ashes. They were cold. She hurt inside, and the hurt was like a hard embrace, and then there was no hurt, there was nothing. Love cauterizes the wound that it inflicts, she thought. The tremor was no more than a tiny fire now, a discomfort instead of a desire. She could smell something like candles burning at a funeral. Estelle is dying, she thought. I smell her skin smolder.

"I need an ale," the Trans Am said, and the car dipped into the Springfield, Vermont, exit ramp.

She could not tell whether her sadness was true. This feeling: Is it mine, yours, ours together, some graver thing? If I bend to it, will it save us?

She wanted to speak, to midwife the thought into meaning with words, but of course she said nothing. She stilled herself, body and mind, as one at the sickbed of a friend. The Trans Am remained silent, his face sullen, muscles tensed.

They stopped at a gas station, an old place spruced up into a convenience market. The Trans Am sent her in to buy the usual six-pack.

She returned with a bag cradled in her arm. He didn't even wait until she shut the door before peeling out of the lot. The smell of burning candles vanished, replaced by the smell of tires burning on asphalt. They were on the road again, riding the slithery snake that is Route 5 in Vermont. He handed her the opener from the glove box, and she took the cap off the bottle.

He grabbed the beer, drank—and grimaced.

"What's this?" His voice accused.

"Molson's."

"This is Molson beer. I drink the ale, Molson Golden Ale."

"What difference does it make?" she asked.

"It makes no difference at all," he said, in a warm, affectionate tone, the timbre of which she had not heard in years but which she knew how to react to. She threw up a hand to protect her face.

The bottle of beer, which the Trans Am had swung backhandedly in the general direction of her head, hit her forearm, glanced off her temple and toppled onto the car seat. The soft flesh of the side of his palm lingered for a second against her face. The Witch bit the hand.

The Trans Am pulled away at the first pain and jerked the teeth right out of the Witch's mouth. The dentures remained clamped in his hand. His face contorted, as if he'd discovered leeches sucking him, the Trans Am shook the dentures from his hand. They dropped to the floor at her feet.

She picked them up and held them in her hands, as a child might hold a baby chick.

Something in her shouted danger—but too late. This time the Trans Am hit her directly on the cheekbone with the back of his closed fist. She knew what was coming next. A man beats you, and he gets angrier blow by blow because you remind him how low he is. He reacts by blaming you. Later, he says, "What's a woman for but to help a man find relief?" And you say, "Sure, I get it." Now you both have a reason for him to beat you. Before she felt the pain of the blows, she felt the fear in her belly. She was not afraid to die or even to suffer; what she feared was mutilation. She tried to protect first her face, then her breasts. A beating wasn't so bad when a man was very drunk because he'd tire quickly. But when he was sober, or after he'd only had a couple, he could go on forever, it seemed, until there was nothing left of you but something that looked run over.

The next blow did not hurt. It took a second for her to figure out why. She was outside herself, suspended somewhere above the car, deep into the night, and yet able to see into the car. Curled and stiff at the far edge of the passenger seat lay Estelle. And she returned to her body again; she *was* Estelle, feeling the hurt, falling into the rhythm of the Trans Am administering the beating. Threes and twos, three blows, followed by two breaths—*Smack! Smack! Smack! Um-poof! Um-poof!* Hit, hit, hit, breathe, breathe. *Smack! Smack! Smack! Um-poof! Um-poof!* Everything has its beginning in pain and rhythm. I am the beginning, Estelle thought. . . . And she was again the Witch, counting, calculating. *Smack!* (one), *smack!* (two), *smack!* (three). Before the *um-poof* of the first released breath, the Witch uncoiled and struck, going for his eyes.

They battled. The Witch had the advantage now. The Trans Am wanted to live. He had to try to hold the car on the road while he kept her off him. She managed to interpose herself between the windshield and his eyes. The car leaned to one side, skidding on two wheels, the sound of it like some strange bird searching for home from a point far above land. She was that bird. She could feel, almost to the point of enjoyment, the car slice toward what seemed like the edge of the horizon. She heard the Witch in herself shout the word "Die," the voice harsh, angry. *Be calm, accept your fate, love those who mean you harm. Dying this way, so full of event but without meaning, like birthing a child that has no heartbeat, is a fit end for the Witch, but not for Estelle. If I should die again, if I should die again, if I should die again . . .*

The moment passed. The Trans Am shoved her aside enough to regain his view of the road and command of the steering wheel. The car settled back down on four tires and drifted toward the shoulder of the road, more or less under control.

Once they came to a stop, they wrestled until the Witch was

sprawled on the seat, the Trans Am astride her, holding her wrists. A car passed, its headlights illuminating the Trans Am's face. It was radiant, like a candlelit statue of a saint.

She stopped struggling, staring at his face for the longest time. He squatted over her, immobile, indecisive; finally, he released her.

"We could have been killed, smashed—really killed." He proclaimed a mystery. His face glowed from the inside.

"We're saved," the Witch said.

"Saved," he said.

They had sex right there, for the first time conventional intercourse.

Afterward, he was almost tender, wiping her face with his handkerchief, as if it could wipe away bruises.

They started back. She was thirsty, so he gave her one of the beers. She lit her pipe, took a pull and handed it to him. Continuing on the road, traveling very slowly, they shared the drink and they shared the toke.

He was, she thought, the kind of fellow who had to feel high to feel anything. And yet he couldn't make himself high. He had to take a drug, or somebody else had to do it for him, or events had to come together accidentally and stun him. He was unhappy, but he didn't know he was unhappy, at least not in so many words, because he'd always been unhappy and so had nothing to compare unhappiness to. He mistook highs for happiness. He was, she thought, the perfect lover for such as her.

By the time they crossed into New Hampshire, the Witch had begun to feel her bruises. She'd protected her face fairly well. It was sore, and it would be swollen and discolored in the morning, but the skin wasn't broken. One ear hurt, and it was hot to the touch. A rib felt funny, as if it was loose, although it didn't give her much pain, and she could breathe all right. Mainly, her arms and shoulders ached from taking most of the blows. She didn't feel nauseated. Usually, after Oliver beat her, she'd wanted to throw up. The pain, taken as a whole, was almost comforting. It screened minor annoyances such as the boredom of driving, the discomfort of loud music; it allowed her to concentrate on her thoughts.

From the start there had been no love in her to give; from the start there had been a Witch in her. She had survived on the belief that she had loved Oliver; yet she had triumphed over him by denying the possibility of love. What troubled her now was a vague feeling of incompleteness accompanied by a craving for love, in the full knowledge she could never have it. Avalon had taught her that. If she could destroy that need, she might be free of it. And then in a vision enhanced by toke and fatigue, she was seeing Noreen. The lettering on her red dress said "I" AM LOVE. She returned her attention to the Trans Am. Even in calmness, anger shone from him.

"I want to touch your face," the Witch said.

"I don't like to be touched."

"A world of hurt builds up in you, doesn't it?" she said.

"Stay clear from my face," he said.

They drove on in silence. A few minutes later, the Trans Am said, "Bring your hand up real slow."

With exaggerated caution, the Witch raised her hand to his face. His cheeks were smooth, and there was a curve where his chin parted in the middle. His lips felt like roses on her fingertips. She sensed the moment when he could bear this intimacy no longer and she dropped her hand to her side.

"When you get pent up, you always have to hurt somebody, and is it always a woman?" the Witch probed.

The Trans Am said nothing.

"After you hurt them, you feel sick or anything?"

"I feel good, I feel relieved." She could feel the threat in his voice.

"Beforehand, you worry you'll hurt somebody?" she asked.

"Not exactly."

"You worry about losing control, making a mistake, getting caught. Tell me if I'm wrong," the Witch said.

The Trans Am wavered between continuing the conversation, which was unburdening him, and ending it because it was exposing him. He understood she wasn't afraid of him for the simple reason that she didn't care what happened to her. Perhaps he'd had a moment or two like that, and he knew the freedom it brought, the power. He was jealous of this power. She could steer him here and there, because he coveted this power. If she should ever weaken and he read fear on her face, he would have the power and she would be destroyed.

"What do you want?" he asked.

"Listen close," the Witch said. "I can help you find what *you* want."

He said nothing, but he listened intently.

"Young, scared, alone—I can make it easy for you," the Witch said.

The Witch lived like a robot, programmed by some mastermind long since gone by. She prepared her meals, she kept her house, she satisfied her customers, she engaged in small talk, she drove her car. But she felt curiously detached from these activities. They were not her life; they were duties carried out to oblige a being different from the one that inhabited her soul. There, in that dark keep, she lived; there she plotted. She wanted—had to—destroy Noreen Cook, to save herself. But she didn't know why. She nourished herself by the compulsion to get on with the dirty business at hand; only the question— why—confused her. Why? No sense looking for answers, anymore than there was sense in looking for the answer to, why the seasons, why the moon? She understood this much: for something to be born, something has to die. There was one too many of her.

She tried to reason out her troubles, and that process only increased her confusion. If, as she believed she must, she destroyed Noreen, she would destroy herself, for Noreen was a part of herself. But that didn't make sense; the idea of sense itself didn't make sense: the ability to reason was a curse for a creature, like carrying a useless horn on top the head. Ideas, images, sounds, memories came and went from her mind like pedestrians on a busy street. She couldn't put them in any order, couldn't make sense of them. Thoughts of Romaine visited her often. Crazy old woman: Are you this one, my own, or the other one? She had to forgive Romaine—she had to get even with Romaine.

Over and over again, a truth sounded inside her: somebody has to die, somebody has to die, Noreen has to die. *Not Noreen—anybody but Noreen*. Possible subjects paraded before her mind like characters in a police lineup from an old television show. Herself? Noreen—no, not Noreen? The Trans Am? Both of them, Noreen and the Trans Am? A stranger? Someone she loved, whose death would bring on her own? Avalon? Donald? Who's guilty here? One? All?

The Witch read about Aronson's death in the *Tuckerman Crier*. His picture was on the front page. He was in a flower shop, buying roses for his wife, when two men attempted to rob the place at knifepoint. Aronson pulled his pistol, disarmed the men, and held them to await the police. But one of the men, only eighteen and apparently strung out on drugs, began to advance toward him. Aronson warned the man to keep back, but he kept coming. Aronson held his fire, and the man attacked him. In the struggle that followed, the gun went off. The bullet exploded in Aronson's lungs and ruptured the aorta. Bystanders called Aronson a hero.

The hero was survived by his wife, one son, and one daughter. The Witch hadn't known Aronson had children, knew

practically nothing about his family except that his wife had
an aversion to oral sex. To conclude her business with Aronson,
the Witch felt it necessary to see his wife, the son, the daughter; thus she considered the funeral as an opportunity. She
didn't want them to know who she was, their loved one's whore,
but she did want them to notice her; she wanted something
of her, her witchness, to bend into their memories. She dressed
in black and purple, wearing a veil to obscure her face.

The funeral was held in a new church on the Tuckerman
flats. When she thought of this area, she visualized the way
it was thirty years ago—cornfields and treeless swamp and
expansive sky, open, between the density of the city and the
density of forested hills beyond. Now, filled in, it was crowded
with streets, houses, apartment buildings, a shopping center.
The changes, the fact that she couldn't reconcile herself to
them, made her experience the strangeness in herself as a lost
moment in time, as if she herself didn't exist except as somebody's memory, probably defective, of a place, an idea.

The church was of red brick, with a roof held up by huge
wooden beams of sandwiched lumber. Oak pews stained blond
pleased the eye and the hand. The brick, bare and unadorned,
left the Witch believing the church was still in the process of
construction. The matter puzzled her, for certainly the interior
would look better with some kind of paneling. Perhaps the
congregation was waiting for Christ to return and decorate the
church according to his own taste. Was there a Christ? If she
knelt before him, what would he say? What would he do? Did
Christ have sex? If so, with whom? If not, why not?

The Witch sat in the rear. To her front was the impressive
sight of members of the VFW, in white belts and dark blue
uniforms. Most were old men, vets from wars gone by. The
uniforms were loose in the chest, tight in through the gut.
Over the years, men narrowed at the shoulder and broadened
at the hip until they began to resemble their women, who,

sprouting hairs on their chins, began to resemble their men. Soon they would merge into one being, so that when one of them passed on, the loss would be all the greater. "What's the point, Jesus?" the Witch whispered.

The casket, buried under flowers, was barely visible, and it was closed. The Witch was disappointed. She always enjoyed looking at the dead. The life gone out of it, a body could neither injure nor be injured; it stirred the memory like the sound of rain. Also, since the purpose of a funeral was to bid farewell to the loved one, why close the casket? You didn't shut the door and say good-bye, you said good-bye and shut the door.

She watched Aronson's wife, escorted by her son, wobble down the aisle to the front row. She was a wide-bodied woman, with white hair blued, perhaps to go with her eyes. She didn't look sad as much as frightened, as if she'd wandered into this funeral and discovered, quite by accident, her husband in the coffin. She wore bright red lipstick. The son was long-legged and gangly, a good half a foot taller than his father had been. His face was regular-featured, almost handsome. Behind them walked a blocky young woman, with a faint, embarrassed smile on her face, as if she'd been caught in a lie. This would be the daughter.

The minister said some prayers, and the congregation sang some songs, and then first the son, then the daughter eulogized their father. The son said he hated to see his father die because he was just getting to know him, and now he never would and that was hard to bear. The daughter said the father had gone off to heaven, and she was looking forward to being reunited with him. The son and the daughter avoided eye contact. They hated one another, the Witch could see, and that knowledge made her surge inside with the power of her witchness.

Somewhere along the line, perhaps during some more singing, the Witch lost touch with the ceremony. She was in her memory, remembering that day Aronson had tried to sell her a gun. While she had worked her specialty on him, he had told her a story:

"There was this fellow, name of Ed. Ed developed a nerve problem over his missus leaving him. Run off. Took the kids and everything. Didn't run off with no man. Just *pfttt!* and run off. Which upset Ed, the not knowing why.... Slow down, Witch. I don't want to spout till I finish spouting off. Good, that's better, just right.

"So poor Ed was left alone in his house, which was all right as long as it was daytime or he was drunk. Well, it isn't daytime all day, and a man unless he's a natural-born inebriate won't— can't—stay drunk all the time. During his sober moments, Ed felt uneasy, unreal, un-, like he wasn't all there, like he'd become something you can pass a hand through, a g-d ghost.

"One night Ed happened to look out the window. He noticed a bush his old lady had him plant the year they bought the house. The bush was big and shaggy now. His old lady used to send him out to trim it, and she'd criticize the job he did. You don't make it round, it looks like Woody Woodpecker— stuff like that. Ed got to hate the bush. He was thinking about his hate when, so to speak, he saw his hate staring back at him in the form of a man crouched behind the bush. Ed said to himself, Don't pay no attention—it's all in your head. So he ignored it.

"That night, nothing happened. He had his whiskey, and he forgot the bright eyes in the bush, and he watched the television news, and he went to bed and slept until he had to take a piss at three o'clock in the morning, as per his habit. He took his piss and went back to bed and got up at six-thirty and ate his Wheaties or whatever and drove to work, no bush on his mind.

"Night arrived, as it will, dark, and drunk was Ed, and not particularly unhappy until he looked out the window. The guy behind the bush seared him with those burning eyes. Ed jumped back, spooked out of his jockstrap. When he was composed, he shut off the lights in the house so the guy couldn't see him. . . . Thank you, Witch, I was starting to falter, but you got my attention up.

"The eyes in the bush increased in brightness. They were yellow in the bull's-eye, redder toward the outer rings, and black on the edges. You see what he was looking at? Fire. Ed said to himself, This is a Fig Newton of my imagination, and I'm to ignore it. But there was no ignoring those eyes. He drank more whiskey, but no matter how drunk he got, the guy kept staring fire at him from behind the bush.

"Ed went to bed and the crazy idea come to him that the eyes were throwing off some kind rays. Naturally, Ed couldn't sleep, so he prowled about the house in his pajamas. Worked up an anger, and that gave him courage to go outside and face down the guy. Well, as you might guess, there was nobody behind the bush. Next night, same thing. And the next. And so forth.

"This went on for two or three weeks, and Ed was going nuts. He saw a psychiatrist, who asked him about his potty training and gave him some pills. Didn't do no good. Finally, one stormy night the wind was blowing and Ed could hear it racketing against the house. He was especially agitated. By now the man with the burning eyes was permanently camped behind that bush. Ed said, Eeeenough! He went upstairs to the bedroom closet, took out his twelve-gauge pump, loaded her up, opened the front door, and blasted the living hell out of that bush. *Boom! Boom! Boom!*"

At that moment, the Witch's labors drew to an end: Aronson finished. The Witch remembered returning her teeth to her mouth, settling down, rubbing the back of her neck with her hand, and asking, "Then what?"

"What do you mean—then what?"

"You didn't finish the story," the Witch had said.

"Oh, yah, well, I forgot for a sec. I kind of lose interest in these yarns after I get my horn scraped. What happened was he blew the bush to smithereens and killed the man with the burning eyes. There was no body, of course, no blood—but the guy was deader than a fart in a hurricane and his shining eyes were darkened for good. *Boom*—no bush; *boom*—no man; *boom*—no fear. Ed never had any doubt after that. He found himself a nice lady, remarried, and moved to Madison, Wisconsin. You understand the point?"

"That a gun can put soul as well as body to rest," the Witch had said.

Aronson had congratulated himself with a laugh.

Old light from the stars slipped into the room from the window, and the whore's bed was in shadow. The Witch, although she sat in a chair a few feet away, couldn't see the Trans Am, but she guessed he had awakened. His clothes were in a clump on the floor where he had shucked them. Only the knife strapped in leather to his calf remained on his person. She could smell his cologne and something else she couldn't quite identify, an almost imperceptible stink. A change in his breathing, through the mouth instead of the nose, told her for sure he was awake and alert now. She imagined he was thinking about reaching over to touch her; she imagined his hand would pass right through her. She sat perfectly still, silent. She wanted him to think of her as a statue, a monument, a black stone.

"Witch?" he whispered.

She remained motionless.

"Witch!" His shout was shrill, his stink suddenly thick and acrid, so that she knew its source now—anxiety.

She did not move or speak, but tried to connect him to herself by conjuring: *Reach for me, touch me*.

The Trans Am deliberately quieted his breath, signifying he

was a player in her game. Minutes passed. The stink of him became so strong it began to nauseate her. Then she heard the rustling of the sheets and a snap unfasten. What he had reached for was his knife.

"Do you like the dark?" she whispered, just loud enough to be heard.

"You're trying to make me afraid," he said.

"You are afraid," she said.

He moved again, positioning himself to plunge the knife into her. She remained perfectly still, silent. His breathing quickened, and the stink of him was transformed into a strong perfume; he was becoming aroused. She didn't care whether he killed her or not, and she understood it was her indifference that for the moment was saving her life. The thought of the terror in him, his urge to couple and kill, gave form and meaning to her tremor. It doesn't matter about us, she thought. I was lost before I was; he was lost by who he was. More time passed. There was only the sound of their breath, in rhythm now, like two rivers joined. She knew if her silhouette moved a trifle, if her breath caught, if she cried out, he would stab her.

Finally, he moaned. A surrender.

"Someone always dies in your dreams," she said.

"It's never me," he said. At that moment, she flicked on the lamp. Light slashed the room like the brush of some mad painter.

The Trans Am was kneeling on the bed, knife upraised, penis erect. The Witch looked into his eyes. They were like flowers, squeezed into blue droplets.

After they had sex, the Trans Am, calmed, sweet-smelling, lay on his back, the knife resting on his chest, point downward.

"How does it make it you feel?" the Witch asked.

"Important," he said.

"I want to touch the blade," the Witch said.

"Why?"

"For the thrill," she said.

He grasped the handle of the knife but did not remove it from his chest. She put her finger against the blade. His hand moved a trifle, and a blossom of blood appeared on the tip of her index finger.

"Now I'll touch you with my bloody finger," she said.

"I don't know." He was suddenly wary.

"The knife is in your hand, the blood on mine—how can you be afraid?"

"I am not afraid," he said.

She allowed a long moment to pass before she raised her finger and touched him on the forehead.

"Feel it? It doesn't hurt, does it?" she said.

"It's all right—cool." He sat up on the bed and craned his head to see himself in the mirror.

"There's a smear on my forehead," he said.

"The Witch's touch."

They dressed and he sat at her kitchen table drinking ale. After he'd had two bottles, she brought him pictures of Noreen.

"New ones," he said.

"You like them?"

"She's scared," he said.

"Quivers like a bird. Touch her and she'll never stop shaking," the Witch said. She took back the pictures.

"All alone in that bookstore—seems so easy," he said.

"But."

"She's got a boyfriend."

"I know for sure the nights when he won't be around," the Witch said.

14

The Passion of Estelle Jordan

The Witch stole down through the belly of the barn, and slipped the spring lock to the storage room of the porn shop. The darkness inside was like a prison sentence. She groped about until she reached the door to the showroom. She opened it a crack and peeked in. Noreen was prepared to close up for the night. The Witch watched her shut off the outside lights, lock the front door, count the day's receipts, and put the money in a deposit bag. She dragged herself through these chores as one rendered half-conscious by habit and boredom.

Finally, Noreen trudged toward the storage room, to get her things and go home. When the Witch threw open the door, Noreen gave a start.

"Estelle?" Noreen said.

"Not Estelle—the Witch."

"I didn't see you come in. How did you get in? I don't get it." Noreen's voice was charged. This, thought the Witch, is how terror begins: with mystery and wonder.

"Big doings tonight," the Witch said.

Noreen nodded, as if she knew all along what was going to happen to her, although her nod also made it clear she knew nothing and that, in fact, she was pleading for an explanation.

"Turn around," the Witch commanded.

"I don't want to turn around," Noreen said, but she did as she was told.

The Witch ran her fingers along the back of Noreen's neck, then unzipped the red dress with a single pull. Noreen giggled nervously until the Witch pulled the dress over her head. In bra and panties, her body revealed, Noreen was frightened as well as lost.

"I don't like this—I don't like the strangeness." Noreen's voice quivered.

"You're scared—I can feel it," the Witch said.

"I don't get it," Noreen said.

"Just think about how you feel at this moment," the Witch said.

"I'm afraid—you've made me afraid."

"A minute ago, out there, you were dead. Now you're alive, every nerve tingling."

"I trusted you, now you're hurting me."

"Trust comes easy-like, trust begs a mother for her love," the Witch said. "A trap. Survive trust and you might live a long time."

The Witch brushed Noreen's cheek with her lips. Noreen's fear tripped through the Witch like some powerful drug taking hold; the Witch grew strong and terrible.

"Lie down," the Witch said.

Noreen lay supine on the floor.

"On her back—it figures," the Witch said. "Turn over."

The Witch bound Noreen's wrists and ankles, using the plastic twine that bundled the dirty magazines. Noreen struggled, but like a lamb in the jaws of a wolf: her terror had denied her the full use of her muscles.

Her work finished for the moment, the Witch strutted about. Then, half dancing, she stripped naked, leaving her skirt, blouse, and work lace on the floor beside Noreen, who had begun to weep softly.

"Not bad, eh? You like?" The Witch addressed an imaginary audience, as she thrust out her loins.

She picked up Noreen's red dress, dangling it before Noreen's face, before wiggling into it. Noreen stopped weeping. The Witch said tauntingly, "The wasp puts on the butterfly's wings."

"My dress! That's my dress." Outrage drained some of the fear from Noreen and gave her courage.

"You don't own nothing, Noreen." The witch pranced about the room, posing in the dress, mocking the gestures of a fashion model.

"What are you going to do with me?" The fear in Noreen returned, redoubled. She spoke not to, but beyond, the Witch, as one praying.

"For the time being, shut you up." The Witch ghosted into the showroom. Behind the counter she found a gag consisting of black leather ribbons and a red rubber ball. With this she muffled Noreen. Trussed and silenced, Noreen lay unmoving on the storage-room floor.

Shutting the storage-room door behind her, alone now in the main part of the store, the Witch began to test herself in the red dress, standing stock-still, trying to feel contact with this body that, as it seemed, was not hers and that was draped by this dress that was not hers either. An image passed through her mind of a girl waiting on the streetcorner for boys to drive by.

The porn shop looked different, as if she'd never been here before. It disgusted her. There seemed to be a permanent smell of piss in the air. Walls were smudged, floors grimy, magazine racks weighed down, the reading matter limp from handling.

In spite of herself, as if guided by an inner command she had no control over, she gathered up a sack of tokens to play the peep shows. The cramped, ramshackle booths evoked a memory of bob houses for ice fishing. Every fall Isaac built a new one, each less well constructed than the previous year's model. He might have saved himself the trouble by taking in the current year's structure before the ice broke up in March or April, but he never got around to it. Sometimes Estelle visited, enjoying the brightness of the frozen pond. Isaac chopped holes in the ice, baited his lines with minnows, rigged the tip-ups, and retired to the comfort of the bob house. He'd sit on a wooden bench, warmed by a fire in a five-gallon milk jug he'd converted into a wood heater. His pleasure was to sip whiskey and watch the weather through a tiny window. "Don't know why but the booze tastes better out here," he'd say, gesturing with the bottle.

She moved from one hard bench to another in the movie booths, dropping in tokens, letting the movies unreel in concert. The booths and the films, like the rest of the porn shop, were worn and shabby. Scribblings marred the walls. Holes had been gouged through to the neighboring booths. Film projectors groaned from overuse and poor maintenance. There were breakdowns in the showings. (The projector ground on while the picture vanished, or the image was gauzy, or there was no projector noise, no picture, nothing but a lost token.) The films themselves were fuzzy, nicked, scarred. It seemed to the Witch that even the performers had aged, as a result not of the passage of time but of the weather in this place. Back-of-the Barn Adult Books 'n' Flicks was growing old, dying.

She searched for that girl who had gypped the men, paid with her body and, perhaps, her life. She never found her.

She left the peep shows and, rummaged about the porn shop, tearing off the plastic covers and looking at dirty magazines. Dazed as if by the sun, she unexpectedly found herself staring into one of the mirrors planted to scare off customers from shoplifting. The mirror was curved, distorting her image.

"Noreen?" A hand in the mirror reached toward her own hand, and she jerked it away. Once again she felt Noreen's fear flow into her, except instead of filling her with strength as it had before, it now drained the strength from her like a fast-overtaking illness. In a moment, she was panicky and frightened, feeling precisely the emotions she herself had foisted upon Noreen earlier. Fear made everything difficult. It was difficult to think, difficult to act. She had to breathe deliberately and deeply to keep from fleeing. Yet she managed to prepare for the Trans Am. She unlocked the door to the customer entry, leaving it half open, and took her place on the stool behind the counter.

Perhaps ten minutes had gone by when she heard the throaty purr of the car pulling into the parking lot.

She remained on the stool, legs crossed, hands together. She didn't have to look to know when he'd entered the store. She could smell the anxiety on him. She turned and faced him. He stood, masked, knife in hand.

"Witch—where's the other one? You promised me the other one." He was shocked to see her.

"I am the other one." Her voice was soaked with fear. Her Witch's tremor flowed to the Trans Am.

The dress had been worn and washed so much, the fibers that held it together were weakened, so when the Trans Am grasped the front of it, it parted down the middle as if by magic, soundlessly and all at once. Naked, the Witch huddled in a small S on the floor. From the beginning, she understood this was not to be one of those teach-you-a-lesson beatings. Such beatings were delivered by hand, like embraces gone mad. The Trans Am's means would be his boots; he aimed to mutilate and destroy her. It was that certainty, the sudden calm it brought her as she succumbed to it, that made her realize human hope was the most ruinous of lies. She felt free, on the verge of something new.

With the first blow, her fear vanished. She felt a thudding

against her flesh, but no pain as such. Sounds—his grunts,
her moans—seemed to come from loudspeakers. The porn
shop, the Trans Am in his mask, were bright and clear, if
jarring. It was as if someone were shaking the sun. She found
herself almost entertained by the heavy swinging boots, as if
she were watching a movie screen and the blows reached
through the screen to her own face and body. She felt no
compulsion to protect herself. She wished only to remain conscious to appreciate what was happening. She understood the
beating itself as a message, not directed toward her in particular but toward all living creatures. The beating said: A life is
given meaning by its end. So be it. To save herself, she had
both to destroy herself and to save Noreen. This, her sacrifice
of the body of the old whore, was her means.

Time passed, she didn't know how much. She glimpsed her
teeth on the floor, smashed.

After a while, the Trans Am grew tired. The thudding stopped;
he gasped for breath. She watched him reach for his face, as
if to attack it. Next, she heard the *rip* sound of parting Velcro,
and the mask peeled from his skull like a second flesh. Beneath, his soft-hard, smooth face was soaked with sweat. As
if blinded, he reached around him, and came up with the dress.
He wiped his face on it.

He crouched over her, peering at her. She lay unmoving.
He pinched the nipple of one of her breasts, and when she
did not respond, he unfastened the belt to his pants. She understood now that he would rape her, but that he had wanted to
wait until her body was limp, lifeless, completely under his
command. He pawed at her, his touch glacial, impersonal as
if he were fondling one of the inflatable dolls on sale at the
porn shop.

His prick entering her was cold and hard. There was no
passion in him, no desire—only will. The porn shop grew

quiet. She thought for a moment she was in a church, attending a funeral, her wandering mind conjuring this place, this end, with this maniac. *Where am I? Help me, Mother.* And she was sitting on a stool and a woman (was it her mother?) was making up her face, talking to her, telling her the secrets of her life.

A long time ago, Noreen, I had a social disease. Doctor examined me, says, "You're scarred inside." I says, "I'll say." He says, "You can't have any more children." My body told me otherwise. I had another. Willow. Only he wasn't made for this world. Hollered for his soul, for the Jordan soul. Willow, my youngest, was sired by Ollie, my oldest, when he was fifteen. Willow was Ollie's and Willow was mine. Oliver used to beat Willow because he was made wrong and because Oliver had a good idea where he came from. Ollie would protect Willow. At the time, I didn't care about Willow or about anything. I was in never-never land, like you're in now, Noreen—like they hit you and it doesn't hurt.

One day there was a fight. I watched it. I watched my eldest son murder his father to save my youngest son. Ollie, after he done the deed to Oliver, he got wisdom. He saw the truth. Which soon, in the glaring pain of it, he was to forget. But at that moment, when he understood, he named me. "Witch— you're the Witch," he says. When I had the name, I assumed the self. When Ollie and I made Willow, pity for myself told me we had fallen in together as kin will, victims of happenstance. How pity lies. Witchness made me see the truth. I used Ollie to rid myself of Oliver. Witchness bore me an eye for seeing the world as it is. I've paid the price for knowledge. Donald denies me. No Witch gave him birth; the Witch is barren. It was that girl back then that gave birth to four sons. You, Noreen.

My life is over, my story made. Never mind that the facts

195

will be changed in the telling; I will give the kinship new heart. After the flesh of me is gone I'll live in the stories, rekindling the kinship, destroyed by it, creating it.

The Witch came to consciousness in degrees. She was on the homestead farm Isaac had failed at, listening to pigs grunt. The sounds reminded her of sex, and she was fifteen with a customer. And finally she was pushing sixty, here, in the porn shop, listening to the Trans Am reaching his climax. The tremor dies forever at this moment, she thought. As the Trans Am finished, the Witch's body shifted involuntarily and his face came into full contact with her own. His lips on her sunken mouth tasted like slushy snow from the street.

She felt him jerk away in revulsion and leap to his feet. As he buttoned his pants he saw her blood on his hands. He reached for his face, feeling it. More blood. He picked up the dress and again wiped his face, tossing the dress casually away. It fell beside Estelle. Slowly, the image on the dress came into focus. The Witch's face was imprinted on the dress. The dear self reached out.

The movement took the Trans Am by surprise. He knocked her hand away. With a grunt, he returned the mask to his face, and stepped back. He circled her suspiciously, like a starving animal appraising poison meat. She never saw him go for the knife strapped to his leg; it blossomed from his hand, a silver flower. He knelt beside her, keeping a distance. Curious, frightened, he stared at her for the longest time. He crept a little closer and began poking the knife at her belly. She could feel the belly respond, like a wave. His eyes widened in horror.

"Something in there," he said, and screamed, his familiar lost-boy scream.

Just before she blacked out again, she saw him raise the knife to plunge it into her belly.

*   *   *

Critter awaited Delphina's homemade pizza, prepared according to the Jordan formula—store-bought crust, store-bought tomato sauce, salt, pepper, oregano, garlic powder, upon which was piled grated cheddar cheese and the key ingredient, ground venison. Critter traded for game meat with Abenaki, who was a wild and peculiar man, even by Jordan standards. The only time of year Abenaki didn't hunt was during the legal deer-killing season in November, when, as he would say, "It ain't safe to be in the woods." Critter himself was no hunter, but could honestly say he liked hunting. He found neither profit nor comfort in tramping about in dark, gloomy forests, and he didn't like getting up early in the morning only to go out in the cold, and, although he wouldn't admit it even to himself, killing animals made him squeamish. What Critter liked most about hunting were the tools of the hunter—guns and knives. Not that he desired to shoot or cut anything. It was just that weapons pleased his eye, as painted pictures might have pleased the eye of another man.

"Smells ready," he prodded.

"Another couple of minutes," Delphina said.

He stiffened, as one suffering an inadvertent insult. It was a gesture that never failed to infuriate his wife.

"Another... couple... of minutes." Delphina was trying to avoid a fight.

"You always say that and you always burn the cheese." Critter delivered this criticism impartially as a judge.

"Serve it up yourself, then." Delphina stormed out of the kitchen.

The tone in her voice (which said, "Shut up, grouch!") revealed to Critter his hidden mood beneath the lighthearted glaze of drink—anger.

Slapped numb by five beers, Critter should have been happy. Why am I so on edge? he silently asked the empty beer bottle in front of him. No answer came, but he was left with a vague resentment against Delphina for making him draw attention to his depths. Noreen wouldn't have done that. Noreen adored him.

Something formed in his mind, a question. Why did distance between man and wife increase as they drew closer? Because of the beer, or perhaps because of himself (Critter wouldn't have been able to say which), the question never quite formed entirely in his mind. It settled in unconstituted to tease him, like a familiar name forgotten but on the tip of the tongue. He suffered the itch of uncertainty.

"Del?" he called.

"What do you want now?" she shouted from the living room. She'd turned on the television.

"Nothing," he said.

He knew one thing that was bothering him, the affair with Noreen. It wasn't so much that she was making demands— the CB, the VCR. He didn't much like spending his hard-earned cash for someone else's pleasure, but he'd foot the bill as he would any other for services rendered. In one sense, he welcomed her demands; they demonstrated to him that he had means, she value. What bothered him was the habit of two women; it was overtaking him, like drink or smoke. He didn't need one more bad habit. (He'd started thinking of his life in terms of habits because the word *habit* didn't have any tender hooks in it.) Not that he wanted to break the habit. He wanted to continue: Delphina at his side, Noreen on the side. The fact was, he'd been relatively content of recent. But like any contented man conscious of his contentment, it was the consciousness of the contentment that, ultimately, discontented him.

If only he didn't have this urge to tell Delphina everything. He was always on the verge of confessing, even while he knew how stupid and fruitless a confession would be. The trouble was his own vanity. He wanted both to tuck it to Delphina, so to speak, by showing her he couldn't be taken for granted, and to unburden himself emotionally. He might be happy, but lately he was also pent up. He needed relief—confession would bring it. But if he confessed, he'd lose not only one of his women, or perhaps both, but his secret. He'd be empty again, the way he was before he took up with Noreen. More than Delphina's wrath, more than the real possibility that she would leave him and separate him from the family that meant so much to him, more than the loss of Noreen, more than the loss of love itself, what Critter feared most was emptiness.

"Del?—Del!"

"What?"

"Serve it up, goddamn it!"

She didn't exactly come running, but she did come, and the pizza was not burnt, and after a few bites he felt a little more at peace.

"Can I get you a beer?" he asked.

Delphina, dear wife, recognized his attempt to smooth relations. "I could use a beer," Delphina answered civilly, and sat at the table.

After a time, she said, "You're so uptight. Honestly, but I think you work too hard. You're never home."

"Miss me?"

"Well, yes—well, not always. Things seem to go better when you're not around. It's like I've got one less child to deal with."

He might have hit her then, reached out without a thought and batted her one right side of the head, but the phone rang. It was Dot McCurtin, Darby's high-tech town gossip.

"There's an emergency call for you on the CB, sounds like the real thing," Mrs. McCurtin said.

Moments later Critter was listening to Noreen's voice, "Red Dress calling Van Man, Red Dress calling Van Man. Emergency! Emergency!"

Seconds after Noreen explained the situation—some sex

maniac working over the Witch in the bookstore—Critter was in the van with Crowbar, speeding toward the auction barn.

"Red Dress, this is Van Man. On the road, to the rescue. Over."

"I think he's killed her." Noreen's voice quivered through the static of the CB.

"Red Dress, name your present location? Over."

"Why, Critter—I'm in my car in the parking lot." Even through her fear, Noreen's tone carried just a suggestion of Delphina's brand of sarcasm, and Critter twitched inside with annoyance.

"Red Dress, get out of there. Start your engine and drive away. Over."

"I can't, I'm too scared. Over."

"If he comes out of the bookstore, he'll see you, and you'll be dead meat. Red Dress, can you run? Over."

"I can run."

"Get out of car, Red Dress, and go hide. Run in the woods. Find a dark place, lay down and wait for the sound of my voice. And, Red Dress, don't move once you lie down. Don't make noises. Over. Red Dress? Red Dress? Over. Noreeeeeen?"

Noreen did not respond.

He'd told her to get out. Had she fled the car? If so, why hadn't she signed off? Critter was really concerned now. He reached in the glove compartment of the van, knowing there was nothing there that could help him, but all the same—reaching. His father used to carry a .357 magnum pistol in the glove compartment, and Critter couldn't get the notion out of his head that somehow the gun would materialize for his reaching hand. When his hand found only paper, Critter felt betrayed.

By now the CB airways were crackling with the peculiar accent of Jordans, a Yankee twang slowed down by a drawl almost Southern in its leisure. The Witch was in trouble. Any Jordan man in the Darby area who had a car or truck in running condition was headed for the barn on Route 21. Even Donald and his junkyard crew, twelve miles away in Tuckerman, had got the message and started their engines.

Critter knew he'd be the first to arrive at the barn. He had no gun; the smart thing to do would be to wait for help only minutes behind. Yet he did not. Something in him was changing second by second. Concern gave way to worry, worry to panic, panic to fear, fear to anger, anger to rage, rage to desire, desire to ecstasy, until he felt everything he'd ever felt in his life all at once; he was bathed in a pure emotional light—and then one thing, one emotion, something he'd never felt before, a single-minded will to do, soul to dare. His vision and mental processes narrowed, concentrated. He could see better, think more clearly; for the moment, the clutter of his life was broomed away in a shower of sparks.

He thought: Get the sex maniac, kill him. Nothing else mattered. He was no longer the husband and father, the businessman and employer, the American bent on happiness and prosperity—cautious, logical, worrisome, cunning. He was a pure Jordan male loosed on the world—headstrong, unpredictable, fearless, direct, dangerous, deadly.

In the seconds after he'd pulled off the blacktop into the auction-barn drive, he formed a plan, a Jordan plan. He had no weapon—no gun, no knife; nothing but Crowbar. And this van. By Jawj, this van could do a number on a guy. He had the van and the dog—and surprise. With no thought given to the consequences, he wheeled into the parking lot, aimed the van at the customer entry of Back-of-the-Barn Adult Books 'n' Flicks, and crashed through the wall.

The van plowed in a good six feet, taking down the door, ripping through frame lumber, plywood, sheetrock, and siding.

A split second later Critter and Crowbar jumped out of the cab into a cloud of dust. Critter saw a guy in a mask, dazed for a moment, and he saw a knife on the floor.

"Get him!" shouted Critter, and Crowbar attacked. The guy ran outside, Crowbar after him barking and snarling.

On the floor lay the Witch, bleeding, naked, oddly vibrating. And then it was as if the Witch had risen up from that battered body, and stood young, beautiful, and cruel. Critter raised his hands to his face, resisting the urge to cover his eyes. A picture flashed in his mind of his son Ollie playing peek-a-boo. He saw now that it was Noreen standing before him. She was wearing the Witch's clothes.

"She saved me, and I saved her." Noreen measured out her words as she spoke them. Critter wondered whether she was stoned. He couldn't get it out of his mind that the Noreen he knew was gone, vaporized, that this person was not Noreen but the Witch in a new form.

A movement from the Witch caught his attention. He watched her belly ripple. Critter had never seen muscles behave that way. Alarmed, he stepped back. The Witch began to pant furiously, her belly as alive as a lake in a storm, and then the waves subsided and soon she was breathing almost normally. He continued to watch, fascinated, stupefied, as the ripples on the belly began to build up again.

"What is this?" he said, more to himself than to Noreen.

"Birth—she's borning something." Noreen's face glistened.

Critter couldn't remember picking up the knife. It merely appeared in his hand. He held it like the Statue of Liberty her torch. The next thing he knew he was running outside through the hole in the wreckage. Moonlight lit up the parking lot. The masked guy backpedaled toward his car, Crowbar menacing him. Critter strode forward, knife held high.

The guy in the mask made it to his car, but too late. Abenaki

Jordan piled into the parking lot with his pickup truck and blocked his exit. Critter and Abenaki pulled the guy out of the car. Critter had expected a fight, but the guy's limbs were like water. He was scared shitless.

Other Jordans arrived, and soon a dozen men stood around, penning in the guy in the mask, pushing him around.

Without consciously meaning to, the group moved as one back toward the bookstore. Bright, blue-white light poured through the hole in the wreckage. As one spying, Critter watched his Uncle Donald kneel on the floor beside the Witch. He saw the Witch's hand reach up and Donald enclose it within his own hands.

For Critter, everything brightened, time accelerated. The night, the situation, seemed unreal; the idea of material being had lost credibility. It was a feeling he welcomed. He felt in control, as one feels in control of a dream, even as it sweeps one out to its sea. He spotted Abenaki, Andre, and Alsace, and he grabbed his half-brothers by the scruffs of their necks. "Let's get him!" he shouted, dragging his brothers with him, as he bulled his way forward and grabbed the mask. The sound of it torn from the face rippled pleasingly through Critter's fingertips.

It was the Acheson kid. Upper Darby snot. Critter hit him in the face, swinging with his forearm so the butt end of the knife handle caught the kid flush. Blood blossomed from his mouth. The kid made no sound; his eyes rolled. He was like a deer brought down by dogs, beyond apprehension, beyond fear, awaiting his end. Critter didn't want to look at the face. He stepped back. "Andre, put the mask back on his face," Critter ordered. Andre hesitated, and Alsace stepped in and did the job. Blood dripped through the mouth zipper.

Donald emerged from the wreckage, carrying the Witch blanketed in his arms. Donald, the Witch, Noreen, and Donald's son, Again, drove off. Critter felt a strange, unaccountable anger, as if something had been taken from him and he didn't even know what it was.

Somebody mentioned telephoning Constable Perkins, but Critter shouted, "No, he's mine."

"Abenaki, you and Alsace put that guy in the back seat," Critter commanded. "I'll drive his car. Andre, you follow us in my van. Everybody else go home."

Critter wasn't sure what he was going to do next, but he knew he didn't want the kid and the car on his own property.

He liked the feel of the Trans Am, not sure and steady like his van or dignified and powerful like his Caddy, but hard and responsive—violent. He drove fast, like a drunk teenager enjoying the feeling of speed. Impulsively, he turned off on Upper Darby Road, roared right past the Acheson place and finally into the Salmon Trust lands.

The road was dirt now, and Critter began to feel himself surge from the inside. He cut the wheel of the Trans Am, and the car barreled into the woods. Abenaki hollered with glee as the car bounced and jounced, plowing through small trees. Critter hollered, imitating Abenaki—*eeeeyow!* Crowbar joined in. Then all the Jordans, maddened and ecstatic, hollered at once.

The Trans Am only went about fifty feet before it got stuck, a big rock under the oil pan, the front end sticking up so the headlights shined into the sky.

"Now what?" said Abenaki from the back seat of the Trans Am. His breath came in lusty gasps. Andre ran from Critter's van, shouting, "Gimme a go at him!" And Alsace answered, "I'll have a turn, I'll have a turn."

Critter spoke the words, "Pull down his pants," and showed the knife before he himself understood his own intentions.

"This is not your lucky day," Abenaki said, and pawed at the Acheson lad, like some deranged lover.

The Acheson kid began to struggle now, whimper and wriggle and whine. Crowbar, as if in mockery, mimicked the whine.

Critter surged with power and strength. He climbed into the back seat, and by himself turned the Acheson kid upside down. Once they got the kid's pants over his hips, it took only a couple of seconds to complete the job. Critter grabbed the kid's balls and with one slice of the knife set them free, letting them drop to the floor of the car. The kid wasn't even sure what had happened.

They laughed as he ran screaming into the dark woods.

Critter fetched the siphon hose from the van. They drew out a couple of gallons of gas from the Trans Am, doused the inside, and touched it off. Whitish headlamp glow seemed to jet off into the night from the orange flames.

After leaving his kinsman at the barn where their respective vehicles were parked, Critter drove himself and Crowbar home. He didn't know whether the Witch was dead or alive; didn't care really. It didn't matter. As for himself and Noreen, their affair was over. That didn't matter either. What mattered was the future of the kinship—himself, Delphina, Little Ollie, Jawj, and other children he would sire.

When he arrived home, he was still full of energy, alert and powerful. He stormed into the house, walking right past Delphina into the bathroom. He rummaged through the medicine cabinet until he found her birth-control pills. He flung the plastic tin on the floor and stomped it with his heel.

15

Peace

Because her eyes were closed, Estelle Jordan felt more than saw the gold light of morning. *Touch the light*. She reached. Her hand moved from the blanket into the bar of sunlight. The shadow of her hand falling across her face, obscuring the daylight through her closed eyelids, caused her to cross from sleep to wakefulness, and she opened her eyes. A few words from the voice in the dream remained—*Touch the light*. She experienced a moment of mild regret at having lost something.

She arose, opened the window of her bedroom, breathed in the morning air, looked far at the greening hills, listened far for crows, looked near at the huge maple tree—she thrilled to the fright of its new foliage—listened near to chickadees. These birds of May, squabbling, complaining, happy in their violence—what optimists they were. They made her feel optimistic herself. Time of year, she thought. Everything new. She watched the birds, listened to them, felt them in her heart. They were a pattern to appreciate, like the faded design of an old quilt, or the lines in a pair of hands, or the rhythm of an old man snoring. And that made her think of Avalon Hillary. He'd telephoned her, asked to drop by late in the morning for coffee.

She dressed in loose-fitting blue jeans, a plain cotton blouse, ankle-top work shoes (the kind that poor girl she'd left behind had stitched years ago in the shoe shop); she brushed her hair, tying it into a ponytail; she washed her face but applied no makeup to it.

Avalon arrived at ten A.M., a bunch of dried weeds in his fist. "Last year's growth," he said.

"Thought you were partial to the green stuff," she kidded.

"I am," Avalon said.

"But you knew I liked them dry and brown." She arranged the weeds in a wooden pot. "You look good, Avalon, trim, cleaned up, new clothes."

"You look good, too, Estelle." He choked on the words, and his eyes said, "My, how she has aged."

She understood. She had seen the figure in the mirror. Almost overnight, her hair had turned nearly white. Deep furrows cut into her face. Her hips had widened and her shoulders were rounding.

"You still can't tell a lie with any conviction," Estelle said.

Avalon blushed. "You had a hard winter, I know, but I guess you're going to make it for a few more years."

"I intend to. I've got one more life to live."

And as before when they were lovers and friends, they chatted for a few minutes. Which was to say that Avalon talked. Things were going well. He'd found a way to get out from under the farm and still keep his land. He'd gone into partnership with a Mr. Charles Barnum, a Tuckerman lawyer; they planned to open a nine-hole golf course.

"I need to keep busy, and this should do it. I said to the landscape architect, 'You decide how to remodel the terrain as you please, but I kind of like that stuck-in-the-mud backhoe where it is. Gives me humility.' He says, 'We can incorporate it in the course as a hazard.' I says, 'A hazard—well, yes.'" Avalon chuckled, enjoying his joke immensely.

Finally, Avalon got around to the personal stuff. "I'm seeing the widow Kringle. We're talking about making it permanent, being we're both used to matrimony. I didn't want you to hear it from somebody else. You did a lot for this old gander, kept him upstanding when he was about to keel over."

"It's better you go with her, better for you, better for me. I'm getting out of the man business—no more customers, no more boyfriends."

"You'll have to make ends meet," Avalon said. "I'll give you a job in the clubhouse."

She knew he'd honor that promise, and hate like Hades seeing her day after day. "The Witch was no fool," she said. "The Witch put away a few dollars. And anyway, I'm a Jordan—taken care of. What with a new baby on the way, Critter's starting a new business, a handy mart in place of the bookstore. I'll be clerking part-time—nights. I always did like night work."

"I don't quite know how to put it in words, Estelle, but I knew what was said about you—I knew what you were. But when I looked at you, I saw another walking beside you."

He didn't embrace her as he left, but backed out of the front door with the mixture of magnificence and awkwardness of one of his bovines backing out of a stall.

The outside dinned. The birds had gone to war. She saw beauty in even their noise and violence. Was there any creature that didn't inflict pain on its own kind? "No—no, siree," she answered herself. The beauty she beheld—was it out there? "No—no, siree. In here." She thumped her chest.

Beauty was the great discovery of her recuperation. Privacy had become solitude, escape had become awareness, of growing things, design, color: beauty. Beauty: which through the very fact that it was not substance and therefore could not be worn out made her aware of herself as flesh, bone, blood, of the sadness of the frailty and impermanence of the human body. Beauty: which was both surrender and conquest. Beauty hurt and healed at the same time. You pricked your finger and it hurt, and a little bubble of blood blossomed into a rose and the fragrance sustained you as well as any food.

She slow-danced through her apartment to feel the beauty of the dear self moving. She fiddled with her plants, to take in their beauty. She fingered through a book until she found a fern, pressed between the pages. She crumbled it in her fingers to feel the dryness, to feel the loss of it in her heart as it turned to dust. She enjoyed a sense of righteousness, of God-almighty light. She spoke, but inwardly. "This that I have, my experience, this dust, teaches me, makes me. Destruction of something beautiful, if it be done with appreciation of the beauty, preserves the thing."

She was geting ready to go out, drive to Donald's house, when the phone rang. It was one of her customers.

"Heard you were in the hospital, laid up for most of the winter," he said, his voice jovial as any salesman's.

"That's so," Estelle said.

"You're home now, though."

"That's so—I'm home."

"You, ah, have a free night soon?"

"My nights were never free. Now they're all free."

"Oh, are they now?" The make-believe cheer vanished from his voice.

Estelle headed him off before he got too mad. "Hang on," she said, genuine cheer in her own voice. "You're not wasting your time. Fact is, this old girl is retired, but I can recommend a lady who can help you out. Trained her myself. She costs a little more. But, listen—young stuff. Think about it."

After she'd finished talking to the customer, she called Noreen.

"I'm sending you another one," she said. "Here's the story on him..."

When Estelle left for Tuckerman, the sun was high in the

sky, showering the leaves with bright, silvery sparks. She paused for a moment on the landing, almost expecting to see the Trans Am. A car could be resurrected from his ashes via insurance. As for the young driver, who could tell? If medical science could find a way to sew the quick back onto a fellow, he'd be out there again terrible as ever. A shiver of fear ran through her. She did not deny it. She would know the world, all of it, good and evil joined, as she, the Witch and the dear self, were joined. So be it. This feeling, this knowledge, this memory shadow of the tremor, was not entirely unpleasant.

When she arrived at Donald's house, instead of taking her place at the head of the table in the kitchen, she walked down to the garage. She ignored Donald's rule banning women in the shop and entered it. Donald stood beside a shiny black car, the welding torch in his hand, mask down. Sparks flew; the light was white and blinding. She shut her eyes. When she opened them it was as if a great span of time had passed; she *was* new. The light from Donald's torch went out. He turned toward her and lifted the mask to his forehead, and she could see his face. In his eyes she recognized a tenderness for her.

So, she thought, this is my peace.

ESSAY

People of the Kinship

Taxi Stories

When I was a student in the late 1960s at the state college in my hometown of Keene, New Hampshire, I drove a taxi for three years. In a big city, the clientele for the cab company consists mainly of the well-off and tourists. In a small community where public transportation is slim or non-existent the situation is the reverse. People who regularly take taxis are people without cars. Or they're shut-ins who use taxi drivers to deliver food, toothpaste, razor blades, stockings and other necessities, but also beer and spirits from the state liquor store. My passengers in Keene and environs included old people, welfare mothers, their kids, drunks, convicted drunk drivers who'd had their drivers' licenses revoked, the sick, the physically disabled, the deranged, the retarded and once in a while a business man from the Dillant Hopkins Airport, always a treat because I could usually count on a tip.

A few of the people I met in the taxi were normal, but most were weird or screwed up or profound or funny or sad. Some of my customers included:

The Light House Keeper. He was about sixty, well-dressed, dapper mustache, dying of emphysema in a furnished room in the former Ellis Hotel. Every couple of days, I or another driver would bring him a bottle of Jack Daniels and two packs of Chesterfield Cigarettes. He used to keep the light on in his room

1

around the clock. All through the night hours you could see his figure stalking about through the curtainless window. Then one night: darkness behind the window. No more calls. From that time on, as I drove on Main Street in the dark hours I often looked up at the window, expecting to see a light on and the keeper pacing in his room, but I never did. Years later the Ellis Hotel was razed, leaving only my memory in the space.

The Congregationalist. She kept her head up, her hands on her lap, her eyes in the past—or so I imagined from glancing at her through the rear-view mirror of my cab. I'd drive her to the First Congregational Church every Sunday, then back to the old folks home on Court Street after the service. She always tipped me twenty-five cents, but rarely made conversation. She didn't seem shy, merely uninterested in a young taxi driver. One Sunday, on the return trip from church, she started asking me questions. She was a skilled interviewer, and I told her all about my hopes and dreams. (I wanted to be a great poet like T. S. Eliot.) Just before I let her off, she gave me some advice. "Young man," she said, "never get old." Something about the way she delivered her words, coldly and directly and with finality sent a shiver of fear through me. I never saw her again, and I've never had a moment since when I haven't been aware of my mortality.

A Voice Named Desire. Often a woman with a sultry voice would call the dispatcher for a six-pack of beer. The voice was teasing, flirtatious and, ultimately, mysterious, its come-hither quality somewhere between Marilyn Monroe and Marlene Dietrich. The voice instructed the driver to buy the beer and leave it on the staircase of the inside hall of the apartment house. The fare, the beer money and a tip would be in an envelope. I was curious about this customer and once, on the spur of the moment, I did something I will always regret. I put the six-pack on the staircase, took the envelope, opened the outside door and shut it loudly. But I did not leave the hall. I wanted to get a look at the mystery woman with the sultry voice. A few seconds later the door opened. She was in her thirties, dressed only in a white slip; her body had a marvelous shape, but her face was covered with running sores. When she saw me, she burst into tears and ran back into her apartment.

Big Ed. One afternoon the taxi dispatcher got a call from a bartender who said, "Star Cafe!" and hung up. Translation: "Come and get a drunk." The Star was on Roxbury Street, just off the main drag. It was a rough beer bar, but I always felt comfortable there, maybe because I never had to worry about committing a faux pas or breaching an etiquette. A guy could relax at the Star Cafe.

My customer was Big Ed. We had been schoolmates at St. Joseph's Elementary School. He was never mean, never a bully, but he was a wild, disruptive boy. Big Ed was now a powerfully built young man, drunk, broke and mouthing off; the bartender was paying the cab fare. In the car, speeding toward Big Ed's home (he was still living with his mother), Big Ed challenged me to a fist fight. He wasn't mad, he said; he just wanted a fight. I declined. He was disappointed, but he did not pursue the matter.

Several years later he was arrested for robbing a corner market in Athol, Massachusetts, caught when the police cruiser passed his car on the street; Big Ed had forgotten to remove his ski mask. Later I heard that while being held a prisoner at the county farm in Westmoreland, he had been sent on a work detail in a dairy barn and had cut a cow in half with a chain saw. Big Ed eventually graduated from the county farm to the state prison, doing life for murder.

Driving a cab showed me just how class-divided Keene was and furthermore how different the down-and-out are from the up-and-coming. It's axiomatic that suffering people have nothing but their pride and that they suffer in silence. My experience in the taxi taught me that this isn't so. Suffering people have only their suffering; it is their sole subject matter. The worse off my passengers were, the more they revealed about themselves. They told me about ancient grudges between loved ones, unfair bosses, alcoholism, sexual abuse, consumptive rages, cruel diseases and various forms of despair, but they rarely bothered to tell me their names.

What struck me about the suffering souls who took my taxis in the late 1960s is how much time they spent thinking. They ruminated, philosophized, schemed. I found them talkative and surprisingly articulate in describing, say, the development of a cancerous tumor. Betrayed by brain, body, society, self or God, they sought refuge in their box canyon minds. We've all seen this phenomenon at work. Watch homeless people. They talk to themselves. They find no shelter in the world, so they reside in their heads. Accordingly, I resolved that if I ever wrote about people like this I would concentrate on their interior lives.

It was during my taxi days that I first read T. S. Eliot's poem "Preludes." After such lines, I thought I knew the Light House Keeper better, and the woman behind the Voice Named Desire and Big Ed, all my acquaintances as well as my friends and loved ones. I felt then a calling to be a writer myself. I thought that if I could do for others what Eliot had done for me, my life would have some meaning.

Shack People

When I created the Jordan clan in the first novel of the Darby series, *The Dogs of March*, I called them "the Shack People." They were based on men, women and children I'd grown up with in Keene and in the surrounding towns of Cheshire County.*

*In *A Little More Than Kin*, the small city outside of imaginary Darby is the real city of Keene. As time went on and the Darby books grew, Keene was changing, not always in the way I wanted it to change for the purposes of my

Our New England forest is messy and crowded, just like the Jordan shacks. I postulated a connection between landscape and people who by necessity live close to the earth. Maybe so, but since driving across the United States a number of times, I've been amazed to find Jordan shacks all over the country. I am now convinced that a libido for shack-living is based more in culture than in topography. If you're looking for it, the presence of Shack People is blatantly obvious on the back roads of Northern New England, the South, Appalachia, Texas, Eastern New Mexico and Southern California, less so in southern New England, the Middle-Atlantic states and the Mid-West, although you'll find them in isolated pockets such as the Pine Barrens of New Jersey; I'm not sure about Florida, the Rocky Mountain states and the Northwest, because I have not visited those areas.

What the motorist sees of the Shack People from the road is disheveled housing, dogs in the yard, an in-bred look to the people; get a little closer and you notice bad teeth, a sloppy appearance and inattention to personal hygiene; know them better and you learn they distrust authority outside their clans and possess a contemptuous attitude toward education, success, law and indeed toward what most of us call our values. You also realize they're no smarter or stupider than anybody else. They just have a different set of priorities.

What fascinated me about the Shack People when I was growing up among them in the late 1950s was that they lived by their own rules. It didn't matter what the rest of us were wearing (dungarees rolled up at the cuff) or what music we were listening to (Elvis and "You Ain't Nothing but a Hound Dog") or what ideas were fashionable (bomb shelters in case of an atomic attack), the Shack People were totally oblivious to us

---

fiction. Hence, real Keene became fictional Tuckerman in *Whisper My Name, The Passion of Estelle Jordan* and *Live Free or Die*. In retrospect, I can see that this action was unnecessary.

5

and our fancies. I can't remember exactly when, but I started to
view the Shack People as a sort of anthropological project in
my backyard. Perhaps by studying these strange peoples I might
gain some insight into my own nature and into human nature
in general. Not that I actually studied the Shack People. This is
all in retrospect. I took a few mental notes—and forgot. It was
only when I started to write fiction about the Jordans that the
ideas about the Shack People that had been there all along began to surface. (It's this awakening from the distracting dream
of what we want to see to the reality before our eyes that is the
value of writing fiction as well as reading it. A writer gains the
same insight into the world through the process of creating a
work of fiction as the reader gains through the effort of reading it.)

The Shack People are the most despised and least understood of Americans, because, I believe, we in the mainstream
define ourselves in opposition to them. Good teeth, clean bodies,
tidy houses, spacious lawns and specious virtues are not only
traits of the American character, they're national fetishes. In
some communities, local legislative bodies actually require
homeowners to maintain properties according to community
standards of appearance. Good learning and good manners
might aid one's advancement in American society, but good
teeth, a clean body and passable stylishness are requirements.
At this writing, we fishes in the mainstream are wearing wild
ties, listening to rap music and debating multiculturalism. The
Shack People are unchanged, still oblivious to us and our "new"
ideas.

The Jordans

My departure point in writing about the Jordans was simple
enough. I don't believe there is much difference in the intelli-

gence or emotional range of people the world over. It is how individuals assign the intelligence and emotions that make the difference. Thus, a young man from the suburbs might build a rocket for a science class in high school and that might lead to a career in engineering. An equally talented young man brought up in a shack, such as Donald Jordan, might work on his car, which in Donald's case leads to his own junk car business. I know such a man in Keene. I asked him how he catalogued hundreds of derelict cars sprawled across his hundred acres of now-defunct farmland, not to mention thousands of parts in his warehouse. He tapped his temple and said, "Computer."

Ollie Jordan, the protagonist in *A Little More Than Kin*, is derived from a man who lived in my neighborhood in Keene. He was tall, gaunt, with rotted teeth, eyes like a starved hound, a face in perpetual five o'clock shadow. He wore a felt hat set at a rakish angle and the same rumpled suit in all seasons, but no tie and sometimes not even a shirt. He walked with a stiff gait, his hands gripping the bottom of his jacket cuffs. To some people, this man might have seemed a laughable figure, a bum left over from the Depression of the 1930s, a loser. In fact he was the leader of his clan, a man who had a great deal of prestige among his own kind. The day-to-day world of American society simply did not exist for him, because he was so busy trying to get ahead in his own world, searching for ascendancy within the clan, supplying succor when he could; surrendering his ascendancy and seeking succor when he had to. This dance of mind and body in the world of things (a bottle of liquor), phenomena (winter weather) and abstractions (economics) is very common for many of us, but with luck our obsession flows nicely into the mainstream of society. For the leader of the clan, the man I would call Ollie Jordan, there was no such confluence.

I was mulling over these matters one March day while I was making a cup of coffee on a small piece of woodland I owned in the town of Westmoreland, New Hampshire. I'd built my fire on a flat stone. While the air where I sat was still, I could hear the wind clacking in the trees above. The stone became the altar stone in *A Little More Than Kin*, and Ollie Jordan, in his mad love for a mad son, became a tragic figure.

The origins of Willow Jordan and Estelle, the Jordan Witch, are a little more complicated, and require more story-telling. Besides driving a taxi in my college days, I worked for a summer as a laundryman at what was then called Elliot Community Hospital in Keene. My partner was a slightly retarded young man about twenty years old. He had fiery red hair, big muscles and a touchy temperament. Once, he took offense to something I said or did (I have no idea what) and stuffed me into an industrial-sized washing machine. I escaped.

Most of the time, though, Red and I got along pretty well. Dirty laundry dropped down a chute from the first, second and third stories into our domain in the building's basement, where the foundation of huge stones lay exposed and the heating pipes were wrapped with asbestos insulation. Red and I would load the dirty sheets, towels, pillow cases, Johnny gowns, surgical outfits and nurse coveralls into a cart. The main rule was always look before you reach. I saw and touched all that is within a human being, things warm, gooey and suddenly smelly. We emptied the laundry into the washers, and after it was washed and spun cool, we shoved the load into dryers as big as the interior of the Dodge Colt I currently drive.

We tossed the clean, dry bedding and clothes into a cart and wheeled it to a table. Here three women took over. They sorted, folded and put away the clean laundry. The women, in their fifties, were losers in the sweepstakes of American life. They'd had the wrong parents, the wrong up-bringing, the wrong education, the wrong mates, the wrong gods, and no luck.

The women never paid me any attention. I was just a snot-nosed college kid, with no meaning to their lives. Not that I made any attempts to break the ice; I was content to maintain the psychic gulf between us. Red, however, had access to the women. They liked to scold him, treating him like an outsized child. He seemed merely to want to be in their presence. Occasionally, on our breaks, when he was in a certain wistful mood, Red would stroke the long gray-black hair of one of the women. He was like any friendless child petting a cat. The woman would go on with her work as if she did not notice, until finally she'd grow bored with Red and cuff him on the side of the head, and he would stop.

Years later I saw Red driving a trash collection truck. He'd grown larger and more powerful, but he looked worried, angry, abused. Red's tragedy was that he was just smart enough to realize he wasn't smart enough. He, combined with my felonious schoolmate, Big Ed, became Willow Jordan in *A Little More Than Kin.*

Two of the laundrywomen were so nondescript that today I have no clear memory of their appearance or personalities. But the third, the one who allowed Red to touch her hair, is very clear in my mind. At around five-foot eight, she was taller than the other two. She was a little stooped, but she had good bones and as a young woman she must have been magnificent. Her skin was pale, her eyes dark and intelligent; the cast of her look was distant, haunted. She had fine features, but she never wore lipstick or makeup of any kind. What was memorable about her was her hair, black, streaked with gray, hanging almost to her waist. You could tell that she washed and combed it out every day. What stayed with me about the tall laundry folder was that her pride as a person and as a woman was in her hair.

Around this same time, in the world outside the hospital laundry, I took note of another woman. She was in her forties, very attractive. She had bleached blond hair, a fantastic build and she always wore a lot of makeup. I would see this woman at night around town in the company of an older man. A month or so would go by and I would see her again with another man. I fantasized that she was a high-priced hooker, a sort of angel of death who would ferry these old guys into the next world on a bier of carnal ecstasy.

One night I was in the lounge of the Crystal Restaurant in Keene (renamed the Chrysalis Restaurant in the Darby novels to honor my love of monarch butterflies), when the blond came in with yet another septuagenarian. For the first time, I heard her voice. She spoke in a strong, coarse version of the Yankee accent. She was in charge and spankingly sarcastic.

In *A Little More Than Kin*, I created Estelle Jordan; it wasn't until I wrote the last line in the book that I had the first inkling of Estelle's dualistic nature. One part of her was like that bleached blond—attractive, assertive, selfish, coarse. This was the face she showed to the world—the face of the Witch. But deep inside was another self, vulnerable and sensitive. The secret self had a secret name, which the Witch did not reveal but contemplated when she brushed her long, gray-black hair. This was the Dear Self. At some point, the Dear Self took control of the personality and contemplated the Witch. It was my perception of these two selves, in conflict, seeking integration, that set in motion the writing of *The Passion of Estelle Jordan*.

The Class System of Darby

When I was starting to write about the Jordans I noticed that there were very few comparable characters in the fiction I was reading. Almost all the books I read were about people from suburbs and cities. When country people were portrayed, the main characters often held the same values as suburban or city people, while the subservient characters, the hicks of the Sticks, were patronized and condescended to. Shack People, if they were portrayed at all, often came off as unreal. For example, even a good writer such as James Dickey writing a good book, *Deliverance*, reduced Shack People to the level of subhumans with not a whisper of complaint from critics or public. When I started the Darby series I wasn't interested in maintaining the stereotypes of frugal Yankees and cracker barrel philosophers who said, "Pahk the cah" and "Ayup." I strived to portray the townspeople as I believed them truly to be. I also deliberately put the emphasis on the neglected classes, what today would be called rural underclass and rural working class. I felt little obligation to highlight the middle classes, since other New England writers such as John Updike, John Cheever and Ann Beattie have written about suburban-type New Englanders extensively and well.

The idea of class is fuzzy in the American mind in part because of the poverty of our language. The class groupings we learn in Sociology 101—upper, upper middle, middle middle, lower middle, working, and lower—tell us little about the classes or about ourselves and have misled us into preserving the American myth that money alone makes for class status. There's some truth to this, but it must be obvious to anyone who looks carefully at rich and poor, black and white, owners and renters that American class structures are shaped by clan, culture and a multitude of other factors, as well as by economics. (For a scholarly rendering of this situation, I recommend David Hatch Fisher's extraordinary cultural history, *Albion's Seed*.)

Within rural New England are a number of distinct social classes with which I've populated Darby. They include, from the most to least: Locals, Commuters, Shack People, Farmers, and Gentry. One way to differentiate among these groups is to report their attitudes around a single issue. For this essay, I've chosen zoning as the issue, because it touches upon matters in the Darby books and because it remains important to people who live rural in New England. I will describe how each group functions in Darby and discuss the characters from the novels who fit into these groups and then present the group's attitudes toward zoning.

Locals: Locals can include teachers, lawyers and other professional people, but the soul of this class is in those who work with their hands—loggers, housewives, sawmill operators, factory workers, waitresses, truck drivers, mechanics, leftover back-to-the-landers and people in the trades, such as carpenters, plumbers, masons and electricians. Some scrape out a living from the town, but many commute to jobs outside of Darby. Locals are distinguished from Commuters by their frame of reference: Locals view the world in local terms. They're regulars at town meetings, and organizers of sugar-on-snow parties, quilting bees, snowmobile clubs and other strictly local activities. They have a sense of history, an old-fashioned conservatism not exactly in line with modern, slash-and-burn conservative ideology; they're conservative in the sense that they are cautious, fatalistic, thrifty and often oriented toward the past as expressed by an interest in, say, collecting old tools or growing wild rose bushes. They like machines and gadgets, because their basic understanding of the universe is Newtonian. Dot McCurtin, the high-tech town gossip of Darby (a very valuable person in a small community) is a classic Local. Another is town constable Godfrey Perkins. So is Old Man Dorne.

Despite their Shack People roots, Howard Elman and his wife Elenore are Locals. In *The Dogs of March* I imagined the Elmans and the Jordans as having similar backgrounds. The difference is that Howard and Elenore are foster children who don't really know where they come from. In a way, they embody the American ideal in that they are freed from the driving forces of heritage and the confinements of kinship. Clan, culture and class mean little to the Elmans, because they've lost their racial, ethnic and cultural memories. Like thirsty wanderers of the desert, they've stumbled into their current class, Locals.

A person doesn't have to be born into Darby to fit the social category of Local. It's attitude and orientation toward local matters that defines a Local. An example of a newcomer who has adopted local ways and been accepted by other Locals is Joe Ancharsky, the storekeeper. Joe is from Hazelton, Pennsylvania. He's based on a type I've seen all over New England. They're, say, auto workers from Michigan or mechanics from New Jersey or coal miners from Pennsylvania, who have a dream to own a country store. After decades of hard work, in their forties and fifties, they finally get the wherewithal to sink their savings into the dream. The newcomers of this breed are very important to New England villages, because they make a financial investment in the community and because they fall in quickly and naturally behind local traditions.

Locals define their group identity through community. The current zoning set-up, whatever it is, goes a long way toward establishing what specifically constitutes the community. Therefore, Locals are usually against changes in zoning of any kind. The poorer Locals are afraid that Commuters will squeeze them out using zoning law as the primary tool. The wealthier Locals are opposed to zoning on the general principle that change is likely to be bad for the town and because they oppose anything the Commuters favor.

Commuters: This is my designation for the middle class, the people who seek to live a suburban life in the country. Commuters can work in any of the occupations of Locals, but the leadership of this group is usually found among professionals—doctors, lawyers, managers, teachers. Most Commuters are newcomers to the community, but not necessarily. Some natives become Commuters when they lose their sense of orientation to the historical town. Commuters have little interest in town matters; their concerns are their children and themselves, concerns expressed in a passion for good schools, town planning and districts zoned to give them privacy. Some are the rural equivalent of Yuppies. They have little sense of or respect for the traditions of the town, and they believe themselves superior to just about everybody. Commuters get themselves onto planning boards and school boards and conservation commissions. Commuters might be conservative or liberal in their political philosophies, but in their relationship to Darby they're liberals in the sense that they're predisposed toward changing the town.

Through the medium of zoning changes, Commuters have already transformed many New England towns into the equivalent of rural suburbs. I used to think that this process was inevitable, but I've noticed a trend in the years following the first couple of Darby books, which is that many Commuters instead of changing the towns have been changed by the towns. Some have become Locals. A war is on between Locals and Commuters for the soul of the Northern New England town, and it's too early to predict the outcome.

Shack People: Not all rural poor folk are Shack People. Many of the poor are neat and tidy; many seek to improve their lot in life; some are even educated with a reverence for learning, personal hygiene and subject-verb agreement. In my class system, such people might be poor Locals or poor Commuters. What marks Shack People is less their economic status than their cultural attitudes. Indeed, some Shack People get rich, buy big houses and turn them into shacks. Critter and Delphina Jordan, who appear in *The Passion of Estelle Jordan,* serve as examples.

Shack people don't actually have an attitude about zoning; to them zoning belongs to that nether world of the society they ignore, but they achieve de facto zoning by their slovenly habits: nobody wants to live near them.

Farmers: Most of the farmers I've known I met in my work as a reporter for the *Keene Sentinel* newspaper. I found farmers to be well-rounded, well-informed, ironic, intelligent and interesting. I have to laugh at suburban and city people who use the word "farmer" as a slur to indicate an uneducated, unsophisticated rural person. They're saying "farmer" but they're thinking "shack people." Farmers know tools, accounting, taxes, land, law and, in New England—given the fickleness of the gods of weather and the nuisances of rocky soil—philosophy. About the only area where Farmers are clearly inferior to suburbanites and urbanites is in their fashion sense.

The farmers of Darby, the few who are left, are often wheelers and dealers in the town. They know how things work; they get themselves elected as selectmen and members of various other boards. Those who quit farming and go on to other work prosper as real estate agents, land developers and contractors. Harold Flagg, the storekeeper I killed off in *The Dogs of March*, is an example of the non-farming Farmer. Avalon Hillary in *The Passion of Estelle Jordan* is my archetypical Farmer; he's a composite of the farmers I met.

Farmers have mixed ideas on zoning. On one hand, like the Locals, they're opposed to zoning out of habit and tradition. On the other hand, they can see great possible profit in zoning, and Farmers are nothing if not practical-minded. Land in an agricultural zone is taxed less than commercial or residential land. If a farmer wants to sell his property, it often makes practical sense for him to re-zone his mind as well as his land. Accordingly, Farmers often find themselves in a philosophical and spiritual maze that includes the topiary of the past, the present, the future, the land, the law, economics, heritage, price controls, free markets, freedom, servitude to animals and retirement in a Florida condo.

Gentry: The Salmons of Darby (pronounced Sahl-mohn) along with the Butterworths and Prells represent a class of people who are living the America dream in reverse. They reside in

Upper Darby in grand houses built between 1890 and 1930 or in remodeled farmhouses dating back to the 18th century. They own a good deal of property, mainly forest land. They're well-educated and cultured, but the family fortune has slipped away, and often the Gentry suffer from cash flow problems. They retain a great deal of prestige in the town and some power. They're New England's equivalent of European royalty: up-front influence, but not enough in the bank to back it up with. I've covered the Salmons, the Prells and the Butterworths in *Whisper My Name*, the third book in the Darby series, and *Live Free or Die*, the fifth and concluding book.

The Gentry take a cautious attitude toward zoning. They lead the movement in zoning for historical or environmental purposes, but they often side with the Locals when it comes to conventional zoning such as commercial or single-family housing zones. The reason for this is partly tradition. Gentry don't want their towns changing into suburbs. Also, the Gentry have little need for codified zoning, since as owners of large plots of land they've already achieved de facto protection from encroaching development.

Can one move from one class to another in the world of Darby? My answer is that as in most other places in the country one must break away. Success is never in the hometown, and is rarely an outgrowth of one's heritage. It is always someplace else. The best and brightest are educated someplace else; they take jobs someplace else; the childhood sweetheart is abandoned for a loved one someplace else. The ideal couple consists of a man and woman from different parts of the country who establish a family in yet a third location, preferably in the suburbs but maybe in Darby. Evidence for this idea is all around us. Businesses, communities, educational institutions, all sectors of power in our society almost never seek their leaders from within the ranks of the home office or the hometown or the current administration, but bring them in from someplace else. It makes for a society that is fluid, dynamic and lonely with wanderers looking for oases.

The Jordan Kinship

The oases we find or settle for or that are thrust upon us often are not places but social structures. One such structure covered in the Darby books, both a part of and apart from the idea of class, is the idea of kinship. I use the word in a special way, and I'd like to say a few things about how this word came to be and what it encompasses.

Early on I struggled with language in trying to differentiate the Shack People from the rest of Darby society. I didn't like using loaded words such as "upper" and "lower" and even the word "class." These words demean all groups. I went after clarification through the conveyances of fictional characters, setting, dramatic situations and action: the Darby novels. In the writing of the fiction, I found *kinship, succor* and *ascendancy*.

In the Jordan kinship, a Jordan gains ascendancy (prestige, power, monetary reward, an advantage in the mating game, a feeling of independence and mastery) by providing succor (employment, leadership, emotional support, companionship and welfare) to less fortunate members of the kinship. When one is healthy, strong, confident and lucky, one seeks ascendancy; when one is unhealthy, weak, hesitant and unlucky, one seeks succor. In this respect, the Jordans aren't much different from most people in America. However, the special uses the Jordans have for "ascendancy" and "succor" not only establish principles of behavior but help give the Jordans an identity that separates them from those in the outside world. Because no one else uses these two words in quite the same way as the Jordans, the language gives them a feeling of exclusivity, a feeling which they require to give them distinction and shape as a kinship. In almost all groups who seek to secede from the mainstream culture, one can find such creative language. Members of the Jordan kinship don't necessarily know each other by name, but they recognize one another through codes of dress, accents of speech, modes of behavior and styles of housing. They know not only that they're the Shack People, they know they're a special version and they're proud of it. Here's an example. Ollie Jordan, in *A Little More Than Kin*, meets his common law life wife, Helen, at the County Fair: "He breathed in the smell of her long brown hair—wood smoke, fried foods, the piss from babies, farm animals—and he knew she was of his own kind."

Kinship as a Phenomenon

Most members of the Jordan kinship are poor. In the eyes of their fellow Darby folk, they rank at the bottom of the social ladder. In the scheme of things in Tuckerman County, they probably don't amount to much. But the idea of kinship, in the sense that that I use that word, is not limited to tiny clans in the hills of Northern New England. Kinship groups are strong and pervasive throughout American life. Members of kinships can be rich or poor, or anywhere in between. They can hold political views and values of every stripe. What binds the members in kinship has little to do with money or politics. As long as the members of an extended family are caught in the grip of a loyalty above immediate family, nation and society, the group can grow into a kinship. Nearly any community or neighborhood will include a dominant kinship. What we fear in such families is not their family affiliations but an x-factor that may threaten us; this x-factor is the power of kinship, a power that rises up from the inside and which serves not us but the members of the kinship. Not all families develop into kinships, and it's more than blood ties that make up a kinship. It's culture and class as well as clan; it's a selfish attitude that the group has about itself.

A group united by kinship can contribute to and be integrated within society at large; for example, the Kennedy family of Massachusetts. One may or may not agree with the Kennedys' political philosophy, but it's undeniable that within the Kennedy kinship is a will to do good for society. Kinship groups like the Kennedys are the exception, however. Most kinships are hostile to society. Kinships might be politically conservative or liberal, but in their internal structures they are self-referential and exclusionary. Members are accountable to the kinship before they are accountable to city, state, nation, church, society and even immediate family.

Sometimes in kinships—perhaps most of the time—the blood bond is not so much biological as metaphorical. The enduring Ku Klux Klan has its origins in clan, culture and class. The Klan constitutes a kinship. A motorcycle club, where the members swear allegiance to the group above all, is a kinship. So-called drug cartels develop along lines of clan, culture and class: kinships. Some kinships are temporary; for example, college fraternities and sororities, and youth gangs. A kinship by my definition is almost always narrow, measuring events and deciding on actions according to its own rules. A business corporation does not constitute a kinship, but the management structure of a corporation might. The same thing goes for the membership of a trade union. Or a university. Or a religious institution. Or a governmental body. The test of kinship is whether members of a group have rules they put ahead of the rule of law and ahead of the instinct to abide by the unwritten codes of society. Thus the Mafia functions as a kinship, but not the Knights of Columbus.

The Jordan kinship poses no direct threat to American society, but a proliferation of kinships does. For so long, our national debate has been waged on the battlegrouncd of democracy versus communism, conservatism versus liberalism, Republican versus Democrat, White versus Black, man versus woman, gay versus straight, rich versus poor, atheist versus believer, native versus newcomer, suburb versus city, developer versus environmentalist, local versus state, state versus federal. But what really drives the world are small groups, shadow bodies within communities, within neighborhoods, within businesses, within political parties, within institutions, within ethnic groups, within governmental bodies, entities very like the ones I've tried to describe as kinships. Kinships are exciting, selfish, powerful, tribal and juvenile, giving rise to youth gangs, spoiled-brat family dynasties, greedy business empires, bullying political parties and, finally, government dictatorships.

Kinships are always among us, but they rise up and grow more powerful when the nuclear family is weak, where youth rides over age, where government largess is distant, where political parties are fragmented and lacking a moral center. In other words, kinships fill a need in a society such as ours, given over as it is to individualism. Kinships supply rules, patterns of behavior, companionship, moral support, welfare and opportunities for prestige: ascendancy and succor.

Most kinships are not at the forefront of consciousness in our society. Most exist invisibly, outside the news, so to speak. But without a kinship, a person is in serious trouble. Every time I go to New York I'm amazed at the number and variety of immigrants, many speaking languages I've never heard before and gesturing in ways I've never seen. I've talked to several of these people, a waiter in a Lebanese restaurant, a young woman from Cambodia, an Irishman college student with an athletic scholarship for his abilities at soccer, a member of an East Indian caste with extensive financial interests in American motels. These people, and from all appearances the other immigrants I've seen, belong to kinships. It was the power of kinships that brought them to this country in the first place. I've also seen thousands of homeless men and women of all ages going through trash containers looking for food, sleeping on the street or in subways tunnels. Most of these people are Americans of long-standing. They were homeless because for whatever reason, they needed succor; having lost the tether to their kinship groups, there was no one to provide that succor.

Literary Matters

The working title for *A Little More Than Kin* was *The Kinship*. Somehow, though, it didn't seem to me that the book earned that title, because it was so narrowly about Ollie Jordan and his own personal madness in his relationship with his retarded son, Willow. I was still struggling to find a title when my friend Terry Pindell of Keene suggested a line from *Hamlet*. The minute he spoke Hamlet's aside about his despised uncle, "A little more than kin, and less than kind," I knew I had my title.

When I was working on *The Passion of Estelle Jordan*, it also passed through my mind to name this Jordan book *The Kinship*. Once again I decided that the novel was too much about one character, Estelle Jordan, to use the inclusive "Kinship" title. I didn't come to the eventual title until I'd finished the last draft. Shortly before the novel was going to go to press I mailed some suggested titles to my editor at Viking Press, Charles Verrill. *The Passion of Estelle Jordan* was the last one that popped into my head as I finished the list. Days later I suddenly realized that I had unconsciously structured my novel along the lines of the Roman Catholic mass. In the mass, a perfect sacrifice is made in order to save humanity from Adam's sin. That sacrifice is Christ. Estelle too must make a perfect sacrifice. In the Catholic faith, Christ's suffering is often referred to as his "passion." *The Passion of Estelle Jordan* had to be the title. I called Verrill. He wasn't in. I called my agent, Rita Scott. She wasn't in, but her colleague, Ray Powers, said Verrill had already picked one of the titles. I broke into a panicky sweat. "Ern," Powers said, "It's *The Passion of Estelle Jordan.*"

I've felt for a long time that although they are part of an even larger entity, the five-book Darby series, *A Little More Than Kin* and *The Passion of Estelle Jordan* belong together. Now that the books have been joined under one cover, I feel they've earned the title I had in mind from the beginning, *The Kinship.*

UNIVERSITY PRESS OF NEW ENGLAND

publishes books under its own imprint and is the publisher for Brandeis University Press, Brown University Press, University of Connecticut, Dartmouth College, Middlebury College Press, University of New Hampshire, University of Rhode Island, Tufts University, University of Vermont, and Wesleyan University Press.

ABOUT THE AUTHOR

Ernest Hebert's most recent novel is *Mad Boys*. His highly acclaimed Darby series includes *The Dogs of March, A Little More Than Kin, Whisper My Name, The Passion of Estelle Jordan,* and *Live Free or Die*. Hebert lives with his wife and two daughters in West Lebanon, New Hampshire, and teaches writing at Dartmouth College.

LIBRARY OF CONGRESS CATALOGING-IN-PUBLICATION DATA

Hebert, Ernest.
    The kinship : with a new essay / by Ernest Hebert.
        p.   cm. — (Darby series)
    Contents: A little more than kin — The passion of Estelle Jordan.
    ISBN 0-87451-630-7
    I. Hebert, Ernest. Little more than kin. 1993.   II. Hebert,
Ernest. Passion of Estelle Jordan. 1993.   III. Title.   IV. Title:
Little more than kin.   V. Title: Passion of Estelle Jordan.
VI. Series: Hebert, Ernest. Darby series.
PS3558.E277K56   1993
813'.54—dc20   93-10978
∞